The Phoenix Traitor

The Phoenix Traitor

Book Two

Amelia Wood

Hardback: 979-8-9853665-3-2
Paperback: 979-8-9853665-4-9
Ebook: 979-8-9853665-5-6
First edition

The Phoenix Traitor is a work of fiction. The names, characters, businesses, places, events, locales, and incidents are either products of my imagination or used in a fictitious manner. Any resemblance to actual persons, living or dead, or actual events are coincidental.

Editing by Judi Wess
Cover art by Theá Magerand
Typesetting by Sarah Lahay

For Aliza and Lucia.

I cannot wait to see what the two of you accomplish in the future.

I love the two of you more than I could ever explain.

Part One

THE DUELS

The Silent Duels is a holiday designed to honor the Serpent and Spider, but all houses will be required to participate.

Only houses may attend or participate. Lesser sons and daughters will take officer positions in the military. Heirs fight for glory and honor.

Fights may end one of three ways.

The overseeing ruler may end it.

The loser may surrender.

The loser may die.

The victor will not be charged with any crimes, and the death will be forgotten in due time.

O! Silentium et furtim.

—THE BOOK OF THE PHOENIX, VOLUME THREE

Chapter

ONE

Prologue

T HE HALLS OF THE temple were silent in the early hours of the morning.

Silent except for the young priestess rushing through them, hurtling around corners so quickly that she nearly slammed into the far wall. Her silver robes flew out behind her, barely tied over her stomach as her bare feet slapped along the stone floors. Her shadow rippled across the walls, cast in sharp relief by the moonlight streaming through small windows near the ceiling.

She was not beautiful, this priestess. Deep burns marred her face and what was exposed of her arms and hands. She was blind in one eye and patches of her hair had been burned away.

But despite that, she was fast as she rushed down a staircase, what remained of her hair waving behind her like a black banner. She hit the edge of the stairs and halted, catching her breath as she peered through an archway and into the sanctuary beyond.

She didn't bother looking at the words inscribed in the archway above her head—she knew them by heart, just like every other priest and priestess who had ever entered the temple's service.

O! Flamma et furor.

Oh! The flame and the fury.

She'd only ignored that warning once, and it had almost cost her life. She stepped into the main sanctuary, eyes darting over the massive, terrible Flame in the center of it.

The Flame was contained in a white stone pit, the only material known to keep the fire caged. It raged in the pit regardless, seeking a way out.

The Phoenix Flame.

The last bit of magic left in Eiad, trapped and contained like a wild animal. Some of the priestesses and priests whispered that The Phoenix Flame should be unleashed, to allow magic to run rampant across the continent and across the world again. To allow it to cleanse, as it did centuries ago.

She couldn't bring herself to agree. It was only a fire, after all, holy or otherwise. It was not as though releasing it would do anything except kill.

The priestess shuddered as she passed underneath the archway, turning slowly to look around the sanctuary. The ceiling was an open dome, allowing the elements in. The black-blue sky above, scattered with stars, shined down on her as she took another cautious step into the massive room. The floor was still stone, but huge mosaics depicting the patron animals surrounded the Phoenix Flame. Behind each patron animal was another archway, inscribed with something relating to the animal itself. Through those hallways were smaller, more dedicated sanctuaries, each unique and special. Each burning with more Flame.

The hall she had just come out of was behind the mosaic of the Phoenix Herself, the largest of them all. Her bare feet slid over the rough gems set in the floor, rubies and gold and onyx glittering up at her, the Flame flicking over them. On the opposite side of the Phoenix mosaic was a large set of double doors, leading out to the temple grounds and the mountain they sat upon.

She turned in another slow circle. She'd been summoned here by a breathless priest who had knocked on the door and told her that she was urgently needed in the main sanctuary.

But nobody was there. Nobody, as far as she could tell.

But then footsteps sounded from the Dragon's hallway, and the priestess turned to see a lone figure walking towards her, the firelight casting the woman's shadow against the wall. She was almost giant-like as she stalked towards the priestess, impeccable silver robes tied tightly across her stomach. A long, curved knife hung from her belt, glinting dully in the firelight.

"High Priestess," the girl breathed, inclining her head.

Where the girl was meek, the High Priestess radiated confidence and grace. She was older, yes, but that did nothing to hunch her proud shoulders or curve her back, which was held ramrod straight. Gray hair was pulled into a large bun at the top of her head, mouth pressed into a thin line. Her skin was lined with age but not sagging, her deep blue eyes narrowing on the girl.

"Good," the High Priestess said, her voice raspy with age. "You came."

"Of course," the girl said. "I was told I was needed in the sanctuary."

"You *are* needed," the High Priestess said. "I do not summon people from their beds in the dead of night if it is not important."

The girl didn't say anything as the High Priestess began to walk past her, soft slippers gliding over the mosaics.

"Walk with me," the High Priestess said, and the girl hurried to fall into step behind her as they passed over a black-and-gold mosaic of the roaring Dragon.

The High Priestess didn't say anything as they moved past the Tiger and the Leopard—although her face hardened as they stepped over the latter.

The priestess couldn't help but wonder if the High Priestess was thinking about what had happened in central Eiad only two months ago. The conflict that was building, the whispers that were stirring.

The High Priestess stopped upon the purple-and-bronze Serpent and stared into the deep Flames. They stood there silently for a long while, the girl shifting anxiously as she waited for the older woman to say something. The silence stretched on uncomfortably, the High Priestess's eyes unfocusing as she continued to look at the Phoenix Flame.

"What do you think of the court?" the High Priestess asked suddenly, ripping her gaze away from the fire to stare at the priestess. "Of the royal family? The Phoenixes?"

The girl grappled for an answer as the High Priestess's eyes never wavered, focused so intently that the girl nearly jumped into the fire to avoid the weight of the stare.

"I...I'm not sure what you mean, High Priestess," the girl said softly, and the High Priestess scoffed.

"Of course you do," she said. "Simply answer the question. What do you think about the court."

"They protect us, don't they?" the priestess asked. "And they fund us?"

"Protection?" The High Priestess snarled. "What protection?"

"They put soldiers here when everything happened with Lady Verity Ignis-" the priestess began, taking a slight step backwards, but the priestess cut her off with a growl. The girl flinched.

"Those soldiers are here to *watch* me," she said. "To ensure that I, too, don't rise against them and side with this Order. They know they are powerless if the might of the temple backs the Order."

"Would the Order protect us from the royal family?" the priestess asked, and the High Priestess rolled her eyes.

"How stupid are you?" she asked, turning once again to the flame. "None of them wish to protect me, and to choose either of them would be a betrayal of my faith. What they wish is to keep me contained here, to ensure that I do not become a threat to their fragile stability, for they *know* what I can do."

"But then....why did you ask me, High Priestess?"

The High Priestess's lips curled into a savage smile. "To see if you were worthy."

The girl squirmed. "Worthy of what, High Priestess?"

The High Priestess leaned into the girl and grasped her shoulders.

"Worthy of remaining," she said, and then she threw her down, down, down into the depths of the Phoenix Flame. The girl screamed as she fell, as the Flame began to rip at her before she even hit the bottom of the pit.

The sound echoed into the night, lifted toward the holy heavens, and the High Priestess turned away.

She did not look back as the girl's screams faded away, and she knew, come morning, nothing would remain.

Chapter

Two

Asher Cinis, former crown prince of Eiad, leaned over the side of a ship and threw up.

Beneath him, the waves rolled gently, lapping against the side of the boat. Cool, salty wind brushed his curls away from his face.

Phoenix above. This was a new type of hell.

"You're pathetic," a man said, coming to stand behind Asher. "Please, try to pull yourself together."

"I didn't ask to be on this Phoenix-forsaken boat," Asher said, clamping a hand over his mouth as nausea rose again in his throat.

"Regardless," the man said, and Asher looked up at him, scowling. Tyvish Choo grinned at him, all long dark hair and light freckles. "You're looking especially green today, prince."

"Shut your mouth," Asher hissed, sinking down and leaning against the side of the boat, head between his knees. One of the other sailors had, quite kindly, told him it might help.

"Relax," Tyvish said, sitting beside him. "Juniper told me to keep an eye on you. I'm just doing my job."

"Don't pretend to care," Asher said, gagging on the words.

"I do care," Tyvish said. "Not about you, necessarily, but Juniper asked, and I'm going to do it."

Asher couldn't respond, eyes fixed on the wooden planks beneath him. His stomach twisted again.

"How much longer?" Asher asked softly, turning his head slightly and catching Tyvish's expression. A slight smile quirked his thin lips.

"A week," Tyvish said.

Thank the Phoenix. He couldn't wait to be on solid ground again. They'd been on the boat for nearly a week already, steadily making their way toward the middle continent.

It had been Luria Van Ela's—the rebellion's leader—idea to send Asher and Tyvish aboard a boat worked by a crew of rebel sympathizers to the country of Verdeca, far in the north of the middle continent.

Asher, frankly, was terrified. Verdeca had a terrible reputation for violence, their history written in blood on snow. The tsar ruled through fear, using the seven elite female guards that surrounded him to punish, enforce, and conquer. Only the combined effort of the rest of the middle continent had been enough to slow Verdeca's endless slaughter, locking them behind a flimsy treaty that nobody expected to hold for much longer.

And Asher was supposed to convince that very same tsar to send soldiers to Eiad and fight in the civil war.

After a while, Tyvish stood, staring down at Asher. "Come on. Get up. At least pretend there's something decent about you."

Reluctantly, and only to keep Tyvish's endless teasing at a minimum, Asher pushed to his feet and followed him, legs wobbling.

"Have you ever been on a boat before?" Tyvish asked, and Asher glared at him. Tyvish was remarkably at home on the ship, walking as easily as he would over hard-packed dirt.

"Of course I've been on a boat before," Asher said. "I've been to both the middle and far continents. They were just… much slower. And much bigger."

"Ah," Tyvish said. "I'm sorry the accommodations aren't up to your normal standards. I'll be sure to commandeer a ship fit for a king on the way back. For his Royal Highness Prince Asher."

Asher scowled but said nothing, glancing again at Tyvish, who was messing with one of the ropes.

Asher didn't know the other man well—they'd only met two months ago, and they hadn't spent much time together. Tyvish was part of the upper circle of the rebellion—despite the irony in that alone, seeing as the Order wanted nothing more than to topple the already-existing upper circle of Eiad. He was allowed to sit with Luria Van Ela, her closest companions, and…Juniper Farley.

An unfamiliar emotion twisted in Asher's stomach, and he grimaced.

Two months ago, he'd put everything he knew on the line for Juniper, a palace servant who, unbeknownst to him, had been secretly working to kill him.

Somehow, Asher had fallen in love with her. When Juniper had fled the palace after the rebellion's first strike, he had gone with her. He'd allowed her to stab Ember Ignis, the Dragon heir, in the stomach, nearly killing her. They'd taken three days to travel away from the palace, growing closer every hour.

The second they'd gotten to the main rebel camp, located in the deep south, Juniper had vanished. It wasn't as though she'd been sent away, as he was now—no, he'd seen her, but she'd made no move to seek him out, and Asher wasn't high enough in the rebellion's rankings to find her.

Juniper hadn't tried. He didn't have a reason why—Juniper had never offered one, and neither had anybody else. Instead, he'd been asked to throw himself into wartime efforts, chopping wood and milking goats in between strategic meetings with Luria Van Ela where he told her all of the information he knew about his parents and the houses.

And after two months of this, his feelings had begun to fade, helped by both distance and resentment.

Tyvish, interestingly enough, had occupied that place in Juniper's life before Asher, but as far as he knew, the Kieallian hadn't moved back into that spot.

He certainly wasn't going to ask him, though. They weren't *that* close.

They ducked into the captain's quarters, where the two of them had been sharing the space, keeping certain conversations private from the ship's crew.

Even within the rebellion, there was no trust. It was a twisted mirror of the houses, who would stab each other in the back just to gain a little more favor with his father.

And Asher couldn't trust anybody at all after the last three months.

"Look," Tyvish said softly, closing the door. "I know…I know you're out of place in the rebellion. I can't say I sympathize with you, because I can't. You're in a weird position, I know. But I need you to get it together before we dock in Verdeca. You've played the game before, Asher, and we need you to play it again. You know what's at stake here."

"Of course I know," Asher snapped. Tyvish was starting to sound like his parents. "I've done this before. But Verdeca is different. The tsar is different. If you think Eiad's royal family is bad…you know nothing. This man makes my mother look like a saint."

"We can't go back without his assistance," Tyvish said. "Not too much longer now. Get ready."

"Verdeca is ruled by a tsar," Asher said, sitting cross-legged on the deck of the ship. The sun beat down on them, weaker than he was used to, and there was a strange chill in the air already. The first taste of Verdeca. Tyvish leaned forward to hear him better. "As of now, he is unmarried and without an heir, although I'm certain that will change within the next few years. If the tsar were to suddenly die, the head of the army would step in. Verdeca usually isn't without an heir for long."

"Stop," Tyvish said, holding a hand up. "Who's the head of the army?"

"We don't know her name," Asher said, frowning. "She's the head of the elite seven guards that always surround the tsar. She's known only as the Wolf, and her second in command is known only as the Fangs. The other women don't have specific titles—if our information is correct, they're sorted into two categories with three in the lowest level and two in the middle. They're fairly young, probably a little older than me, and they're expected to serve the tsar until either he or they die."

"And below the seven?"

"Verdeca's army is incredibly advanced. They rival ours in every way, and I don't doubt their numbers are higher. They're a larger country both in terms of land and population. Men make up the majority of the army, as far as Eiad knows, but I suspect a significant portion is still female, if we consider the importance of the seven. We have no way of knowing their true numbers, which puts us at a slight disadvantage. They've been fairly closed off since the treaty was signed."

Tyvish's face contorted. His own home country—Kieall—had been a part of that treaty. Tyvish wasn't old enough to have been in Kieall for more than a year or two during the war, but Asher wouldn't have been surprised if the other man's parents had fled during it. The Verdecans had not been good to any of the countries, but Kieall had been particularly singled out.

"The fact that he's willing to speak with us is something that must be acknowledged," Asher said. "There's a chance he only allows me in, but if he doesn't, keep your head down and your mouth shut. We'll be in their country—they have every right to kill us if they so choose. Do you speak Verdecan?"

Tyvish shook his head. "I don't. I haven't been around a lot of people who can speak it."

"My Verdecan is...weak," Asher said. "My hope is that, at the very least, the tsar speaks the common language or has a translator who can speak it."

Tyvish hummed softly. "Very well. Anything else I need to know?"

"Stay away from the Wolf and Fangs," he said. "They might not even speak the common language either. And Phoenix above, *do not* attempt to approach the tsar. He'll send for us when he's ready, and even then, keep as much distance as you can. The Wolf's only duty is to protect the tsar no matter what. She won't hesitate to go for the throat. And please, *please* don't forget that I'm no longer Prince Asher Cinis. My parents stripped me of my title and name. I'm simply Asher of the rebellion. Or just Asher."

Tyvish dipped his head. "Very well, Asher of the rebellion. I'll trust you to see us through this."

Asher watched the docks of Verdeca approach, gulls screaming their arrival.

Beyond the gulls...the docks were completely silent. A half-dozen boats rocked quietly in the harbor, all of them empty. They flew only the flags of Verdeca—a howling wolf set against a snow-gray background. A group of people—perhaps numbering eight or nine—stood on the dock and watched their approach.

On the deck, the crew fell silent, watching the people on the dock.

The boat rocked into port, and Asher stared down at the Verdecans.

They stared back.

It was completely and utterly eerie.

Asher had heard rumors of how the Verdecans looked, and they hadn't been wrong—tall and slim soldiers, always dressed in the silver and whites of the country's flag. Each of the eight people standing below possessed either silver-blonde or stark red hair, and they all wore a sword on their back.

He couldn't see from where he stood, but he knew most of them would have pale violet eyes.

The eyes of the old gods, some called them.

When the boat had fully pulled into port, Asher made his way to Tyvish's side.

"Remember," Asher said softly. "Keep your mouth shut."

Tyvish nodded, following Asher off of the boat.

Asher stepped into Verdeca, inclining his head toward the group. A woman, red-haired and terribly scarred, stepped forward, dipping her head slightly in response.

"Welcome to Verdeca, Bears," the woman said, a slight accent curling her words. "The tsar is pleased to receive you. My name is Annika, and I am of the seven. Those standing behind me are of the tsar's court—we have been chosen to escort you to the Summer Palace. Please, follow me."

Of the seven.

She was neither the Wolf nor the Fangs then, although Asher hadn't expected her to be. Those two would be found at the tsar's side.

Asher hadn't missed that Annika had called them Bears—he hadn't missed that Verdeca *knew* he had been stripped of his name.

They followed the Verdecans toward a group of waiting horses, Annika gesturing to two dappled gray mares.

"It will only take a few hours to ride to the Summer Palace," Annika said, gracefully swinging into the saddle. "We will ride at an easy pace. You are welcome to speak to my companions, however, most of them speak little of the common language. We have been…isolated for many years."

Asher nodded his thanks. He'd figured this was how things were going to be—a few people who spoke the common language somewhat well, and the rest who wouldn't be able to understand a single word he said.

The red-haired woman dropped back to ride alongside Asher, neither of them speaking for a long moment.

"You are…you are the former prince, are you not?" Annika asked, and Asher nodded.

"Yes," he said. "Asher."

"Asher," Annika said, her accent twisting the word. "I must admit, we were all quite shocked when the tsar told us of your coming. It has been long since someone wanted to ally themselves with Verdeca."

"My parents will call the rest of the middle continent to their aid," Asher said. "But Verdeca…everybody knows that Verdeca only stopped conquering because they couldn't fight from all sides. You would be a formidable ally."

Annika hummed. "Yes, we would be. Those Phoenixes would go running if they saw the Wolf."

"Can you tell me about her?"

"I can tell you what is already known," Annika said. "Her name is Viktoriya Bolshi. She came into her position under the current tsar, unlike me, who came in underneath the previous.

She was taken from the prisons—she had been convicted of murder—and went through the trials to become the Wolf. She will be at the tsar's right hand."

"And the Fangs?"

Annika's face darkened. "There is less known about the Fangs. Her name is Sofya Seminoava. She, too, was taken from the prisons, although her crime has never been disclosed. Only she, the Wolf, and the tsar know what she did. All we know is that she was set to be killed, and then we pulled her from the prisons. She was very nearly the Wolf. She stands at the tsar's left hand."

Set to be killed.

Murder or treason, then. Asher found it hard to believe the tsar would let a traitor stand on his guard.

That meant both the Wolf and the Fangs were true murderers. Not in the way that being in the army would dictate. The type of killer that made people keep their children close and their curtains shut.

But it didn't matter. Asher still had a job to do, and he couldn't go back to Eiad without doing it.

The Summer Palace of Verdeca was all stone and wood and glass, glittering under weak sunlight. It sat atop a high cliff, short towers jutting into the sky, overlooking the beach and waves below. The road leading toward it was stopped by a short gate, just high enough to keep a horse from jumping over it.

The gate opened with only a gesture from Annika, however, and they trotted through.

"You will be received tomorrow morning," Annika said, riding between Asher and Tyvish. "Tonight, you have been invited to dine with the court but not with the tsar."

Invited. As though they could decline.

"Will the Wolf be there?" Tyvish asked, and Annika shook her head.

"No. You will meet the Wolf and Fangs tomorrow, when you meet the tsar. But do not concern yourself with them—as with the tsar, only speak to them if spoken to. I doubt either of them will engage with you."

They rode underneath a covered archway, Annika guiding the group into a small courtyard, where she dismounted and gestured for Asher and Tyvish to do the same. The court fell in around them, keeping them surrounded.

"Follow me."

"Which level of the seven is she part of?" Tyvish whispered to Asher, his voice so low that he almost missed it.

"Probably the lowest," Asher said, eyes roaming the door Annika was leading them through. Delicate carvings of wolves and vines had been etched into the wooden surface, teeth and flowers blending together.

"I am pleased to say that you will be dining on the finest selection of dishes that Verdeca has to offer, prepared by the tsar's own chefs."

"Is there a reason the tsar isn't dining with us?"

Asher's heart stopped dead in his chest, and he slowly turned toward Tyvish.

Phoenix above. They were going to die here.

Annika turned slowly, tilting her head. "Are you a fool?"

Tyvish glanced at Asher, who couldn't do anything except stare at him.

"I—"

"Do not forget where you are," Annika said softly. "The tsar does not owe you his reasons, and he does not owe you your life. *I* do not owe you your life; however, I will spare it. Do not speak that way again. The others will not be as kind as I am."

Tyvish sputtered for words, but Asher gripped his shoulder, shaking his head. "Shut. Up."

Tyvish nodded, and Annika led them onward in icy silence.

"Tell us of Eiad," a court woman—Mischa, perhaps, although Asher was having a difficult time remembering their names—said. "Tell us of how you get your names again, yes?"

Asher shifted uncomfortably. To what he was sure was Tyvish's delight, the court was fascinated by him, ignoring the other man almost entirely. It didn't surprise Asher, but that didn't make it any less annoying.

But he had to do this, and they were only on the fifth course of nine.

Asher smiled. "We're named for our houses. It's... an honor, really. To be worthy of one's house. It's how we distinguish ourselves, beyond the other obvious things."

"Oh, how interesting!" a man exclaimed from further down the table. To Asher's surprise, a little over half of the court was fluent in the common language, and most of the others could at least keep up with the conversation, violet eyes darting between Asher and the others. "Are the Dragon's eyes truly gold?"

"Yes," Asher said. "Some say it's a mark of the fire that the Phoenix gave to the Dragon."

"Fascinating," Mischa said. She was an older woman, far older than Asher's parents, and she dripped with wealth. Precious, silver gems hung heavy around her throat and from her ears and shimmered in snow-white hair. She, as most of the others did, wore fine silks and furs, always prepared for the winter. It was indeed chilly, even here in the Summer Palace.

"We are so pleased to have you here," another man said. "The tsar…he is very peculiar about who he seeks an audience with. You are very lucky, Asher of the Bears."

Ah. That was another thing he wasn't quite used to—the court, unable to cope with his lack of a title, had simply assigned one to him.

Asher of the Bears. It was better than Asher the traitor.

"We are indeed blessed," Asher said. "He is a very fair man."

He knew that was a lie, and so did they. The current tsar, unable to wait for his father's natural death or abdication, had taken matters into his own hands and subsequently took over, establishing himself as tsar. He'd already publicly spoken about the treaty with the rest of the middle continent, and how he intended to shatter it, doing what his father could not.

Annika, who had taken it upon herself to sit between Asher and Tyvish, leaned toward him.

"They like you. You are doing well."

Asher turned his smile on her. "Of course I am. I grew up in a court as well."

"Oh, the *stories* of the Phoenix Court!" Mischa exclaimed. "How interesting to divide yourselves by animals. How many of you are there again? Ten?"

"Thirteen, with the Phoenixes," Asher said. "Draco is the smallest, with just one member, although Aranea—of the spider—is close behind."

"Oh, and the largest?"

"Serpens of the snake and Corvus of the crow. They have no shortage of heirs."

"How strange," Mischa said. "I would like to see Eiad one day. Perhaps when your rebellion is in power, I can come and see it."

"That would be excellent," Asher said, although…

She was so confident that they would win but Asher could not be. He knew his parents, he knew the houses, he knew the army they had.

He knew their allies.

Without Verdeca, it would be a bloodbath for the rebellion.

With Verdeca, it would be a bloodbath for everybody.

"Where are you from?" Mischa asked, suddenly turning her attention on Tyvish, who froze.

Asher couldn't help but lean toward him—he knew nothing about Tyvish. He, like the rest of the rebellion, kept his past quiet. It was the easiest way to protect themselves from the house's fury. From what was building.

He knew executions would start soon—his parents would start rounding up those they *thought* could be associated with the rebellion and kill them in the streets. He wouldn't be surprised if Ember Ignis was allowed to oversee most of the killings. Ember wouldn't be satisfied until she saw the deaths of both Luria Van Ela and Juniper Farley, though.

"Kieall," Tyvish said. "At least, my parents are. I was born in Kieall but raised in western Eiad."

"Ah, Kieall," Mischa said, her voice wistful. "The Land of Cities, is it not?"

"Yes," Tyvish said softly. "The Land of Cities. My parents always described it as beautiful but in a different way than everything else. I think for them, the beauty was in the people. The culture. They're the only ones who left. The rest of my family is still in Kieall."

If Asher had put it together correctly, Tyvish's family had fled from Verdeca's endless warpath, escaping to the relative safety of Eiad before they set Kieall on fire and watched the ashes turn to ice.

Nobody spoke for a long moment, forks clinking against porcelain plates, gold-encrusted goblets gently *thunking* against the table.

Eiad had wealth—there was no denying that. But Verdeca?

Verdeca was different. Their roots ran deep, even here, but he had to assume that in the north, in the far reaches of the country, tradition—and the wolves—ran rampant.

Chapter

THREE

E MBER IGNIS WOKE WITH a scream, hands clawing at sweat-soaked sheets. Her heart thundered as she gasped for breath, bile rising in the back of her throat. The room spun as memories and nightmares blurred behind her eyes, melding and shifting and always changing. Teeth and hanging trees, her mother's eyes and dragon scales.

Two months had done nothing to ease the nightmares. Two months had done nothing to quell the shaking in her hands or the nightly vomiting. The only thing that had healed was the wound in her stomach, now turned to a raised, pale scar.

She could still hear the sound of her mother's neck snapping.

Over and over and over and over again, echoing into the deepest recesses of her mind whenever she closed her eyes. It was all she could hear for hours on end, when the guilt and depression hit her so deeply that she could do nothing except sit and stare at the wall.

Eating was difficult.

Sleeping was worse. So much worse.

Ember swung out of bed, bare feet digging into the carpet, nightgown whispering around her legs as she slowly made her way towards the lavatory. Her stomach roiled and Ember rushed forward, barely making to the toilet as a bout of dry heaving brought her to her knees and wracked her body.

Ember wiped her mouth with the back of her hand, disgusted. She'd allowed herself to become soft. Weak. But she had no motivation to *try*. No desire to get up and laugh and smirk and scheme.

Not with the memories hovering over her shoulders, night-dark claws digging into her skin and bones.

Ember stepped back into the bedroom, barely sparing a glance towards the other person in the bed. Lucasta Tersus turned over in her sleep, murmuring softly.

Neither of them had slept alone since the murder of Ember's mother, Verity. Nightmares plagued both of them, although they were nothing alike. Men stalked Lucasta through her sleeping hours, reaching out with bloody hands and crushing teeth. For Ember...

The silver hanging tree flashed in front of her eyes, and Ember flinched, rifling through her drawers and silently dressing before slipping out of the room, closing the door softly behind her.

Ember stopped outside of her own bedroom, staring at the closed door and the Dragon wallpaper that framed it. She'd only been inside a few times over the last two months—mostly to move her clothing and books to the guest room. Maids were allowed in, to dust and keep up the appearance, to change the sheets and scrub down the sink, but Ember couldn't get back in that bed, no matter how many times her sheets were washed.

She'd found a dead man in that bed, and when she slipped underneath those covers, all she could see was his face, flashing in front of her eyes until she finally broke and went to sleep in Lucasta's bed.

There was nothing romantic between her and the other girl—Lucasta couldn't love like that after what had been done to her. It was a miracle that the girl was even able to love at all after the atrocities she'd lived through.

Ember continued, passing the door to Verity's bedroom. Nobody, not even the servants, were allowed in there. Ember held the key to the room on a necklace, the key resting heavily between her breasts.

The home was just beginning to wake as she made her way downstairs, gliding across the floors. Servants lit fireplaces, coaxing them to life. Ember didn't care whether or not they were lit, but Lucasta insisted, and she was loath to deny the small, desert-wild woman anything.

The door to the gardens opened easily and Ember stepped outside, taking in a deep breath of fresh, mid-spring air. Eiad was finally warming up after a long winter and a cool start to the spring, and she turned her face towards the sun, basking in it.

She didn't know if she would ever stop appreciating the sunlight, the way it rolled and comforted and soothed. The wind blew, crisp and bringing with it the smell of flowers and grass and...apples.

Ember gagged, the moment stolen.

She'd had all of the apple trees poisoned once she'd gotten home from the palace as she lay recovering by the window. The open window had let in the smell of the blooms, and something in her had irrevocably broken.

The trees had been poisoned and removed. The smell remained.

The scent of apples haunted Ember through every hallway of the Draco Estate, in the gardens, in carriages and cabinets. This had been *their* home—Ember and Verity. A matched pair.

The house no longer felt welcoming without the other half. Something in Verity had made everything work, and Ember knew, in the depths of her heart, that she was not enough to fill that void.

Lucasta stumbled down the stairs around midday, and Ember looked up from where she sat at the dining table, a stack of papers in front of her. For the two months she'd been... incapacitated, the running of House Draco had largely gone by the wayside. The palace certainly hadn't stepped in—there hadn't been a word from them for weeks, as even temple services had been canceled—and Lucasta hadn't been taught how to keep one of the patron houses afloat, and *he...*

Ember shook her head. She wasn't going to think about him. She had finances to focus on at the moment and he wasn't here anyways.

But pages upon pages of numbers were, and Ember sighed, shifting in her seat as Lucasta came to sit beside her, murmuring softly to a servant, who quickly rushed away.

"Good afternoon," Ember said, and Lucasta rolled her eyes, rubbing sleep from them.

"I had a long night," she said. "I could hear that you did, too."

Ember shrugged, unwilling to reveal more—but Lucasta would know. She always knew, and Ember wasn't hiding anything by staying silent. But it still made her feel as though she had *some* semblance of control over the situation.

The servant returned with an orange and a knife, and Lucasta began peeling it, her tattoo catching the light and drawing Ember's eye.

It felt like an age ago that Lucasta had received that tattoo. It had come after Verity's murder but before Juniper Farley had stabbed Ember, and the months that had passed since then were nothing short of torture.

"Lady Ember," the butler, Roland, said from behind her, and Ember turned to find him standing in the doorway with a letter clutched in his hand. "From the palace."

Everything stopped.

The palace.

Nobody had heard anything from the royal family since Asher Cinis's betrayal. Even when she had been recovering in the palace, healers working tirelessly to ensure she didn't bleed out, the royals had never come to speak to her. Instead, they'd sent a scribe, who noted all of the details she could remember about that night and then left her.

Ember reached a trembling hand out for the letter, and Roland placed it gently in her palm. She could feel Lucasta watching her as she reached for her knife, slicing the envelope open before pulling out the letter inside.

Lady Ember Ignis,
You are required to attend a palace meeting tomorrow
at six in the evening. Attendance is mandatory.
We cannot wait to see you there,
King Whelyn Cinis and Queen Feather Cinis.

Chapter

FOUR

A SHER HEARD THE FULL court before he saw them, waiting outside the doors to the tsar's throne room. Everything was silver and carved with wolves, dripping with diamonds.

"These people are…"

"Don't say it," Asher said softly. He didn't know how Tyvish had planned on finishing that sentence, but he knew he didn't want the Verdecans to hear it.

"What if he says no?" Tyvish murmured. "What are we supposed to do?"

"Leave gracefully and be thankful he let us keep our lives. We have other options if the rebellion is willing to let us go to the far continent. Most of those countries have little allegiance to anybody except for themselves. And I suppose we could go after the islands if it came to that. We might be able to sway them."

"But this is our best option, right?"

"Right," Asher said. "Verdeca is the closest, and we can get them to Eiad the fastest. And frankly, they're the strongest. You know what Verdeca could've done to this continent if they wanted to expend the manpower."

Tyvish nodded, face pale. "I'll let you do the talking."

Asher nodded.

Oh, if only his parents could see him now. All of their training, all of their schooling, was finally being put to good use. The scars on his back tingled.

His mother couldn't hit him here.

"Enter."

Annika's voice, and then retreating footsteps.

The doors flew open, and Asher stepped into the throne room.

At first, he could see nothing, the sunlight streaming in through high windows blinding him. As his vision cleared, he could see the court, dressed in silk and furs, whispering and watching. He noticed Mischa, who gave him a small, encouraging smile, half-hidden behind a feathered fan.

And then he saw the wolves.

Three massive wolves, the size of small horses, laying at the very bottom of a short staircase. Two white, and one, the biggest, was black, ears pricked, yellow eyes tracking his every move. Lips drew away from massive, dripping fangs in silent snarls, unspoken threats.

Do not come any closer.

Asher's eyes lifted from the wolves to the next step, where Annika and two other women stood, each of them standing so terrifyingly still that they didn't look real. He could hardly tell if they were breathing, clay women dressed in intricately carved silver armor. They clutched swords between their hands, the tips firmly planted on the ground.

One of them looked horrifically liked his mother at first glance. His palms began to sweat, and he couldn't quite catch his breath as he stared at her, forcing himself to note the differences. His mother's nose was bigger than this woman's. Her hair a shade darker.

Besides, he didn't think his mother had the type of discipline to stand in one place, quietly, for that long. He wrenched his eyes away from her, unwilling to be caught staring.

Up a step. Two more women, standing equally as still. One of them was a giantess of a woman, towering far above her companion. One of her eyes was completely cloudy, the other a green so bright that it was uncanny.

And then...

The third level.

He couldn't bring himself to look at the tsar—not yet. The Fangs, first.

Sofya Seminoava.

She was easily the smallest of the guard, and she had not one sword but two, crossed over her back, arms tucked behind her. Her armor, unlike the rest, was pure white, nothing engraved in it except a snarling wolf's head. Silver-white hair was braided in a crown around her head.

When he looked at her, she stared back with a deep curiosity, sparking within pale eyes.

Asher cringed away from her and turned his eyes upon the Wolf.

Viktoriya Bolshi.

She was not still like the others—no, Viktoriya Bolshi rocked on her heels, bounced on her toes, arms folded over her chest. She, too, wore the white armor, also possessing twin swords. Her hair was short, curling around her ears, and when her eyes met Asher's, she grinned, flashing her teeth, her smile that of a rabid creature rather than a person.

Mad. She was stark raving mad.

This was the woman at the head of the army?

Finally, he looked at the tsar, at the man lounging in a chair that glittered like ice. His hair was not the typical white-blonde but light brown. His eyes were deep violet, his mouth set in a harsh line across his face. The tsar was young—no older than twenty-five, and as Asher swept into a low bow, he didn't miss the silver circlet that adorned the tsar's forehead.

"Rise," the tsar said, voice echoing through the space.

Asher straightened, Tyvish doing the same at his side, and the tsar gave him a small smile.

"Welcome to the Summer Palace of Verdeca, Asher of the Bears," the tsar said. "And to your companion, Tyvish of the Bears." His voice had no hint of an accent, his words flawless.

Odd. Even Eiadians spoke with an accent.

"Thank you for your hospitality," Asher said, inclining his head. "Verdeca is a beautiful country."

"It is," the tsar said, eyes scanning the throne room, never landing on one spot for more than a few seconds. Paranoia, perhaps. Harmless restless energy, maybe. "And you wish for me to tear it apart for your war."

"Yes," Asher said simply. Better not to lie, his father had once said. Let them know what they were in for. "I have come on behalf of the Order of the Bear to seek Verdeca's assistance in the coming war against the royal family and houses of Eiad."

"Your coming is unsurprising," the tsar said. "You knew I would never ally myself with your parents—not after they allied themselves with the rest of the continent."

The tsar leaned forward, tipping his head to the side. Beside him, the Wolf bounced on her heels, nearly feral. Asher was surprised she wasn't frothing at the mouth.

He was going to unleash that same Wolf on his parents. On Ember Ignis. On the parts of Eiad that still believed in the might of the houses.

He couldn't think about that now. He was here to do a job for the Order, and he was going to do it well, no matter what it took.

"I thought your coming here was brave enough for me to grant you an audience," the tsar said. "And...I am willing to enter into an alliance with you."

Asher's heart stopped.

This was a trick. Nothing was this easy in a court—nothing was this fast. There would be a price to this—and either he or Tyvish would have to pay it. Asher had expected games, negotiations, back and forth conversations, maybe even for days or weeks. Sometimes, these kinds of negotiations could go on for months. He'd braced himself for a long fight.

This was too simple.

"But," the tsar said, "I don't trust you. You are a traitor. Who's to say you won't get tired of sleeping on the ground and fighting in filth and starving and run back to your parents? Who's to say you won't flee? I have met men like you, all too eager to run to the group that promises you the most. Men like you cannot be trusted. Men like you are unworthy of my army."

"I—"

The tsar held his hand up, and Asher clamped his mouth shut. Better to keep his head on his shoulders than say his piece.

"I know you wish to argue. I would feel the same way. But I said I was willing to sign an alliance, and I am—but you must do something for me, first. You must prove yourself. Prove your loyalty not only to me, but to your own rebellion. Prove that you will not run—either back to your parents, or to somebody else."

"I will do whatever I must," Asher said, and the tsar nodded, relaxing again. He didn't like saying that, didn't like making promises like that, but Asher didn't have any other options. Tyvish's hand brushed his, a comfort. At least he didn't have to stand here on his own.

"My country has…forgotten what war tastes like. This court," he said, waving a lazy hand. "This court has forgotten it. My people have grown soft and fat on the riches of my father's wars. Many of them do not remember what it was like to see blood covering snow. They forget what burning flesh smells like, and the way it feels to kill a man, the horror and the rush. I want you to make them remember. I want you to rally Verdeca again. Call upon the people and *make them fight*. Whatever army you raise will be yours to take to Eiad, along with the seven who stand beside me. Raise the people, convince the lords and ladies to send their men, and you can take them all to Eiad with you."

He was going to give them the seven. Even if Asher was unable to convince anybody else, unleashing those women upon a battlefield would be enough to slightly turn the war in their favor. It wouldn't be enough, but perhaps they could slow the endless marching of his parents' army.

And this deal...he could take this deal.

"I will gladly undertake this task," Asher said, bowing again.

"Good," the tsar said. "There are two matters to be dealt with regarding this. First, if you are unable to return within a month and a half, he will lose his head."

A long, spindly finger pointed at Tyvish, and Asher's heart dropped into his stomach. Somebody in the room gasped loudly, and a hundred little whispers broke out around them. It felt like standing in a bird cage, listening to jewel-colored songbirds. He glanced at Tyvish, who had paled.

They couldn't speak, not in front of the tsar, but Asher bumped his leg against Tyvish's. This wasn't a death sentence, necessarily. Not an immediate one, at least. The tsar raised a lazy hand, and the court's chatter immediately stopped, all eyes back on them.

"The second matter," the tsar said. "Is of a guide. It would be unwise to set you loose in Verdeca without the aid of a knowledgeable companion—either the frost would get you or my people would. I am assigning the Fangs to you."

Asher's eyes snapped up to the small woman.

Her jaw set, but she said nothing.

"Sofya Seminoava is a wise woman," the tsar said. "She comes from the northern reaches of Verdeca—she is a woman of the people, unlike most of the sniveling folk in this room. She will serve you well as a guide and a protector. I would give you the Wolf, but…Viktoriya is far too unpredictable for my liking. And I need her with me."

Viktoriya grinned, and the tsar turned toward her, offering a small smile of his own.

How strange.

"I suppose you should leave," the tsar said. "Sofya will meet you at the main entrance of the palace with a horse. I'll send a saddlebag up to your room that you're welcome to fill with whatever you'd like. As for providing you weapons, well… Sofya should be more than enough. You'd only get in her way if you tried to help her."

Sofya, as it happened, was still staring daggers through Asher.

"Sofya," the tsar said, gesturing to her. "Go."

"As you wish," Sofya said softly.

She stepped down, pausing beside the wolves.

"Doya. With me."

The black wolf rose silently and padded after Sofya on silken paws, tail lashing as she passed them.

"Go now," the tsar said. "And hurry. I can't wait to see what you accomplish, Asher Cinis."

Asher was allowed to see Tyvish first. They stood quietly outside the palace, staring at the guards ringing the building. The coastal wind whipped at his curls, blowing chilly sea-salt air into his face. Gray clouds rolled overhead, threatening a storm. Everything was so quiet here.

"I'm sorry they want to take your head off," Asher said finally. Tyvish shrugged, but he wouldn't look at Asher. "I'll do my best to keep that from happening."

"I appreciate it," Tyvish said.

Asher wouldn't necessarily call them friends, but they'd grown closer over the last few weeks. The two of them had been able to set their mutual dislike of each other aside to make the traveling more bearable. In some ways, they had even begun to bond with each other. They were the only two people here from Eiad, after all. different roles.

Despite that they were both seen as necessary for Verdeca. And now, they were going to be pulled to different parts of the country.

"Are you going to be okay?" Asher asked.

"I'll do my best," Tyvish said. "I don't know what I'm going to be doing around here. I guess I'll learn Verdecan and spend time with the lords and ladies. I get the impression you would like that more than me."

"I can't raise the entire country to our side," Asher said. "I'm sure some of the people here have troops. You could try to convince them to help us. They already seem to like us. The idea of us, at least."

"I can try," Tyvish said. "I suppose I'll start at dinner tonight. It sounds miserable, though I don't envy you. I can't imagine having to go with her."

"The Fangs?" Asher said. "How bad could she be?"

Sofya Seminoava was much smaller than Asher had anticipated. When she had stood on the dais she had commanded a sort of power.

That same power remained when she stood beside him, but it was different, more muted, especially without Viktoriya near her.

She was completely terrifying.

She didn't speak when he joined her, one hand holding the reins of her horse's saddle, the other resting on the wolf's head.

Unlike Sofya, the wolf only looked larger up close. Lips pulled back to reveal massive teeth, ears swiveling toward him. This time, it was not a silent growl.

"I'm Asher," he said, giving a short bow. Sofya laid a hand on her wolf's head, silencing her, before tipping her head to stare at him better.

Her eyes were silver, pale as the country that surrounded them, and entirely devoid of feeling.

"I am no tsarina," Sofya said. "And I am not the Wolf. Do not bow to me again."

She swung onto her horse, staring down the road.

"Doya," she said. "Go."

The wolf needed no further encouragement—she took off with a yelp of delight, a shadow against the snow that disappeared from sight within moments.

"She's beautiful," Asher said, hauling himself into the saddle. "I had a dog once."

Sofya glanced at him, kicking her heels into her horse's side. "Doya is not a pet."

"Of course not," Asher said, falling into step beside her. "She's massive. I'd like to see you put a collar on her."

"Doya is a Verdecan wolf," Sofya said. "She is of the old blood. There is magic in her veins, unlike yours. Do not speak any longer. I have nothing further to say to you."

"Very well," Asher said, keeping pace with her as Sofya sped up, leading down the road that Doya had raced down only moments before. The road that would lead them deep into Verdeca, deep into the icy heart of a country that did not feel.

Chapter

FIVE

VIPER TRUNCA SAT SILENTLY in the grass, a snake curled around his forearm. He stroked the reptile absently, the snake constricting and releasing around him periodically. Smooth skin slipped under his fingers, the feeling almost hypnotizing.

He cast a glance toward three of his sisters, rushing and laughing and skipping through the grass, straying toward the fence that enclosed their yard. They looked so young, so innocent, bathed in the golden glow of the setting sun. Adder was four, the youngest of eleven, blonde ringlets bouncing around her face as she screeched in delight and darted away from Asp, both of them barefoot and wearing nothing more than undershirts and shorts.

Spring was good for the Trunca family, even if nothing else was.

The snake began to slither up his arm, towards his sleeve, and Viper moved it to his other arm. It hissed in annoyance but wrapped around him quickly, easily, slithering slowly. A macabre bracelet.

Another sister sat at his side, legs drawn up to her chest.

"Do you want to hold the snake?" Viper asked, extending his arm out to her. Coral looked up at him. She was a wraith, a specter made of short auburn hair and the same blue eyes he had. She, out of the youngest five, looked and acted the most like their mother, and Viper had no idea how he was supposed to speak to her. Not to mention the fact that she was only twelve. Barely old enough to understand the intricacies of court, but Coral picked up on them regardless—and then promptly ignored them. Her loud, often rude comments had led to their father keeping her from any further palace meetings.

"No, thank you," Coral said, staring at the snake. Her gaze was tinged not with fear but blatant distrust. "I don't like them."

Viper almost laughed.

Almost.

He hadn't laughed too much recently.

"I know. Could you take her inside, then?" he said. "Make sure you close the tank well—we don't want her to get out again."

Coral frowned. "I didn't leave the tank open."

Viper resisted the urge to sigh. Coral was…different, compared to himself and the other three. Hers was a quiet sort of strength, soft-spoken like their mother.

Unlike their mother, however, Coral actually had a backbone, and she held her arm out silently for the snake, which Viper easily transferred to her. She stood and made her way into the estate behind them, the door closing softly behind her.

He let out a long breath, turning his attention back to the younger girls. Adder stumbled, and his heart leapt. He launched himself to his feet, already ready to rush to her aid, but she caught herself easily and tore after Mamba, screeching with excitement.

A grudging smile rose over Viper's face. His sisters brought that out in him—the pure, unchecked joy of the younger girls never failed to bring him his own happiness.

They *were* his happiness. Nothing else—and nobody else—came close to them.

"It's getting dark," he said, approaching the girls. Adder looked up at him with wide, pleading eyes. She had blue eyes, too, and they stared up at Viper with an unspoken plea. "We need to go inside before Father gets home."

Mamba made a face. "I don't care when Father gets home."

Viper felt similarly but this was the wrong group to voice those opinions too. Although Mamba, who was ten, and Asp, who was nine, could control their tongues, Adder could not be trusted. She repeated everything she heard, parroting it off with her small voice.

"More time, Vipie?"

"Not today, Addie," he said, bending down to scoop her into his arms. She giggled, pressing close to him.

"Up! Up!" Viper sighed, rolling his eyes but obliging nonetheless. He tossed her up into the air, and she screamed in delight as she came falling back down, crashing into his arms. Mamba and Asp had begun their trek back towards the house, their joined hands swinging between them.

Viper let out a deep breath before following after them, setting Addie down and holding her hand, guiding her into the tentative safety of the house.

Lord Krait entered the house with a flurry of curses and barked orders, flinging his coat towards the nearest servant and storming into the dining room, where Viper, his sisters, and their mother sat.

He sat down with a loud, large *thump*, beady eyes staring down at the family.

Viper hated that he and his father had the same hair. The same eye color—although Krait's were often squinted so much that he couldn't see the color—, and the same facial structure. Despite his age, Krait Trunca was surprisingly healthy. Physically, yes, but it was his mind that gave Viper the most problems.

"What's wrong, dear?" Viper's mother, Gianna, asked. Her voice was soft, soothing, placating.

Although it wasn't entirely her fault, his mother always had been weak.

"Those wretched Phoenixes," he began but abruptly cut off when servants filled the room, carrying dinner. It wouldn't do to speak badly about the royal family when any of the servants could be reporting back. And right now, the Phoenixes were as difficult to predict as Krait himself. Addie was currently occupied with a small toy, keeping her attention away from the conversation.

Once the servants had cleared, leaving behind a baked halibut for each of them, his father began again.

"They've invited all of the lords and ladies for a meeting," he said. "No word for *months*, and now they seek to summon me like a dog?" Krait scoffed.

"You'll have to go, though, dear," Gianna said, delicately cutting into her fish.

"Of course I'll have to go," Krait said. "It's the principal of the thing."

Viper leaned over to cut Adder's fish for her, ensuring that the chefs had followed his instructions to only season hers with salt and pepper. She didn't like anything else.

Adder pointed at the fish's eye and giggled. "Fishy!"

Viper repressed a smile as he speared a piece for her, placing the fork in her small hand.

"You'll need to come with me, Gianna," Krait said. "For appearances. Viper as well."

Viper stiffened at the sound of his name. "I need to watch the girls."

Krait waved his hand dismissively. "We have servants to watch your sisters. You're the oldest. You should be there."

"Summon Boa. She'll come back."

"Your older siblings have responsibilities. Studies and jobs to attend to. You'll come to this meeting. Besides, we've already spoken to Boa, and the earliest she can come home is for the Solstice. You'll be able to see her then."

Viper could feel his mother's eyes on him, and he ignored her, stabbing a piece of fish violently. Coral tugged on his sleeve. He bent towards her, allowing her to whisper to him.

"Why is Father angry?"

"Speak to me directly, Coral," Krait said, and although his voice was still harsh, abrasive, he had lowered it.

Viper had always appreciated that Krait at least *tried* to treat Coral properly, even though there was still a long way for him to go. But Viper didn't dare say that to his father, especially not as Coral stared at Krait with wide, panicked eyes. He didn't often address her directly. She turned toward Viper, and he smiled softly at her.

"You can talk to him, Coral."

"Why…why are you angry, Father?" Coral asked, her hands trembling.

The movement sent a pang through Viper, and he tore his eyes away from her hands to focus on Krait's face, which had softened slightly.

"I'm not angry," he said slowly. Allowing her to take a moment to understand and process his words. "I'm frustrated. The royal family is…not making decisions that the houses believe they should make. They should've summoned us long ago."

"And Viper doesn't want to go?"

Krait's eyes flicked to Viper's. "No, he doesn't. But he has to."

Nobody spoke for the rest of the meal.

Chapter

Six

E MBER HAD BEEN SITTING in front of her mirror for almost
an hour.

Her eyes traced the lines of her own face again and again
as though she were memorizing them. In truth, she was trying
to see if the cream and powder a maid had applied was actually
covering the deep hollows under her eyes. She was dressed
comfortably, in pants and a golden tunic that hung loosely off her
frame. It would hide the fact that she had grown thin and sickly.

Lucasta would accompany her today, and Ember could
hear the other girl downstairs, occasionally barking orders at
the servants.

She pulled a brush through her hair again, watching as
it fell limp around her shoulders. Everything about her looked
drained. Empty.

"Are you ready?" Ember jumped, turning to find Lucasta in the doorway. She wore pants and a tunic as well, although she filled hers out much better. Where Ember had gotten worse, Lucasta had—at least physically—become much better. Her hair shone; her eyes glimmered. She seemed alive.

Ember was a walking corpse in comparison.

"I'm ready," Ember said softly, glancing down at the invitation on her vanity and forcing herself to take a deep breath. Her hands trembled violently as she followed Lucasta out of the room.

The palace had hardly changed. Green towers still shot into the sky, candles glinting in the windows. Guards patrolled the upper turrets and the grounds below. The carriage came to the front of the palace, where a courtyard stood.

Ember swallowed, her head pounding as she stared and stared at the courtyard. The roof had been removed, leaving it open to the stars above, but her eyes weren't on the sky as she slowly stepped out of the carriage, Lucasta's hand in hers. The weight grounded that hand, but the other was still fluttering at her side, uncontrolled.

Servants stepped forward to escort them into the palace. Four of them. Ember squirmed uncomfortably.

This seemed awfully like a guard.

They all carried a knife on their hips, a blood-red ruby set into the silver hilts.

They walked silently into the palace, and Ember nearly choked, stumbling back.

The smell and taste of blood flooded her mouth and nose, thick and metallic, driving out everything else. Ember coughed, desperately trying to push the taste out of her mouth.

"Why do the hallways smell like that?" Ember asked, rounding on the servant next to her. The women stopped, but none of them spoke, simply staring at her. "Answer me."

"We are under strict orders not to speak to you. Please come with us, Lady Ember."

"Why does the palace smell like blood?" Ember asked, pulling her hand from Lucasta's, who had also come to a stop, folding her arms over her chest. Watching. Ready to intervene.

"Please come with us, Lady Ember."

"*Whose blood am I smelling?*" Ember's words came out in a panicked scream, the taste of blood in the back of her throat. "*Tell me!*"

"Lady Ember," one of the servants said, and Ember didn't miss the girl's hand straying to her knife. "Please come with us."

Her throat was closing, her breath catching as she desperately tried to find a way out.

Where she wanted to go, it didn't matter. But anywhere was better than here, in this palace that reeked of blood and fear.

Lucasta slipped her hand into Ember's and tugged her along, still following the servant.

Her heart stopped when Lucasta leaned in and whispered, "The hallways don't really smell like blood, Ember."

They fell in around them once again, herding them down the hallway until Ember stood in front of the doors that would lead into the meeting room.

She hadn't been here since…

Lucasta squeezed her hand. "Breathe."

"I'm trying," Ember snapped and released Lucasta's hand. "Follow me in, okay?"

A flicker of emotion passed over Lucasta's face, but it was gone in an instant. She gave Ember a short nod. "Of course."

The first servant pushed the doors open.

Ember released a long breath and stepped into the room.

She hadn't expected the way her body would seize up as she stepped into the room. Her eyes were always moving, always seeking, searching for *something*.

Perhaps even for someone, although she quickly shoved that down. The room was almost entirely full, every available seat—except for the two House Draco chairs—taken by a lord or a lady or an heir. Lesser sons and daughters took up the rest of the space.

She had arrived only before the royal family, it appeared.

She stood in the doorway for what could've been a heartbeat or a year. Every eye turned towards her, some widening in surprise, others squinting in suspicion.

Ember tilted her head up and took another step into the room. And another. Forced herself to continue.

She hesitated by the chair reserved for the Lady of House Draco. Even when Verity had been missing, Ember had chosen to sit in the heir's seat.

But she could do that no longer.

Ember slid into the seat, a tremor passing through her body.

This felt entirely *wrong*.

All of it—from the stares that continued to follow her, to the servants along the walls, all armed with a knife—was wrong. Strange.

New.

And nobody had told her anything.

"Lady Ember." Ember stiffened at the sound of her name, forcing herself to turn towards House Passer. Lord Lark Canticum smiled at her. "Are you quite alright?"

"Yes," Ember said softly. "I'm doing rather well."

Ember had no doubt that every single person in the room knew she was lying. Lucasta slid into the seat behind her, a comforting presence at her back.

She forced herself to not scan the room again, although her eyes immediately jumped to one of the large windows, which had been mended.

In her head, the sound of glass shattering echoed, and Ember flinched, eyes squeezing shut for a moment as she rejected the memory.

She could feel him looking at her, but Ember couldn't look at Viper Trunca. He made no move to speak to her, no move to do anything except sit and stare at her.

Ember ignored him and surveyed the rest of the table. It was strange for there to be an empty place between House Tigris and House Ibis, the Leopard's spot remaining empty. The tapestry behind the empty chairs had been replaced by a Phoenix banner instead.

Filthy traitors.

They would be punished, eventually.

Ember's eyes skipped toward House Olor, a swan tapestry hanging on the wall behind them.

House Olor was currently being led by a woman who had only married into the houses, and she squirmed uncomfortably as she, too, looked around. Blue's mother. Blue sat behind her, and he and Ember made eye contact for a brief second. Blue gave her a shallow nod. They hadn't spoken much, either, although not by choice. Blue's mother had promptly whisked Blue and his younger brother away from Eiad and to the beach country of Sal. If Ember's speculations were correct, they'd only returned because the royals had summoned them. It had done well for all of them, Ember could tell. All three of them, once uncomfortably pale, now had a healthy glow. Blue's hair had lightened from a deep, ocean blue to a soft, sky blue. It was nearly to his natural shade of white.

He opened his mouth as though he was going to say something, but at that moment, the doors flew open and the king and queen walked in.

The air in the room shifted, like a storm on the horizon, and Ember straightened as she took them in.

They'd burned her mother's body without her.

They hadn't even let her say goodbye.

Ember didn't think she could do this. Her hands clenched into fists under the table, and she forced herself to release them. To stand with the others as Whelyn and Feather stepped into the room and looked over all of them.

She had forgotten how to be angry, she realized. She had forgotten what it felt like to hate, as she lay in the darkness. It had all paled in comparison to the grief.

She could feel it now, though, the slightest prick in the back of her mind.

How dare they?

"Please, sit," Whelyn said, gesturing at them. Had he always had such pronounced wrinkles around his mouth? "We have much to discuss, and I see no point in these empty formalities."

Well, *that* was surprising. The king had always been a stickler for tradition. Ember didn't know what had caused Whelyn's shift—perhaps it was the death of her mother, the infiltration of the palace, or the loss of House Pardus.

But Ember was fairly sure that it was Asher's abandonment that had cut the deepest.

She'd felt it, too, although hers had felt suspiciously like a knife in her stomach.

So they all slowly sat. The queen didn't bother with roll call, and neither of them had papers of any sort in front of them.

The king folded his fingers in front of him and leaned forward. "Obviously," he said softly, "we have things to discuss."

The lord of House Equo, Charles Palin, seized his opportunity, unable to sit in the silence. "Obviously? King Whelyn, with all due respect, the houses have been discussing this from the moment we were dismissed from the palace. We should've acted weeks ago. So what, exactly, has made you change your mind?"

"My husband," Feather interrupted, and Ember's eyes darted over to the queen, "does not have to explain himself to you. The court is second to the Phoenixes, or have you forgotten?"

Ember set her jaw. Despite the exhaustion that lingered in her very bones, she could feel fire creeping back in, laced with hatred. Her mother's last words rang in her ear.

Vengeance.

"Your question is a valid one, Charles," Whelyn said. "And I agree that we need to act. These weeks have been a period of necessary healing for all of us."

Several people rolled their eyes, and Ember resisted the urge to do so as well. She could feel that the queen was keeping a close eye on her.

"Fine," Lord Palin said. "Let's act."

Whelyn nodded. "Let's get started."

"First and foremost, there is the matter of the Silent Duels," Whelyn said, and Viper sat forward. This would be interesting. The Duels had been a consistent sore spot for the last few years. Most members supported them, but a few, notably the lower houses, had begun to push back, viewing them as an unnecessary waste of House talent.

"We cannot have the Duels," Lady Nocte, of House Ibis, said immediately. "It is impractical with all that we have going on at the moment."

"If we don't host the Duels," Scarlett of House Vulpus countered, "then we'll look weak. If we present the Duels—which have always been a show of strength—it'll only show that we haven't laid down to die yet."

"We could simply make it more exclusive," Viper's own father said. "Houses only."

"Perhaps, but that presents complications as well. We may want to take a vote. Lords and ladies only."

"No deaths this year either," the king said. "It would not do well for us to lose valuable members of our court during this time."

There were a few unhappy murmurs. A good Duel would end with a death or, at the very least, a near-death. Lesser children didn't often fight like that, but it was common for the heirs to go at each other with unchecked violence. To keep them from doing that was nearly unheard of, especially as the Book of the Phoenix explicitly allowed it.

"It's near impossible to have a Duel without a death," Charles Palin said. "Besides, it's good for morale."

"Quite the opposite," Violet Soo, of House Aranea, said. "Simply stage the Duels. It's easy enough to make somebody *look* dead while they remain perfectly well. Cut the right spot, end the fight quickly. Everybody is happy then. It's enough blood, but without the loss. We get to keep all of our best fighters."

Whelyn seemed to consider it for a moment before nodding.

"Very well. Each heir is responsible for discussing these things with their family. All in favor of hosting the Duels?"

Most of the lords and ladies put their hands up, but a few—most notably, Ember—didn't.

"The vote is in favor of hosting the Duels," the queen said. "It would be pointless to argue on it further, although I must admit I *am* curious to hear what Lady Ignis has to say on the matter."

Ember stiffened, and Viper watched as her breathing picked up. He knew, without even having to look, her hands were trembling under the table. Lucasta leaned forward slightly, her eyes flashing in concern.

But Ember cleared her throat, eyes locking on the queen.

And Viper, despite himself, leaned forward to listen.

"I…I think it would be unwise," Ember said, her voice shaking slightly. It broke him to hear the tremor in her voice. "The Order has been silent after Asher Cinis's betrayal. They will not stay quiet forever. The Duels would be a perfect opportunity for them to strike."

The queen waved her hand dismissively. "They wouldn't dare."

In that instant, the queen made a mistake.

Something sharpened around Ember—she sat up straighter, folding her hands on top of the table. Her anger kept them from trembling, apparently, as they sat perfectly still. Her gaze didn't waver.

"I'm sorry?" If they hadn't been already, every single person in the room turned toward Ember.

Uncomfortable tension stretched on, the women at both ends poised to explode. The queen's face was darkening from a light pink to a deep purple.

Ember struck first, just as quick and dangerous as Viper's namesake.

"The Order *dared* when they hung my mother." She bit out each word, barely restrained anger echoing in each word. "The Order *dared* when they infiltrated the palace and threatened all of our lives. *The Order dared when they stabbed me!*"

Silence followed her words, until the king spoke.

"I understand your concern," he said softly. "But Scarlett is correct. We cannot look as though we're hiding. And the vote has decided against you. We proceed with planning for the Duels."

Ember's face set, decisively violent.

"The Duels will proceed as normally as possible," the king said. "Limited invitations. Heirs and lesser children participate. Lady Ignis will continue to represent House Draco—we must show that she is strong and well after the attack."

"Very well," Ember said softly. "I will fight."

"Good, good," Whelyn said. "There is another issue that we spoke of as well—the issue of the temple."

"Bah," Lord Palin said. "The temple is a waste of our time. I say we leave them well enough alone on Mount Saffi."

"And allow the Order to sweep in?" Lady Olivea Forrest, of House Alces, asked. "That would be foolish. If they were to convince the temple, they would be able to crush us between them."

"I doubt the temple will ever choose to side with the Order," the king protested. "But…it would not do to ignore the might of the temple, lest we upset them. I believe it may be time to send a delegation to them. Queen Feather and I will consider our options. I'm sure we'll have an answer for you after the Duels."

"Very well," Lady Soo said.

At this, the king sat back, looking slowly at the court. His eyes drooped. "You are all dismissed."

Chapter

SEVEN

VERDECA'S COUNTRYSIDE WAS NOTHING but an empty tundra for miles.

Now and again, they could see Doya, racing over the endless ice, but then she would vanish again.

Sofya was silent at his side, but she set a relentless pace.

"We will reach the town of Mir before dusk," she said, breaking the silence for the first time in hours. "There we will find lodging…and there you will have your first opportunity to speak to my people."

My people.

"The tsar called you a woman of the people," Asher said. "What did he mean by that?"

"I am from the far north," Sofya said, eyes tracking Doya across the ice. "That is where the tradition remains the strongest. That is where the wolves come from. That is where the gods are. So I am of the people because I am of the old blood."

"Like Doya?"

"Like Doya."

Silence again. He could hear nothing except the horses' hooves on the ice, and the wind endlessly whipping toward them.

"I know we're heading east," Asher said. "But straight east?"

"Northeast," Sofya said. 'The south—both southwest and southeast—is so stupidly loyal that the second they hear you are raising an army, they'll flock to the tsar—most of the lords and ladies of the south were at court with him today. They are…hungry for war. From their homes, they can see Qin and Prajan and all the rest of those countries, and they are envious. They want that again. They miss the taste of blood in their mouths, and they wish to feast again. But the north is removed from that. The further east, and the further north we ride, the less likely they will be to join up. They have allowed their weapons to rust and have locked their armor away. They have their ways, in the north, and they have their families, and I doubt they want to fight some silly war."

"It's not silly—"

"Enough," Sofya said. "No more questions from you."

She glanced at him, pale brows furrowing.

"Are you not cold?"

"A bit," Asher said, snuggling further into his coat.

"You will need warmer clothing before we reach the north. I will see what I can do to keep you from freezing to death. I do not wish the tsar to be upset with me if you die."

"Thank you," Asher said, and Sofya turned away, a black tattoo suddenly appearing from underneath the fur collar of her coat as she shifted her shoulders. "What's your tattoo of?"

Sofya glared at him. "Have I not told you to be silent?"

Asher shrugged. "We have to spend two months together. I'm just trying to get to know you better."

"I do not care," Sofya said. "I have no desire to know you."

Phoenix above. A strange part of him almost wished the tsar had sent Viktoriya instead—she at least seemed more fun, even if she was a bit crazy.

"I'm just—"

Sofya sighed, reaching up and yanking her collar down.

A wolf stared back.

Asher rode up closer to her, tracing the harsh lines of the tattoo. It had not been done with care—there were stray lines, strange shapes. But it was a wolf nonetheless, a black wolf with burning red eyes.

"They brand you in the prisons," Sofya said, pulling her coat back up and hiding the tattoo. "I am sure Annika told you that Vika and I are of the prisons."

Vika. Viktoriya.

"She did," Asher said, guiding his horse away again. Putting space between the two of them felt wise. "But she said nobody knows what you did."

"That is because I did not care to tell them," Sofya said. "Vika's crimes were well known. She killed the slavers that came for her sister. Eight of them, when she was just ten. People were outraged when she went to the prisons, so her story has been told countless times. It is not quite as grand as some try to make it seem. I hear it was quite terrible."

"Is that why she's…"

"Crazy?" Sofya asked, her tone harsh. "Wild? I would not use those words around her. That is an act. Vika is quite serious, but it scares the court to think of her as a rabid beast on a tether. They respect her more, and the tsar knows that, so he allows her to do whatever she wants. She keeps them afraid. And when they are afraid, they obey faster."

"How long was she there?" Asher asked, and Sofya glanced at him.

"She is twenty-four now, and we were released two years ago."

Twelve years.

"She is death-marked," Sofya said. "She was branded, too. She had a year left."

"And you?"

"Fourteen years," Sofya said. "They wanted to kill me, too, but then they forgot about me. I rotted in the darkness."

"I'm sorry," Asher said, and Sofya scoffed.

"Do not lie," she said. "You would have forgotten me too, if I had been in your prisons."

And then she pulled ahead, fleeing his questions and the darkness that lingered.

They walked into Mir's tavern without speaking to anybody. They made a strange group—the Fangs of Verdeca, a disgraced former prince, and a massive wolf.

Whether it was Doya or Sofya that made the other patrons fall silent, Asher didn't know, but their attention quickly shifted to him, dozens of pale eyes tracking his path across the room. Asher, with his dark skin and tight curls, was an oddity here. He would be pinned as an outsider immediately, without ever opening his mouth.

Nobody spoke. They simply watched, heads tipped in consideration as he and Sofya slid into a table, Doya laying at their feet. A barkeep, who had been in the middle of serving another table, noticed Sofya's armor and slunk behind the bar, watching them suspiciously.

Somebody spoke softly in Verdecan, and Sofya cocked her head, responding quickly before turning to Asher.

"They wish to know who you are," she said. "Some of them speak the common language—most do not. I will not be your translator."

"Sofya—"

"Fangs," she said. "And this is to be your army. You must learn how to communicate with them."

"I don't speak Verdecan."

"Then you will have to learn."

Asher nodded, jaw clenched, heart pounding, and pushed himself to his feet, Doya leaning up against his leg.

"My name is Asher of the Bears," he said. "I was formally the crown prince of Eiad, but I renounced my title and my claim to the throne to fight against my family, the houses, and the rest of Eiad's elite, in hopes of building a fair Eiad."

"Why you here?" a woman asked, her accent so thick that he could barely understand what she was saying. Now that he really looked, Asher could tell these people were not soldiers—they were mostly older people, wearing home-spun clothing and sipping ale from chipped tankards. The woman who had spoken had gray streaks shot through red hair, and withered hands clutched the table. She glanced at Sofya, who didn't waver, and then to Asher. "We fight again?"

"I—yes," Asher said. "I've come to ask you to help fight for the Order of the Bear."

The last word had hardly left his mouth before the people were leaping up, all clamoring at once. Asher took a step back, and Doya growled low in her throat.

A warning.

Sofya was a moment behind her, her voice ringing out across the room.

"*Botsist!*" They quieted slightly, although they continued grumbling. "Listen."

"I will not force you," Asher said, nodding at Sofya gratefully. She simply set her eyes forward, scanning the crowd, although he hadn't missed how her hands had flown to her swords. "I understand you've lived peacefully for many years, and that you are hesitant to fight a war for a country you don't care about. But you must understand. Without Verdeca, the houses will again take control of the country, and then they will come for you. Your enemies—Prajan, Qin, Geloj Swesh, Oscela, and Kieall—will come for you on the orders of my family. They will burn Verdeca to the ground, simply because you did not offer your aid."

"We no fighters," the woman said, and Sofya turned to him, shrugging.

"She's right. These are country-folk. Perhaps long ago they were fighters, but no longer. They have settled down and traded swords for shovels."

"Can you ride?" Asher asked, tipping his head. The woman frowned, as though it were a silly question.

"Yes."

"Then take a horse and go south. Tell the south to rise up and—"

"No," the woman said, and the other patrons began grumbling again. She sat down with a thud. "No south."

Sofya grimaced. "I did not warn you. The country is... divided. You did not get a warning because I did not think you would suggest such a thing."

"Like Eiad?" Asher asked, whipping around, and Sofya shook her head, to Asher's relief.

"No. There will be no fight—they both respect the power of the tsar and the seven, but...they do not like each other. No southerner would fight for a northerner."

"But I'm neither," Asher said. "So even if they were just carrying the message, the answer would be no?"

"Right," Sofya said, beckoning the barkeep with a wave of her hand. "It will be no."

"Please," Asher begged, turning back to the watching patrons. "Please help me."

"No," the woman said, sitting back down. "No war. We tire."

The others sat as well and Asher, a bit disoriented, slumped into his seat, staring at Sofya, who was speaking softly with the barkeep. "What...what just happened?"

"You just learned what it is like to raise an army in Verdeca," Sofya said, watching the barkeep scamper away. "You are not one of us—they will not fight for you without true reason. They do not care about your war; they do not care about your country. Even *if* your country goes after Verdeca next, we will fight back. It will not be the massacre you speak of."

"You don't know what my parents are capable of."

"You do not know what *Verdeca* is capable of," Sofya said. "My country could slaughter yours without even a thought. These people will only fight if there is a *true* reason, and you did not give it."

"I thought this was supposed to be the easy one," Asher said, and Sofya laughed.

"You are a fool," she said. "And they know that."

Asher's face burned but he didn't respond—how could he, after all? He'd already failed.

"Why wouldn't the tsar just call them to arms?" Asher asked, unable to stay silent for long.

"You wish for these people to die for you," Sofya said, still watching the people. "You need to look them in the eyes and ask them yourself. The tsar could call them—but he is, despite his flaws, a man of the people, as much as he can be. He may not have dwelt among them as I did, but he respects them. He knows what they could do to himself and the court if they so chose. He keeps the people as happy as he can, and in return, they do not overrun the palace."

"Then you ask," Asher said.

"No," Sofya said harshly. "Do not ask me that again. This is *your* task. If it is important to you, you will find a way. They are still people. They are just teaching you that threats of power will not work on them. You believe your country strong, violent, hateful, but you have seen *nothing*. You know nothing of war or people or violence. And while you are here, you will learn. But I will not do it for you, and I will not hold your hand. I am only here to ensure you do not die in the wilderness."

Doya whined, low and pitiful, and Sofya clucked her tongue at the wolf. "*Terpinye*, Doya."

"What's her problem?" Asher asked, and Sofya glared at him.

"She is hungry," Sofya said. "She wishes to hunt, but I have forbidden it until tonight. She scares people."

"Of course she does," Asher said. His own stomach growled as a tankard of *something* warm was placed in front of him, as well as a bowl of stew, thick and meaty. "What's the drink?"

"Honey wine," Sofya said, blowing steam off of the top before raising her own tankard to her lips. "Only the south has the ability to keep bees. It is impressive that they have it this far north."

Asher raised the cup to his nose, inhaling deeply. It smelled of spices and honey and wine, and he drank, relishing the warmth that bloomed in his stomach. "It's delicious."

"Yes," Sofya said softly, taking another drink. "I remember when I had it for the first time."

Asher didn't dare speak—he was desperate to learn more about Sofya and what had landed her in the execution cells.

She took another sip and cleared her throat. "It was during the trials to become the Fangs. We had just finished our third challenge—the last needed to be part of the lowest rung, the *Nizhiny*. They had us swim the length of a frozen lake. The guards had to break the ice so we could enter the water at all, and it froze over our heads. We broke out on the opposite bank. Some died in the water, some died in the days and weeks afterwards because of what it had done to them. But I did not. When I was on the bank again, they wrapped me in a blanket and handed me a cup of *vilvy*. I have had an addiction to it since."

"I can see why," Asher said, and Sofya smiled.

"What did you drink in Eiad?"

"Everything," Asher said. "I'd rather not talk about it." Sofya's smile vanished, and she nodded, her silver eyes cold and sharp again.

"Yes," she said. "I heard the stories. I will not ask again."

EIGHT

I WILL FIGHT. **I** will fight I will fight I will fight I will fight I will fight.

Ember simply couldn't believe she'd said that, her words from yesterday continuously ringing in her ears. The Duels were only two weeks away and she hadn't practiced in months. There wasn't a chance that she'd be able to hold a knife, much less actually wield one against an opponent. And she knew, too, who they'd put her up against. It was the same every year. Blaze Minus, the heir of House Tigris, who only fought with his bare hands in a loincloth.

It was disgusting, and Ember felt as though she had no choice but to beat him, year after year.

But this year would be different. She wouldn't provide much of a fight, if she could even fight at all. He'd be able to toss her around like a little, broken doll. It didn't matter that the king and queen had put in the rule against deaths—Blaze would make short work of getting her to the brink.

"I cannot be weak again," Ember whispered, looking at herself in the mirror. Her eyes darted down to the knife on her vanity. The Dragon head's hilt grinned up at her and Ember set her jaw.

At the very least, she had to *try*. Had to try and survive the way she had for so very long. Ember grabbed the knife, pulling the sheath out of her drawer. She strapped it to her arm and slid the knife in, smiling softly at it.

The weight was comforting and helped to ease the shaking in her hands. She'd have to ask Lucasta to help her find some way to weigh her hands down for the Duels themselves. At least then, she'd be able to stab or slash.

Ember sighed, pushing away from her vanity. She stopped a servant in the hall, murmuring softly to her. The woman nodded, rushing off as Ember followed, much slower. She ran her hands over the railing of the stairs, savoring the feeling of the cool wood underneath her fingertips.

Lucasta was waiting at the bottom of the stairs, a hopeful expression on her face. "You're going to practice?"

"I have to," Ember said softly. "Or the fight will be over in moments. I have to give them something."

"You *don't* have to do anything," Lucasta said, falling into step beside her. She made a face.

"You've never been to the Duels. You don't understand," Ember said. "The crowds...they'll be screaming for my blood. Blaze will be obligated to hit me a few times so they can see

Dragon's blood. It's fine, though. They're staging it this year. Nobody's really going to get hurt."

"What a filthy holiday."

"It is the most brutal," Ember admitted. "But most of the others aren't much better. The Hunt especially…"

Lucasta shuddered. "Don't tell me."

Ember met the servant at the door, reaching out for what the woman held—a basket of knives. Lucasta made to follow her outside, and Ember held her hand up.

Lucasta sighed. "Let me help."

"No," Ember said softly. "I need to do this alone."

"You aren't alone, Ember."

"I…" Ember couldn't bear to tell her that even if she was physically surrounded by other people, the burden of House Draco and the future of her place in the houses, fell solely upon her and her alone. And what she would have to do to cope with Verity's death…no, she had to do that alone, too. "I have something else I want your help with."

Lucasta cocked an eyebrow, and again, there was that flicker of unfamiliar emotion deep within her dark gaze. "Go on."

"Weight helps with the shaking. I need a way to weigh down my hands during the Duels. It'll help a little, at least."

"Very well," Lucasta said, nodding. "I'll start looking into options. Maybe rings? Or a bracelet?"

"Whatever you can figure out," Ember said. "I'll try whatever you give me."

With that, she slipped outside. The wind whipping her plait around her face was refreshing, soothing her thoughts.

The faintest smell of apples brushed past her, and Ember's stomach roiled, but she closed her eyes, instead focusing on the smell of the grass, of the flowers in the distance.

She needed to concentrate.

Ember dropped the basket, finding one of her targets leaning against the side of the house, a spiderweb connecting it to the wall. She dragged it out into the garden, driving it into the soft ground. Mud squelched under her boots as she made her way back to the knives.

She brushed her fingers over the Dragon-head knife on her forearm before pulling a knife from the basket. She tested the weight in her hands, thrilled to see that it, too, was doing something for the shaking. Her palms were slick with sweat, and Ember swallowed before pulling her arm back and flipping the knife towards the target.

It went wide.

Ember hadn't expected much else, but frustration lodged in her throat nonetheless.

She hadn't realized how bad she'd actually gotten.

That frustration didn't subside as she made her way through the basket, knife after knife passing through her hands. There were twenty in total, and once Ember had thrown the twentieth, she looked up at the target.

She had only managed to hit it twice, and both were stuck into the furthest edges of the target. Ember let out a growl of annoyance, stomping over to collect her knives.

Just go back to bed.

The thought rose, unbidden, to the front of her mind, and Ember stiffened, a knife in each hand.

It would be easy enough to go back to sleep. To send servants to clean up the knives and the target, to bathe and slip back into her bed and wait for Lucasta to figure out how to fix this.

She so desperately wanted to.

But…

"Do not," Ember muttered, "allow yourself to be weak again."

So she gathered her knives and began to throw again.

Viper dipped a brush into paint, staring at the canvas in front of him. Adder's portrait smiled back at him, all blonde ringlets and bright, blue eyes. His mother had both sketched her and painted it, but she'd sent Viper to add proper highlights to Adder's hair. Coral sat on the ground beside him, watching him paint. She was sketching, although she hid her canvas from him when he tried to see what it was.

"You're not as good as Mother," Coral said. Her tone was neither scathing nor critical—she was simply pointing it out.

"I know," Viper said. "I don't practice as much as she does. I suppose I should."

Coral nodded, worrying with the ends of her hair. "I think you should, too."

Viper sighed, sitting back in his chair as he stared at the painting. It was nearly done, which was a relief. His mother had wanted it to be finished by Adder's birthday, which was shortly after the Duels, and thankfully, it looked as though it would be.

"Father says I have to fight next year," Coral said, making a deliberate line on her canvas. She squinted at it for a moment before erasing it. "I don't know what I'll use."

"For what?" Viper asked, only halfway listening to her.

"For my weapon," Coral said. "Father says that Serpents are supposed to use whips."

That, admittedly, was something Viper struggled with as well. Technically, all of the houses had a choice weapon, dictated by the Book of the Phoenix, and House Serpens's was a whip. As on the nose as it was, it had been that way since the beginning of the houses.

It was much harder to learn how to wield a whip than a knife, though, and while Viper had been trained with both, he preferred the knife. The whip was too unpredictable, too difficult to use with perfect accuracy. Besides, as good as a whip was in close, single combat, it would be of little use on a battlefield. He knew House Draco's was a dagger and nothing more, which was only *slightly* concerning.

Viper set his brush down, running a hand through his hair. He needed to stop thinking about Ember. She'd made it abundantly clear that she didn't want his concern.

"Are you worried?" Coral asked. "I would be worried."

"I'm not that worried, Coral," Viper said. "I'm a lesser son. Nobody cares about my fight."

"But you're the oldest," Coral protested. "Boa had to fight as an heir last time because *she* was the oldest. It's only fair."

"Boa was named heir, remember? Taipan stepped down. And besides, I'm not interested, Coral," Viper said. "The decision comes down to the king and queen, and they're too busy to care anyway."

Coral set her jaw and opened her mouth to say something, but at that moment, the door to the studio flew open and Viper turned to find Mamba standing there, her face flushed with excitement.

"There's a woman here to see you, Viper," she said. "And she's *beautiful*."

Viper's heart leapt. *Ember?* But no, it wouldn't be Ember, that simply wouldn't make sense.

She'd made it clear that she didn't want anything further to do with him, and part of him resented her for it.

"Let her in," Viper said. "I'll meet her in the living room in a moment." He took a second to take off his painting frock and ensure there wasn't any paint on his face. His hands were covered in paint, but there wasn't anything he could do about that now, and he simply shoved them into his pockets as he made his way out of the studio and into the hallway, passing a dozen closed doors. He and his siblings all had their own rooms, but most of them stood cold and empty now, with his older siblings scattered to the winds. The only time it had even truly hurt had been with Boa—he'd been so young when his other siblings left—some for different continents—that they felt more like cousins than brothers and sisters. The Trunca children, when they left, often did not come back.

Viper stepped into the living room and froze.

Lucasta, seated on the couch, gave him a nervous smile. "Viper."

The last time he'd seen Lucasta had been the last time he'd seen Ember, too. He swallowed hard.

"Lucasta," he said, nodding. He sat across from her. "What are you doing here?"

"I need a favor," she said, avoiding his eyes, and Viper sighed, already moving to stand.

"I figured. You and Ember never bother to seek me out unless you need something."

Lucasta's face set. Unreadable. "That's unfair. Please don't get up."

"We both know I'm right—"

Lucasta raised a hand, cutting him off. Viper's face burned, but before he could say anything else, before he could spit venom at her, she sat forward, and something like worry flashed in the deep recesses of her dark eyes.

"It's to keep her from dying at the Duels—and I suppose, beyond that. I know your king banned killings this year, but in her state…it would be so easy. Her opponent could do it accidentally."

Despite, himself, Viper stilled. "Go on."

"She *cannot* fight the way she is. We're both aware of that. She isn't getting better—thankfully, she's not getting worse, but her hands are just as bad as they've always been. And that's not even taking into account that she hardly sleeps or eats, and she hasn't practiced in months. She started practicing *for the first time* when I left. She's not the same woman, Viper."

"But I don't understand why you're *here*," Viper said. "I don't understand what I can do to help her."

"She asked me to find a way to weigh down her hands. The weight is the only thing that keeps them from shaking. It's our way of giving her a fighting chance, so to speak."

Viper shook his head. "I will not help you."

"Viper—"

"Lord Trunca is just fine," he said. "Do not come back here. I wish you the best, Lady Tersus, in both your quest to help Lady Ignis, and in life, but I have no desire to further associate myself with either of you. I'm sure you can find your way to the door. Have a nice day."

Chapter

NINE

VIPER CLOSED THE DOOR softly behind him, Adder and Mamba bathed in moonlight in the room he'd just left. He leaned against the door, running a hand over his face.

Two days. Two days had passed since Lucasta had come to ask for his assistance. Two days had passed since he'd refused her.

He, beyond what the houses inherently owed to each other, had no allegiance to Ember Ignis. He was a lesser son. She was a lady. If she needed help that badly, she could go to the other lords and ladies. The guilt that curled in his stomach, whispering that he was a terrible person for leaving her to *die* in the arena, shouldn't have been there.

But it was nonetheless.

The guilt whispered that she hadn't known what she was saying, that she had only spat such venom to keep him safe, as she'd said over and over again. It whispered that she was only trying to keep him out of the brewing conflict as much as she possibly could.

He still resented her for it. He still hated that she thought he needed to be protected at all.

Viper needed a distraction. Something to occupy his mind, something to pull his thoughts away from Ember Ignis and the blood that surrounded her. He found his heart tugging him toward his mother's painting room—of course. The portrait of Addie still needed to be finished and it wasn't like he was going to be able to sleep tonight anyway.

He was surprised to find light streaming underneath the door when he approached it, and he knocked softly, entering to find Coral asleep on the floor, a couple of candles burning around her. His mother sat on her stool, in front of a blank canvas, and she turned as he entered, smiling softly. Auburn hair, streaked with gray, tumbled over her shoulders, lovely and unbound.

"I thought you might come here," Gianna said, beckoning Viper closer. When he stood beside her, staring at the emptiness in front of him, she placed a brush and a small jar of gold paint into his hands. "The girls told me about that woman coming to visit you. Lady Ignis's friend. The prostitute, was she not?"

"She was," Viper said, his low tone matching hers. "But no longer. She stands as the Dragon's right hand now. I wouldn't be surprised if Lady Ignis names her heir."

"Lady Ignis," Gianna said softly before standing with a sigh. She smiled again, and only then did Viper notice the wrinkles around his mother's eyes had deepened. He often forgot that as he aged, she did as well, and perhaps he didn't need to be so harsh on her. She was nothing more than a product of her environment, just like he was. "Come, Coral. It's time for bed." Viper's sister grumbled something as she stirred before pushing up, sketchbook clutched close to her chest, and followed Gianna out of the room.

The door closed behind them with a soft *click*, and then Viper was alone with his thoughts. He slid into the seat his mother had just vacated and swapped the brush and paint for a soft pencil, the tip hovering just over the canvas. He closed his eyes against his torrent of thoughts, desperately trying to shove down Lucasta's voice.

Keep her from dying.

He was not responsible for her life.

They were having Ember's ceremony today.

Viper knew that she hadn't been back to the palace after waking up from Juniper Farley's attack, knew that she hadn't been present for the burning of Lady Verity Ignis's body. That *had happened when she was still on the verge between life and death, her fate balancing in the middle. Viper hadn't gone either, but both Blue and Lucasta had attended. It had been a short ceremony, and although the Phoenix Flame left no ashes, an urn was created nonetheless, black and gold. Blue had placed it in Ember's bedroom after the burning.*

Now she was coming back to the palace, and he promised himself that he would be there for her every single step of the way. He waited in the throne room with everybody else, taking the space in. He'd been in the throne room only once, when he'd watched Asher Cinis say his vows to the crown when they were all about sixteen.

It hadn't changed much since then—the room was a large, open space with massive, floor-to-ceiling windows flanking the room. On the far end of the room was a raised, wooden dais, stairs leading up to the two thrones at the top. There had once been three, but Asher's was gone, disappeared to Phoenix knew where. The floors were slick wood imported from Tali, and for the occasion, large wooden benches had been brought in. A black runner was laid on the floor, leading up to the dais, and twin Dragon tapestries framed the doorway.

Viper desperately tried to yank himself from his thoughts, from his memories, but now that he had allowed himself to confront them, they came all at once, in a terrible rush that he had no control over. His hand moved, sketching lightly without purpose, without direction, but the sound of the throne room was in his ears now, drowning out everything else.

The throne room was packed, and Viper shifted uncomfortably between his father and Coral, who had her hands over her ears. He ruffled her hair, and she forced a smile. Viper was inclined to agree with her about the noise—the space echoed. He stared at the far wall, where a massive mural of the patron animals and the Phoenix had been painted, depicting the Phoenix's ascension to Her home in the sky.

Slowly, painfully, the throne room quieted. The houses took their seats. The king and queen stepped onto the dais, both of them immaculately dressed. They both wore crowns.

He didn't have much time to dwell on them, though, as the doors at the end of the throne room opened, everybody stood, and Ember stepped in.

She was a marvel.

She wore black and gold and red, and he simply could not take in all of her at once. The dress they'd put her in started at her throat, tight across her shoulders, arms, and torso, and fanning out at her waist. Bare feet peeked underneath the skirt, but it was her face that drew everybody's attention. Gold eyes outlined with kohl, pursed lips painted red.

Her eyes were so incredibly empty.

In that moment, Viper forgot everything except for her. Except for that woman. Except for the Dragon that now strode down the runner, dress whispering softly around her feet. Her eyes were firmly fixed on the dais and what the queen held—a diadem in the shape of a roaring dragon. Golden wings would fan out on either side of her, and the Dragon's own head would rest on her forehead, beady red eyes staring out upon the crowd.

Ferra Ignis had worn that crown, and so had Verity. Generation after generation of Dragons had borne the weight of the diadem, and now Ember would be forced to do the same.

Just as quickly as he'd removed it, though, he placed his attention right back on Ember. She passed his row, and her eyes jumped to him for the slightest second. He dropped his gaze to find that her hands were shaking, but she buried them in the folds of her dress and finished the walk. The king motioned for the houses to sit, and they did so, Viper leaning forward so as not to miss a single word.

Ember stood at the base of the dais, her head high despite the shaking in her hands.

"No," Viper said out loud, pulling away from the canvas and shutting his eyes against it. "Not yet."

He didn't know who he was pleading with—himself, Ember, the Phoenix Herself. But his prayers were not answered, and he could not help but go back to his work.

"Ember Ignis, daughter of Verity Ignis," the king said, and Viper wished he could've seen her face in that moment, when that man said her mother's name. From where he sat, though, he could only see her back, and the way her hands trembled. "Do you accept your sacred duty to respect and obey all the commands of the Phoenix herself, all the days of your life?"

"I do," Ember said, her voice ringing out across the throne room. Chills rose on his arms.

"Ember Ignis, granddaughter of Ferra Ignis, do you accept your sacred duty to continue and expand the workings of House Draco?"

"I do."

"Ember Ignis, descendant of the Dragon, do you promise to protect and defend House Phoenix and the goddess of this land?"

"I do."

"And finally, Ember Ignis, the Dragon heir, do you accept your position as the lady of House Draco, the only woman who may continue the future of your house?"

Ember's voice cracked. "I do."

The king reached behind him, and the queen placed the golden diadem in his hand.

"Kneel, Ember Ignis, the heir."

Ember sank to her knees, bowing her head. Slowly, the king lowered the diadem onto her head. Ember's head dipped lower for only a moment before she raised it, the diadem glinting in the sunlight.

"Rise, Ember Ignis, the Dragon."

She rose.

And Viper had known, in that moment, that he would never be free of her grip. Not as she turned and faced the crowd, looking down upon them all as she stepped onto the runner and made her way out of the room. The siren song of Ember Ignis had wormed into his heart and made a permanent home there, always calling him back to her.

Viper reached for the brushes and paints that his mother had left scattered on the table, pulling them toward him at random, barely registering the colors he was picking.

He'd sought her out afterwards, at the small reception that had followed in the courtyard. Ember had been surrounded by a group of lords and ladies, all of them speaking to her animatedly, hands moving and eyes wide. Ember simply sipped from her flute of champagne and nodded along every so often. Lucasta was at her side as well, oftentimes speaking more than Ember. A little shadow that acted as a second set of ears and eyes.

After a long while, Ember detached herself from the group, and Viper moved in to meet her, holding out another flute to replace the one she'd drained. He could feel Lucasta watching them but found that he couldn't tear his eyes from Ember.

"Viper."

"Ember."

They stood there, staring at each other. Her eyes roamed his face with a hint of desperation, but what she was looking for, he wasn't sure. His own heart thudded—they'd been playing this game for weeks. He would flirt, she would shut him down. She would flirt, he wouldn't be able to react properly. There was a tension there that he couldn't quite figure out, and it stretched between them now, an invisible tether linking the two of them.

Finally, she spoke, her voice strained, and her eyes darkened.

"You cannot speak to me anymore," Ember said, and Viper had reeled, taking a step back. Surely he'd heard her wrong—surely she wasn't dismissing him, after everything they'd gone through together? But Ember continued. "You are...too close to me. The Order will know that for a fact now that they have Asher. He has no reason to protect either one of us, and I know they still want me dead. I will not put you in more danger. I refuse to do so. So you must stay away from me for your own safety. I am not doing this to be cruel, Viper. I am doing it to keep you safe,

because if they take you…if they go after your family, hoping that your collapse will trigger mine…I could never forgive myself for that."

Her voice was low and rushed, her words tripping over each other. The party swirled around him, lights and laughter, but the only thing he could hear was his own heartbeat and the way Ember wouldn't look him in the eyes.

"I can take care of myself," he said finally, his voice cracking, and he hated it, hated how weak *he was around her. "I don't need you to protect me."*

"I thought the same about my mother. Look how wrong I was. And she was a lady, Viper. They shouldn't have been able to get her."

"You keep Lucasta around."

"It's different."

"How?"

"I…" Ember flushed, pulling her eyes away from his face. "If you really must know, I can't sleep alone. Not after Blue's father. She doesn't mind, and I don't feel comfortable asking some servant girl to climb into bed with me. So I need Lucasta."

Viper rolled his eyes. "You're making excuses."

The blush was creeping up Ember's neck now, and her eyes locked onto his suddenly, something like fear burning in the depths of her eyes. "Don't you dare."

"Oh," Viper said softly, "I dare."

"Do you understand what I'm trying to say?" Ember asked, "I'm trying to keep you safe. I will not allow them to take you too."

"Oh, I understand," Viper spat, and his face curled into a sneer. If they were going to play the game, they were going to play

it correctly. He wouldn't back away from her. "Don't worry, Lady Ignis. I'll stay away from you. I'm not interested in wasting my time on somebody so selfish."

Her face had changed then, and she took a step back from him, brow furrowing in confusion before her expression sharpened.

There she was—the Dragon, rearing her head. This was Lady Ignis, daughter of Verity Ignis. This was not Ember.

But this was who she had to be to outlast the Order.

"Remove yourself from my presence, Lord Trunca. I am a lady of this court, and I have no further time to spend on lesser sons."

He'd knocked back the rest of his champagne as he walked, shoved the glass into some servant's hands, and stormed out of the courtyard.

He didn't look back.

Viper forced himself out of his thoughts, paint smearing his hands and clothing and forehead, and stared at the canvas.

He knew—just as his mother had known—what he was going to paint.

It was Ember who stared back at him—Ember as he knew her and the Dragon, a terrible mix of pale skin and black scales, wholly golden eyes, devoid of their whites and their pupils. Black hair that rippled into flame, a mouth that was at once bared in a snarl and twisted in a scream, fangs flashing. She wore nothing except her scales, turning from woman to Dragon, the change between the two so small, so imperceptible, that Viper knew he could not have painted it again if he tried for the rest of his life.

Viper's chest heaved as he stumbled away from the still-drying painting. He'd painted her diadem, just as it had been that day.

He'd painted *her* just as she'd been that day. He'd painted the moment his words had hit home and she'd shifted. That slight, terrible difference that nobody else would've picked up on, the hardening of her eyes and the smallest set of her shoulders.

But he had seen it.

Viper knew he shouldn't hold such a thing against her. She was only doing what she thought was best, she was only trying to protect him so that he—or his sisters—didn't swing next.

But he wasn't a child. His sisters were protected by himself and his parents and the guards stationed around the estate.

You are too close to me.

He'd heard the hesitation in her voice when she'd tried to define what, exactly, they were to each other. But what she'd said had been true. He was too close to her. But it was not the Order he feared. It was himself. It was the fact that, no matter how much he'd raged the days after that had happened, how much he'd cursed her name, he could never truly hate her. He could never shake off the claws that Ember Ignis had dug into his very spirit.

And he wouldn't allow her to be destroyed by Blaze Minus in the arena, either. He wouldn't leave her fate in Lucasta's hands alone, capable as they might be.

Viper would have to help her, if only to kill the monster that lurked in his gut.

Chapter

TEN

"LADY IGNIS IS NOT in," the man at the door of the Draco Estate said, moving to close the door. Viper, before he could truly think through what he was doing, shoved his foot in the small crack, forcing the door open. The man's eyes widened.

"I'm not here to see Lady Ignis," Viper said. "I'm here to see Lady Tersus. Is she here?"

"I—"

"I'm here, Viper," Lucasta's voice floated over the man's shoulder before her head appeared, dark hair long and unbound, a small streak of white pinned back. "Let him in, Roland."

"Without Lady Ignis home?"

"Yes," Lucasta said, taking the handle from the man and opening the door wide enough for Viper to slip in. "And

I'd prefer to keep this a secret from her, if you wouldn't mind."

The man scowled but nodded, closing the door behind Viper before stalking off.

"Where's Lady Ignis?" Viper said, and Lucasta rolled her eyes.

"Just call her Ember," she said. "We both know you're only doing that because you're bitter. And I don't know where she is. Contrary to what you may believe, she and I aren't attached at the hip."

"You would be bitter too," Viper muttered, and Lucasta shrugged.

"Ember knows she can't get rid of me," Lucasta said. "I'm too valuable. And besides, I think she actually likes my company."

Lucasta led him into a sitting room, gesturing toward the couch before curling into a chair of her own. They'd sat in this room only a few months ago—the first time Lucasta had stayed the night with Ember.

"I have some ideas," Lucasta said, no longer bothering with the pleasantries. "And if we can agree on one, we need to find somebody to execute it, because we're out of time. The Duels are next week."

"I know," Viper said softly.

"Bracelets won't work—they'll just be annoying, and I doubt they'll help with her hands all that much, but rings, maybe?"

"They have to be heavy enough to weigh down the shaking, so the rings might work, but...thick rings might be a problem with the knives."

"They could be efficient weapons," Lucasta countered, and Viper shook his head, considering.

"I...what about gloves?"

Lucasta glanced up, tipping her head to the side. "Gloves?"

Viper nodded, leaning forward. "Gloves, lined with iron. Heavy but slim. Tight around the wrists to ensure that they don't slip off but loose enough that she can still use her hands as much as she could without them."

"That's actually a really good idea," Lucasta murmured softly. "But somebody will have to make them. I was never privileged enough to frequent the seamstresses that the houses use—would you be able to find and commission somebody?"

"My mother will know somebody," Viper said, nodding. "And I can pay for it—it's not as though House Serpens can't afford it."

"Excellent," Lucasta said, and her gaze softened. "Thank you. I appreciate the help. I know she will, too."

"Keep me out of it," Viper said. "I'll let you give them to her."

Lucasta shook her head. "No. You give them to her. I'm not allowed to go to the Duels, and even if I was, I'm tired of things being so...off. Maybe this will help the two of you reconnect."

"Maybe," Viper said softly. "Maybe."

The temple sanctuary was warm with afternoon sunlight, streaming directly onto Ember where she sat in a pew. This was where they'd burned her mother, Lucasta had told her. This was where whatever remained of Verity Ignis had been cleansed from the world, leaving behind nothing except painful, terrible memories.

Underneath her exhaustion, something was brewing. She'd spent all morning practicing with her knives, and part of the afternoon in front of her mirror, remembering what it felt like to be beautiful. Ember had even managed to rest her hand on the doorknob of her mother's bedroom one time before shuddering away from it.

The Duels were giving something back to her. The routine of it all, the necessity of re-honing her body into the weapon it had once been. It gave her the space to be angry again.

The Phoenix Flame was roiling in its bowl.

The argument about the temple was coming back to her now, and a terrible idea. The king had mentioned a delegation to send to the temple in an attempt to sway them to their side, but she knew that she wouldn't be chosen to go with them. The royal family would want to keep her close, to keep an eye on her doings.

But they wouldn't want her anywhere near them if she was a danger. For the last few months, Ember had been docile, easy to keep under their thumb, but she couldn't be expected to act like that forever. She wanted to speak to the High Priestess though, to understand the true power behind the temple. Could the Phoenix Flame and its bloodlust be used on a battlefield? Would the High Priestess even allow it?

She knew the royals wanted answers to those questions, too, but she would be damned before she assisted them without getting something out of it. Ember wanted the temple to be loyal not to the royal family, but to her.

"Funny seeing you here," a voice said behind her, and Ember tore her eyes away from the Flame. Blue Corvu slid into the seat next to her, not looking at her yet. They hadn't spoken to each other since Juniper's attack, and they had never discussed their parents' deaths before. She knew he and Viper had been friends before, but the two of them had never been particularly close themselves.

"I frequently come here," Blue said. "I don't necessarily believe I'm religious, but...we all need something to turn to these days, don't we?"

Ember glanced down at Blue's hands, where they were twisted in his lap. She tapped his ring finger, where a silver ring with a sapphire set in the middle rested.

"New?"

"In a sense," Blue said. "My father's house ring."

"The one from the severed finger?"

"The one from the severed finger," Blue confirmed. "A little macabre, I know, but I don't have much of him left. Nobody will talk about him. It's like they forgot it happened."

"They didn't forget," Ember said. "It's just...not important anymore."

"At least your mother was high up. My dad...he was just a nobody lord with a drinking problem. He died just to show the royals that the Order wasn't playing games. That's all it was. At least Verity's death *meant* something," Blue said, and Ember could hear the frustration creeping in. She had admittedly not given much thought to what Blue's family had gone through with the death of his father. They were a lesser house, and there were still three of them left.

It felt terrible to admit that, even just to herself.

"Your father's death meant something," Ember said softly, but Blue shook his head.

"No, it didn't. It just proved that the Order had the capacity to go after their own. Your mother's death was a *true* blow to their power. To kill a Dragon in their own palace? Unspeakable. To kill a drunk man with a little too much money in his pocket? It happens every day in this Phoenix-forsaken country. He wasn't beloved, like House Pardus, and he wasn't respected, like your mother. Nobody in the court knew him well. A lot of that is his fault, of course, but it can be difficult when it feels like nobody cares."

They stared at the Phoenix Flame together.

"I'm going to ask the king and queen if I can be part of the temple delegation. To try and connect with my faith. Something like that," Blue said. "I don't really know. Being in Sal was good, but I hate being back here now. Getting out again would be nice. But I don't think they'll agree to it."

"I want to speak to the High Priestess myself," Ember said. "And I don't think they'll let me go, either."

"I suppose we could act out," Blue said. "Give them a reason to send us away. Show them that we aren't willing to just obey their every word. After all, our parents died because of *them*, and they haven't even had the decency to officially address it. I remember the last time a lord died—we were in mourning for four days."

Ember turned toward him, and their eyes locked.

"Act out how?"

Blue shrugged.

"Act out at the Duels. Force their hand. They said no deaths, right? All staged?"

They stared at each other for another long moment before Ember smiled.

"I suppose they did," she said, and the two of them sat in silence until shadows deepened in the temple and the sky above glittered with cold stars.

Chapter

ELEVEN

A SHER WOKE TO THE sound of wolves.

He sat up, eyes darting from the nearly dead fire to Sofya, sitting across from him, to Doya, who was howling.

There was a music, a beauty in the howling of the wolves. He couldn't see the other wolves, but he could hear them, their voices blending and mixing with Doya's as she tipped her head back again.

They'd stopped for the night, halfway between Mir and the next town, slightly off of the main path but still exposed against the ice, nothing to give them cover except the sleeping mats and blankets Sofya had brought with her. Asher had slept in his coat—it was too cold to do anything except wear all of his layers.

And it was only spring—nearly summer. Phoenix above, this place would be a freezing hell come fall.

He was trying his very best to not think about his parents. He could imagine them, back at the palace. They would've had a long day of meeting with house members, planning the approaching Silent Duels. They would've eaten dinner separately—his father in his study, probably accompanied by one of his mistresses, and his mother in the dining room, perhaps hosting guests, perhaps alone. Sometimes, it was only the two of them. Was she still having those dinner parties, he wondered, after what happened to Verity?

Verity. Ember.

The last time he'd seen her, she was grasping the hilt of a knife shoved deep into her stomach. He knew she was alive, but nothing beyond that.

It felt strange, to be so removed from it all. By now, everybody would know what he did. Everybody would know that he ran while Ember clung to life in the palace courtyard.

Would they still blame him if they knew what he was running from? What he still felt like he was running from, even now?

"In the north," Sofya said suddenly, jolting him from his thoughts as she prodded the fire, "they say that when you die, you will hear the wolves beckoning you home."

"You have an afterlife?"

"Of course," Sofya said, glancing at him. "How terrible it would be to have nothing after death. The gods will welcome you, and you will run for eternity with the wolves and those who you love. It is a pleasant thought—that I may be able to see my mother and sister again."

"I'm sorry they passed," Asher said. Sofya waved her hand dismissively, but there was something forced about the movement, betraying her feelings.

"Do not worry," she said, her tone offering no room for argument or questions. "I have come to peace with their deaths."

"And your father?"

Sofya's face darkened—a rare flash of rage. For a killer, she rarely let the mask slip. "I do not know. I do not care."

"I understand," Asher said. "My father is a lot of things, but my mother...it would be better for everybody if she died. And I know that's a terrible thing to say, but—"

"It is not," Sofya said, as Doya began howling again, head thrown back toward the sky. "She hurt you, did she not? You should feel that as much as you wish. You do not have to forgive your mother."

"She's still my mother," Asher said softly, but even as the words left his mouth, he felt the sting of a whip against his back, and his mother's laughter rang in his ears. Often, after they had a relatively peaceful dinner together, she would call the captain of the guard to her side, and it would begin.

"She is not," Sofya said, and tipped her head, so similar to Doya's movements that Asher couldn't help but glance at the wolf. "You flex your back when you speak of her—did you know that?"

Asher stilled. "I...no. I hadn't known."

"I had a tell, too," Sofya said, eyes darkening, although she didn't elaborate further. "Vika made me stop. You do not have to hide it, but perhaps you should try. It is a weakness others may exploit. Did your mother strike you?"

"*She* didn't," Asher said. "She just had the captain of the guard do it."

"I am sorry," Sofya said. "It is a terrible thing to be hit."

"It is," Asher said, and they lapsed into silence, both of them staring at the flames. He didn't understand how it was so easy to tell Sofya about these things, when he had been unable to reveal his secrets to people he'd grown up with.

Doya had finished howling, the voices of the other wolves dying out, and was now curled up beside Sofya, massive head resting in the Fangs' lap.

He still couldn't believe the sheer size of Doya, but it was her coloring that was the most interesting to him. The other wolves he'd seen—both the real wolves, and their depictions— were all white, a color that was much more suited to hunting in the snow.

But perhaps Doya was so fast, so powerful, that it didn't matter if prey saw her—they wouldn't be able to escape the wolf's teeth and claws.

Sofya laid down again, Doya immediately pressing up against her.

Phoenix above, he was lonely. Nothing had changed when he'd joined Juniper Farley and the rest of the rebellion—he was scorned there, too, turned away and ignored by everybody. Including Juniper.

"What was it for?" Asher murmured.

"Be silent," Sofya said, but snapped her fingers nonetheless, and Doya rose from her side to join Asher. "Speak to her if you must. She does not tell secrets."

Sofya turned her back fully—not a movement of dismissal but of understanding. A movement to give him privacy. He knew she was going to listen nonetheless, knew that it was in her very nature to do so, but he appreciated the gesture regardless.

Doya laid beside him with a huff, laying her massive head into his lap, her breath warming his leg. He hesitated to touch her, as Sofya did—he didn't trust her, and she didn't trust him. Not yet, at least.

But he spoke to her nonetheless.

"She won't speak to me," Asher murmured, eyes trained not on the wolf or the flames or the darkness surrounding them, but on Sofya, who gave no indication that she was listening. "Juniper won't. I…I gave up everything for her, but she doesn't seek me out. And she knows I have no way of getting to her either. She's keeping her distance. But I don't know why. I don't know what I did."

Doya's eyes fluttered shut, and Asher lay back, gently placing his hand on the wolf's head, between her ears. She leaned into his touch, and Asher suppressed a smile.

Around them, the wolves fell silent, voices fading into the deep night.

They saw trees the next morning, to both Doya and Sofya's delight. They appeared out of nowhere, first spread apart and then clumped together, green branches clumped with snow, red berries littering the ground around their roots.

The wolf took off immediately, tail lashing, and vanished in between the trees, a shadow that rippled and moved within. Sofya was slower but her pace had increased, too, her horse's hooves kicking up powdery snow directly into Asher's face. He shook snow from his curls as he spurred his horse on after Sofya.

He was relieved to see the trees too, although he feared what might've been lurking in them—the wolves were not the only animals who survived in Verdeca's endless tundra. There were stories of massive, white bears, foxes that slunk through the undergrowth, massive deer with antlers that could rip a man from nose to thigh.

Sofya, too, disappeared into the trees with a shout of joy, Asher following close behind.

She was gone. Doya, too.

Asher pulled his horse to a stop, turning it in a tight circle. His horse exhaled nervously, prancing in place, and Asher urged her further into the woods, deeper down the path.

In the darkness of the trees, a shadow moved.

The hair on the back of Asher's neck stood on end—was that Sofya? Doya? Something else entirely, hunting him through the trees?

His horse's hooves crushed berries underfoot, staining the snow red.

Asher drew his knife.

Another movement—definitely canine shape, tracking his movements with its own.

"Sofya?"

He didn't understand how she had disappeared so quickly, how she had managed to hide both herself and a horse so fast.

A whistle cut the silent air, and Asher's horse reared as Doya burst from the trees, snarling. He landed with a thump as the horse took off down the path, and Sofya's laugh echoed through the trees.

The dull end of a knife pressed against Asher's throat, and he stilled.

"I wanted to remind you," Sofya said. "Of what you are dealing with. *This* is what Verdeca is—she is a country that is cold and unforgiving, and you have trespassed upon her to ask her to bleed. I am simply reminding you of what my people can do to you if they want."

Another whistle, and Doya, herding Asher's horse, and Sofya's horse emerged from the trees, whinnying softly. He heard her sheath her sword.

"Get up," Sofya said, and then hissed in pain as Asher's knife cut across her legs, across the pants that she had not bothered to layer with armor. In her sweater and pants, she was just as unprotected as he was.

Sofya's blood dripped into the snow, and her jaw set. Asher pushed himself to himself to his feet, pants soaked through with snow, and grinned as Sofya unsheathed both of her swords.

He knew he had made a mistake the second he heard Doya growl.

"It's not fair if you use Doya," Asher said, but Sofya was no longer speaking—her eyes were locked on his, tracking him as he shifted his weight.

Silver and black flashed through the air as Sofya's swords swung at his right and Doya leapt at his left side. He was only fast enough to block Sofya's swing—Doya knocked him to the ground, jaws around his throat, not yet biting down, but holding him there so that he could feel the pressure of the wolf's massive teeth around neck. The pressure increased, her jaws tightening, and Asher spluttered, hands flying to bury in the wolf's fur, desperately trying to push her off of him.

"*Vypsuk!*" Sofya said, and Doya released him, stepping back, saliva dripping from her jaws. "*Nvosky, Doya.*"

Doya slunk away from Asher, although dark eyes still watched him, tracking him as he stood.

"Fool," Sofya said. "Get on your horse. We must go."

Asher's hand reached up to touch his throat, a necklace of shallow puncture wounds ringing his neck.

He was terrified of them.

And he knew that neither wolf nor woman feared him in the slightest.

Chapter

Twelve

V   IPER WAS HOPING—NO, praying—that he and Lucasta
had come up with something good. The Duels were
here, and the crowd would've already gathered, impa-
tiently waiting for the show they were promised.

All of the spectators had been informed that there were
to be no deaths, but serious injuries were still allowed. There
would be punishments, of course, if one were to break those
rules.

Lucasta had promised to collect him before Ember
left for the Duels—after all, Lucasta hadn't been given an
invitation. Which was all the better, according to her.

"It's a blood sport," she said. "I'm not interested in seeing
that."

Viper had a suspicion that Lucasta simply didn't want to see Ember get hurt.

Some parts of him felt similarly.

Some parts of him simply couldn't care.

Viper dressed slowly, ensuring that everything was right. His mother had sketched the outfit and commissioned it, and he was relieved to find that everything fit well.

Every inch of it had been designed to mold to his figure, leather pants and a long-sleeved tunic that was overlaid with a pattern of violet and bronze scales. He wore light, flexible boots tightly laced to his feet, and he strapped a whip to his left hip and a bandolier of knives across his chest. Two extra knives rested on his right hip and inside one of his boots, respectively. A Serpent's-head helm fitted him easily, strapping to the leather tunic to ensure there wasn't a weak point in his neck. Only his face would remain uncovered.

Viper stepped into the hallway, holding a small, rectangular box. It was made of slick black stone, a roaring Dragon inscribed in gold on the top. *That* particular detail had been Lucasta's doing—a final moment of ingenuity.

Around him, House Serpens was just beginning to wake. His father and mother, Coral in tow, would arrive shortly after him to claim their seats, but the other three sisters would be kept at home, far from the violence and bloodshed. One day, they, too, would have to face that.

Viper despised that, despite the fact that it was a part of their religion, especially as they were House Serpens. The Silent Duels had been designed to honor the Serpent and the Spider, but it was an awful holiday. None of the other holidays, the Hunt included, even rivaled the Duels in terms of casualties.

It was a 'good' year when only one person ended up dead by the final fight. Whether they died in the arena or from injuries afterwards, it didn't matter. It made him sick. What god demanded such sacrifices from Her chosen few?

But that didn't mean he would refuse to participate. That didn't mean he'd allow himself to get beat up by whatever heir they chose to throw at him.

Viper stepped outside, turning his face to the predawn sky before getting into a carriage. He brushed a thumb over the box in his lap, his finger skidding over the gold Dragon inscription.

He didn't think he was ready to see her.

But there were no other choices.

The carriage started down the road, wheels rumbling over stone as they headed toward the Phoenix Palace, and then past it.

The Silent Duels weren't held at the palace or any of the estates—it was held in an arena a few miles north of the palace, designed and built solely for the purpose of hosting the Duels. Viper could see it even now, rising above the trees. It was a building of colossal proportions, made of the same green stone the Phoenix Palace had been created from. It was all one large, perfect circle, with the bottom of the arena being cool sand. Viper had skid across that sand more than once, his blood sprinkled across it.

The walls of the arena were made up of seating, the bottom row reserved for the royal family and the lords and ladies of the first three houses. From there, the walls rose, the seats filled by the rest of the lords and ladies. After that, heirs sat while the lesser children participated, but they were replaced by those same children when they went to fight. The topmost rows were for the guests that the royal family specifically invited—they would be empty this year.

Underneath the arena was a labyrinth of waiting rooms, where some of the fighters chose to dress and arm themselves. There was a massive dining hall as well, and they were fed before and after their respective fights. Two staircases led up from the waiting rooms to two sides of the area, where gigantic metal grates would be raised to allow them in.

From there, the Duels would commence.

Viper shifted his seat, gently touching the whip at his side. His father would want him to use it at least once, perhaps for some showy, finishing strike. He still didn't know who they'd put him up against, although he could wager a guess. They paired them up in a similar way every year, with Ember and Blaze Minus having the last fight. It would be different, though, without House Pardus.

"They'll put Ibis with Equo," Viper muttered to himself. "Which means I'll have Alces."

He didn't particularly know how he felt about fighting Allan Forrest, heir of House Alces. Normally, he'd be up against some lesser child from House Corvus—there weren't nearly enough in the other houses to waste on him, although last year he'd fought the heir of House Vulpus, Vervid, who had spectacularly trounced him.

Viper had seen Allan fight before—the choice weapon of House Alces was a massive axe, and Allan wielded it with surprising proficiency. He could see it too, the handle carved into the shape of a massive elk, with the blade gleaming silver and sharp under the sun. If Viper was lucky, the fight would end *without* his blood coating that axe.

Chapter

THIRTEEN

E MBER COUNTED HER KNIVES strapped to her hips again, fingers skipping over the hilts. She had arrived about an hour ago and had been quickly rushed into one of the waiting rooms.

It was a cell—albeit a nice one—furnished comfortably with a couch, a chair, and a vanity. A pitcher of water and a glass had been left on the vanity for her, as well as kohl that she had already used to line her eyes. The court loved their dramatics.

She'd dressed in the chilly darkness of the space, ensuring that her clothing all fit well. Black, scaled armor covered her entire body, but it was her weapons that would draw people's eyes. A golden sword was strapped to her back, a massive onyx stone set in the hilt. She wasn't perfect when it came to swordsmanship, but it could do something against Blaze and his monstrous fists.

Her hips and thighs were strung with throwing knives, and a small, round shield bearing a roaring Dragon was strapped to her forearm.

She didn't know if it would be enough. But she didn't have any options.

She tightened the sheath that her Dragon knife rested in, ensuring that it wouldn't fall off of her while she fought.

"You're to come and eat something," the guard at the door said, a hand on the sword at her hip. "King's orders."

Ember forced herself to keep her face blank.

He burned Verity.

Without you.

Some things felt unforgivable.

She shook the thought from her mind and nodded at the guard. "Very well. Lead the way."

The guard turned, leading Ember through the maze of cells and large common rooms. Some of the cells were barred with large, metal grates rather than wooden doors, and Ember shuddered when a shadow in one of the corners moved, revealing a sickly, mottled bear.

Despite its condition, the creature managed a half-hearted roar at her, and Ember shied away from the cage. Her hands twitched.

The hallway let out into a large dining hall; a massive, wooden table laden with food set in the center of the room. Chairs surrounded it, and twin fires burned on either end, warming the place. Lesser children roamed around the table, some of them eating, although most were simply staring into space anxiously.

She couldn't blame them. She remembered being pushed into that arena the first time. The way the world had stilled and quieted, everything tilting for the slightest second.

And then the crowd had roared her name, and Ember had attacked.

She would not dare make the first move this time.

Ember sat beside Blue's younger brother, who was nervously chewing a piece of toast, his eyes skipping around the room so quickly that she could barely follow them.

"Norvin."

The boy stiffened at the sound of his name, turning towards Ember. His eyes widened.

"Lady Ignis."

"Don't bother," Ember said, reaching for an orange. Her fingers trembled as she began to peel it, and she could feel the boy watching her. "I am not a lady today. Only a fighter, just like you."

She didn't miss the way the boy reached back to anxiously touch the slim, silver swords strapped across his back. House Olor's weapons, the twin swords.

"I'm not really a fighter," Norvin said. "I'm only thirteen."

"You're going to fight. Thus, you're a fighter. A *victor* is something else entirely. But as soon as you step out into the arena, you're a fighter. Try to win, though."

She finished peeling the orange, handing it to him.

"And do not, for the sake of your brother," Ember said, leaning in, "lose."

The guard gave her an approving nod as Ember approached her, pointing her down a new hallway. "Go up that way to reach the stands. The fights are supposed to begin any minute now."

Ember didn't bother to tell her that she'd already gone up those stairs many, many times before to watch the others participate.

Only this time, she would have to sit with the royals.

Somehow, despite her true position, she was still straddling the divide between heir and lady, playing both parts as well as she could but always falling slightly short.

Ember jogged up the stairs, once again checking to ensure that she had everything she needed. She hit the landing, reaching down to adjust one of the knives on her hips, when she heard footsteps behind her and turned, spotting a golden-blonde figure in the darkness.

Her breath caught.

Viper.

He stood a few steps down at her, looking up. He wore scales, like her, and she didn't miss the sharp blue of his eyes, peering out through the darkness.

"Lord Trunca," Ember said softly, looking at him. She remembered their last conversation all too well. She had both regretted it and didn't at the same time. She knew for a fact that the Order would seek to use him against her, the way they had with Verity. The right thing to do, the *kind* thing to do, was to push him away. Even if he hated her…at least he would be alive. At least his little sisters would be alive.

But she couldn't deny the fact that her stomach fluttered as he climbed the rest of the steps, meeting her on the landing. She couldn't deny the fact that she missed having him around.

Despite herself, Ember ceded a step, unable to bear the weight of that gaze.

"Lady Ignis," he said, and it was then that she noticed he was holding something, a little box clutched close to his chest. "I…"

"Don't," Ember said. She could not bear this, could not have this distraction before she had to fight. Her hands shook faster, betraying her. "Please."

"I have something for you," Viper said, holding the box out. Upside down. "To help you today."

Ember's entire being stopped as she stared down at the box. She watched, as though in a different body, as her hands, still shaking, reached out to take it. It was smooth and heavier than she had expected, and she turned it over to find a glittering, golden Dragon grinning up at her.

Oh, it was beautiful.

Her heart broke and healed and *ached* as she opened the lid of the box.

He gently took the lid from her as she lifted one of the items out of the box.

Gloves.

They were stitched of black silk, and the weight of them was unfamiliar—so unfamiliar that she immediately slipped them on, a perfect fit except where they were loose at the wrists, twin strings dangling from each of them.

The shaking in her hands had receded so far that she barely noticed it.

"There's a way to tighten them," Viper said softly. "May I?"

Ember nodded blearily, still staring at her gloves.

Viper stepped forward, and this close, Ember was sure he could hear her heart pounding. She could smell him—paint and oranges. She stretched out her hand towards him, and Viper gently took it, turning her wrist over, leaving her hand palm up.

"The seamstress stitched iron into them," he murmured. "I hope they're heavy enough."

Ember's breath caught as he brushed his thumb over her wrist, over the pulse racing there. The slightest smile turned the corners of his lips, and Ember's heart stopped entirely as Viper took the twin strings and tugged them, wrapping them around the bottom of her wrist and tying them in a bow on the other side. His hands were quick, deft, and it only took him a few seconds to do both gloves.

But those seconds had felt like *years,* and when he released her, Ember took a deep breath, dizzy.

She did not like the effect he was having on her. She was supposed to be avoiding him, shunning him, casting him from her thoughts. But there he stood, like some new god, dressed in scales and knives.

Ember supposed she looked the same.

They stepped away from each other, and Viper dipped his head. "I suppose we should go up."

Ember nodded, allowing him to brush past her and open the door at the top of the stairs.

The roar of the crowd filled her ears, and her senses sharpened once again as the tang of blood surrounded her, wrapped her in its metallic embrace.

Everything fled her mind as she stepped into the sunlight.

It was time.

Chapter

FOURTEEN

VIPER HELD THE DOOR open for Ember but stared at the wall when she walked past him, the wake of her steps leaving behind the faintest smell of crackling flames and apples. She said nothing to him as the door shut and they found themselves standing in the arena, having emerged somewhere on the second floor.

She went down.

He went up.

Viper moved towards the third floor, where the rest of the heirs were already waiting. There weren't many of them this year—with Ember sitting down with the royals, it left only Blaze Minus, House Ibis's heir, Lonan, House Equo's heir, Sorrel, Viper, Blue, Vervid, Robin of House Passer, and Allan Forrest.

Viper didn't belong among them.

He wasn't truly an heir. He was only playing the part, and he received more than one prickly look from the others as he slid in between Blue and Robin. She gave him a half-hearted smile, clutching a slim throwing spear between her hands.

Blue, however, had different intentions.

"Are you ready for this?" His face was blank, impassive.

"No," Viper admitted. "But what choice do we have?"

"None," Blue said softly. "We are of the blood. But Ember...I don't think she even *can* fight anymore."

Then I will fight for her.

Viper shoved the thought deep, deep down into his stomach, to the depths of his being, forcing himself to not look at her where she sat below, next to Queen Feather.

The arena *roared.* The stones shifted under their screams.

There had been no blood yet, but the crowd was already in a frenzy, frothing at the mouth to see it.

But this would be *nothing* compared to how they'd react to Ember.

Viper turned back to Blue.

"She has to fight. She has to give them her show."

"I know," Blue said softly. "But it still feels wrong."

"We're already here," Viper said, bumping Blue's shoulder with his own. "We might as well enjoy the fights."

While we still have them, Viper didn't bother to add. The shadows in Blue's eyes spoke volumes.

The lesser children fought well, but Viper's mind wandered nonetheless. There was too much to keep up with, too much to think about, and he knew for a fact that the last thing he was supposed to be focusing on was the way Ember's pulse had skipped under his fingers when he'd touched her wrist.

Her heartbeat was a song that he simply could not push away.

Blood stained the sand at the bottom of the pit, gleaming in the sunlight like a collection of scattered rubies. The final two competitors moved off of the sand, and Viper stood, following Robin out of the stands and down the stairs, back into the depths below.

His heart beat erratically, and he touched his weapons again, ensuring that they were all there. When they reached the bottom of the stairs, they were immediately split up and herded to respective sides of the arena, and he checked to ensure his boots were laced correctly.

The screams of the crowd were deafening when the first two competitors, Robin and the heir of House Corvus, Bylon, entered.

He knew instantly when the fight began, because the arena fell quiet.

Viper couldn't see the fight at all, but he could *feel* it. Every thud upon the ceiling could've either been Robin with her spear or Bylon with his crossbow thudding to the ground. He wished he could've watched. They were only allowed back in the stands after their fight, which meant both Robin and Bylon would see every single one of them go through the arena. Viper both envied and abhorred that idea.

At least, though, he'd be able to see Ember.

Blue jogged up the stairs next, and Viper knew that Vervid would be waiting for him on the other side of the arena, just as the House Vulpus twins had done for Blue's own brother. Viper simply couldn't remember who had won that fight.

He watched Blue retreat up the stairs, drawing his twin swords as he did. Vervid would have slim, lethal throwing knives.

Viper listened to every slam and skid above him, but he had no way to tell if Blue had won or not.

It didn't matter, though, because the guard at the top of the stairs, sending next to the grate, was beckoning him forward. Viper made the climb in a daze, touching the whip at his side but not freeing it.

Not yet.

Cool air flooded through the grate, and through the thick bars he could see the sand, stained with blood, and the other gate, where he knew Allan would be standing with his axe.

Someone called to the woman at the gate, and she slowly turned the cogs that raised the door, the ancient metal shuddering.

Viper stepped out of the darkness and into the arena.

He was blinded for the slightest second as he passed into the arena proper, and although he was dimly aware of the crowd that screamed for his blood, he was more aware of the figure on the other end, emerging from his own gate.

Allan grinned at him as they came together, all mousy brown hair and a flimsy jawline.

"You aren't ready for this," he said, flipping the axe in his hand. "Lesser son."

"Oh, but think about how funny it'll be when I beat you," Viper said, unsheathing one of his knives. "The heir, beat by some nobody."

Allan snarled, his smile suddenly gone, and lunged.

Silence fell.

Viper rolled at the last second, sand flying from where the axe struck. He was up in an instant, drawing a knife from the bandoleer strapped across his chest, flinging it toward Allan, but he was quick too, ducking and arching his axe through the air, silver flashing in Viper's peripheral, but he threw up a knife, blocking the hit.

It reverberated through his bones and teeth, through his very blood.

Viper held firm, pushing back against Allan. The other boy stumbled, and Viper struck, rushing Allan and hitting him in the stomach with his head, knocking them both to the ground. They rolled through sand and blood, grappling with each other.

Viper pinned Allan, rearing back before stabbing him through the hand with one of his knives. The sickening sound of flesh breaking and bone cracking echoed throughout the arena and Allan bucked, eyes widening. Viper stared at the blood bubbling up around the knife.

And then he smiled.

This was the Duels.

This was *his* holiday. There was no way the outcome of this fight could be anything other than his victory.

And he was going to make his house proud.

Viper stood, kicking the axe away from Allan. It rested a few feet away on the sand, glinting dully.

With a quiet grunt, Allan ripped the knife from his hand, favoring the other. The metallic smell of the Elk's blood wrapped around Viper, and he understood, for the briefest moment, the bloodlust of the crowd.

There really was something intoxicating about it.

Allan attacked with renewed ferocity, drops of jewel-bright blood sprinkling the sand.

Viper grinned, freeing the whip at his side.

It was time to end this.

He cracked the whip, the sound terrible and exhilarating all at once. Viper snapped it toward Allan, catching him around the ankles and bringing him to the ground. He could do nothing but squirm and buck as Viper knelt beside him, pressing a knife against his throat.

"Yield," he murmured.

Allan struggled underneath him, trying to reach a second knife, but Viper knelt on his wrists, holding him in place.

"Yield."

A fight traditionally only ended three ways, and Viper couldn't kill him. Nor did he want to. He shot a quick glance toward the royals, who had their heads bent together in close conversation. Allan stopped struggling, simply going limp underneath Viper.

The hatred in his eyes rivaled Ember's.

"I yield."

His voice carried over the arena, into the stands, and Viper released him, stepping away.

And the crowd screamed for him. Screamed and clapped and stamped their feet, a roiling, roaring mass of people that, for once, were all focused on him.

A group of medics came and hauled Allan out of the arena, and the moment passed. The crowd quieted and Viper was ushered up to his seat, to watch and wait for Ember.

Chapter

FIFTEEN

EMBER WATCHED, IMPASSIVE, AS they carried Allan Forrest past her on a cot.

Her entire being had focused on the fight, and when it had ended, she'd relaxed, unable to help the relief that had swept through her body.

She ignored the gloves—although they were working wonders—and she instead checked her knives again. Adjusted the sheath that held them against her body. Watched in wonder as her hands stayed miraculously still at her sides.

This had been Lucasta's work, of that she had no doubt. It had been clever, though, to bring Viper in. Lucasta's attempt to bring them back together again, although Ember couldn't fathom why.

"Nervous?" Ember turned with blank eyes toward House Ibis's heir, Lonan.

"I am the blood of the Dragon," Ember said. "No. I am not nervous."

That shut Lonan up pretty quickly, especially when the guard at the top of the steps called down to him. He stiffened for the slightest second before heading up the stairs, a bow and a quiver of arrows strung over his back. House Equo, who he was to face, would probably have a long-sword and a shield.

Ember brushed a hand over her own shield, relishing the feeling of the gloves.

She didn't want to take them off.

She waited in the frigid darkness by herself, listening to the crowd scream and quiet abruptly, leaving her with no sound but that of her own breathing and the cheers of some of the lesser children, who had been allowed back down to eat. She could hear Allan's low, dramatic moans as they took him deeper into the labyrinth. He wasn't going to die from a wound in his hand, after all. If Viper hadn't poisoned his weapons—which wasn't explicitly against the rules but was heavily frowned upon, especially this year—he probably wouldn't even lose his hand.

A massive cheer broke the silence, and Ember stiffened.

It was almost time. Ember drew two slim throwing knives and headed up the stairs, watching through the grates as House Ibis and House Equo both walked off the sand, neither of them looking particularly injured.

That was quick. Obviously, one of them had chosen to surrender before it got too bloody.

Which meant Ember was *really* going to have to give them a show—and she would. Blue's suggestion had been a good one. If she was able to keep herself under control, she would be able to provide the only death in the Duels and secure her spot to Mount Saffi. She could hear disappointed whispers from where she stood, her entire body ramrod-straight as she trained her attention on the sands. Focused.

She flexed her gloved hands and stepped out onto the sand.

All she could hear was her own name, screamed a hundred times. The sound of it echoed through her very being and Ember dropped into a fighting stance as Blaze stepped out.

A few of the people in the crowd made scandalized noises, taking him in. Ember curled her lip. Blaze was clad in nothing but an orange loincloth, his tanned, golden skin streaked with orange and black paint. Dark lines of kohl had been drawn around his eyes and he was barefoot, without a single weapon covering his skin.

But it was his face that drew people's attention. It was his face that made Ember's heart stop for the slightest second.

The self-inflicted scar that marred his face was remarkably similar to the one that belonged to the leader of the Order. The woman who had commanded Verity's death.

Not her.

Ember shook her head, clearing her thoughts, as she and Blaze both stepped further into the arena. The sun beat down on her, hot and unrelenting, and only a stiff, warm breeze blew the hair off of her neck. The crowd fell silent.

Her scales shifted as she moved, and Ember smiled softly.

She was going to win this fight, and she was not going to do it the way the royal family wanted her to.

Already she noticed every single one of Blaze's weak points—the hollow of his throat, the soft spot between his neck and shoulders, the backs of his heels, his groin. Most of his body was covered in large, thick muscles, impenetrable. Perhaps his stomach—

Blaze lunged, massive hands stretched out for her neck and Ember ducked, throwing all of her weight against him.

He didn't even give an inch. Not one.

Clearly, he thought this was his fight to win.

But he certainly moved when her knives slipped over skin and muscle, creating shallow cuts across his chest and stomach. Blaze lunged back, eyes wide with fury.

With bloodlust.

Not her.

She needed to keep it together. The fight would be over quickly if Blaze managed to get the upper hand. She *had* to win.

Ember flipped the knives in her hands, pressing her attack. Her blades flashed as she and Blaze threw themselves at each other, Blaze snarling softly when he caught her plait in his hand and *yanked*.

He dragged her against him, pressing his chest against her back, pinning her in place. His arms began to tighten

Caged.

Ember gagged and thrashed, dropping one of her knives.

Right into his foot.

Blaze growled and released her, stumbling away.

"*Bitch,*" he hissed.

"Likewise," Ember snarled, drawing a new knife.

But she may have pressed him too far.

The sun cast his scar into sharp relief, and Ember shook her head.

Not her.

Blaze moved fast—far faster than she had expected from a man his size, slamming her to the ground. He wasted no time in wrenching the knives from her hands, throwing them clear across the arena. Ember scrambled away from him, hauling herself back up to her feet, but Blaze was on her again in an instant, grabbing her legs and yanking him toward her. Ember bit her lip to hide her scream, Blaze looming above her. He ran a hand down her body, hooking on one of the knives strapped to her thighs. Ember thrashed freeing one wrist long enough to unsheathe one of her knives slightly, not drawing it yet. She needed him to move, to bare his throat.

The sun haloed around his head, casting his face into dark shadow. He shifted slightly and for a sudden, terrifying moment, the scar on his face caught the light.

Not her.

Ember thrashed, desperately trying to clear the thought from her mind, but now she could see nothing except that woman, cackling as Verity's neck snapped.

Ember drew her knife and stabbed him in the throat. She barely registered the sound it made when the blade passed through his skin, the slight resistance put up by his flesh.

She did not let go when he released her. Blaze choked, eyes blowing wide with fear and panic and pain.

Her her her.

She twisted the knife when he reached up to claw at it, but she held steady, hot blood coating her hands and the new, brilliant gloves. It ran down her arm in a steady stream as she twisted again.

Ember grit her teeth as drops of his blood splashed across her face, landing on her lips and eyelids. The taste of it was repulsive, but she didn't—couldn't—release the knife.

Another twist.

She was dimly aware that the crowd had begun to scream in horror. She saw the guards that rushed towards them, and from the corner of her eye, she saw the king and queen watching her.

One with pity and repulsion, one with nothing but hatred.

Twist.

She had broken the rules.

Somebody dragged Blaze off of her. Miraculously, he still fought, bucking as they dragged him towards the other end of the arena, away from her.

His blood would soak through the sand, joining the endless generations that had come before him, and Ember smiled.

She lay on her back, her sword digging into her back, the sun warming her face and the blood that covered her, and Ember began to laugh.

Laughed, even as guards surrounded her, commanded by the king.

Laughed, even as they dragged her away, through the blood of the other heirs, a sacrifice to an unloving god spilled out on sand.

Laughed, even when a muttered command led one of them to slam his elbow into her head.

And the world went mercifully dark.

126

SIXTEEN

"YOUR VERDECAN IS TERRIBLE," Sofya said, handing Asher a cup of honey wine—*vilvy*, she had called it.

"I'm trying," Asher muttered, but they both knew that was a lie. Only a few of the people in this town, Kvas, could understand the common language. He'd attempted to rally them in Verdecan, calling upon the endless years of tutoring he'd been subjected to, but he hadn't been able to spit out more than a few words, one of them being "potato".

Sofya, true to her word, had done nothing to help him. She'd simply allowed him to trip and fall over his words, landing spectacularly on his face. A few of the listeners had been gracious enough to not laugh. The rest of the group, Sofya included, had not been so kind.

"You could help me, you know," Asher said.

"I could," Sofya said. "But you would learn nothing, yes?"

"Then teach me Verdecan," Asher said. "At least enough to make my case."

Sofya sighed, long and dramatic. "Perhaps. I'll think about it."

"Thank you," Asher said, blowing steam off the top of his drink. "Where's Doya?"

By the time they'd arrived at the town, the wolf had vanished.

"Hunting," Sofya said. "I cannot keep her contained when she is surrounded by the woods. She longs to hunt, and I will oblige her. The people have been warned to stay out of the woods tonight. She has not accidentally killed before, and I do not think she will, but it keeps the people content."

Asher ran his hand over the marks Doya had left on his throat again, fingers skipping over the scabs.

"Do not touch them," Sofya said. "If you are lucky, it will not scar. But it probably will. She bit down too hard."

"It's okay," Asher said. "I didn't hurt you, did I?"

"No," Sofya said. "There will be no marks in a few days. The cuts were shallow."

"Good," Asher said. "I'm sorry. I shouldn't have struck back."

Sofya's mug hit the table with a resounding *thud*.

"Do not apologize," she said. "I attacked you, you attacked me, I sent Doya after you. Such is the nature of things. I do not blame you."

She looked up suddenly, and Asher followed her gaze to see a group of men march into the tavern, stomping snow from their boots and looking at Sofya with rage in their pale eyes.

"*Lepinsk!*"

That was one word Asher had picked up—*Fangs.*

"I will handle this," Sofya said. "*Do not* involve yourself. Be silent and allow me to speak to them."

One of the men stalked over, built like a mountain, draped in furs. A thick beard and long, curly hair transformed him from man to beast.

"*Tvoy volk melik ubil bvuck!*"

"*Bvesk,*" Sofya said.

Asher, who hadn't been able to follow the conversation at all, glanced between them.

"Doya killed a buck they were hunting," Sofya said. "I'm just going to pay them for it. It is not Doya's fault, after all."

Asher didn't bother to ask how they knew who Sofya was without her armor—something about her very presence made people turn.

Sofya placed a few coins into the man's hand, and he scowled before turning his attention on Asher.

He tipped his head to the side.

"Who he."

Sofya answered. "Of Eiad."

"Are you soldiers?" Asher asked, and Sofya translated. The man shrugged and said something to Sofya.

"In a sense," Sofya said. "They are the protectors of this particular village. So not soldiers like me, but fighters nonetheless."

"Will they fight for Eiad?"

Sofya tipped her head again. "Perhaps."

She turned toward the man, her Verdecan fast and unintelligible, and he nodded along, eyes flicking from Asher to Sofya, as though he could not quite tell what was going on.

When the man responded, eyes locked on Asher, and Sofya grinned, Asher wanted to scream with joy.

"He will fight," Sofya said. "And he is going to ask his men if they will as well. He thinks some of them will, but some will want to stay, to defend the village."

"What about women?" Asher asked. "Are there any women in the village who will help?"

Sofya shook her head. "I…the seven is different, because of the legends that surround those women. There are some women in the main bulk of the army, but not many. It is mostly men."

"Very well," Asher said. "But I want him to ask, anyways. Just in case. Every fighter helps."

Sofya nodded, translated, and the man gave him a sharp nod.

"I ask," he said before thundering off, toward the group he had left at the doorway.

"Good job," Sofya said. "These are the type of men that you must ask. They are the ones who still remember, who keep their swords sharp. It is a shame that the true military—the barracks, the camps—are in the south. But perhaps your messenger will be able to help."

Five men left Kvas the next morning. Five, and a small, slight woman, barely bigger than Sofya, but clutching a massive spear with steady hands. Asher watched them leave from his dirty window, galloping down the path toward Rossolinky Palace, before the sun had even risen. He watched them until he could no longer see them in the darkness, until he didn't know why he continued to stand and stare out the window.

"We must keep moving," Sofya said, coming into his room without knocking. She had pulled her hair out of its normal crown braid and into twin plaits, trailing down her back. It made her less severe—it softened her face, made her look like a young woman instead of a stern matriarch.

"You have beautiful hair," Asher blurted, and Sofya frowned. Asher's face burned—where had *that* come from?

"Thank you," she said, her tone hesitant. "Come. It's time to leave. We can make it to two towns today and a third by nightfall if we're quick. They're all grouped together under the protection of a lord. We will stay with him tomorrow night. He has insisted."

"Which lord?" Asher asked.

"He isn't at the Summer Palace," Sofya said. "You would not know him. His name is Lord Maximovich. He is…he and I…we do not like each other. But he is scared of what the tsar would do to him—he is scared of what the tsar would let *me* do to him if he were to directly disrespect me. He simply believes it unnatural to have Vika and I at the head of the army, for we are not noble born. I am sure he will adore you because of your position."

"Former position," Asher corrected. "I'm not a prince anymore."

"Hmph," Sofya said. "Perhaps. We will just have to see. But come. We have much of the road to cover, and the sun is already rising."

"You're in a good mood today," Asher said, glancing at Sofya. She hummed softly.

"Yes," she said and gestured at something that she had tied to her belt. "The woman at the tavern gave me a flask of *vilvy*. I am very happy about it. Would you like some?"

Asher blinked in surprise. "No…no, that's okay. Keep your drink."

"Very well," Sofya said, unclasping the flask and taking a long drink from it. "Ah. It reminds me of freedom."

"Can I ask you something?" Asher asked, and Sofya glanced at him.

"You may ask whatever you'd like. I may not answer, but I will at least consider it."

"How did you become the Fangs?"

"A series of challenges," Sofya said. "Designed by the tsar and the former guard. Vika and I were the best at them, so we were able to take these positions."

A purposefully vague answer—Asher hadn't been specific enough in his asking.

"Is that always how the women are chosen?"

"Yes," Sofya said, drinking again. "But the last time, only noblewomen were allowed to compete. Our current tsar raided the prisons for his guard. That is not unheard of, but it had been a long time since a tsar did such a thing."

She was leaving this open, too, almost prodding him into the direction of asking her why she was in the prisons at all, but he knew that such a question would only lead to her sword at his neck. He reached up to touch the scabs on his neck again.

"My turn to ask a question," Sofya said, and turned star-colored eyes upon him. "Why did you become a traitor?"

Asher didn't say anything for a long moment, and Sofya offered him the flask again.

This time, he took it, allowing the sweet liquor to warm his throat and stomach before answering.

"I did it for a woman," Asher said. "And I did it to flee my parents and the person they wanted me to be. I could not be the next king of Eiad, and everybody around me knew it. They were waiting for me to fall."

"A woman," Sofya mused. "A foolish reason. She is not even here with you now."

"She's busy," Asher said. "She's…I believe she's going to be queen if the rebellion takes over."

"You plan on putting a new queen on the throne?" Sofya asked. "Truly?"

"I don't plan on doing anything," Asher said. "But I believe that's the rebellion's plan. To seat her on the throne."

"Interesting," Sofya said.

"My turn again," Asher said, handing back the flask. "How many challenges did you have to complete?"

"Twelve," Sofya said. "Three to pass the first level, four more to pass the second, and five to become the Fangs."

"Can you tell me about them?"

Sofya shrugged. "There is no rule that says I cannot. But I do not want to. I do not like to dig up those memories."

Chapter

Seventeen

EMBER WOKE WITH A roaring headache.

A massive, terrible headache that pulsed from all sides of her head, beating a rhythm behind her eyes. She groaned as she cracked them open, starting suddenly when she noticed where she was.

The throne room.

An interesting selection.

And she wasn't alone.

She could hear voices around her, speaking in soft, low voices. Viper's voice was particularly recognizable, toeing a line between frantic and soothing.

"She's waking." The person who spoke was unfamiliar, and then somebody's hands were on her.

Ember's eyes flew open, and she bucked away from the person, hands flying to her knives.

Or, at least, where her knives should've been.

Someone had stripped her of both her weapons and gloves, and she noticed her hands had started up again.

Perfect.

Ember looked around with wide eyes, taking the people in. A small crowd surrounded her, Blue and Viper among them. A dog wove through the crowd, and Ember vaguely recognized her as Asher's hound.

The king and queen watched from their thrones, and the rest of the group was made up of house lords and ladies. A few heirs as well, although Blaze and Allan were notably missing.

Bile rose in a wave as Ember remembered Blaze. Remembered his hands and the way it had felt to drive her knife into his throat. His blood was still dried on her hands and arms. She hadn't meant for it to be so brutal.

Her attention jumped to the man who had tried to touch her, who still knelt on the floor. He stretched his hands out, smiling.

Placating her, as though she was a wild animal.

So Ember snarled.

"Lady Ember," the queen said, her voice bored, "please control yourself."

Ember stood slowly, head pounding, turning to the queen. She lounged in her throne, staring at Ember with the same expression somebody might look at a cockroach with. Ember ground her teeth together.

"Then don't have strange men touch me *when I'm asleep.* I'm sure you remember, Your Highness, the gift that the Order left for me? I am not particularly inclined to tolerate such things."

Blue stiffened at the mention of his father. The queen scoffed and opened her mouth to speak, but the king cut her off.

"Lady Ignis," he said softly. Gentle words, as though she would shatter at any moment. Her teeth ground together. She would not break so easily again. "Do you know why you're here?"

"Because I killed Blaze Minus," Ember said. "Despite the new rules."

"Blaze Minus is not dead," the king said. "Phoenix willing, he won't die, but his life hangs in the balance."

Hopefully that would still be enough. She really didn't want him to die, but sometimes, sacrifices had to be made.

"I got carried away," Ember said. The queen outright laughed, the sound ringing hollow. Only the presence of armed soldiers kept Ember from leaping upon the dais and attacking her.

"I don't believe you," the king said and looked at the rest of the crowd. "Leave us."

All of them turned to go, but the king spoke again. "Not you, Viper Trunca. The same goes for you, Blue Corvu."

The two of them froze in place, the dog leaning against Blue's leg and whining pathetically.

"That damn dog," the queen said, moving to stand, but once again, the king stopped her.

"*Enough, Feather.* Leave the dog," he said, voice laced with exhaustion. "She's not important right now."

"What's going on?" Ember asked, crossing her arms. She had to keep up appearances. "He's not dead. You dragged me here, covered in blood, and stripped me of my weapons. You dropped me on the floor like some type of criminal. So I would like to know why I was hauled here, rather than taken home."

"Because you are a danger," the queen said simply, and Ember flinched. "To yourself and to this court. You are far too unstable to keep here, and you willingly broke the rules. Word will quickly spread of what you did to Blaze Minus, and from whispers arise rumors. And rumors, you silly girl, are dangerous. We cannot have the Lady of House Draco turning against her own kind. You may be the Order's enemy, Ignis, but you are not our friend."

Ember lifted her chin. Was it working? She didn't dare look at Blue and give them away.

The king sighed deeply. "As you know, we have been discussing who to send to Mount Saffi. I believe you may be the right choice. It would be two birds with one stone, don't you understand? You can sway the temple to our side *and* heal. It would be good to get you out of the public eye, as well. We cannot have rumors that you've lost your mind. We need the people to believe that you are strong, that you recovered from your mother's death."

"And do not try to argue," the queen said. "It's already been decided. You'll leave tomorrow morning."

Ember forced herself not to smile. Instead, she cast a glance towards the other two, standing clumped together with the dog. "And what about them?"

"They will accompany you," the king said. "Both of them, alongside Lucasta Tersus. Hazel as well, I suppose."

The dog's tail wagged, and Ember shot it a dirty look. Blue was suppressing a smile.

"How long will it take?" she asked, and the queen shrugged. Ember grit her teeth at the dismissiveness in the motion.

They still didn't take her seriously. Even after they'd thrown her up against their strongest soldier, they couldn't see her as more than a little girl. She would never be anything except the heir to them.

She might be the lady, but she would never be *Verity*.

"If the weather is in your favor, it's only a week to reach the base of the mountain. Before making the climb to the temple, you must spend a week purifying your soul and your body before you're allowed on the holy road. From there, it is only a few days to the top, with plenty of stops along the way. You may stay for a month at the top of the mountain before coming down. The timing will be the same—if not faster—on the way back, as another week is required after stopping your journey down the holy road."

Ember gave her a curt nod. Her hands shook. Where were her gloves? Why had they taken them? "And my house? Who will run House Draco in my absence? My staff needs to be paid, the estate must be kept, and—"

"*We* will take care of it," the queen said, a small smile curving her lips. "Never fear."

"Very well," Ember said. "I suppose all is settled then. If you would please excuse us, I must go inform Lady Tersus of this." They turned to leave, Ember struggling to keep control over her emotions. Over the sheer joy pooling in her stomach.

The queen called out after them, but Ember didn't bother to stop, Feather's parting words ringing in her ears.

Do not disappoint us, Dragon.

Part Two

THE PILGRIMAGE

Those who wish to honor the Phoenix on the Mount must partake in a pilgrimage in order to properly show respect. A week of spiritual and physical cleansing—from all sins of the flesh and fervor— is required for all who seek the top of the mountain. Pilgrims must walk from the base of the mountain to the top on foot. No horses or carriages will be permitted to pass through the Feathered Gates.

—Taken from the journal of
the ancient priestess Saffi

Chapter

EIGHTEEN

V IPER SAID GOODBYE TO his sisters in the morning.

It was so early that the sun had yet to show its face. His bags lay at his feet, packed and ready for the month he was about to spend away.

He didn't like leaving his sisters for so long. Too much could go wrong, and there was the problem of people not understanding Coral. If his father brought her to court, forced her to sit through meetings and questions and whispers, could she stand that?

Neither of them was supposed to be in that room.

Fate simply seemed to enjoy playing with the children of House Serpens.

Viper pressed a kiss to Adder's head, setting her down. "Vipie?"

"Vipie has to go for a little while," he said softly, bending down to her level. "You have to be a good girl for Mother and Father. Be sweet to Coral. Can you do that?"

Adder let out a sob, throwing her arms around his neck. "But...but they don't like to play with me! Coral doesn't like me! And my birthday is soon!"

Viper sighed softly, kissing her temple. "Mamba and Asp will still be here," he said. "They'll play with you. And it won't be very long, Addie. I promise. I'll be home soon, and then I can give you your birthday gift. I'm sure Mother will give you a cake and some presents, okay?"

Adder nodded tearfully and released him. Viper stood, kissing Mamba and then Asp. Coral and his parents had yet to make an appearance and the carriage would pull up any moment now.

Neither Mamba nor Asp was crying. They were both old enough to remember when Boa left, and she had yet to come home, too busy to spend time with them. At least they knew Viper *was* coming home.

Footsteps rang out in the hallway, fast and frantic, and Coral swung around the corner, eyes wide. Her auburn hair was mussed around her head, and she grinned at him, crashing into him full force. He could no longer pick her up the way he could with the other three, but he hugged her tightly nonetheless.

"Father wants me to go to the palace with him," Coral said into his shoulder. "I don't want to."

"I know," Viper said. "But sometimes we have to do things we don't want to. Perhaps you could bring one of the little girls, if that would help?"

Coral shook her head. "I can't. They won't like it either."

So selfless, that quiet little sister of his. Viper let go of her and stepped back, watching Mamba and Asp argue about who was going to get the last sweet roll from dinner last night.

His heart ached.

The sound of wheels on the drive startled him, and Viper looked around for his parents one last time before picking up his bags, allowing Adder to 'help' by holding his hairbrush. He handed his things off to the carriage driver, waving to his sisters as he stepped into the carriage.

He was relieved to find that he was the first one. He still didn't know how he was supposed to approach Ember.

Something had shifted in the darkness of the tunnels and Viper didn't know if he was ready to face it. Anger and affection warred inside of him in equal measure, both of them desperate to reach Ember.

Viper settled back, taking the carriage in. It was large and spacious, with plenty of room for the four of them and the dog. Plush, black velvet benches were on both sides of the carriage, and small lamps flickered as the driver snapped the reins and started them off. Wood floors and walls made the carriage feel warm and comforting.

And it was surprisingly stifling.

Viper immediately unlatched the window, opening it to allow the cool air in. He tipped his head back, basking in the breeze as the carriage thumped along the road. If they had chosen to pick him up first, there was a fairly good chance that Blue would be next. Viper didn't know how Blue felt about this pilgrimage, but maybe it would be good for him.

Viper refused to believe that it would be good for *him*. Being around Ember for that long...

No. That simply wouldn't do.

He released a long breath, turning to stare out of the window.

The faster this was over, the better.

Ember and Lucasta sat beside each other at breakfast, neither of them speaking and neither of them eating.

Despite this being what she'd wanted, it still felt strange. They'd been given almost no time to prepare for such a long journey,

Ember had found herself sitting outside of Verity's bedroom in the middle of the night, breathing and staring at the handle.

She couldn't bring herself to open it. Especially not when every creak of the stairs sounded like her mother coming upstairs. Not when the door rattled—just once—when Lucasta had slammed her door down the hall, as though her mother was on the other side, waiting for her to simply open the door and come inside.

Perhaps she'd be able to open it when she came back.

Now, she and Lucasta sat in strange silence, Lucasta furious over the early wake-up call. "Obscene," Lucasta hissed. "This is a *crime*."

Ember snorted. "I highly doubt that."

"It *should* be a crime, then."

Lucasta attacked her toast with renewed vigor as Ember watched her. She dropped her eyes to her gloves, which had been recovered and washed after the Duels. She'd tied them herself—sloppily, but she couldn't bring herself to ask Lucasta for help.

And she certainly wasn't going to wait for Viper to do it again.

The memory of him gently lacing her gloves was tainted now, but she hadn't forgotten how her pulse had jumped when he'd touched her.

In the strangest way, all of her memories of Viper were blood-stained, red and gold in her mind.

"Have you ever done this before?" Lucasta asked suddenly, pushing away her empty plate and taking Ember's. "One of these pilgrimages?"

"No," Ember said. "My mother did it twice, but I was never invited along. It wasn't something I was really interested in, though."

"Ah," Lucasta said. "We have something similar, in Gleoj Swesh."

Ember froze.

Lucasta never spoke of her life before. It had been an unspoken agreement between the two of them. The little she had revealed painted a very messy picture in Ember's head, pieces of a country she knew little about.

But it wasn't her place to ask questions.

"Oh, really?" Ember asked, forcing herself to relax.

Lucasta nodded, eyes fixed firmly on Ember's plate. "I... my...it's different, of course. Our gods are different. Each of the six gods and goddesses has their own temple and you must journey to one to pay your respects. There are smaller temples for all six as well, but to truly worship, to truly show respect, you must go to the big temples. To go to all six...it doesn't take months—it takes *years,* especially if you spend the proper amount of time at each temple."

"Years?" Ember repeated, watching Lucasta polish off the rest of her toast.

"Years," she said. "You're supposed to spend half a year to a year at each temple so you can properly understand and create a relationship with the god or the goddess. By the time you leave the sixth temple, you'll transcend to a new level of holiness. You can't go until you're twenty-five. I wish I could've gone."

Ember opened her mouth to ask more questions, eager to jump on the opportunity, but Roland knocked on the door before coming in.

"Lady Ignis, Lady Tersus" he said, inclining his head, and Ember didn't miss how Lucasta frowned at the title. "The carriage is here. Your things have already been loaded."

Ember nodded. "Thank you."

She and Lucasta stood, following Roland out to the carriage. Inside, much to her dismay, she could see two figures moving.

Perfect.

Both of the boys were already in the carriage and as the door swung open Ember could've sworn she caught the smell of paint and oranges.

They sat in uncomfortable, unbroken silence. The only sounds were the thumping of Hazel's tail on the floor as she dreamt and the polite conversations that occasionally passed between Blue and Lucasta, but those were broken off just as quickly as they began. Both of them had fallen asleep shortly after they'd set off. Beyond that, there was only the wind streaming into the open window, the commands of the drivers, and the *clip-clop* of the horses' hooves upon the stones.

Viper didn't know how much of this he could take.

He was supposed to spend an entire *week* in here? With her?

Ember was a stone where she sat, gloved hands folded in her lap. She'd obviously tied them herself—the knots were barely holding the gloves in place. He resisted the urge to reach out and fix them. She'd probably bite his head off.

She was no longer Ember—this was Lady Ignis again, much to his disdain.

Viper tapped a finger against his knee, forcing himself to look anywhere that wasn't here face, gazing steadily out the window. He didn't know what she was looking at or for—the areas around the Phoenix Palace were inhabited by small villages and wealthy, houseless individuals. Every so often a massive estate designed to mimic one of the court's would appear in the distance, often settled on rich farmland, nothing but dirt now, but by the time they came back, they would be full of crops, ready to be picked shortly afterward.

It was still strange that they would barely be home in time for the Summer Solstice—although he was glad they weren't missing it. It was one of the only holidays he truly enjoyed. There was no blood spilled, unlike the Duels and the Hunt.

Beyond the Solstice, every holiday was reserved specifically for one or many of the houses. The Feast of Feathers, for example, was a harvest feast specifically designed for the four avian houses. The Duels, of course, were for the Serpent and Spider, while the Hunt favored the predators. The Race of Heirs, the last holiday of the year, was for the Stallion and the Elk.

Viper resisted the urge to smile when he remembered last year's Race. He'd been forced to act as heir again, with none of his siblings being willing to drag themselves back for nothing more than a stupid horse race.

House Serpens hadn't won the Race in years, and Viper had wanted the victory. Badly.

So he'd attempted to break one of the horse's legs. It was neither his finest moment nor one he was proud of, but he certainly hadn't expected the horse to belong to the heir of House Draco. When she'd approached him, fire dancing in the depths of those gold eyes, he'd recoiled.

Ember Ignis was terrible in her anger. Terrible and beautiful all at once, and he'd flinched when she'd raised her voice at him, screaming about how the horse was worth more than his entire human life.

Viper had barely registered anything she'd said. He'd been swimming in gold and when she'd stomped away, he couldn't tear his gaze from her.

He'd taken it all from her and then he'd been stupid enough to seek her out at the party shortly afterwards.

Viper allowed himself to look at her—just once.

At the same time, Ember turned her head to stare at him in return.

The others' steady breathing assured Viper that they were both still asleep as he looked at Ember. Really, truly looked at her.

She was far thinner than she had been before Verity's death, which he'd expected, but she was smaller than she'd been when she'd been stabbed. She'd pulled her hair back into a low plait, and her face was free from all cosmetics, leaving it bare as the sun caught on her eyes, turning them molten. The sun danced along her cheekbones, the slope of her jaw, the small whips of hair that escaped around the sides of her head.

She was studying him, too, although something seared in her gaze. Viper flushed as she ran her eyes down him again in a low, lazy look and then brought them back to his face. Her lips parted slightly, and his heart began to hammer in his chest as he realized she was looking at his mouth. His breath—and by the looks of it, hers as well—sped up. Her eyes darkened slightly as her pupils dilated. She wet her lips, leaning forward slightly.

Viper tipped the slightest bit forward, and then Blue woke up with a massive stretch.

He almost killed him.

Ember sat back suddenly, furrowing her brow as though she didn't quite know what had just happened. Viper had to admit he didn't really know either. And Ember was right back to sitting like a little statue, determinedly looking out the window.

Fine. He could do that too.

Viper fixed his gaze straight ahead, at the wood paneling directly above Lucasta's head. If she was going to sit like that for the rest of the ride, then he was going to do the same thing.

Apparently, Ember had forgotten that he knew how to play the game too. She was better but he was learning, with every smile and turn of a sleeve and the slightest, teasing notes. He'd grown up in the courts too, more in the shadows than Ember. In some ways, that only made him more observant. Nobody cared where or when a lesser child came and went, and so he'd taken those opportunities to poke about the palace or whatever estate the party was being held at.

He knew how to weather this.

He knew how to weather her.

He was not fine. Viper was not even close to fine.

Lucasta, to his immense relief, had woken up and now she, Blue, and Ember talked softly with each other. Viper listened—not because he was eavesdropping, but because there was nowhere else for him to go. He couldn't very well avoid them in this carriage. He did, however, stand and stretch his head out of the window, calling to the driver.

"Where are we stopping tonight?"

"Some merchant's house," Blue answered instead. Viper had a feeling his words hadn't even reached the driver—the wind had picked up steam and whipped his words away as they continued north. "They offered it to us for a night on the way there and a night on the way back."

"How do you know that?" Viper asked, staring at Blue. "Who told you?"

Blue frowned. "The queen. Didn't she send one to you as well?"

Both of the girls had gone terrifyingly still. Predators, with all of their attention trained on poor Blue.

"Send what?"

Ember didn't pose a lot of questions. She only demanded things, as though she was entitled to the sum of human knowledge.

"The...the letter," Blue said, reaching into his horrible orange jacket. He emerged with a small, cream-colored letter.

Ember swore viciously. "From the palace?"

Blue nodded in confirmation. "The queen, specifically. Here, you guys can read it."

Viper and Ember grabbed for the letter at the same time, but he was faster, snatching it out of Blue's hand. Ember set her jaw, and Viper smirked before dropping his gaze to the envelope. He slipped the letter out, eyes darting over the words scrawled in elegant handwriting.

> *Mr. Corvu*
> *As you will be making the pilgrimage to the*
> *Mount Saffi temple with Lady Ignis and the others,*
> *I entrust to you a detailed plan for where you will*
> *stop each night. There are further instructions*
> *concerning the week that must be spent before you*
> *reach the mountain.*
> *Thank you,*
> *Queen Feather.*

"What did she say?" Ember asked, just as Viper said,

"A detailed plan?"

"What plan?"

Blue squirmed uncomfortably. "I thought you would've gotten one too. Especially you, Ember."

"Obviously," Ember said, and Viper could see that she was gritting her teeth. He handed the letter to her, and she took it without thanks, careful to keep their hands from touching. "I did not. She's still mad at me, I assume."

"Here's the second part," Blue said, pulling out another piece of paper. This one was far longer, with a day-by-day plan written out. "You can keep it—I've already studied it."

Ember took it from him with predatory calm, running her eyes down it, Lucasta peeking over her shoulder. "She left no instructions beyond us arriving at the base of the mountain."

"But the original letter said she would," Lucasta said. "'Concerning the week', remember?"

"I remember," Ember said, flipping the paper over. "Nothing. All it says is that somebody will be waiting for us. Quite frankly, that isn't the most reassuring. But I suppose we don't really have another choice, do we?"

"No, we don't," Viper said, and Ember stiffened. Whatever heat had passed between them a few minutes ago was completely gone.

"This may have been, like, a test," Blue said. "To test me. To test *us*. Maybe she knows."

"That's stupid," Ember said.

"Knows what?" Viper asked, and the two of them turned to look at him.

"I went after Blaze on purpose," Ember said. "I could've pulled back if I'd wanted to. I need to go to the temple. The High Priestess has power that we do not."

Blue scowled, reaching down to scratch Hazel between the ears. "How could she know? You and I were the only ones who were even present for that conversation. I don't think they're smart enough to spy on us to that extent."

Lucasta leaned over and slammed the carriage window shut. "The drivers are paid by the royals. They could easily be reporting back."

"Or they're Order members."

They all fell silent at that.

Hazel whined, breaking the quiet, and Ember glared at the dog. "Are all of our...esteemed...hosts prepared for her?"

"I don't know," Blue said. "You know everything I know. Honestly. I'm not hiding anything."

"I believe you," Ember said. "But I can't believe the *nerve* of the queen. I'm the *Dragon* and she won't trust me."

Nobody responded, and this time, the silence spoke volumes. Ember rolled her eyes and sat back, saying nothing.

They continued to ride in silence, and Viper didn't know how he was supposed to deal with this for an entire week.

Nineteen

ASHER SQUIRMED AS A small child stared daggers into his eyes.

"I...do you speak the common language?"

The little girl, draped in fur and silk, said nothing as she raised her fork to her mouth and took a bite.

"You have a lovely home," Asher said, lying through his teeth. Lord Maximovich lived in a stone keep, with cold floors and vaulted ceilings. Everything echoed, and the entire place was freezing despite the massive fires that burned throughout. The lord himself sat a few places away, at the head of the table, with Sofya at his right and his mousy wife at his left.

Asher had been placed beside Sofya, across from the lord's eldest daughter, Yesipova, who couldn't have been more than twelve and was thoroughly uninterested in him.

Sofya, to Asher's relief, had offered to assist in the translation for the lords and ladies only, although Maximovich spoke enough of the common language that she was really only there for clarification.

Asher stabbed through a piece of meat as the child across from him continued to stare and stare and stare with dead eyes.

"I apologize for Yesipova," Maximovich said, drawing Asher's attention. The lord was not, as he had imagined, a massive man with a sword in one hand and a leg of lamb in the other. He was small, flighty, and appeared to be eating less than Yesipova. All of them—the lord, lady, and daughter—possessed thin red hair and dark violet eyes, and although Maximovich's weren't quite as dull as Yesipova's, there was still a strange emptiness in them that Asher couldn't figure out. "She is…different."

"No need to apologize," Asher said, his words almost swallowed up by the conversation that reigned on the other side of the table, where various members of Maximovich's family sat. The woman on Asher's right side had introduced herself as Vitsina, Maximovich's sister and Yesipova's aunt, seated across from her husband.

She tugged on his arm now, and Asher leaned into her. "Yesipova is a rude little brat. Don't let my brother fool you."

Vitsina spoke the common language better than anybody else Asher had met so far—better than the tsar, better than Sofya. She'd briefly explained that she had spent a few years in Eiad before she was wed, traveling the far south of the country to truly taste the heat.

"Is she always like that?" Asher whispered back, and Vitsina nodded.

"Terrible child. But Agapova refuses to have another child, and thus we are all stuck with her."

Vitsina turned away, and Asher leaned in to whisper to Sofya, who jumped slightly. "What position does Vitsina hold here?"

"Because Yesipova is not of age, if both Maximovich and Agapova were to die, Vitsina would step in, as dictated by tradition. She is, admittedly, the more intelligent of the two. Maximovich suffered a terrible blow to the head during the border wars and lost most of his intelligence."

Ah. That explained his eyes, then.

"Vitsina is…ambitious," Sofya continued. "Very ambitious. She married up, and she has yet to have a child because she knows that if her husband dies, she inherits his men and his keep, and she won't have to pass it on to her husband's heir."

"So she could, potentially, inherit her brother and husband's assets?"

"Correct," Sofya said. "She has placed herself in a potentially incredible position."

Servants came and cleared the meat from in front of Asher and the others, swiftly replacing them with small cups of what appeared to be fruit suspended in a strange liquid.

"*Kissel*," Sofya explained, catching Asher's worried expression. "Just eat it. It's good."

"So, Asher," Maximovich said, drawing Asher's attention. "Why are you here?"

Sofya squinted, obviously confused, and Asher forced himself not to look at her.

He and Sofya had already explained *exactly* why they were there to Maximovich as the beginning of the meal.

He felt Vitsina, beside him, turn in confusion as well.

"We…I'm…I'm here to ask you to send your men to Eiad to fight in the civil war."

"Ah, yes," Maximovich said, furrowing his brow. "I remember now."

"It…it's his injury," Vitsina said softly. "It keeps him from remembering things."

"I do not like you," Yesipova said, breaking her silence, and Asher turned to stare at the small child.

"I'm sorry?" Sofya said, her tone suddenly harsh.

"I do not like him," Yesipova said, gesturing to Asher with her spoon. "Remove him, Father."

"What?" Asher said. "I—"

"Enough, Yesipova," Maximovich said, and the hall fell silent around them. "Do not be rude to our guest. *You* are dismissed."

The little girl got up with a huff, pointing at Asher with a single, long finger. "Fool. You do not belong here."

With that, she stomped away, the door of the banquet hall slamming shut behind her.

Slowly, painfully, the conversation picked up again, although Asher and Sofya remained silent. She turned to look at him.

"Can you speak any other languages?" she asked softly, and Asher nodded.

"I can speak a decent amount of Qinnian," Asher said, and Sofya immediately switched to Qinnian.

"You're lucky that Yesipova doesn't have her father's ear," she said, her Qinnian far stronger than her Eiadian. "But you must be more careful. We may not be so lucky with the next lord or lady. Be careful with the children."

"Are we speaking Qinnian now?" Vitsina said, leaning in on Asher's other side. "How exciting. Are we trying to keep my brother out of the conversation?"

Sofya flushed. "I—"

"It's quite all right," Vitsina said. "He doesn't speak Qinnian, and I doubt anybody else here does either. Language is simply my craft."

"Will Maximovich consider Yesipova's statement at all?" Sofya asked, and Vitsina shrugged.

"I doubt it. Yesipova does the same thing to all of his guests. He's only taken her seriously a couple of times, and that was with others agreeing with her. As long as you keep Agapova and me happy, you should be in no danger of being removed."

"Has the tsar presented an incentive for me to send my soldiers?" Maximovich asked, switching the conversation back to the common language.

Sofya answered. "You are not required to send your soldiers, and if you do, the only thing you will receive is a guarantee that I will not sweep down upon your keep."

The lord paled slightly as Sofya tipped her head, a predator in motion. "I will be going to Eiad alongside whatever soldiers you send," Sofya said. "I cannot promise their safety, but I will do my best to keep them alive. I will arrange proper burials or burnings for those who do not survive, and I will personally see to it that their families are notified when the war has been won."

"You believe you will win, then?" While the question may have been spoken in Sofya's direction, Asher knew it was truly for him.

"With Verdeca, yes," Asher said. "We cannot stand against the might of the houses and their allies without your men, but with Verdeca, we have a chance to win the war."

"The war, too, would allow you to get revenge on the other countries of the middle continent," Vitsina said, piping up. "Perhaps it is worth considering, brother."

"I could not disagree more," Agapova said, and Asher jumped. So far, Maximovich's wife hadn't spoken a word, and her voice was an uncomfortably deep rasp. She coughed slightly, as though each word pained her to say. "I do not wish to risk the lives of such good men."

"You would risk them for the border wars," Vitsina spat. "You would risk them taking over Lord Nazarov's keep. But you would not risk them for this?"

Agapova switched to Verdecan, her words fast and clipped, and Asher leaned into Sofya as she translated for him in Qinnian.

"Agapova is ranting about Lord Nazarov and how his land rightfully belongs to her husband—this is untrue, of course, but it is the story that she clings to. Agapova is of the old faith, and there is a great temple—the temple of the Oracles—inside of Nazarov's borders. She lusts after it."

"Speak Eiadian, all of you," Maximovich spat, as the conversation at the other end of the table began to soften, people leaning in to listen to the argument. "There is no reason not to."

"Dismiss the others," Vitsina said. "They have no reason to be here—they are only going to gossip later."

Maximovich barked a command in Verdecan, and the rest of the table—notably excluding Vitsina's husband, who Asher still had yet to meet—stood to leave with mutters and whispers, but at least when the final man stepped out of the dining hall, the door slamming shut behind him, it was quiet.

"Happy?" Maximovich asked, and Vitsina rolled her eyes.

"Don't act as though you're doing me a favor," she said. "You know I'm right. You let them whisper too much, and it sows discontent within the people. You are a fool to disagree with me, Max."

"I am not disagreeing with you, Vitsina," he said, and Asher and Sofya exchanged a look.

"Siblings," Sofya muttered. "My sister and I were the same way."

"*Enough*," Agapova said. "This is unimportant."

They all fell silent, Asher squirming uncomfortably. He had no idea how he was supposed to break into this conversation—he felt entirely unwelcome in this particular space.

"We must make a decision," Vitsina said. "If we are to send our men, we must decide now."

"*Our* men?" Agapova asked. "You speak of *Maximovich's* men."

"Pronin and I have a decision to make as well," Vitsina said, nodding at her husband. "But I wish for our decision to align with Max's."

"You say that there is no reward, correct?" Agapova said, directing the question in Sofya and Asher's direction. "So then why should we do such a thing?"

"Because it will prove your loyalty," Sofya said. "You wish to look good in the eyes of the tsar, do you not? He will not look favorably upon those who do not send their men without good reason."

"And you say that you will be going?" Agapova asked.

"Yes," Sofya said. "I and the rest of the seven."

Agapova and Maximovich exchanged a glance. "Must we send *all* of our men? We need protection, too. What if Nazarov wishes to attack us?"

"Nazarov is not going to attack you!" Vitsina said, her voice jumping with frustration. "Give it up, Agapova! You are the only one who cares about such a thing!"

"Vitsina," Pronin said softly. "My love. Be silent."

Vitsina's icy gaze turned onto her husband, and the man shrank away from her.

"Choose wisely, Max," Vitsina said. "I do not wish to see the Fangs when she is not our ally."

Maximovich's eyes darted between his wife and his sister before landing on Asher.

"You may stay here tonight," he said. "I will have an answer for you in the morning. You are all dismissed—yes, even you, Agapova."

His wife clamped her lips shut, and then they were all standing, Asher at Sofya's side as they left the room.

"Walk with me," Sofya said softly, guiding Asher in the opposite direction of Vitsina, Agapova, and Pronin.

They turned down another hallway, Asher shivering as cool night wind blew through open spaces set in the stone walls.

Sofya glanced over her shoulder, leaning into him. She spoke Qinnian again, but kept her voice low, as though concerned that Vitsina was going to pop up again.

"I have a feeling he'll side with us," Sofya said. "With Vitsina. She commands more respect than Agapova, even if only for her position as Pronin's wife. Agapova was a farm girl before she married Maximovich, but Vitsina was educated alongside her brother. She knows the art of war far better than Agapova does."

"I hope so," Asher said. "We need their men."

"We do," Sofya agreed. "We need all of them. But we will simply have to wait. Once we have his response in the morning, we ride to the Temple of the Oracles—the one Agapova so desperately wants. From there, it is less than half a day's ride to Lord Nazarov's keep, but I wish to spend time at the temple. I am of the old faith, just like Agapova. It is important to me—it will not take me long."

"Very well," Asher said. "Take all the time you need."

Sofya gave him a wry smile. "There is not enough time in the world."

Chapter

TWENTY

EMBER TURNED OVER IN bed, reaching out for Lucasta. The other girl slipped her hand through Ember's easily, both of them staring up at the ceiling.

They'd arrived early in the evening, the merchant—a trader in silk rugs and spiced wine—eagerly awaiting them at the door. His home was obviously meant to resemble the Phoenix Palace, similarly to the woman who had previously owned Lucasta.

Ember wanted to spit. She hated that word.

Owned.

Not any longer, thank the Phoenix.

Ember shook thoughts of that woman from her mind and returned her attention to the ceiling. The room was nice enough, but it smelled sterile, as though nobody had ever slept in it. The man, too, had been rather confused when Ember had requested a bed big enough for her and Lucasta.

She hadn't missed the man's eyes flicking between her and Viper, but she'd quickly squashed that particular idea.

They'd eaten as well, but there had been nothing worth noting. She'd been exhausted from spending an entire day putting on a front with Viper and even Blue. Neither of them had appeared to notice, but Lucasta certainly had, giving Ember concerned glances when she'd refused most of her food. Most of her stomach was full of water and not much else.

Ember sighed, squeezing Lucasta's hand and closing her eyes, her entire body relaxing into the bed.

She'd have to do it again tomorrow. And the next day. Every day for an entire week, not to mention the way she'd have to act as they traveled up the mountain.

But soon—soon they would be at the temple. If she could convince the High Priestess quickly, they'd be back home before their allotted time was up.

Ember attempted to slip into sleep, but her mind was awake and reeling, unable to figure out how she was going to make it through this.

"I think our best chance is to act as reverent as possible," Blue said, folding his hands in his lap as the carriage plunked on. "I'll even dress differently. There's nothing I can do about my hair, though."

"It won't matter," Ember said. "My mother told me about the High Priestess. She's not to be trifled with, and she's not to be lied to. It's probably best if we act like ourselves—but follow all of her rules. Don't talk back, don't seek her out unless she seeks you out, is that understood? All of you. We have to be careful to not push her away. We need her."

She allowed her eyes to rest on Viper for the slightest second, and a smirk curled his lips. "Understood, Lady Ignis."

Oh, he was *insufferable.*

His hair was gold in the sunlight, ruffled slightly by the breeze flowing through the window. His eyes dropped to her lips for the slightest second, and Ember pursed them, curling her hands into fists.

"Don't play games with me," Ember hissed, ignoring the glances Blue and Lucasta cast between them.

"Oh, I'd love nothing more than to play games with you, Lady Ignis," Viper said, sitting back. "But a game is only fun if you have someone to play with."

Ember flushed, rapping on the top of the carriage. It came to a stop, and she pushed past Lucasta, stepping outside. The drivers looked at her in surprise as she clambered up beside them, sharing the seat.

"I...Lady Ember?"

"I want to ride out here for a while," Ember said. "You're welcome to ignore me. In fact, I command it. Don't pay me any attention."

"I win again," Lucasta said, pulling a handful of cards and coins toward her, grinning.

"Of course you won," Blue said, snatching a coin from her pile, flipping it over his knuckles. "It's *your* game."

"We've played six times. You should be better by now."

Blue muttered something obscene under his breath, but Viper's attention had already shifted, watching Ember as she counted out another stack of coins from her little bag, placing them on the table.

"Let's try again," Ember said, smiling. "I have a good feeling about this time."

"Don't," Blue said. "You already know you're going to lose. She cheats."

"Oh, please," Lucasta said. "Are you playing or not?"

"You ran me out of money!"

"Ugh, fine. Here." Lucasta slid coins back to Viper and Blue, grinning all the while. "You can shuffle, if it makes you feel better."

"Give them here," Blue said, holding his hand out. The sound of Blue shuffling the cards filled the room, accompanied only by the soft snoring of Hazel underneath the table. Ember ducked her head for a moment, pulling her hair back with a ribbon, away from her face. Her cheeks were flushed from laughter, her eyes glittering in the candlelight.

They'd taken over the main dining room of this particular merchant's house, he and his wife choosing to leave them alone after dinner with nothing but a deck of cards and a few books. It had been Lucasta's idea to teach them this game—*Uvetz*—an Oscelan game. She had won every round, but Viper didn't really care.

He could feel the tentative joy in the room, the little happiness that was trying to creep in and infect them. It threatened to make them forget about what was going on—make them forget the blood coating their hands, the steel they would soon wield.

But he was okay with that. He was okay with forgetting, even if it was only for a little while.

"Your deal, Ember," Lucasta said, Blue pushing the cards across the table to Ember. Gloves closed over the deck, tied over hands that no longer shook.

Under the table, their legs brushed, and Ember jumped, eyes flying up to his face for a brief second before she began dealing.

Viper let out a long breath, his body still reeling from the shock of the brief touch they'd just had. Blue scowled at his cards as Ember threw Viper his last card. He picked them up, barely glancing at them as he watched Ember inclined her head toward Lucasta.

"You won last time. Your turn."

"Ah, the joy of being the winner," Lucasta said, and Blue opened his mouth in retort, spitting *something* out about Lucasta hiding cards in her sleeves, but Viper had already tuned them out.

They only had a few more days of travel before they finally arrived at the base of Mount Saffi to begin the cleansing. From there...the temple, and the High Priestess. And there was so much on the line that he didn't know what they were supposed to do if she denied them. He didn't know how they were supposed to go home if they failed.

Chapter

Twenty-One

"Although it may displease Agapova, I will send my men to Rossolinky Palace," Maximovich said, dipping a spoon into a thick bowl of gruel. "I believe Vitsina is correct. And I do not wish to give the tsar any reason to look at me with displeasure."

Asher dipped his head. "Thank you. Your support is greatly appreciated."

"Of course," Maximovich said. "I myself...I am not fit for battle the way I used to be, and Agapova was not raised for war, but perhaps Vitsina can ride with them."

"I would be honored," Vitsina said and glanced across the table at her husband. "Pronin and I have decided the same. I would be happy to lead both groups to Rossolinky."

"We can discuss it further ourselves," Maximovich said, turning back to Asher and Sofya. "I presume you must be on your way?"

"Yes," Sofya said. "Your hospitality has not gone unnoticed, Lord Maximovich. The same to you, Ladies Agapova and Vitsina, and Lord Pronin."

"Your horses have been well fed and kept here," Maximovich said. "You will find them in the stables. Where your wolf is, I cannot say, but my people were under strict orders not to hunt any wolves in the area—and highly encouraged not to hunt at all. She will be safe."

"Thank you," Sofya said. "Although I was not worried about Doya. I was more worried about your people."

Maximovich grinned. "As was I. Gods be with you, Sofya Seminoava."

"Try again," Sofya said. "Say the word *exactly* as I say it, yes? Hello. *Pavat.*"

"Pav-at."

"Closer," Sofya said. "Much closer than before. Are you picking anything up?"

"A little," Asher said. "I can at least understand the main point of whatever the conversation is. I think."

"It will get easier," Sofya said. "I learned Eiadian when I was in school. One of my classmates was half-Eiadian, and she was my best friend, so I learned it for her."

"Your Eiadian is very good," Asher said, and Sofya turned to stare at him.

"You called it Eiadian," she said. "Strange. Strange indeed."

"Slip of the tongue," Asher said. "Half of Verdeca calls it Eiadian. It's been sinking in, I think."

"Perhaps our other customs will be sinking in, too," Sofya said. "Perhaps you will learn to make *vilvy* before you are sent back to Eiad."

"Sent back with you," Asher said, and Sofya offered him a small smile.

"Indeed. Myself and your army."

"And the seven," Asher said.

"Yes," Sofya said. "The tsar did promise that, and he will indeed deliver."

"Can you tell me about them?" Asher asked. "The other women?"

"Yes," Sofya said. "But I'm going to say half of it in Verdecan, so keep up. I will speak slowly and clearly so you can understand."

"Fine," Asher said.

"I will start in Eiadian and slip into Verdecan," she said. "I suppose I should start with the *Nizhiny*. You met Annika—she is one of the two who remain from the old seven. The tsar dismissed the other women, for they were unable to protect his father. But Annika and the other woman were on missions, and thus could not be held responsible. They oversaw the challenges we participated in to become part of the seven. After Annika, there is Yeltsova and Zarubina. They were from one of the smaller prisons located in the cities—petty crimes. Yeltsova was a pickpocket in the city of Magatlas, and when she was caught, they imprisoned her. Zarubina was from the same prison, but she had been imprisoned for her father's debts. The amount was not much, but his refusal to pay it landed Zarubina in prison. They were impressive in the challenges, more so than many of the others. The tsar took notice of them, and they were offered positions in the *Nizhiny*."

"Annika, Yeltsova, and Zarubina," Asher said. "Got it."

"Good," Sofya said. "Then, there are the *Seredina,* the second level. There is Oksana, the tall woman with the blind eye. She is the oldest member of the seven, both in experience and in age. It will not be long now before the tsar gives her the option to retire. She is very powerful, but she is aging. It is not her fault. There is also Mazhulina—she was part of the group who came in with me. She is quiet and secretive, although not in a bad way. The tsar uses her as a spy, for she will not give up his secrets. She spent many years in the southern part of the continent before the treaty was signed. She was poised to collapse many governments before she was forced to come back."

"You switched to Verdecan," Asher said. "Right at the end. I understood some of it."

"Good," Sofya said. "Repeat what you understood."

Asher scowled. "Something about coming back? She was doing something and had to stop?"

"You missed a few words, but yes," Sofya said. "Mazhulina was going to destroy the Oscelan and Kieallian governments, but the treaty was signed and the tsar knew that if she went through with the plan, it would break the treaty. Verdeca was very tired at that point, and we needed time to recover, and so the treaty benefited us all. Anyways. After Mazhulina and Oksana, it is just me and Vika. Wolf and Fangs."

"'Just' you and Vika?" Asher said, laughing. "You are the most feared soldiers in perhaps the entire world."

"Oh, I know," Sofya said. "I have heard the stories they tell about us. They say that we eat the hearts of men, that we are surely witches, that we have exchanged our souls with a demon for our power. But it is nothing like that. The challenges forced us to adapt, to get better, to *learn*. When we were given the positions, we were trained by Annika and Oksana for months before we were ever allowed to go on a mission."

"So you don't eat the hearts of men?" Asher asked, and Sofya rolled her eyes.

"No," she said. "For I do not like the taste."

The Temple of the Oracles was nothing to look at, at least in comparison to the temples of Eiad, with their soaring ceilings, stained glass, and white stone pits filled with the Phoenix Flame. It was only gray stone, with small slits cut into the walls to let in light and air, and the door was a solid piece of wood that swung open with a creak when Sofya touched the handle. There were no carvings, no glass, only stone and wood.

"You may wait outside, if you wish," she said softly, clipping a small pouch to her belt. "Doya will guard the entrance—animals are not allowed within the inner sanctum."

"I'd like to come with you," Asher said. "If only to see."

"Very well," Sofya said. "I will do my best to teach you about what I am doing. The first thing you must know is about my name."

She slipped into the room, and Asher followed, closing the door behind him and plunging them into semi-darkness.

Asher gazed around, taking in the space—smooth stone walls, stone floors, and a staircase that appeared to descend into hell. A single torch burned by the entrance of the tunnel, casting Sofya's face into sharp relief.

"In Verdeca—although the tradition has begun to fade out in the south—names are given in a very specific way. The first name is often familial or from mythology. Many people are named for heroes or demons or ancient royalty, but just as many are given the name that their mother or grandmother had. My name is from mythology—it is the name of a demon. Then there is our surname—mine is Seminoava. This is also familial, as I believe it is in Eiad. But it is our second name that is perhaps the most important. That is our god name."

"Your god name?"

"Yes," Sofya said, plucking the torch from the wall and heading down the stairs. "Each person born in Verdeca is given the name of a god or goddess for their second name. If you are a woman and are given a god's name, it is changed, and the same for those men who are given goddess names. I was given the name Veharas, the female version of the god of blood and terror, *Veharus.*"

"And you have no say in your name?"

"None," Sofya said. "Although I have heard of adults who find themselves more called to a different god and may change their name. But there are more stories. There are stories that every hundred years, a child with a god's name *is* the god incarnate. A child named for Krukante, goddess of the harvest and soil, whose farm produces incredible yields even in a drought. A young girl named for Trusov, god of animals, who has an uncanny friendship with Verdecan bears. A son with the name Cegrene, of the flame and fury, who can coax a roaring flame from a puddle of water."

She glanced at him as they turned a corner that revealed more stairs, more darkness.

"The year I was born, it had been a hundred years since a child with *Veharus'* name was born and was so vicious, so terrible, that he could not have been anybody except the old god. My mother did not think anything of it when she gave me the name—she gave it to me for the painful childbirth that brought me into the snow. But perhaps she chose well. Perhaps she knew what I would become."

"Which god name would you give me?"

"That is an interesting question," Sofya said. "Perhaps Cegrene, for *Cegrena,* the goddess of flame and fury. But I do not know. That is based only on your lineage. Oh—can you hear that?"

Asher tipped his head to the side as Sofya fell silent, and then he heard it—running water.

"What is this place?" Asher whispered, and Sofya smiled.

"It is a temple," she said. "Worship is quite different for those who believe the old faith. We do not sit in benches and listen to holy people ramble. We go to the heart of our gods, and there we find our faith."

Another corner rounded, the sound intensifying, and then they were standing on the ground floor, gazing at the clear, rippling lake, and the small waterfall that splashed into it without end. A small set of stairs led into the pool before plunging off into the depths.

Above them, the ceiling shone with brilliant light, dozens of bright blue-green spots illuminating the pond below.

"They feed each other," Sofya said, sliding the torch into a sconce by the final step. "The lake feeds the waterfall, and the waterfall feeds the lake. They cannot exist without each other."

The water poured endlessly from a dark, terrifying hole in the wall, and beyond that, there was nothing.

"What are those?" Asher asked, pointing up at the ceiling, at the small dots that pulsed there.

"Bugs," Sofya said. "God-bugs. They are found only in the holy temples of old, and if they are removed, they die. But here, they thrive brilliantly."

"You cannot step into the holy waters," Sofya said. "For you have not been cleansed, and you are not of the faith. But you may come as close as you wish."

She pulled the sheathed sword from her back and placed it at her feet, shucking off her boots and socks before reaching for the buttons on her tunic.

"I forgot to warn you," Sofya said. "I must be nude. You may look, you may not. It is only a body, after all."

She pulled her tunic off, revealing an undershirt, and Asher glanced away. Sofya laughed softly.

"So modest," she said. "You are so strange in Eiad."

"I—"

"You do not have to defend yourself," Sofya said. "I did not say it was a bad thing. It is only different."

He heard the soft whisper of her pants hitting the ground.

"I've turned around," Sofya said, and Asher turned, careful to keep his eyes on the back of Sofya's head as she reached for the braid on top of her head and pulled small pins from her hair, releasing a silver cascade down her back. He watched the muscles ripple in her shoulders as she stepped up to the lip of the pool, taking in a long, deep breath.

As she released it, she stepped into the water.

He could see the brief moment that the water shocked her, the cold seizing her body, and then she dove in, disappearing for a moment before Asher could see her underneath the water. She emerged near the middle, smiling softly. Her hair floated around her in a silvery halo.

"It is not so bad," Sofya said. "Not when you have swum in colder. Would you mind handing me the pouch on my belt?"

Asher nodded, stooping beside her clothing and un-clipping the small pouch. He handed it to her, their palms brushing for the briefest moment. He trembled, the cold shooting through his veins, and Sofya grinned.

"You are not used to ice." She opened the pouch, shaking a few, deep red berries into her palm. "Watch."

She dunked her fist underneath the water, and when it emerged, the juice ran down her palm, down her arm.

Sofya dragged her hand across her face, painting it in strips of red, swam out into the middle of the pond, and then she began to pray, her voice soft but echoing within the chamber. Asher understood nothing except *Veharus,* repeated over and over again as Sofya closed her eyes and lifted her hands, staying afloat with nothing but her legs.

Asher sat at the edge of the pond, at once unable to tear his eyes away from her while feeling as though he was not supposed to be witnessing this at all. The hair on the back of his neck stood on end as Sofya's voice soared toward the stone above them, whispering words that he could not understand but could *feel* within the very depths of his soul.

Something deep within him stirred—something that had not been awoken since his cousin's death and his own dismissal of the Phoenix.

It was the strangest feeling, a feeling that he could not decide if he liked or not. It felt as though there was someone—no, *something*—in the cavern with them. It was not bad, but it was strange, unfamiliar, uncomfortable. It wrapped around his heart, drawing him toward the very lip of the pool.

Sofya's voice began to fade out, and Asher reached up and touched his face, brushing away the tear that had appeared at the corner of his eye.

He watched her swim toward him, pulling herself out of the water. She shook herself dry beside him, spraying him with ice-cold droplets.

He hissed, scrambling up and away from her as she laughed softly.

"Did you enjoy seeing that?" Sofya asked. "I know your customs are...quite different. I have heard some things."

"It was..." Asher struggled for the words, struggled to say *something* to explain to her what he had felt, but he could barely remember how to think. "I want to learn more about your gods. About your religion."

Sofya glanced up at him, tipping her head as she wrung the water from her hair.

"Very well," she said. "We have six weeks left. I will teach you all I can."

"And if I choose to be cleansed?"

"Then I will have to find a holy person of your patron god to cleanse you," Sofya said. "I am not a holy person, nor do I think you would be of *Veharus'* line anyways . But we will speak about that when we get to it, yes? You may decide that you do not want to convert."

"Thank you," Asher said, and Sofya smiled, reaching up to touch his face with hands like frost.

"We will see if your fire can be frozen."

TWENTY-TWO

THE MOUNTAIN RANGE CAME out of nowhere.

One moment there was nothing on the horizon, and then they turned slightly, rounding a bend, and it rose above them in all its might, a jagged jawline of gray stone and patches of white snow. From where they were on the road, the mountain was so small that Viper almost felt as though he could pluck it from the earth and put it in his pocket like a handful of loose rocks. When he opened the window, sticking his head out, the wind whipped away his breath, the chill bringing tears to his eyes as he watched Saffi approach.

He couldn't even see the temple at the top, but he knew it was there, lying in wait like a beast in a cave. He could barely even see the small village that had sprung up around the base of the mountain, but if he strained, he could just barely pick out shapes that might be buildings.

"Viper."

He turned at Ember's quiet call, finding all three of them staring at him.

"We need to keep talking," Ember said. "About the High Priestess."

"What about her?" Viper slammed the window shut, relaxing into his seat beside Blue.

"I have…concerns about her loyalties," Ember said, eyes fixed on her hands as she fiddled with the strings on her gloves. "She knows we're coming but sends no response. And she can't be ignorant to what happened to my mother. By now, everybody in Eiad knows about the Order. So my question is this—if she is loyal to us, as the king so wholeheartedly believes, why hasn't she reached out? Offered support? Sacerdos are hardly soldiers, but they're healers, and we could use their help, and she knows that."

"I don't know," Viper said honestly. "The temple has always been withdrawn, hasn't it?"

"In a sense," Ember said, glancing up at him slightly. "The far north—past Saffi—didn't practice the religion of the Phoenix. The temple, including this High Priestess, helped the king during those conversions. She's been happy to step in before."

"That was when it benefited her," Lucasta said. "Getting involved now doesn't get her anything."

"Oh, it certainly does," Ember said, scowling. "It gives her a place in this country after we burn the Order into nothingness.

And if she thinks the Order will be any more merciful than us, she's wrong."

"She might just keep out of it," Lucasta said.

"Neutrality could be just as dangerous," Blue pointed out. "For us, at least."

Viper watched Ember as she turned her head to stare out the window, at the rapidly approaching mountains. Her eyes darted around, never quite settling, and he could practically *hear* her thinking.

"I'll handle it," Ember said quietly. "At the end of the day, this is my task."

"Don't be stupid," Lucasta said. "You know you'll need us."

Ember glared at her, but her eyes were soft, and the slightest smile curved the edges of her mouth.

"Very well," Ember said. "When I need you, I will call on you."

They lapsed into an easy silence, and Viper couldn't help but look out again, at the town that was shaping into actual houses and structures. A little closer, and he could see figures moving around inside, separated nearly in half by a fence that appeared to wrap entirely around the mountain's true base.

"The town isn't part of the temple," Ember said, and Viper glanced at her. "I'm sure the gate was the High Priestess's doing. Keeping the unworthy out of her spaces."

"We're unworthy, aren't we?"

"Oh, absolutely," Ember said. "Unfortunately, she doesn't have a choice in the matter of us coming up. One way or another, she will have to meet me."

When they pulled into the town, Ember was the first to get out.

Phoenix above. It was freezing. She crossed her arms over her chest as she turned in a slow circle, taking it in. A tavern, right on the edge of the fence, was empty in the middle of the day, but the doors were propped open with chairs, and inside, a few women moved around, one of them openly starting at Ember.

She turned away, noting the houses, the stables, the little stands that lined the roads. It felt…empty.

"Where is everybody?" Viper asked, coming to stand behind her.

"Out," the woman in the tavern said, drawing everybody's attention to her. "There's no work here, unless you're a barmaid."

Beyond the fence, however, was quite the opposite. Men and women in silver robes—sacerdos—moved about, none of them paying attention to the carriage and the people only a few feet away from them.

No—that wasn't quite right. Two people *were* watching them, a short, older woman with tightly pinned white hair and a younger man, his hair cropped close to his head. Both were wearing sickles, the silver of the blades hidden by their robes, The sun caught on the woman's, practically blinding Ember, and now she could see nothing but the serrated edge, dangling there.

Armed sacerdos. People who claimed to be nothing more than religious peacemakers were wearing sickles.

Ember glanced at Viper, barely inclining her head toward the woman's hip. He followed her gaze, brow furrowing when he noticed the sickle.

He opened his mouth to speak, but Ember shook her head, widening her eyes.

Carefully now.

"Lady Ignis." Ember turned, finding the two carriage drivers standing behind them. "We're to stay here until you return. Are we free to go?"

"Yes," Ember said. "We will send word before we leave the temple, so that you're prepared for us."

"Thank you." They moved toward the horses, and Ember turned toward the two waiting sacerdos, locking eyes with the woman there.

This was where it would begin. Ember knew that the second they crossed over the threshold, they would be entirely at the mercy of the High Priestess and her sacerdos.

That was fine. She needed the weapon the High Priestess was hoarding. She needed a way to ensure the Order would not walk away from her wrath.

"Welcome, little Dragon," the older woman said as Ember approached, pale blue eyes shifting to the other three as the man began unlocking the gate. "The Swan, the lesser Serpent, and the scorpion."

Lucasta snorted, and the woman's eyes narrowed.

"You have approached this line to gain access to the most holy of temples, have you not?"

"We have," Ember said.

"You are invited into the Village of Saffi to partake in a cleansing of the flesh and fervor, which is required of you to pass through the Feathered Gate and approach the temple. Do you take on this task?"

"We do."

"Then come and be cleansed."

The woman turned sharply on her heel, and Ember followed closely, noting the male sacerdo as he fell into step at the back of the line, locking the gate behind them.

They'd passed over the barrier, and now they had to be more careful than normal—shielding their words from everybody, house or rebel or holy. Viper gave her a minuscule nod, turning away as they emerged into the village proper.

It was…quaint. The buildings were all made of moss-covered stone, so old that Ember was scared they would crumble underneath her fingertips. The roads had been paved with a similar stone, well-trod from generations of pilgrims and sacerdos crossing back and forth on them. In the center of the town, a fountain bubbling merrily in the center, the Phoenix depicted in stone in the center.

"How—how does the fountain work?" Blue asked, piping up near the back of the group. "I thought only the Talians had that type of technology."

"It is similar to what the Talians do," the male sacerdo said, his voice a rumble of thunder. "It's fed by the hot springs we have here, underneath the mountain. It's been here longer than any of us have."

"Interesting," Blue said softly.

The woman stopped at the fountain, where the road split in four, turning to face all of them. Scars crossing the woman's paper-white palms, years of sacrifice outlined in flesh.

"Keep to the roads at all time here," the woman said. "For you have no need to go anywhere else. To leave the village and enter back into your shameful lives, you simply follow the path back. Any sacerdo can unlock the gate for you and let you out. If you continue forward, you'll arrive at the woods, where we keep a garden and places to worship. You are welcome to partake in these spaces, however, you are not to disturb any sacerdos that may be praying there. To the left are the hot springs, which Kerio just described to you. The road splits into a fork there—take the left path, for the right leads to the Feathered Gate. Follow me."

She led them down the path to the right, where houses were placed on either side, all of them forgoing windows for cutouts in the stone instead, doors flung open wide. At the end of the road, two massive buildings stood beside each other, constructed of the same stone but circular in shape, different than anything else in the village.

"The temple and the common space," she explained. "The common space is used for meals, which will be signaled by three bells, three times a day. If you miss a meal, you must wait for the next one to be fed."

Blue muttered something, and the woman glared but didn't say anything. "Ladies, to the right, if you'd please. There is room for you on the second floor. The Serpent and Swan are on the left."

"What about our things?" Lucasta asked.

"What use do you have for them here?"

"I—"

The woman scoffed. "I know. They will be delivered to you at the true temple, don't worry. While you are here, however, you are expected to wear the sacred robes and distance yourself from such material gratification, is that understood?"

"Yes," Lucasta said, but her jaw had set, and her eyes were like dark flint.

"Good," the woman said. "If you require anything at all beyond what we provide, ask a sacerdo to help find me. My name is Seppa. Enjoy your time here with us."

That was that, then. Seppa continued toward the temple while Kerio lumbered into the men's building. Ember didn't miss the way Blue's eyes tracked the silver-clad man all the way into the building, until he disappeared into the shadows.

"So," Lucasta said. "I suppose we'd better go in."

"I suppose," Ember said, glancing at Viper. "Find us at dinner tonight."

"Of course," Viper said, swinging an arm over Blue. "Let's go see what hell we have to sleep in for a week."

TWENTY-THREE

THE BEDS WERE HARDLY big enough for one person to fit in, much less two. Ember stared down at the cot they'd given her, next to Lucasta's and another woman's. They all slept in the same room in two straight rows.

"I'm going to have to apologize to everybody," Ember said, joining Lucasta at the cutout in the wall, staring across the street at the men's house. "Not one of them is going to get a good night's sleep while I'm around."

"Maybe you won't have nightmares here," Lucasta said, leaning against Ember's arm. "Maybe being somewhere else will help."

"Maybe," Ember said softly, resting her head on Lucasta's. "Phoenix willing."

The bells began to ring, and the two of them broke apart as Ember's heart steeled itself again.

When they arrived for dinner, Viper wasn't there. Blue sat alone at the end of a long table, underneath an arching ceiling, Hazel at his feet. She was watching the silver-clad sacerdos swarming around them, but Blue...

Blue was watching Kerio a table away, to Ember's immense amusement.

"Staring at the back of his head won't make him turn around, you know," Ember said, sliding in beside him, and Blue glared at her.

"I'm not supposed to bother him, remember?"

"You're fine," Ember said, examining the bowls, forks, and glasses already set out on the table, a few carafes of water. "You're not bothering him by sitting with him at dinner."

"It's fine," Blue said. "Besides, I had to wait for you two because Viper abandoned me."

"Where did he go?" Ember asked, ignoring the knowing glance Lucasta threw at her.

"Hot springs," Blue said. "He said he wanted to go while they were empty."

"Understandable," Lucasta said, fiddling with the white streak through her hair. "When do we eat?"

"Soon, Phoenix willing," Blue said. "I assume we're not going to be allowed to eat without praying first."

"Probably not," Ember said. She was pleasantly surprised that she actually *was* hungry though, craving a meal for the first time in what felt like years.

It had only been a few months, she had to remind herself. It had only been a few months.

The hall around them suddenly began to quiet, the roaming sacerdos finally finding places to sit—a few of them at the same table as Ember and the other two—and Ember looked up to find Seppa with her arms raised, eyes fixated on the heavens above.

"Blessed of the Phoenix," she intoned, never breaking her stare. "We have been gifted another day by the grace of She who watches, the Phoenix, and we are grateful."

"We are grateful indeed," the sacerdos responded, and Ember watched as Seppa lowered her arms so they were directly out in front of her, palms lifted toward the sky.

"The Phoenix has blessed this food for us to eat, and we are grateful."

"We are grateful indeed."

"And because we are grateful, we will use this food to continue fueling our work in the name of the Phoenix above."

"We will continue."

Seppa's hands dropped fully, and then, from doors Ember hadn't noticed before, several rows of sacerdos streamed out, carrying massive platters of food between them, placing them on the tables as they moved through them.

"Finally," one of the sacerdos sitting next to Lucasta leaned forward for the food in front of them—potatoes and chicken, by the look of it—spooning some into her bowl. She looked up at Ember, grinning, and Ember couldn't help but stare at a face that was so familiar it was almost staggering.

The priestess was a near-perfect copy of Asher Cinis.

Dark skin, although slightly paler from living in the mountains, and even though she had her hair pulled back in dozens of little braids instead of curls, it was her face that almost exactly the same as Asher's. She had his nose, his dark eyes and eyelashes, the same full lips that were curved in a smile. *His* smile.

It was Whelyn's face, too.

"You must be Ember Ignis," the priestess said, passing the spoon to Lucasta.

"I—"

"It's your eyes," the priestess said. "Dead giveaway. Everybody knows Dragons are the only ones who have gold eyes."

Ember could *feel* Blue staring at the woman, and although she wanted to keep looking just as intensely, she forced herself to take the spoon from Lucasta and serve herself and Blue.

"Yes," Ember said. "I'm Ember Ignis. This is Blue Cinis, and Lucasta Tersus."

"Tersus," the woman said. "I've never heard that name before."

"I'm not nobility," Lucasta said, picking up her fork and digging into her food. "That's why."

"Ah," the woman said. "I'm Cerraine. I too, am not nobility."

"Just Cerraine?" Ember asked.

"Just Cerraine," the woman said. "I was raised in the temple, like a lot of the other sacerdos, and we were only given first names."

"Interesting," Blue said. "You know what else is—"

"Do you spend most of your time here?" Ember asked. "In the village?"

"No," Cerraine said. "I'm going back up in a couple of days."

"Very nice," Blue said. "Now—"

Ember cleared her throat so loudly that a couple of the other sacerdos looked over. Blue glanced at her, and Ember raised her eyebrows for a brief second. She waited until the understanding registered in Blue's eyes before looking back at Cerraine.

"Do you do a lot of work with the High Priestess?" Ember asked, and Cerraine shrugged.

"It depends," she said. "I've been here for so long that I work with her more than a lot of the other sacerdos, but she does most of her work alone. She's…a very private woman."

Great, Ember thought, taking another bite of her— admittedly better than she expected—food. She would ask for Cerraine's help, then.

"Viper's going to miss dinner," Lucasta said, tipping her head slightly toward an empty bowl on her right side. "Perhaps someone should go take something to him?"

"Excellent idea," Ember said, already turning to Blue, but he had refocused on Kerio, over Lucasta's shoulder.

"Where is he?" Cerraine asked. "If he's in the springs, I would recommend getting the clothes that the other sacerdos would've left out for you in the rooms. You're welcome to go into the men's housing so long as you don't linger."

"Thank you," Ember said, taking the new bowl and fork from Lucasta and filling it to the top, tucking an entire carafe of water underneath her arm before slipping out of the dining hall and toward the houses.

Cerraine had been right—when Ember made her way inside, she found the beds that the two boys had taken over, marked by Blue's outer jacket and Viper's shoes. Both beds had a pair of shimmering silver pants, and Ember took the one on Viper's bed, slinging it over her shoulder. She had already grabbed her own, a soft top and the same pants, and then she headed out to the road to make her way toward the hot springs.

It wasn't difficult to find them—the road led her directly to them, as Seppa had said. A small opening in the base of the mountain led her inside a place so dark she couldn't even see her own hands. The silence was overwhelming, and her breathing sped up, eyes darting around the smooth rock walls.

Too dark too dark too dark.

She couldn't exist in the dark. Too many things lurked in it, too many pairs of bloody hands and screaming mouths.

When the Order kept Verity, did they keep her in darkness this deep?

And the quiet—the ever pressing quiet. She had lain in a bed for weeks as her skin slowly stitched itself together, almost entirely asleep, and in that sleep, she did not dream except of her mother.

There was only deep darkness and silence and pain, and nothing else had existed. She could barely breathe; she could barely do anything except take another shuddering step forward.

"Stop," Ember whispered, quickening her pace. Her hands were slick under the gloves, heart pounding. "Stop."

She rounded a corner and then, miraculously, there was light.

Not much—only a few lanterns hung around the space gave off any light, but it was enough to see. The cavern's walls had been smoothed by years of weathering and erosion, although the ceiling still dripped with stalactites. The hot springs themselves were three deep, crystal-clear pools of steaming, sapphire-blue water.

Beautiful.

Her eyes landed on Viper immediately.

He was the only one in the cave except for her, and he sat in one of the springs, head resting against the lip of the pool.

She suddenly wished the pools were murky.

She stepped toward him, purposefully scraping one of her feet on the ground. Viper's eyes flew open, and he turned to stare at her, neither of them speaking for a long moment. She pinned her gaze to his forehead, unwilling to let herself look anywhere else. Viper seemed to have no such issues—his eyes roamed from her face to her feet to the bowl in her hands. Finally, Viper broke the silence.

"Are you going to get in?"

Ember hesitated, contemplating turning around and fleeing back to the house, but…

She was tired and the soak would help her aching muscles. Not to mention the fact that she was dirty from all the time spent on the road. And Phoenix above, she couldn't face the darkness again so soon.

"Yes," Ember said, daring to take another step toward him. "I brought your pajamas, by the way."

"Thank you. I brought the soap and a towel, but I completely forgot about the pajamas," Viper said, sounding genuinely relieved. "I thought I was going to have to walk out of here naked."

Ember flushed, thankful he wasn't able to see her in the dimness of the cave. The candlelight gilded his hair, turning it into a crown, and she tore her eyes from him, focusing instead on the water of the hot springs.

"Don't look at me."

"Of course," Viper said, sitting up and turning his back to her. Ember traced the lines of his shoulders, of the muscles in his back. A bead of water started at the nape of his neck and made a lazy, slow trail to the pool.

So slowly she hardly dared to breathe, Ember set down the lanterns and the clothing, reaching for the buttons on her tunic.

"Hurry up," Viper said. "My shoulders are getting cold."

"Shut up," Ember snapped, shucking off her tunic and undershirt, shivering as she pulled the rest of her clothing off. She slowly undid her hair and then slipped into the water beside him, unable to help the sigh of relief as the heat seeped into her muscles. Her eyes fluttered shut as she basked in the heat.

"I'm done," Ember said, and Viper sank back under the water. "Just don't look."

"Oh, I wouldn't dream of it," Viper said, his voice so close that her eyes flew open. He was only a few inches from her, their shoulders brushing. She hadn't realized how close they'd been when she'd chosen where to get in. Stupid, so stupid—why hadn't she just chosen the other side of the pool?

And there it was again—that rolling purr of a voice, so new and strange that she barely knew how to respond to him.

He was getting better at playing the games of the court. Or maybe she'd just never noticed him before.

But maybe she didn't mind as much as she originally thought she did.

She couldn't seem to tear her gaze away from him. One of his hands came up, out of the water, to brush away a lock of hair that clung to the side of her face. His hand lingered there, thumb brushing small circles over her cheekbone, and she couldn't get enough breath in her lungs, couldn't do anything except listen to the sound of his breathing and her own heartbeat as his hand slid down, cupping the back of her neck.

The slightest pressure on her neck had her moving closer to him, head instinctively tipping toward the side. Ember watched Viper's lips part, and she closed her eyes as their lips brushed and lightning shot through her veins.

Somebody cleared their throat behind them, and Ember shoved away from Viper, glancing at the sacerdo that stood in the hallway.

Seppa.

The older woman *hmphed* before making her way toward one of the other pools. Her back was to them, now, but the damage had already been done. Ember settled back into the water, face hot, ignoring Viper's gaze on her. She rested her shoulder against his and closed her eyes, forcing herself to relax.

Chapter

TWENTY-FOUR

L ORD NAZAROV DID NOT bother to invite Sofya and Asher to dine with him that night. He met them at the gates of his keep, flanked by his wife and an older, hunched man who stared at Asher with not the usual curiosity but unadulterated hatred. The lord himself was small, sickly, with yellowed skin and eyes that were so bloodshot they almost appeared entirely red. By comparison, his wife was the picture of health, although she, too, was yellowed, and she coughed every few moments into a handkerchief that was spotted with blood. Snow fell lightly around them, dusting Asher's hair with powder and clinging to Sofya's eyelashes and Doya's fur.

"Lord Nazarov," Sofya said, striding up to him. Doya was a step behind her, ears perked but hackles down, her tail lashing slightly. "Thank you for receiving us."

"You are welcome here, Fangs," Nazarov said, in a strange mix of Verdecan and Eiadian. Asher suppressed a smile—that was the first time he'd been able to understand anybody other than Sofya when they spoke Verdecan. The lord's voice was a terrible rasp that made the hair on Asher's arms stand on end. "The boy is not."

Sofya froze, and Doya stilled at the movement, dropping slightly into a crouch. Nazarov's eyes flicked between the woman and the wolf, before landing on Asher. "I'm sorry?" Sofya's voice was quiet.

It was a warning, Asher realized. She was giving him a chance.

Nazarov grimaced before gesturing to the old man, who was practically frothing at the mouth as he stared at Asher. His back was so curved that he was nearly bent in half, and there was a whip curled on his hip. Asher cringed as he recalled the sound a whip made when it sliced through the air, the wet, dull sound that followed when it met his back.

He remembered his mother's laughter.

When the old man caught him looking, he chuckled softly and ran a finger over the leather.

Asher forced himself to tear his eyes from it, back to Nazarov and his wife. No weaknesses. Not here. Not in front of Sofya.

"My advisor, Syukosev, has proclaimed that if the Eiadian steps foot within the keep, our disease will only worsen," Nazarov said.

"Foolishness," Sofya said. "Lord Nazarov, you are already far too sick to worsen much more. And I have been around him for several weeks and I have not fallen ill. He is safe."

"Wrong!" the old man, Syukosev, yelled, jumping in front of the lord with surprising nimbleness. Asher yielded a step; Sofya did not. "You landed in Verdeca five weeks ago, did you not? That is when our proud lord and lady fell ill! They were the picture of health before you arrived!"

"Do not be a fool," Sofya said. "The Eiadians landed only a week ago. Lord Nazarov has been sick for much longer. Asher's coming has not worsened it."

"You would not know!" Syukosev said, as the lady behind him coughed again.

"Surely this cold is bad for them—" Asher began, but the old man snarled at him.

"Be silent! My god name is for *Utphine!* She is the goddess of health and disease! I would know, I would know! I am the chosen one of my goddess!"

Syukosev drew the whip with an all too familiar *hiss.*

Asher flinched. He could feel Sofya watching him. So much for hiding it.

"And unless you would like to see why I was named for *Veharus*, I suggest you let us in," Sofya said quietly, suddenly grasping the hilt of her sword.

Syukosev's face flushed. "You will bring plague upon this mighty keep! You fool!"

The sound of Sofya's sword being pulled from the sheath silenced him.

"Did you call me a fool?"

Another warning. Doya growled, sinking fully into a crouch.

"Y-yes," Syukosev said, but his words were quiet, and he took a step back as Sofya flipped the sword in her hand, the picture of ease and comfort, and swung.

Syukosev did not even have time to scream before his head hit the ground, blood staining the snow. Blood sprayed from the wound, splattering Asher and Doya with scarlet drops.

Asher gagged as the man's body collapsed, his head rolling a few feet away, the berries he'd eaten earlier making a sudden reappearance.

It took only seconds.

"Clean that up," Sofya said to Nazarov. "I expect that we'll see you at dinner tonight. Prepare something good—red meat, I think. Come, Asher, Doya."

Asher stumbled after her, through the blood leaking from Syukosev's neck, and into the stone keep. Sofya made no move to sheath her sword, not even as they passed silent servants, eyeing the blood-soaked blade in her hand, to the wolf trotting behind her, to Asher, who still couldn't quite believe what had just happened.

He had forgotten again. He had forgotten what Sofya Seminoava was. She was not just another woman. If he kept forgetting, if he kept allowing himself to relax around her, it was going to cost him his life.

Sofya led him up a flight of stairs and into a bedroom, gesturing to the bed. "Sit."

Asher did as she asked, moving as though in a daze. Sofya plucked a towel from the pitcher beside the bed, running it along the edge of her sword and staining the white fabric red.

"I am sorry," Sofya said, kneeling beside him, lightly drumming her fingers on his knee. "But I cannot let them forget. And I could not allow him to interfere with our plans. We must push on. Without his whispering, the lord will be much more inclined to agree with us."

"Why...why didn't we just handle it the way we did with Maximovich?" Sofya stilled for a moment, and then smiled softly.

"You spoke Verdecan," she said. "A little bit, right at the end. Good job. Your accent is poor, but I am proud nonetheless. And to answer your question—it would not have worked. Syukosev had Nazarov's ear—as well as his wife, Babkina's—but not in the way Agapova and Vitsina had Maximovich's. He respected their opinions and understood their points, but the decision was his. The decision Nazarov would have made with Syukosev's advice would have been Syukosev's decision, and those are not his men to command. He is too weak to be a lord but too slimy to be a proper commander."

"Do they have any children?" Asher asked, and Sofya shook her head, gesturing for him to scoot over and then lying beside him on the bed.

"None—Babkina is unable to get pregnant. His heir is first, his brother, and then his nephew, but the boy is only a few years old. Nazarov though...he is so sickly that it would not be surprising if his brother stepped in soon."

"His wife wouldn't take over?"

"She is just as sick," Sofya said. "If he dies, Babkina would not be far behind. But no, she would not take over. She would be allowed to remain in the keep, I believe, but would also be offered the chance to move if she wished. His brother is...much stronger. He is younger, with little land, but he keeps that land well, and his people are happy and well-fed. I have seldom heard a negative word against Lord Fedin, nor his wife, Lyapina."

"Interesting," Asher said and then turned to look at her. "Why are we in this room?"

Sofya laughed softly. "A few years ago, shortly after I became the Fangs, the tsar sent me and Vika to meet all of the lords and ladies of Verdeca and inform them of who we were—they were told to memorize our faces and shudder if we passed through their lands in anger. Vika had a very bad fever as we passed through Nazarov's lands, and he offered to let us stay here. This was the room I was placed in while Vika recovered in the room across the hall. It is exactly how I remember it."

Asher looked around the room, at the red-silk feather bed they lay on, the sheer canopy above the bed, the small windows, the desk and chair pushed in the corner.

"I'm sorry I reacted like that," Asher said, lying down beside Sofya, attempting to relax.

"It is okay," Sofya said. "I understand. Unexpected violence can be…quite jarring."

"No," Asher said. "I should be more used to it. I *was* more used to it. But now…"

"You have not been in the palace for almost three full months," Sofya said. "You were living in a new place that is not free from all violence, but from that which seems needless and unnecessary. And I think, too, it was hard for you to see me like that. I have not truly been the Fangs around you yet. But you will have to get used to it."

"I know," Asher said. "I know. The war is coming."

"It is," Sofya said. "Now. Let's keep practicing your Verdecan, yes? Perhaps you can learn a few more phrases before dinner tonight."

Dinner, apparently, was a quiet affair in Nazarov's keep.

There were only four people at a round table, and nobody was speaking. Babkina's face was now a terrible mixture of the yellow sickness and red splotches from crying. Nazarov kept twitching every so often, mouthing silently to himself as he stabbed through his food.

Much to Sofya's disdain, they'd served chicken—dry, unseasoned, completely overcooked chicken with nothing except lukewarm water to wash it down.

This was worse than sitting across from a rude little girl. At least the food had been good at Maximovich's keep.

Asher cleared his throat, unable to stand the silence, but flinched away from Nazarov's stare when the lord turned to look at him.

"Verdeca is lovely," Asher began, and the lord scoffed, waving his hand dismissively.

"Do not bother with your silly lies. You are only here because you want something from us."

"Yes, but—"

"Enough," Sofya said, turning to Nazarov. "You have a terrible cook."

Babkina's face flushed, and her fork clattered to her plate. "I cooked the chicken myself!"

"You did a poor job," Sofya said coldly, sitting back in her seat. "Just as you both did a poor job allowing that worm of a man to control your every move."

"He was a trustworthy advisor—"

"And now he is dead," Sofya said. "You know why we are here and what we want. Will you send your men or not?"

"Why would I risk their lives for a cause I do not care about?" Nazarov asked. "What incentive do I have?"

"If you wish to join Syukosev, by all means, deny the request," Sofya said. "If you do not—if you wish to continue being lord over this keep, rather than your brother, I would send your men."

"You...you dare threaten me? A lord of Verdeca?" Nazarov spat, rising slightly. Sofya's hand flew to the hilt of her sword, and he stilled, sinking back into his seat. "You will not always get what you want that way, Fangs. One day, the tsar will tire of you and you will be nothing more than another useless woman."

"Perhaps," Sofya said. "But for today, it has worked, yes?"

"Yes," Nazarov grumbled. "My men will leave in the morning for the Rossolinky Palace."

"Excellent," Sofya said, pushing out from the table. Doya, who had been resting in the corner of the room, stood as well. "Babkina, I strongly suggest you stop cooking. You are poor at it. Come, Asher."

Asher stood silently, eyes flicking between the lord and lady before following her out of the room.

"Nazarov commands about seven hundred," Sofya said. "Combined with Maximovich's two thousand, you have already called almost three thousand to your aid."

"That's not enough," Asher said. "My parents will call their allies. Kieall alone will send five thousand from their cities."

"We are far from done," Sofya said. "Do not forget that the south will rise up, too. Do not worry. We will gather as many soldiers as we can. I am worth ten, as is Vika. The other women in the seven are worth five at least, if not more. And do not forget Doya and Vika's wolves. They will come with us, and we will loose them on the battlefield. The three wolves are worth many soldiers on their own."

"Good," Asher said. "We'll need all of you."

"Come with me," Sofya said, leading him down a hallway. "You have asked to learn about the gods, so I will teach you about them. Nazarov keeps an impressive library—it is quite ancient, and while the keepers of the books have been dismissed, the books remain. Many of them are religious texts. There was… little else to do when Vika was sick except to read."

Sofya's steps did not falter as she led Asher down a flight of stairs, well-lit by flickering torches. At the bottom of the stairs, Sofya pushed through a wooden, ancient door that groaned in protest, revealing the library.

To Asher's surprise, moonlight flooded into the room from an overhead skylight, casting the shelves below in silvery light. Underneath the moonlight, Sofya was transformed from a woman to a small god, shimmering and shining, the swords on her back glinting.

"The books were organized well before they were abandoned," Sofya said. "Do watch your step, though—many of the stones have come loose over the years."

The library was small, contained entirely within a few shelves, with a couple of dusty tables and chairs shoved into the corners. Sofya lit the cobwebbed torches that surrounded the room as Asher ran his hand across the spines of the books nearest to him, eyes scanning the titles. Some were written in the harsh characters of Verdecan, others in Eiadian, and some in language that he could not understand at all—languages he was sure were no longer alive.

"Back here," Sofya said, calling to him from the last row of shelves. "I have found the god-books."

Asher made his way to her, skirting around one of the discarded chairs, and found Sofya stretching up on her toes to reach a book on the highest shelves, just short enough that she couldn't quite grasp it.

"You'd be more intimidating if you were tall," Asher said, easily plucking the book from the shelf.

Sofya scowled. "You are insufferable. I see why you were sent here."

"I was sent here because of my parents," Asher said, grabbing the next book she pointed to. "For one, they taught me how to talk to people like your tsar. And for two, there's a bounty on my head that's so massive half the country is after me."

"You do not talk about them much," Sofya said, and Asher shook his head.

"Bad memories," he said. "I don't love reliving them."

"I understand," Sofya said, carrying the books to the nearest table and dropping them. She hesitated for a moment. "I have many bad memories of my own. I was in the prison for many years. They kept me in a cell by myself."

"Sofya—"

Sofya's hands clenched on the back of her chair.

"I do not want your pity," Sofya said softly, sitting down and opening the nearest book.

"I'm not offering it," Asher said. "I can't sympathize with you about being kept alone."

"It is a terrible thing," Sofya said. "A terrible thing to be locked in the darkness alone."

"How are you sane?" Asher asked, sitting beside her as Sofya flipped a few pages.

"I channeled that fear, that terror, into becoming a better soldier. The people who are responsible were long dead by the time they pulled me out to fight for my life. I am still not okay—not entirely. But I get a little better every day, and that is all that matters. Perhaps I will never be the person I was before the prisons, but I also do not know if I want to be. Can you read any Verdecan?"

"No," Asher said, staring down at the book she'd moved in front of him. He didn't dare ask her any further questions—she'd revealed far more than he'd expected already. Sofya huffed a sigh of annoyance.

"All of that knowledge and wealth at your fingertips and you could not even be bothered to learn."

"Can you read Eiadian?"

Sofya scowled.

"Enough of that," she said. "The first thing you must know about the gods is how many there are. Verdeca has fourteen. Seven gods, seven goddesses. I will tell you of the gods first. You remember some, I trust?"

"Veharus, blood and terror. Trusov, animals, I believe?"

"Good," Sofya said. "Ades, winter. Oteus, summer. Enas, arts. Rudite, knowledge. Sordur, fertility."

"I'll never remember all of their names," Asher muttered, and Sofya smacked him on the arm, hard enough to smart even through the layers he wore.

"Be silent. Goddesses, now. Which do you remember?"

"Cegrena, flame and fury. Krukante, harvest and soil."

"Very good," Sofya said. "Ratlena and Ritlena, day and night. Vakone, bone and justice. Niuna, of the sea and sky. Melene, of the afterlife and wolves."

"I'll pretend to understand," Asher said, and Sofya's scowl deepened.

"You asked to learn, did you not? It is not my fault that you have no brain." Asher bumped her with his shoulder, stilling for a moment when Sofya's scowl vanished, and she turned to glance at him.

"You are so casual with me," she said. "I am surprised, given what I did earlier."

"It…it's easy to forget," Asher said softly.

"Why?"

He couldn't sense a trap in the question, so he answered honestly. "Because you're not what I expected, and I think that scares me more than anything you could do. You're aware of the stories—Sofya, you are a creature under a bed designed to scare Eiadian children. The Fangs…you're not a person, in Eiad, you are a *monster*. But you're not a monster, are you?"

"I do my best not to be," Sofya said softly. "I do as I am told. And sometimes I am told to do monstrous things. I cannot say it is not my fault—if I chose to turn on the tsar, it would take all of the seven, Vika included, to cut down Doya and I. I could run. No man, no woman except for Viktoriya can kill me, and even then…it would be close. I could stop if I wanted to. But why should I? I was afraid, too. At least I am merciful. At least I am quick."

"Do you truly believe you are Veharus incarnate?" Asher asked, and for some reason, his voice had dropped, a hushed whisper in the corner of a forgotten library in a country he never should've been in.

The question hung in the air between them, shifting through the dust, and Asher couldn't tear his gaze away from Sofya's eyes as she tipped her head to the side.

"Yes," Sofya said simply. "I can feel it when I fight, the knowledge of the gods. He guides my hands and blades. I am the greatest soldier in a hundred years—I am better than Viktoriya. And I do not think I am the only god reborn. They have been waking—can you feel it? Your Dragon. You. There are more—I am certain that there are more, but perhaps they have chosen to keep quiet for now. The old gods are waking, and I fear what will happen when I am asked to cut down the people of Eiad. I will not hesitate to do as I am told, and it will be horrifying. I will rain hellfire upon your people. Are you prepared to see that?"

"Not yet," Asher said, and he didn't quite know why, but he leaned into her, almost instinctively. Sofya did not move— she didn't lean in, but she didn't pull away either. "How are you better than Viktoriya if she's the Wolf?"

"Because she is better at the talking. The lying. I am...I am good at the killing. I have more of a stomach for it."

He didn't move any further as Sofya's eyes tracked the angles of his face.

"Why did you not stare, in the temple?" Sofya asked. Her voice was quiet, too, her eyes frantically searching for *something.*

"I don't know," Asher said. "I...not like that, Sofya."

He heard her breath catch, watched her head tilt with the same predatory grace she always carried herself with.

A noise from the stairs startled them, and Asher jerked back, both of them turning in tandem to see Nazarov appear at the bottom of the stairs, glowering.

"There has been news," he spat. When Asher began to rise, he shook his head. "It is for the Fangs. One of the other lords has sent a warning. He does not want you to continue into Verdeca. He bids you turn back, lest you face the consequences. See, Fangs, there are others that want you to give up on this as well. Get this plague out of Verdeca, or you will die with him."

"Baseless threats," Sofya said. "For all we know, Nazarov, they are threats from *you*. The lords of this country know better than to threaten me, and besides, they cannot beat me. I also have the blessing of the tsar. They aren't stupid enough to take those types of chances with me."

"Perhaps not," Nazarov said. "But that is the warning nonetheless."

"Which lord was it?" Sofya asked, lounging in her chair.

"The note did not say," Nazarov said. "So I cannot tell you. My apologies, Fangs."

Sofya waved a lazy hand. "No matter. Thank you for bringing the news."

Nazarov, wisely sensing the dismissal, turned and made his way back up the stairs.

"You aren't worried?" Asher asked, and Sofya shook her head.

"Of course not," she said. "They cannot beat me. Even if they do send mercenaries after me, even if there are many, I can still hold my own. Besides, I have you."

"I'm not much help," Asher said, and Sofya turned to look at him.

"We'll have to work on that, then," she said. "Now, then. We leave early tomorrow morning. It would be best if you would get some sleep before then."

212

Chapter

Twenty-Five

Viper pulled himself out of the bath, watching Ember where she sat in the water, firmly facing away from him. Dark hair, nearly blue, was plastered to her back, shining gently in the candlelight, like the pelt of some exotic animal. Seppa had left a few moments ago, and he felt it was finally safe enough to get out of the bath and speak to Ember again. He toweled off his hair, scowling at the clothes the priestesses had left for him.

"There wasn't a shirt?" Viper asked, pulling the pants on. Silver and flowy, they were rather comfortable and fairly warm, but he didn't have anything to wear with it, and he felt strange with his chest exposed like this, especially around Ember.

"That's all that was on the bed," Ember said. "And it's not like there was anywhere else to hide it."

"I'm dressed," Viper said. "And I'm turning around. You're so dramatic, you know."

"Oh, *excuse me*," Ember hissed, the sound of rushing water accompanying her words. Her wet footsteps sounded on the stone. "I don't particularly *love* the idea of you ogling me."

"Don't flatter yourself," Viper said. "I doubt there's anything worth ogling."

Something whacked him in the back of the head and Viper, without thinking, spun to face her. Ember was already dressed, looking at him with cool amusement, one shoe in her hand and the other at his feet.

"Don't be an idiot," Ember said, wringing her hair out before flipping it over her shoulder and coming toward him, stopping in front of him. She looked down at him, lips quirking in amusement. "You and I both know there's *plenty* you want to ogle."

She snatched her shoe off the ground and slid her foot into it, stalking out of the cave and away from him. Viper stared at her retreating figure for a moment, barely able to restrain himself from mentioning the almost-kiss, but he thought better of it at the last moment. If Ember wanted to talk about that, if she wanted to try again, she would. Bringing it up would only make her shut down.

Viper rushed after her, clutching his towel and a lantern.

"There is a priestess," Ember said when he caught up to her, her eyes darting around the road. "And she is...she could be...she is Asher Cinis's twin, Viper. His spitting image."

Viper stopped and turned to look at her, tipping his head to the side. "Whelyn Cinis is infamously disloyal."

"I know," Ember said. "She was raised here, so I doubt she knows. She…Phoenix above, Viper. I wonder if the High Priestess knows. She has to. Asher looks like Whelyn, and she looks like Asher."

"I assume we're not going to tell her," Viper said, and Ember shook her head, tucking a lock of hair behind her ear. "Unless she could inherit the throne?"

"She can't, and we won't," she said. "Bastards can't take the throne, and it isn't our business to tell her. Besides, she's content. I just wanted to warn you so it didn't blindside you. It almost killed Blue."

"Unsurprising," Viper said. They'd reached the main part of the town now, standing beside the fountain. Ember shifted a couple times before thrusting her hands out, presenting a bowl of *something*, a fork stuck through the middle.

"Dinner," Ember said, not quite meeting his eyes. "Seppa made it pretty clear that if we didn't eat with everybody else, we wouldn't be able to eat at all, and I didn't want you to go hungry."

Viper hesitated for a moment before reaching out to take the bowl from her, their fingertips brushing.

They stood that way for a moment, fingertips touching, separated only by the gloves.

"Thank you," Viper said softly. "I appreciate it, Ember."

She shuddered slightly when he said her name and pulled away. She reached under her arm and presented a carafe of water, filled to the top and closed with a cork. "Enjoy."

"I will," Viper said, taking that from her as well.

She turned and crossed the square to the women's house, vanishing into the shadows.

He watched the entrance of the house long after she had entered it, and it was only when he heard a rumble of noise coming from the dining hall that he turned and went into his own house, his fingertips still buzzing from that little touch.

Ember went looking for Blue as soon as the bells began to ring. She found him in the same place, Hazel a seemingly constant companion at his feet, and although he wasn't staring at Kerio again, he was staring at Cerraine, across the room and chatting animatedly with another sacerdo.

"Blue," Ember said, sliding in beside him. "About last night."

"I know," Blue said, turning to look at her. His eyes burned with a type of fire she hadn't seen from him before. "Asher's sister."

That word alone was staggering—the bastards of King Whelyn Cinis were rarely referred to as Prince Asher Cinis' siblings, but he was prince no longer, just as debased as his sisters and brothers. They'd all known about the bastards, of course, but it was different to see one, so close to the temple, a place of such high holiness that Ember could barely comprehend what must have been going through the king's mind that day. And who was Cerraine's mother? A sacerdo? Or somebody from the neighboring town, a nobody woman looking for a little *ovum*?

Did it matter?

"She could be Feather's daughter for how much they look alike," Blue said softly. "I didn't think we'd find one here."

"I didn't either," Ember said. "She doesn't seem like she knows."

"She doesn't," Blue said. "I almost guarantee it."

"What's with the scheming?" Viper asked, sliding in across from them. "You two *look* like you're up to trouble."

"Turn around," Ember said. "She's right there."

Viper's brow furrowed for a moment, but he did as she asked, turning his head just enough. Ember watched as the recognition dawned on his face, as his eyes darted across Cerraine's entire figure, before clearing her throat.

"I told you so," she said.

"I…You didn't lie," Viper said. "Phoenix above. Whelyn."

"I think Asher might die if he saw her," Blue said.

"We would only be so lucky," Viper said.

"Phoenix willing," Ember said at the same time, glancing at him. Viper grinned at her.

"Don't tell me you want our esteemed prince dead," Viper said, and Ember shrugged.

"He's probably outlived his usefulness to the Order by now anyway," she said. "They'll get rid of him as soon as he isn't helpful."

"Probably," Viper said.

It was strange to be talking about Asher in such a way. Two months ago, they could've been hung for even *suggesting* the death of the crown prince, but now…

Phoenix.

Things were different, now.

Asher's name no longer carried the weight it once did. He'd been stripped of his title, his inheritance, his very *name.*

He was nobody, now. Nobody, and yet at the same time, everything. Whether he'd liked it or not, his parents had raised him in the court, privy to things even Verity Ignis hadn't known, and for that reason alone, Ember knew the Order wouldn't dare kill him, for the slim chance that he remember *something* that could aid them.

The silence was awkward and was broken only when Lucasta finally arrived, a moment before Seppa's raised hands quieted the group.

"Not this again," Blue muttered. "You missed it, Viper."

"Thank the Phoenix," Viper hissed back. "This looks absurdly boring."

"It will be," Lucasta said.

"Blessed of the Phoenix," Seppa began, and Ember glanced at Viper. His lips were pressed together so tightly they were almost gone. She choked on a laugh, face flushing. "We have been gifted another day by the grace of She who watches, the Phoenix, and we are grateful."

"We are grateful indeed," Ember joined in with the sacerdos this time, her voice shaking with restrained laughter.

Viper's brow creased as Seppa's hands began to lower, and then his face set again when her hands didn't lower fully.

"The Phoenix has blessed this food for us to eat, and we are grateful."

"We are grateful indeed."

"And because we are grateful, we will use this food to continue fueling our work in the name of the Phoenix above."

"We will continue."

"Food," Blue said simply, nodding toward the sacerdos coming out to serve them, and Ember turned back to Viper.

"I wish we could skip this part," he said, although his expression immediately perked up when two sacerdos slid a tray laden with eggs, thick slices of ham, two massive loaves of bread, and a handful of oranges. "Maybe not, on second thought."

"The food's better here than it is at home," Blue said.

"It's simpler," Ember said, watching Lucasta reach for an orange.

"Simple can be good," Viper said, spooning food onto his plate.

"It can be," a new voice chimed in, and all four of them turned to find Kerio standing over them, rocking awkwardly on his heels. This close, Ember could truly see how huge he actually was. He would tower over her, and she was already taller than most people. "May I sit?"

Blue choked, face turning a particularly nice shade of red as he dropped his head. Ember patted him on the back.

"Of course," Ember said. "You live here, after all."

"I don't," Kerio said. "I live in the temple."

"So does Cerraine," Lucasta said. "Do you know her?"

"Yes," Kerio said, sliding in beside Lucasta, diagonal from Blue. "I've been here for a long time. I know almost every sacerdo except the new initiates."

"Longer than Cerraine?"

"Yes," Kerio said. "I, like Cerraine, was raised in the temple. She's a year or two younger than me."

Ember and Viper exchanged a glance. "How much do you know about her?"

Kerio squirmed. "Not a lot. Could you all remind me of your names? I'm sorry."

"Don't apologize," Viper said. "I'm Viper Trunca."

"Lucasta Tersus."

"Ember Ignis."

All four of them turned expectantly toward a scarlet Blue, who cleared his throat. "Blue Corvu." His words came out in a strange squeak, and Ember used chewing as an excuse to hide her face and the laugh that was bubbling up in her throat.

"It's a pleasure to meet all of you," Kerio said. "I'm sorry about Seppa. She…she is used to a very specific type of noble. So far, the four of you seem perfectly normal."

Viper snorted. "You'd be shocked."

"I'm not nobility," Lucasta said. "That might be why I don't seem like a noble."

"That probably would have something to do with it," Kerio said. "What brings you all here?"

"We're here to meet with the High Priestess," Ember said. Kerio's eyes darkened slightly as he cut into a piece of ham.

"For the war."

"You know about it?" Viper asked, and Kerio nodded.

"Of course I do," he said. "Everybody knows what happened to Verity Ignis."

The sound of her name on a stranger's lips was strange. It was rare to hear anybody talk about Verity within the court— she was a taboo topic now, her name spoken only as Lady Ignis. Ember's mother wasn't a martyr. She was a victory for the Order, a terrible victory that, no matter what else happened, they would always have. A group of nobody, houseless people had managed to kill the second-most powerful woman in the country, and they had gotten away with it.

Ember could feel the others watching her, even Kerio, so she cleared her throat. "I'm glad you know—that all of you know. Perhaps realizing what they did to her will help convince the High Priestess of what the Order would do to her if they got the chance."

Chapter

TWENTY-SIX

A WEEK AFTER THE disastrous dinner with Nazarov, Doya was restless. She had been keeping pace with Asher and Sofya, but then she began to slow, ears pricked and tail lashing. Her nose followed the wind—but it was whipping so viciously that Asher wouldn't have been surprised if she couldn't pick up a scent at all.

"Stop," Sofya said above the wind, eyes darting around the road. They were ringed in by thick, green trees, and although they hadn't seen anybody on the actual road for hours, that didn't mean nobody was there. Slowly, cautiously, she pulled a knife from her boot and handed it to him. "Do not dismount."

Sofya swung down from her horse, drawing her swords. "Show yourself."

Nothing, even as Doya's crying increased, as she desperately tried to sniff out what had originally set her off.

In the trees, something moved, and Asher squirmed uncomfortably. The horses were restless, too, kicking up their heels and snorting every few seconds.

Phoenix above.

Asher knew they'd heard the warnings, but he'd dismissed them with Sofya's casualness; he'd put them aside as actual threats. Would anybody really be foolish enough to attack Sofya, especially in broad daylight, with her wolf at her side?

Would anybody really be foolish enough to attack *him*?

Another shadow through the trees—Doya saw it then, taking a step toward the tree line as her growls grew louder and deeper.

They moved like the wind.

Asher couldn't keep track of all of them—there were at least six, clad in white cloth and green leaves, faces covered by hoods.

All of them held knives.

Sofya held her ground, and she did not tell Asher to flee.

They leapt down from the trees, screaming in what was almost Verdecan but not quite.

Doya took down the first, tackling him out of the air with a mighty bark. The man didn't even have time to raise his knife before the wolf tore his throat out, blood spraying across her muzzle.

Sofya was moving like a storm, swords flying up to block the attack that the others pressed on her—all of the others, except one, who approached Doya cautiously, as though he could truly overpower the wolf from behind.

He, at least, had time to scream before Doya's powerful claws ripped his gut open.

The terrible sound of steel slicing through flesh had Asher's attention moving, his pulse jumping as he realized it was not Sofya who was bleeding, but one of the attackers, his throat torn to shreds by the serrated edges of her swords—edges he had not realized she had on her swords. Now, more clearly, he could see that there had originally been eight, but now three of them were dead or dying, and Sofya was holding back *five*.

Five men, each twice her size and armed with two knives.

But still, the Fangs did not falter.

For the slightest second, Sofya's head turned enough that he could see her eyes—her pupils were almost entirely gone, silver blown out in a way he had never seen before.

This was not Sofya, he realized.

A sharp whistle had Doya rushing to her aid, slamming through one man's legs and sending him toppling into his companion. The wolf made quick work of both of them, her snarls a sharp melody over the constant rhythm of Sofya's swords.

Three now.

Sofya was still defending, still keeping them back.

When her Verdecan rang out, Asher understood it perfectly.

Veharus would not spare you, and neither will I.

Both of her swords splayed out in a magnificent arc, and there were two more men on the ground, two more men that Doya finished within a moment, and then there was only one.

Sofya did not hesitate before she pointed both of her swords at his throat.

"*Kneel,*" she hissed. He could hear her regional accent now—the word was thicker, almost incomprehensible, and it was then that Asher realized it was the same dialect the attackers had been speaking. "*Now.*"

Doya, finally finished with his companions, slunk behind the man.

He, wisely, knelt at Sofya's feet.

"Explain yourself," Sofya said, using one of her blades to tilt his head up, so he had to face her, had to look into the eyes of an old god, a god who relished in the blood on her hands and the fear in the man's eyes. She used her other sword to cut the fabric from his face, allowing it to fall into the snow, revealing thin lips and a galaxy of small scars.

The man spoke, in the same thick dialect, and Sofya tipped her head to the side before glancing at Asher. "Can you understand him?"

"No," Asher confessed. "His accent is…too thick. Or the words are different?"

"Both," Sofya said. "He is from the far northeast. I would recognize the accent of my people anywhere. I will translate, as best I can. All he has said so far is that he was sent here by one of the lords of the northeast, but he will not give a name."

"To do what?" Asher asked, and Sofya shrugged, turning back to the man and repeating the question in Verdecan. She was clearly struggling to keep her accent clean, fitting of the tsar's court, but she was slipping when speaking to someone of her hometown.

Asher found that he rather liked her accent. It was more guttural, more raw in the northern dialect, and although he couldn't catch everything, words slipped through that he could understand.

The man answered, gesturing as much as he could toward Asher without alarming either Sofya or Doya, who was licking blood off of her paws in the same way an Eiadian lady might lick juice from her fingers.

"To kill you and keep the tsar from entering an alliance with you," Sofya said, and gestured with her swords, narrowly missing the man's head. "Go."

The man didn't need another warning. He shot off, disappearing into the trees, and Sofya turned to look at her wolf.

"Go, Doya," Sofya said softly, pointing into the woods. "Hunt."

Doya stood slowly, stretching, and then bounded into the trees with a howl that quieted the world and made Asher's heart stop. He knew that the man, deep in the woods, would know what that howl meant. What would soon be stalking him through the trees. He wouldn't be able to outrun the wolf, and even if he managed to climb a tree or hide in a cave, he would have to emerge eventually to find food. Either the wolf would kill him, or hunger would. At least Doya would be quick.

"Why did you let him go only to have Doya hunt him?" Asher asked, watching Sofya as she pulled an oilcloth from her saddlebags and began to clean her blades.

"Because," Sofya said. "I want him to remember what it is like to be afraid. And then I want him dead. Someone will find them here. Based on what Doya did to many of them, and the marks from my blades, whoever finds them will know who it was. And that is all the better. The stories will continue to spread, and perhaps it will prevent further attacks. Whatever lord sent them will know better next time."

She sheathed her swords, tipping her head toward him. "You did not run."

"You didn't ask me to," Asher said, coming up to her. Before he could stop himself, before he could actually think at all, he reached up to wipe a drop of blood away from the corner of her lip, his hand lingering.

She didn't pull away, didn't push him away. She didn't move at all.

"You should have run," Sofya said, her eyes darting from his hand to his mouth to his eyes, where their gazes locked. Asher flattened his palm against her face, brushing another drop away with his thumb.

"You were Veharus," Asher said. "Veharus, not Sofya."

"I know," Sofya said. "I am surprised you could tell."

"Your eyes," Asher said. "Your pupils almost disappeared. I've never seen silver eyes before, you know."

"Only gold?"

"Only gold," Asher confirmed. "And only Dragons."

Sofya's eyes fluttered shut, blonde eyelashes gently brushing her cheekbones, and there it was again, his terrible, traitorous heart, which had once longed so for Juniper.

And that had landed him in the middle of Verdeca with the most dangerous woman in the world.

He couldn't play that game again—wouldn't dare play that game again. Especially not with Sofya Seminoava. Especially not with the Fangs, with Veharus lurking within her eyes. Juniper was just a woman.

Sofya was a god.

Asher pulled back, and Sofya's eyes flew open, a flicker of emotion deep within them before she blinked and her eyes were clear again. Woman again.

"We need to keep going," Sofya said. "We are down almost two weeks. If you want your friend to keep his head, we must continue quickly, for soon we will have to turn back."

Asher swung onto his horse, Sofya gracefully hopping into her saddle beside him, and they set off silently once again, neither of them daring to speak of what had rippled through them when Asher's hand had lingered on her face.

Chapter

Twenty-Seven

S EPPA WOKE THEM EARLY on the seventh day.

The old woman so clearly wanted to get rid of them it was almost pathetic, but Ember didn't dare say that to her face. She and Lucasta dressed quietly in their own clothes and boots—all of which had been cleaned at some point by invisible hands—and were given a pack with enough food and water for a day's worth of travel. They followed Seppa out toward the fountain, where four people waited.

The boys had been roused already and stood quietly, Blue's hand resting on Hazel's head. Kerio and Cerraine stood a few feet away, both of them having swapped their long robes for pants and tunics, boots instead of soft slippers.

"Kerio and Cerraine will be your guides up to the temple," Seppa said. "It will take you two days to reach the top, but there are stops along the way where you will find places to rest and refill. You will find no other sacerdos, and although you've never done anything for yourselves, I trust that you can figure out a way to take care of yourselves."

Lucasta's mouth flew open, but Ember touched her arm gently.

They needed to pick their battles. When they came back down, she would let Lucasta rip into Seppa, but for now, they had to choose their fights carefully. They needed a set alliance before they began arguing with elder sacerdos.

"Thank you," Viper said.

"I suggest you get started now," Seppa said. "My final warning, Dragon—pick your words with care. The High Priestess is not a forgiving woman, and we all remember your mother."

"I'm not my mother."

Seppa snorted. "Certainly, just as Verity was never Ferra. The bloodlines grow weaker with each generation, but it is for the best."

The words barely registered at first, but when they hit, it was like she'd been slapped across the face.

Ember didn't respond. She didn't even let the expression on her face change—she simply turned toward the others.

"Ready?"

"Ready," Viper said.

"Great," Cerraine said. "Follow me, everybody."

They fell in awkwardly behind Cerraine, walking in pairs with Seppa alone in the back.

"You can say whatever you want to her when we come back," Ember said softly to Lucasta.

"It doesn't matter," Lucasta said. "They see me as one of you. I'm not entirely sure if that's a good thing or not."

"I don't know either," Ember said.

The walk was the true pilgrimage, Viper realized after they'd hiked for a few hours. They'd walked in silence for a while, all of them too tired to even think about making conversation.

Then Blue had started up with Cerraine and Kerio, filling the space with pleasant and empty chatter, and Hazel was panting, and then Lucasta had moved ahead to comment on something Kerio had said.

Viper then found himself walking beside Ember.

Neither of them spoke for a long moment when he first fell into step beside her, both listening to the conversation going on ahead of them, a heated debate about whether oranges or apples were better.

"Which would you pick?" Viper asked, watching her face out of the corner of his eye. "Oranges or apples?"

"Apples were my mother's favorite," Ember said. "We had trees in the garden, and she would go out there and pick them herself. It was the only work I can ever remember her doing by hand. Picking those damn apples. We'd have them for months after she got done. Everything we ate would have apples in it. Her perfume was made of them. I used to revel in that smell. Now I can't smell apples without vomiting."

"So you'd pick oranges?" Viper asked, and Ember smiled sadly.

"No," she said. "Even with that, I would still pick my mother's fruit. I killed the trees, you know. Had them poisoned. I regret it, sometimes. But I couldn't stand having them there. They'd start growing when we get back. By the Feast of Feathers, they'd be ready to be eaten. I couldn't go through that without her. I know her room still smells like the perfume, though. I can smell it through the door."

This was the most open Ember had been so far about her mother. Even when Verity was still alive, or had just been kidnapped, Ember had never revealed details like this of her mother. She'd revealed what had been necessary when it came to finding it, but never more. Never anything this personal.

"Have you gone in her room?" Viper asked, and Ember shook her head.

"No. I—I can't. I can barely stand going in my room. I sleep with Lucasta every night because I can't get in my own bed."

"Blue's father?"

"Blue's father," Ember confirmed. "As for my mother's room...I have nightmares about her death every night, even this long afterward. I think I always will. I don't know if going in there would make them better or worse, and I don't want to take the chance."

"Maybe you should," Viper said. "I would offer to go with you, but I know how you are. Alone or not at all?"

"Alone or not at all," Ember said. "You know me so well, Lord Trunca."

"I was always watching," Viper said.

"I know," Ember said. "You and the rest of the lesser children. We always knew you were there. It's…strange. Being with you now. Without my mother's death, this wouldn't have happened."

"No," Viper said. "It wouldn't have."

"I suppose, then, that at least something good came from it."

"Lucasta came from it."

"That, too. I am incredibly grateful for her. I…struggle with showing that to her, but I do my best. I give her everything I can. Once we've eradicated the Order, I'll let her do whatever she wants, wherever she wants. I'll pay any amount of money to give her that freedom. She deserves it more than most people I know."

"You don't deserve freedom?"

Ember's smile turned wry. "I'm of the blood, Viper—*you* are of the blood, whether you want to be or not. We were never meant to be free—we were meant to obey."

How strange that Blue had said the same thing to him, during the Duels. It was strange, too, how resigned they both were, but perhaps that was the way of the heirs. It was their job, after all, to obey. It was their job to keep the bloodlines alive, whether they wanted to or not.

"Wouldn't it be nice to be free?" he asked, and Ember turned fully.

"I don't know," she said. "I've never been free, so I can't say. Maybe. Maybe not. But it doesn't matter. It isn't what the Phoenix intended for us."

He was spared from having to respond when Blue called back to them. Viper hadn't realized how far back they'd dropped until Blue's voice was snatched away on the wind.

"Hurry up you two! Come see this view!"

The first stop appeared at nightfall. It was exactly what Ember had been anticipating, a house that was nothing but three main rooms—a massive upstairs bedroom, a small washroom and a storage room that doubled as a kitchen and eating space on the ground floor, most of the empty floor space taken up by a large table and various barrels and crates pushed against the walls. Kerio and Cerraine moved with confidence inside, immediately finding matches to light the few candles that surrounded the space, closing the blinds and locking the doors.

"You didn't have locked doors in the village," Viper said. "Why here?"

"We didn't build these," Cerraine said. "But we've always been told to keep them locked at night. Bears roam these areas. Ironic, isn't it?"

"Very," Ember said. She missed her throwing knives, but it wasn't as though they would do much against such a massive creature unless she managed to get it through the eye or the jugular.

"Pick any bed," Cerraine said. "I don't know if there's enough for all of us to have our own, but I'm happy to share with Kerio if need be. We'll need to get started early again tomorrow morning so we can get there as quickly as possible. Kerio and I have work to do, and I have to imagine that the four of you have your own work to do as well."

"We do," Ember said. "Thank you for coming with us."

"Of course," Cerraine said, grinning. "Happy to help."

Ember couldn't help but wonder if the other woman knew who her father was—if she did, was she choosing to ignore it and keep it to herself? And if she didn't, hadn't she wondered? Ember knew that both Asher and Whelyn had gone to the temple in the past few years, and if Cerraine had been around, she wouldn't have been able to deny the fact that they looked similar.

Did the High Priestess know?

Ember had to assume she did—the High Priestess seemed to know more than she was supposed to, even about non-sacerdos, and the High Priestess would certainly be familiar with the way Whelyn and Asher looked.

"How old are you, Cerraine?" Ember asked, watching the expression on the priestess's face change.

"If the High Priestess is telling me the truth, I'm about eighteen," Cerraine said. "Soon to be nineteen, though."

Younger than Asher, but not by much. *That*, not the king's adultery, was surprising. It had only started to truly edge into the light in recent years, but this meant that their esteemed king had been unfaithful far longer than Ember had realized.

"I'm nineteen," Ember said. "I was just curious."

"Kerio's an old man," Cerraine said, swinging her pack onto the table and nudging the priest, who was already sitting. "Almost twenty-two, if I'm right."

"Ember's going to be twenty in the next few months," Blue said.

Now *that* was a particularly strange thought. It would be her first birthday without Verity, without Asher, without House Pardus. Ember knew that it would pass quietly. She didn't want to draw attention to it, didn't want anybody to try and celebrate.

Perhaps she could celebrate her twenty-first, if she was still alive.

"That means I'm the oldest person here," Lucasta said. "Already twenty-two."

"And you?" Cerraine's question was directed at both Viper and Blue, and both boys paused in their raiding of the barrels and crates around the room to look up.

"Twenty-one," Blue said.

"Nineteen, like Ember," Viper said. "Although she'll turn twenty before me. I guess that means I'm the youngest."

"But you're not an heir, right?" Cerraine said, taking a seat at the table beside Kerio.

"No," Viper said. "My sister Boa is. She's almost thirty."

"Seventh of eleven," Blue said.

Cerraine's smile—*Asher's* smile—flashed. "You'll never get to inherit, then."

"No," Viper said. "But I don't particularly want to. These two are doing a good enough job for all of us."

Ember shrugged. "I try."

Lucasta slid into the chair on Ember's other side, slapping something on the table.

"Cards, anybody?" she asked, grinning. Blue groaned but reached for his money pouch anyway.

"How do you play?" Cerraine said. Lucasta's smile turned wicked, and Ember settled back in her seat, forcing herself to come to terms with the fact that Cerraine was not Asher, and, just like Blaze, this person had done nothing wrong, even if their near-twin had.

Even if the smile on Cerraine's face was so hauntingly familiar that Ember could barely stand to look at her.

TWENTY-EIGHT

THERE WAS NO LORD at the next keep—but there was a lady.

Kind of.

The child who sat lounging in a massive chair—it wasn't quite a throne—could barely be counted as a teenager, much less a true lady of Verdeca. She glanced over lazily when Sofya and Asher walked in, barely looking up from the book in her hands.

Asher didn't miss the flicker of surprise that passed over Sofya's face when she saw the girl—Asher had been warned that Lady Chuprova had a young daughter, but that the lady herself would be meeting them, and hopefully, the daughter would be nowhere in sight, unlike Yesipova.

But now, it seemed that the lady was missing, and only the child remained.

"Siyana Pavlova," Sofya said, stepping up to the edge of the stairs leading to the chair. "Where is your mother?"

Siyana sat up, discarding her book on the arm of the chair. "Dead."

One word, and it was enough to send Sofya a step back, confusion coloring her face. "Dead? When?"

"Two days ago," Siyana said, tucking a lock of deep red hair behind her ear. "She was sick. And she could not fight it anymore. Now I am lady."

"You are not," Sofya said sharply. "You are not of age. You are—how old are you, Siyana?"

"Lady Siyana, please," the young girl said. "I am thirteen."

"Thirteen," Sofya spat. "Thirteen is not old enough to manage a keep. You are supposed to be nineteen before you are allowed to rule."

"There is nobody else," Siyana said, gesturing around the empty room. "My father. Dead. Mother. Dead. I have no uncles or aunts, no living grandparents. No siblings or cousins. I am the last of my name."

"Surely there is somebody else," Sofya said. "Did your mother have advisors? Did your father?"

"Yes," Siyana said. "Father did. Mother dismissed them all. She dismissed almost everybody. There are a few servants—they are somewhere within the keep, trying to keep the fires lit. But there is nobody else."

"And nobody knows?" Sofya asked. "You have not sent word?"

"We have," Siyana said. "To many of the other lords and ladies, but...nobody came when we burned Mother's body. It was only me and the servants."

The young girl's face contorted, everything scrunching as she held back tears. "Why did they not come, Fangs? Why did nobody care?"

Sofya took a step forward. "Come down from there, Siyana, and we will sit and talk. Just you and me, yes? And we will try to figure something out."

Strange—so strange that Siyana did not hesitate to stumble down the stairs, to drop the act of a haughty lady, and hurl herself into Sofya's arms, and stranger still that Sofya wrapped her arms around the girl, holding her tight.

"We may talk wherever you wish," Sofya said. "Is there somewhere my friend can go?"

My friend.

Asher suppressed a smile—now was not the time to dwell on such a thing.

Siyana sniffled, and then nodded. "Come with me."

Sofya dropped back to walk with Asher as Siyana led them into the halls of her chilly, lonely home, speaking softly in Qinnian so the young girl could not understand. "I will speak to the tsar about what is to be done, but rest assured, she will not be staying here. I will send a messenger to Maximovich and Agapova. Perhaps they will be willing to take her in, just for a little while. Someone must take over her lands and men until she is of age. Until then...she needs to study underneath a lord and a lady, to learn what it truly means to rule. The tsar will help."

"She's very comfortable with you," Asher said back, and Sofya smiled gently.

"When Vika and I traveled across Verdeca—the same trip where Vika was sick—we stopped here. Both of Siyana's parents were alive then, and she was much younger. She grew very familiar with me and was truly a shadow in the week we spent here originally, and the one on the way back. She is a shy girl, sensitive, very smart. She reads much, and she was always very proficient in her studies. Siyana was destined to become a scholar, but when we were around, all she wanted was to be a soldier. Gods, she is so young. If only we had known—I would have rushed. Perhaps she would not have been alone."

"There was nothing you could do," Asher whispered back. "Nothing, Sofya."

"I know," she said. "But that still doesn't heal my heart. It weeps for her. Children should not be left alone in the dark."

"This is the library," Siyana said, interrupting them and pointing at a door. "I can take you to a bedroom, though, if you want."

Asher and Sofya exchanged a glance, and Sofya spoke up. "Perhaps a bedroom. It is already late, and if he grows tired, I want him to be able to retire."

Siyana frowned. "There are only two bedrooms ready, and one is mine. You will have to share."

"That's okay," Sofya said, and Asher's pulse leapt. "We will figure it out. Show us to the bedroom, Siyana."

The girl nodded and continued onward, but Asher and Sofya were silent now, walking side by side down the dark hallway.

Such a terrible place for a child, cold and empty. Even his own childhood, horrific as most of it had been, had joy in it at times, birthdays and celebrations with the other children. Before his mother had been cruel, she had been kind. Before his father had been distracted, he had been doting.

But he had never, ever been alone the same way little Siyana was now.

When they approached another door, Siyana stopped again. "Right here. The fire is lit inside, and there are sheets. I can have somebody bring you dinner and wine if you want."

"That would be perfect," Asher said. "Thank you, Lady Siyana."

She nodded, beaming at the title, and as he went to step into the room, Sofya caught his wrist, thumb pressed over his heartbeat.

"I will be up later," she said softly. "Siyana is still young—she needs to retire early to keep her energy. Wait for me."

"Of course," Asher said, and Sofya released him without another word, catching up to Siyana and quickly engaging her in a conversation about what books she had been reading recently.

The wine was good.

Really, really good.

Siyana, apparently, was entirely unaware of how much she had sent. He didn't blame her.

And Asher realized that he had not been alone in quite some time, and that sitting in the room by himself allowed all the memories of his mother and father to come rushing forward in a torrent.

He'd reached for the wine then.

Just a glass, he promised himself. Just a glass, to wash down his food, and then he would sit in silence and wait for Sofya.

But he couldn't resist.

Not when every crack of the logs in the fireplace was a whip racing toward his back, wielded by a man who desired nothing but the queen's affection. Not when he caught his reflection in the glass and hated how similar it was to his father's face, glaring back out at him.

Seeing the whip that Syukosev had threatened him with at Nazarov's keep.

He had not realized, not truly, what his parents had done to him.

It was no longer the scars on his back that stung, but those inside his mind, burned there by hurled words and endless violence and hatred, a torrent of it that came rushing forward from wherever he'd shoved it down.

Asher had another glass, and another.

He added more logs to the fireplace, staring deep into the flames as though it would provide him with answers. He had gotten better about it—sharing a cabin with Tyvish had kept his nightmares at bay, perhaps because of some unconscious fear of waking him up. And these past few weeks, with Sofya, something about her had helped shove them down entirely.

But he was alone again, and Asher had never really liked to be alone.

Vax, his cousin, was not here—not even his tombstone was here to keep Asher company. He had no dog, no horse, not even servants that he could incoherently mumble to for a few hours before passing out in his bed, a drunken mess that had never really deserved what had been handed to him.

"What am I doing here?" Asher whispered to himself, but his words were slurred and strange, and he realized that instead of a glass, he was clutching the second bottle of wine by the neck. He lifted it to his lips, intent on swallowing the rest, when the door opened, and Sofya stepped in.

Asher turned toward her—slowly, for his head was pounding—and watched Sofya immediately take stock of the situation. He watched her notice the discarded first bottle, the second that he clutched in his hand, and Asher lurched to his feet.

Sofya's hands reached for her blades, and Asher placed the bottle on the table, putting his hands up.

"I'm not going to hurt you," he said, speaking in a terribly slurred mix of Eiadian, Verdecan, and Qinnian. Sofya lowered her hands slowly.

"You have been drinking," she said softly, in Eiadian. "Gods. I should have known not to let her send wine up, but I was foolish. I thought…"

"Its…not…your fault really. Mine only," Asher said, gripping the back of the chair as the room spun. The only thing that stood still was Sofya, a statue in the middle of the room. She was *so* pretty, he realized, in a different way than the women he'd loved before. Or the women he *thought* he'd loved. He'd tried to convince himself that he'd loved Ember, once, to make it easier when they would inevitably have to marry. And then Juniper, who he'd given everything up for.

"Asher," Sofya said, and with a drunken jolt he realized she'd said his name again, and he loved it, he loved his name on her tongue. The way her accent curled the end, turning it not into the name that his parents had given him, but something far more beautiful. Something far more holy. Sofya didn't spit his name with disgust like so many others did.

"Say it again," Asher said, lurching past her and sprawling on the bed. "Please."

He turned to see Sofya watching him. "Say what?"

"My name," Asher said, and groaned, pulling a pillow over his head. "No. I'm sorry. No, Sofya."

The bed sank slightly as Sofya sat beside him. He could feel the tension in the air, even in his drunken state, coiling like a beast ready to strike.

Sofya said his name on an exhale, coming out quickly and all at once, the syllables slurred together as though she was drunk, too. "Asher Cegrene."

Never Cinis, with her.

And thank the Phoenix for that.

"My god name?"

"Yes," Sofya said. "Flame and fury. It suits you, I think."

"I don't know," Asher said, pulling the pillow down just enough to peer at her, to peer at where she reclined on the many pillows. They had not shared a bed at all, not even at Nazarov's keep, when they could've. She had requested a second room.

But now…now, she was staying. Even when he was terrible and making a fool of himself, she was staying beside him. Even when she could go sleep on the floor of Siyana's bedroom and keep the little lady company, she was staying.

Asher, through the fog in his mind, could not decipher that. Perhaps it was only because there were no other open rooms, or perhaps she felt bad for him.

Or, maybe, she simply wanted his company.

"I'm sorry, Sofya," Asher said. "Sofya, Sofya, Sofya."

"Enough," Sofya said. "It's time to go to sleep."

"Not in this," Asher said, gesturing to his clothes. "I have. A belt on."

"Then take it off," Sofya said. "Sleep in your underclothes for all I care."

She unsheathed her swords and unbuttoned her coat, dropping it on the floor before shimmying out of her own pants, leaving her in nothing but a piece of fabric binding her breasts and underwear. "See? I did it."

She was under the blankets then, and he was on top of them, and that wouldn't do. Asher grappled at the clasp on his belt, shoving his uncomfortable pants off before he, too, shed his coat, his shirt going with it.

And then he joined her under the many blankets. It was cold, for a moment, especially with the space between them. Asher piled pillows around them—but not dividing them.

He would not block her from seeking him out, if that was what she chose. He did not think she would. She was the Fangs, after all. She could have her pick of men, and Asher knew, in the depths of his heart, that she would not want some drunk, former prince who was good for nothing except embarrassing everybody he ever made contact with—anybody he ever loved.

His parents, first, and then Juniper. Both had gotten rid of them in their own ways, both had made it clear they did not want him around.

But Sofya Seminoava stayed. She burrowed further underneath the blankets, turning to face him in the weak firelight.

"Being alone is hard," Sofya said softly. "I understand. You are not the only one who has suffered. We are so similar, you and I, and so different."

"I love when you speak Verdecan," Asher confessed, unable to look at her until her hand came up gently, turning his face to her.

"Goodnight," Sofya said softly and whispered something in the northern dialect that he could not understand and in this light, she stopped being the Fangs, stopped being Veharus, stopped being a monster. She was only Sofya, her face dappled by shadows. Her hair was liquid silver around her head, the curve of her neck outlined in moonlight.

She really was like a god, and she was going to destroy him.

"Tell me what you said," Asher begged. "Please."

"Another day," Sofya said. "If you remember, then another day. Goodnight, Asher."

He groaned in protest but couldn't find it within himself to argue any further. Sofya's hand dropped from his face.

"Goodnight, Sofya."

Chapter

TWENTY-NINE

THEY APPROACHED THE TEMPLE quickly.

At first, it was a feeling that they were getting closer, a shift in the air. There were whispers that weren't the wind, voices swirling that almost spoke in a language that Ember understood but not quite. The words were out of reach, flying away just as she tried to snatch at them, and so she did her best to ignore them as they continued to climb, up and toward the top.

It was far colder than she'd expected, and she shivered as she climbed over a patch of snow. Those had appeared about half an hour ago and were only increasing in frequency.

"Is there snow year-round?" Ember asked Kerio, who was beside her. He'd been walking in stormy silence all day after losing terribly in *Uvetz* the night before, but he brightened at her question.

"Yes," he said. "Some of the other sacerdos—Cerraine included—hate it, but I love the snow. I love winter. I think it's lovely. We get fresh snow through the fall and winter, and then it just sticks throughout the spring. There's not a lot during summer but it's certainly there."

"I'll have to disagree with you," Ember said. "Winters are brutal in central Eiad—I can't imagine what you go through up here."

"The Phoenix provides," Kerio said. "If you stay on the temple grounds, you'll be fine. It's those who wander off who don't come back. She can't protect everybody all of the time."

For a moment, Ember wondered if the voice on the wind was the Phoenix Herself, but she shook the thought from her head. No—she was hearing things. The old gods no longer existed that way anymore. All of them had fled this mortal plane long ago.

Up ahead, toward the front of the group, Lucasta rounded the corner alone, and Ember heard a noise rip from the other woman's throat, not of fear but of awe. She increased her pace, passing both Viper and Blue, and came to stand beside Lucasta, who was taking in the Temple of Saffi.

It was a marvel. A wonder. It was suddenly no surprise as to why so many, even those from other countries and religions, came to see the majesty of the temple.

It was, like every other temple in Eiad, completely rounded, but instead of being made of white or gray or even the rare green stone of the Phoenix Palace, it was entirely black, surrounded by snow that didn't get closer than a few inches to it. The entry was one massive, rounded arch in the stone, without doors. Stained glass windows had been placed periodically on the walls, and although she couldn't see what they depicted from here, Ember knew they would be of the patron animals, based on their colors alone. The roof of the main room wasn't closed by glass like most other temples but left completely open to the elements.

"Incredible," Viper whispered softly, taking another step forward.

"Isn't it?" Cerraine asked. Ember's eyes slid away from the temple proper to the small buildings that surrounded it—a few larger buildings, and a lot of much smaller ones. Most were rectangular, but there were also more rounded buildings, spread out clockwise from the temple.

"What are those?" Ember asked.

"Dining areas, bath houses, and bedrooms," Cerraine said. Ember craned her neck and stretched onto her toes to see *over* the main part of the temple to find that it continued, pushing further back. "Each patron animal gets their own, smaller temple as well. Those are the smaller circular buildings. A couple of the big ones are actually part of the main temple, but the lesser ones had to be built separately, for the sake of the design."

"Fascinating," Ember said.

"Come on," Kerio said. "We can show you the Phoenix Flame."

Ember stilled. They were standing underneath an archway she hadn't noticed before, and she stared up at the writing engraved on it, written in what could only be the old language.

"What does it say?" She asked.

"*O! Flamma et furor*," Kerio said. "Oh, the flame and the fury!"

Ember shuddered as she passed underneath the arch, the words ringing in her ears.

That wasn't the only thing she could hear, though.

The voices she'd heard on the way up the mountain were shifting, now, molding and shifting into a singular, pulsing voice. The words were still nearly out of reach, just past her fingertips, and as she followed Kerio, the voice grew louder, nearly screaming at her in that ancient language. Her hands flew up to cover her ears, but it was only Cerraine who looked at her.

"You hear it too, then," Cerraine said. "It's maddening at first. You'll get used to it."

"What *is* it?" Ember asked, ignoring the stares that the others gave her. Cerraine fell into step beside her.

"Take them ahead, Kerio," she said. "I'll go with Ember."

Phoenix. It was roaring in her ears now, and Ember took a step backward in an attempt to relieve the pain, the stress of it, watching her friends as they continued into the temple. Only Cerraine stood beside her.

"It's the Flame," Cerraine said softly. "You're hearing the Flame, Ember."

"The Flame can't speak," Ember said.

"You're right," Cerraine said. "But the Phoenix can. This—this is Her mouthpiece. Not many can hear Her, Ember. I'm sorry that you can."

"That doesn't make any sense," Ember said. "The old gods aren't *here*. They don't exist anymore."

"Don't they?"

They stared at each other for a long time, Ember clutching her ears as Cerraine tipped her head. "You can't deny it. She's here, even if the rest of them aren't."

"I can't understand it," Ember said, and she hated the tears that sprang to her eyes. She would have to grapple with the implications of the Phoenix speaking with her later.

"I can't either," Cerraine said. "Not out here. When you step into the temple, it will change. You'll be able to understand it, and it'll be quieter."

"Then why aren't we going in?"

"Because She is *dangerous*," Cerraine said. "The Phoenix was never a kind god. You know that. She can tell you things about yourself that you don't want to know, and she *will* coax you toward the Flame. You *must* ignore Her."

"Why?" Ember said. "Why can we hear Her but the others can't?"

"I don't know," Cerraine said. "Some of the other sacerdos can hear Her, some can't. The High Priestess can—she won't admit it, but I've seen her by the Flame. It's hypnotizing."

"Okay," Ember said. "Please."

"Okay," Cerraine said and held her hand out. "Come with me then, Ember."

Ember hesitated, nearly unwilling to remove her hands from her ears, unwilling to touch another person who wasn't Lucasta or Viper, but there were gloves, and she didn't know what was going to happen when she entered that temple.

So Ember, slowly, carefully, slid in her hand into Cerraine's and allowed the other woman to lead her up the road, up the stairs, and into the temple's sanctuary.

Inside, the Flame was a monster.

It was a beast in a cage in the Phoenix Palace. But here?

Here, it was barely contained. It was easy to forget in every other temple what the Phoenix Flame was.

Here, nobody could forget the Flame was the last act of a once-almighty god, leaping and twisting and reaching out with golden tendrils for the people who surrounded it. The cutoffs of the Flame were hungry.

Here, this Flame was *ravenous*.

Cerraine had been right.

The screaming stopped immediately. It leveled out, became a rumbling purr, and the words were changing too, the language shifting into something recognizable. The dialect was strange and unfamiliar, but the words that the voice spoke—that the *Phoenix* spoke—were familiar now.

It was calling her name.

It was calling her name in her mother's voice.

Cerraine's hand tightened over hers, not letting her go, but Ember was already attempting to tug herself away from the other woman, fumbling with her glove strings.

She left Cerraine shouting and holding the glove behind her as she took another step toward the Flame, reaching for the knife on her forearm.

Viper spun at the sound of Cerraine's scream, his eyes darting toward Ember, stumbling toward the Phoenix Flame as though in a dream. Shadows rippled over her face as she took another staggering step, standing on the lip of the pit.

The Flame reached out to her with greedy arms.

Ember unsheathed her knife in a fluid motion, the blade catching the light and sending it spiraling across the room.

Viper hadn't registered when he started moving, but he was, hurling himself toward her as Ember's knife pressed into the palm of her un-gloved hand, cutting across in a fluid motion. Blood bubbled instantly, pouring from the wound into the Flame. It leapt at the offering, snatching drops of blood from the air.

Viper grabbed the back of her shirt and hauled Ember backward just as she attempted to take another step forward, throwing both of them to the ground in a heap.

For a moment, he could do nothing except stare at Ember, who lay motionless a few inches away from him, her bloodied palm pressed into the floor.

She took a shuddering breath and Viper stood, head spinning.

"What the hell was that?" Blue asked.

"The Flame," Cerraine murmured. "I told her not to. I tried to keep her away."

"You didn't do a very good job," Blue spat. Cerraine rounded on him instantly, mouth flying open, but Ember groaned, and suddenly Viper didn't care about the argument whatsoever, crouching beside Ember.

"Are you okay?" Ember looked up at him, her pupils blown out. "Ember. Are you okay?"

"Yes," Ember said, pushing herself into a sitting position. "Phoenix. What happened?"

"The Flame did," Cerraine said, producing a small roll of cloth from her pack. "Give me your hand."

Ember held her hand out willingly, and Viper watched as Cerraine carefully wrapped the wound before covering it with Ember's glove, tying it neatly.

"I didn't...I hadn't realized..."

"It happens," Cerraine said. "But now you know. You can still hear it, can't you?"

"Yes."

"Keep away from it," Cerraine said. "Avoid this room entirely if you can. That's what I do. It is the only way."

Behind them, someone gasped.

Viper looked up, and Cerraine leapt to her feet.

"High Priestess."

Viper and Ember scrambled up at the same time, Viper taking in the older woman who stood only a few feet from them.

The High Priestess had been beautiful, once. He could see it in the highness of her cheekbones and the arch of her eyebrows. Her face was marred by wrinkles, her lips pursed so tightly they almost vanished entirely. White hair was pulled into a high bun behind her head, and she wore the same silver robes as the rest of the sacerdos and a red rope across her midsection cinched it. A sickle of black stone hung at her side. She was nearly taller than Ember, although the younger woman still had the slightest edge.

It was her eyes, though, that drew attention, a deep, sparkling blue so at odds with the raging gold behind her.

"Dragon," the High Priestess said.

"High Priestess."

"You are not welcome here," the High Priestess said. "Go."

Chapter

THIRTY

"I F WE RIDE WITH minimal stops—every other night— we can make it to Rossolinky Palace in one week from our furthest stop. It is much, much closer than the Summer Palace, so we should have no issues getting back in time. I fear cutting it close, but I also fear that we haven't collected enough support quite yet."

"How many men are we at?" Asher asked, trotting alongside Sofya. She'd slowed for a brief moment to pull a flask of warmed *vilvy* from her saddlebags, sharing it back and forth with him.

"Over ten thousand," Sofya said. Asher nodded, taking another swig from the flask. After Siyana, they had stopped at four other keeps, and although the lords and ladies there had been pleasant enough, Asher strangely kept wishing for Siyana's keep, for the warmth of Sofya beside him as he slept. Beyond *vilvy*—and only in small amounts—he hadn't had anything to drink since that night, and Sofya hadn't commented on it, even though Asher remembered. He hadn't yet pressed her to reveal what she'd spoken a week and a half ago in the northern dialect, and she hadn't offered again.

But Asher could feel it there, hanging between them, desperate to rear its head and reveal Sofya's secrets.

"I do not like this area," Sofya said suddenly, reaching for the flask and taking a long drink. "I am familiar with it, though."

Asher glanced around—at the sparse trees, at the snow covering the ground, at the light animal prints that had been stamped into it. They'd passed through a small village about two hours ago—that was where Sofya had gotten her *vilvy*, providing the honey in exchange for two flasks.

He could see nothing amiss, but even Doya seemed on edge, once again walking with them rather than dashing off in pursuit of something to eat.

"Why?"

"Because," Sofya said. "This is where the prison is."

She didn't have to explain more than that—Asher knew instantly that the prison she spoke of was the one she had been kept in.

"It's still standing?"

Sofya nodded. "Unfortunately. Vika and I…we wanted to burn it to the ground, but the tsar refused our request. He does not do that often, and I am not fool enough to disobey when he does."

"I can burn it down if you want," Asher offered, only half-joking, and Sofya turned to him with a tight smile.

"I cannot allow that," she said. "Regrettably."

Asher grinned back at her. "Just say the word, Sofya, and the place goes up in flames."

"Veharus above," Sofya muttered. "You are a terror, Asher."

Asher suppressed a smile at the sound of his name. "Can I ask you something?"

Sofya glanced at him. "Within reason."

"What was the hardest challenge you had to overcome to become the Fangs?"

Sofya was silent for a moment, worrying her bottom lip with her teeth, before responding. "There were many that were difficult, but it was the hardest when they dumped us into the woods after our third challenge—which was a combat challenge against a moose—and told us to find our way back within a week. We had nothing but the clothes on our backs, but they had hidden many things in the woods, and that was how we survived. But it was midwinter and… there was little food. Women began to hunt each other down for food."

Asher swallowed hard. "Did you?"

Sofya turned toward him, tipping her head to the side. "Is that a question you want the answer to?"

"That response tells me enough," Asher said, and Sofya nodded.

"I assumed it would. I am not proud of it. But I am alive, and that is what matters."

"Yes," Asher said. "Agreed."

"Now," Sofya said. "I get to ask a question."

"Fair enough," Asher said, and Sofya considered it for a moment before asking.

"Who was worse, your mother or your father?"

"Worse in what way?"

"To you," Sofya said. "Who treated you worse?"

"My mother," Asher said. "She was...very violent. My father was distant, and didn't care much for me, but my mother had the captain of the guard whip me when she was displeased, even though most of the time I hadn't really done anything to deserve it."

Sofya's face darkened. "That explains Nazarov's keep, then."

"I didn't mean to react," Asher said.

"Sometimes, we can't help these things," Sofya said. "You see me here—it's been years, and I still feel nervous. It takes time, like I told you before. Everything takes time. Will you kill her? Your mother?"

"I—no. I don't think I'd ever get the chance. I don't know if I'd be able to go through with it, even if I did. I'm not really that kind of person."

"Will *I* be asked to kill her?" Sofya asked, turning to look at him. "Will your rebellion ask me to kill them both?"

"Maybe," Asher said, squirming uncomfortably. "I...I haven't really thought about their deaths yet. They feel untouchable, I guess. I felt the same way about Verity Ignis, too, but they managed to kill her anyway."

"Their deaths will come," Sofya said softly. "At least one of them, but most likely both. Your rebellion cannot take over when your parents remain."

"I know," Asher said, equally as soft. "But...still. They're going to kill everybody I know—everybody I grew up with."

That was a sobering thought. He hadn't been particularly close to anybody in the houses, but that didn't mean he wanted them dead. The lords and ladies had known him when he was small, ruffling his hair and passing him extra sweets at parties. The heirs and lesser children had been his playmates, until all of them got too old for such things.

Would he be able to stand it, if they killed Blue in the streets, the same way his father had been murdered?

Could he watch them hang Ember, watch as she kicked and screamed? As the light drained from the last pair of golden eyes in Eiad?

"Everybody who did not protect you," Sofya said, and Asher shook his head.

"They didn't know. Only a few people knew—and I don't think my father actually understood the extent of my mother's abuse. The only other people who were even aware were servants who helped me lick my wounds, and the captain of the guard."

"Do not worry," Sofya said, glancing at him. "They will not strike you again. I will not allow it."

"If I don't get to burn down the prison, you don't get to kill my parents."

Sofya scowled. "That is hardly the same thing. Killing your parents will benefit everybody. Burning down the prison does nothing except giving me and Vika a very terrible sense of satisfaction."

"It's interesting that you and Vika came from the same prison," Asher said, and Sofya shrugged.

"Perhaps. But that is where they keep the most dangerous criminals, from across Verdeca. Viktoriya is not from the northeast—she is from the northwest, far, far away. They took her there to hold her. Luckily, when they took me, they did not have far to go."

"Luckily," Asher muttered, glancing back at her. "How did you get Doya?"

"Oh, a much better story than the challenges," Sofya said. "The tsar gifted the wolves to me and Vika when we were given our positions. There was a big ceremony for all five of us—the tsar opened the palace to the public, and there were thousands there, court and peasant alike. When it came time to announce our names to the public, he handed us both a box. Inside of Vika's were two little white wolf pups, brother and sister, from the last tsar's wolf. Verdecan wolves are incredibly rare—litters are often one or two pups, three at the most, and they are always, always white. That is what the stories say, at least. So it was quite a surprise to everybody when I opened my box and found Doya. He explained that the mother of Vika's wolves had given birth to a black wolf, a third pup nobody had expected, which are commonly thought to be cursed, wretched, unlovable. She was larger than her brother and sister, and while Vika's wolves went back to their mother that night, to nurse, the wolf rejected Doya. I fed her milk from a spoon for weeks, until she could eat solid food. I trained her myself, allowed her to sleep in my bed, and taught her commands that could keep both of us safe. I trust her with my life, without compromise, because I know she will keep it safe."

"She loves you," Asher said, and Sofya nodded.

"Yes. And I love her. She is my best friend. Most wolves do not live beyond ten or eleven years, but Verdecan wolves are expected to live for at least twenty. We will be together for many years, and for that I am so grateful. And when I die, I will be able to join her on the endless ice and we will run together forever."

"I should get a wolf," Asher said, and Sofya laughed—a genuine laugh that stung his ears in the very best way.

"Good luck," she said. "If you can find a pup and convince the mother to let you have it, perhaps you will be able to raise one."

"Or the mother will rip my throat out," Asher said.

"That is more likely," Sofya said. "Are you ready to be back in Eiad?"

"Yes and no," Asher said. "I...I feel this strange tension. Like something is waiting there."

"Something *is* waiting there," Sofya said. "The other gods. They have all gathered in Eiad, and they will rear their heads when they hear about us."

"Do you think you'll survive?"

Sofya looked away, hands gripping the reins, and shook her head.

"I think I have been too lucky. Eventually, the luck will run out. I feel it too. I feel that not only do gods wait in Eiad, but so does death," she said, touching her right side. "He has been waiting long for me."

Chapter

THIRTY-ONE

SHER GRUNTED, DESPERATELY TRYING to shove Doya off of his chest. The wolf's jaws were gently locked onto his neck again, and Sofya stood a few feet away, watching.

"The command is *off*," she said. "You know the word. Just tell her and she'll stop."

"That feels like a trick," Asher said, wrestling with Doya, who only snarled slightly and tightened her hold.

Sofya walked over, squatting beside his head and ruffling the fur behind Doya's ears.

"Please, Sofya," Asher begged, squirming. "I'm freezing."

"Freeze," Sofya said. "You should be able to get her off with a command or physical force. She is not even trying."

"Let me fight you," Asher said. "Come on. This is hardly fair."

"Of course it is fair," Sofya said. "Doya is not immortal."

"Maybe not, but Phoenix above, she's *heavy*."

Sofya patted him on the head before turning to her wolf, barked the word "off" in Verdecan, and Doya released him, stepping back and leaving a string of saliva around his neck.

"We will try again later," Sofya said, glancing up, where the sky was rapidly deepening from orange to black. They were standing outside another temple, although, as Sofya had explained, this was a newer one, built with pews and stained glass. There was no underground lake, no god-bugs, or anything of the sort. It was closer to an Eiadian temple than an old Verdecan one. They'd attended the service only a few hours ago, but it hadn't felt like what had happened in the cave. But it had been necessary—the lord of this particular keep, Lord Razin Yegorovich, was deeply religious, and appearing at the temple service would make them look far more sympathetic.

"I think we must tell him that this is a godly mission," Sofya said, drawing her swords and tossing one to him, sliding into a fighting stance. "That there will be a place for the Verdecan gods in the new Eiad."

Asher tested the weight of the sword in his hands, keeping an eye on Sofya as she swung her foot behind her in a circle, so steady on her feet that Asher didn't think anybody could actually knock her over.

But he needed to train, and who better to spar with than the best soldier in the world?

Sofya did not move. She was a statue, barely breathing, barely blinking as Asher desperately tried to figure out what he was going to do to best Sofya. He didn't think it was possible.

"I think you're the only soldier we need to bring back," Asher said, and Sofya laughed.

"One-on-one, I am unbeatable," she said. "But when there are numbers...I need assistance."

"So I really have no chance, I guess," Asher said, and Sofya nodded.

"Yes. But the practice cannot hurt, can it?"

Sofya moved, darting forward and swinging at his head so quickly that he barely had time to block it, grateful beyond belief that she only had one sword. Sofya hardly let the swords make contact before she threw a punch at his head with his left hand, cutting low with her sword, toward his knees.

The punch hit, but thankfully, the sword did not.

Asher stumbled back, head throbbing as Sofya leapt back, grinning. She hadn't aimed for his eye or his nose, and Asher was sure that it was because she knew he wouldn't have been able to block it.

"You're too fast for me," Asher said. Sofya didn't answer— she simply pressed the attack again, moving slightly slower, allowing him to keep up. Doya, behind him, snarled as Sofya dropped, sweeping his legs out from underneath him as he was focused on her sword, arching through the air and catching the sunlight on the blade.

His back hit the ground, head slamming into the snow, and Sofya was on him in an instant, leaping on him and straddling his legs, keeping him pressed down as she leveled the blade of her sword against his neck, the serrated edge just barely brushing the bulge in his throat.

Neither of them moved for a long moment. Sofya weighed next to nothing on his legs, just a wraith of ice and wind, and as she slowly pulled her sword away, Asher's free hand flew up, catching her wrist and brushing his thumb over the pulse that raced there.

"You lose," Sofya whispered, and Asher smiled slightly, releasing her.

"Against you, I'll always lose," Asher whispered back. "Always."

Lord Razin Yegorovich insisted on leading a traditional prayer before they ate. A traditional prayer that lasted thirty minutes.

And this was the *shortened* version, at least according to Sofya.

Asher squirmed in his seat, staring at the soup in front of him that was surely cold by now, but he was so hungry that he knew he'd eat it all anyway.

The lord raised his hands toward the ceiling, continuing to chant in a Verdecan dialect Asher didn't understand at all. The words *felt* familiar, but when his brain desperately tried to process them, nothing came to mind.

Beside him, Sofya was barely suppressing a scowl, hands clutching her thighs underneath the table as she, too, stared at her soup.

Asher reached over, placing his hand on top of hers, squeezing gently. Sofya glanced over at him, providing him a tight-lipped smile as Lord Razin continued to ramble on and on and on.

Down near the end of the table, somebody groaned loudly, and Razin abruptly cut off, eyes flying open. Asher drew his hand away, glancing down toward the end of the table, where a man, young and handsome, grinned at the frowning lord.

"Our guests are hungry," the man said, speaking Verdecan with a strange accent that Asher could mercifully understand. "They know that you are a pious man, Lord Razin, but you are starving them. Let them eat."

"Quiet, Lord Dorokhin," Lord Razin said. "Cutting the prayer short allows demons to infiltrate our food. Is that what you wish? Destruction upon our esteemed guests?"

"Don't be absurd," Dorokhin said. "You've scared off the demons, I promise. You're about to scare off the rest of us, too, if you don't let us eat."

Razin's arms dropped, and he sighed, rubbing the space between his eyes. "Very well. Sit down, all of you."

Razin sat with a loud *thump*, and everybody else followed.

Asher didn't hesitate, picking up his spoon and immediately diving into his soup, relieved to find that it was still lukewarm. It was definitely some kind of fish, and potatoes floated in it, and it was delicious. They'd also been provided with some warm, spiced tea that was still hot thanks to the covered mugs they'd been served in.

"Our food here is…simpler than in other places," Lord Razin said. "We believe it serves the gods more if we eat simply, as our ancestors did."

"We used to not have any seasonings," Lord Dorokhin, the young man from near the end of the table, said. "Thankfully, our merciful lord revoked that rule a year ago. What a relief for all of us!"

"A relief indeed," Sofya agreed. "But I agree entirely with you, Lord Razin. There is nothing of more importance than doing what serves the gods."

"Humph," Lord Razin said, turning to look at Asher. "What does someone of his nature know of the gods?"

"He knows plenty," Sofya said, nodding at Asher. "I have been teaching him the ways of the gods for the past few weeks."

"But you are of the old faith, are you not, Sofya Seminoava?"

"I am," Sofya said. "But they are the same gods."

"In name perhaps," Razin said. "But you of the old faith worship so differently, believe so differently, that they are almost not the same at all."

"What is your god-name, Fangs?" Lord Dorokhin asked, leaning forward to look at Sofya and Asher.

"Veharus," Sofya said, and a shudder passed through the group. A few people began whispering to each other, but both Dorokhin and Razin were completely focused on Sofya, their attention diverted from Asher.

"How unusual," Razin said. "Veharus is a rare god-name."

"I am aware of this," Sofya said. "But it is fitting, is it not?"

"It is," Dorokhin agreed. "And for you, Eiadian? Have you been given a god-name?"

"He has not," Sofya said. "Not officially."

"We have holy people of all the gods here," Razin said. "If you wish to have him cleaned and christened, you are welcome to do it in our temple. We would be honored."

"Thank you," Sofya said, leaning back to allow a servant to whisk away her bowl and place a small plate of meat and vegetables in front of her. Asher stared down at his own plate. More fish—but that wasn't a problem. He immediately dove in, listening to the conversation but not speaking, not drawing any extra attention to himself.

"But we are here for another reason, Lord Razin."

"I am aware," Razin said, cutting his own fish. "But do you not think it rude, even sacrilegious to speak of war over a meal blessed by the gods? War in a country that the gods are not worshiped in?"

"The gods will never be worshiped in Eiad if we do not bring them there," Sofya countered, glancing at Asher. He cleared his throat, drawing the attention of the table.

"There will be a place for the Verdecan gods in the new Eiad," he said, parroting off what Sofya had told him before. "You will be able to establish temples, bring your holy people, have your holidays. Eiad will be a place for all to worship, including those of the Verdecan faith."

"This is a war for the gods," Sofya said. "A war to bring the gods to a heathen country who has never known their mercy."

"And you are certain that Verdeca will win?"

"Verdeca has me," Sofya said. "Verdeca has the seven, and the brave men and women who are marching to Rossolinky Palace right now to join the tsar and fight for their gods. Verdeca cannot lose so long as we have enough men."

"I cannot provide much," Razin said. "Only five thousand men, many of them simply from the high villages of the northern ranges. They are not clean soldiers, Fangs, but you know that. You know what type of men I speak of."

"I do," Sofya said. "And they are brave, and true, and they will fight for Verdeca without question."

"They are your people," Razin said. "I can hear it in your accent."

"They *were* my people," Sofya countered. "I have not lived in the mountains for many years now. I do not think I can continue to call myself one of them when for most of my life, I did not live there."

"Your accent will always betray you," Razin said. "It's not clean enough to sound like the court, although some words… some words are. But yes. I will send my men to Rossolinky Palace."

"Thank you," Sofya said, inclining her head, and Razin nodded tightly.

"Keep my men safe," Razin said. "And do not let them forget about our gods, or we will surely lose."

Chapter

THIRTY-TWO

T HE HIGH PRIESTESS'S WORDS didn't register at first.

In all honesty, not much was registering for Ember. There was the Flame, which had quieted slightly after her offering, the throbbing pain in her hand, and there was the High Priestess, standing there with disgust written across her face.

Ember heard the words a second after the others did. Viper's face changed instantly, confusion sparking in the depths of his eyes.

"I—"

"They're pilgrims," Cerraine said, and Ember was surprised to find how steady the other woman's voice was when she spoke to the High Priestess. "They participated in the cleansing."

"They are here to ask of war," the High Priestess said. "Because the king is too cowardly to face me himself."

"His Highness is busy," Ember said, but the High Priestess raised her hand, cutting her off.

"Whelyn is a fool," she said. "And he is afraid. That is all it is."

"Please," Ember said. "Just let us talk to you, and perhaps we can—"

"I will give you a chance to plead your case," the High Priestess said. "As Cerraine said, you did complete the cleansing. You are welcome here as pilgrims. I will give you *one* chance. My answer will be the same regardless. But I wish to see how you do it. To see how it compares to your mother."

Ember's jaw set. Mention of her mother hurt, but she couldn't show that in front of the High Priestess. She had a feeling this woman could exploit even the slightest weakness, and she desperately needed the High Priestess to see her as somebody worth respecting. "Very well."

"Tomorrow," the High Priestess said. "I will call for you when I am ready."

She pushed through their group, heading deeper into the temple.

There was a long silence, and then Viper spoke.

"She's terrifying."

"Utterly," Cerraine agreed. "At least she's giving you a chance."

"Not really," Ember said. She flexed her hand, relishing the sharp pain that sparked with the movement. She could feel the others watching her, waiting for her to react. "I suppose we'll have to try something else, then."

"Don't do anything stupid," Viper said softly. "Don't give her the opportunity to hurt you."

She didn't miss the way his eyes flicked toward her stomach, where her scar was. She hated that—hated that he believed she was fragile, that she needed protection. She could defend herself just fine.

"You worry too much," Ember said, ignoring his gaze. "I'm going to see the Dragon's sanctuary."

There was a man in the smaller sanctuary.

He was the first thing that drew her attention—not the small cutoff of the Phoenix Flame, not the painted mural of the Dragon on the far wall, not the flowers scattered around the room.

No, the first thing she noticed was the man.

He was a hulking brute from behind, hair tied in a long braid at the base of his neck, shoulders so broad she was surprised he'd fit through the door.

And then he turned to look at her, and Ember yielded a step.

He was massive—bigger than Blaze Minus—with a thick beard that covered most of his face, leaving only his full lips and large brown eyes, under brows like caterpillars. His skin was dark, falling somewhere between her own shade and Asher's. Large, golden hoops dangled from his ears and nose. His clothing, all in shades of brown, hung loosely around his figure, and he was barefoot, bangles clinking around his ankles and wrists.

He spoke.

"What are you?"

The question was so strange and surprising that Ember's brow furrowed. His voice was laced with a rumbling accent, so surely he'd misspoke.

"I'm Lady Ember Ignis," she said. The man shook his head.

"*What* are you? Your eyes."

Oh.

"I'm the Dragon," Ember said softly. The man's eyes brightened.

"I found you," he said.

"I'm sorry," Ember said. "But who are *you*?"

"I apologize," the man said, inclining his head. "I am Nekun of Oscela, son of the *Pasha* Jaghatai."

Ember immediately bowed in response.

Oscela was headed by a group of powerful families—the *Cehan*—with the *Pasha*, often the patriarch of the richest and oldest family, ruling over the others. The son of that man was known as the *Pasha Daha*—it was the closest thing Oscela had to a traditional prince. This man was royalty.

And he was, for some reason, standing in an Eiadian temple, kneeling at a shrine of her patron animal.

"I did not realize," Ember said.

"It is not a problem," Nekun said. "I did not realize either."

His words from a moment ago came back to her—*I found you.*

"What brings you to Eiad?" Ember asked, fiddling with the strings on her gloves. Nekun smiled, revealing bright white teeth, and gestured in her direction. His hands were gigantic, palms the size of her face, and his fingers were adorned with rough-cut rings and tattoos of symbols that she couldn't make out in the quick glance she got.

"You," he said. "That is why I am here. My father sent me."

You.

"Welcome to Eiad," Ember said. Her palm throbbed. "We are happy to have you here."

"Thank you," Nekun said. He didn't elaborate on what he meant, simply turning and surveying the room.

Ember followed his gaze, taking in the space properly for the first time. At the far end of the circular room was a small bowl of the Phoenix Flame, flickering merrily. Unlike the large Flame, this one didn't speak at all, similar to the cutoff of the Flame that resided in the Phoenix Palace. The floor was sprinkled with flowers—yellow carnations—and dried bundles of flowers and herbs hung from the ceiling.

Somewhere, bells began tolling.

"Dinner, probably," Ember said when Nekun turned to look at her. "Would you care to accompany me?"

"Tomorrow, perhaps," the prince said, giving her another beaming smile. "Today...I am going to explore. I will be here tomorrow morning, shortly after first light, if you wish to speak to me again. Good evening, Lady Ignis."

"Good evening, Prince Nekun."

She watched him leave and tried to ignore the sinking feeling in her stomach.

Chapter

THIRTY-THREE

WHEN THEY LEFT LORD Razin's keep, Sofya set an unforgiving pace.

They were running out of time.

Asher hadn't realized how many weeks had passed, how many days had gone by from when they'd started off from the Summer Palace.

They had eight days left before Tyvish's head was separated from his neck, and that simply couldn't happen. He felt guilty for not giving him much thought throughout the last few weeks, distracted as he was with Sofya and the lords and ladies. He hoped Tyvish was okay, though. He didn't want to go back to Eiad without him.

He *couldn't* go back to Eiad without him. Not only would he (begrudgingly) miss the other man, but the Order would never forgive him. Tyvish was beloved by many people within the rebellion, Luria van Ela, their leader, most of all.

Asher knew they had taken too much time to simply do nothing—too much time at each keep, each temple, each stop along the way. They'd stopped too many times to spar or split a flask of *vilvy*.

And now they were going to have to ride like hell until they got there. They couldn't push the horses too hard, unwilling to risk having to slow at all, but Sofya kept them at a steady gallop, racing across the snow that was slowly melting, turning to mush underneath the horse's feet. Summer was coming into full force in Verdeca, the world around them shifting from gray and white to brilliant greens. Flowers had begun to spring up alongside the roadway in brilliant reds and purples. He hadn't even realized Verdeca would bloom at all. A few times, Doya had stopped to roll around gleefully in the flowers.

Asher desperately hoped Tyvish had utilized his time well and had rallied the south to come to their aid.

Doya had disappeared long ago, almost as soon as they'd stepped out of Razin's keep and into the bright Verdecan sun.

"We will make it," Sofya said, glancing at him, hands tightly gripping the reins. "Do not worry. Your friend will not be killed."

"Would he really kill him?"

"Of course," Sofya said. "My tsar does not bluff."

Asher thought about Tyvish's death for about two seconds before deciding he wanted to change the subject.

"If the south is raised, how many soldiers will we go to Eiad with?" Asher asked, watching Sofya as she furrowed her brow, considering the question.

"At least thirty thousand," Sofya said.

"Good," Asher said. "My parents…their allies will send many soldiers. But perhaps thirty thousand will be enough."

"Perhaps," Sofya said. "It must be enough. We have no other allies. Surely there is nobody else for the rebellion to call."

"You're right," Asher said. "And I've never been allowed to know the numbers of the rebellion, so I can't say what our final numbers will be for sure."

"That is no worry," Sofya said. "We will find out when we land in Eiad."

"I wish I could see my parents' faces when they find out you've aligned yourself with the rebellion," Asher admitted. "I wish I could see them find out it was because of me."

Sofya glanced at him, smiling slightly. "We will bring them to their knees, Asher Cegrene. I promise you that."

"My parents would kill themselves before they knelt before me," Asher said, and Sofya's smile only grew.

"I will not allow it," she said. "And once they have knelt, I will let you do what you wish."

"I just want them dead," Asher said. "I don't care if that makes me a terrible person. They deserve it. They *all* deserve it. My parents and the houses and all of the rich and houseless who have backed their ways for years."

"They will get what is coming," Sofya promised.

When they stopped for the night, pulling the horses into a small copse of trees beside a sluggish stream, there were only a few hours left before the sun lit the sky again, and Asher was swaying on his feet, thighs throbbing as he unrolled his bedroll beside Sofya's. Neither of them had bothered with a fire—once the horses were relieved of their saddles, they'd both collapsed without speaking, Doya stretched out between them like a furry, breathing wall.

They woke again at first light, saddled the horses and filled their flasks, and were back on the road, Doya keeping pace at first before she tore off into the trees after spotting a rabbit in the shadows. She vanished into the darkness, and Asher didn't know how he was supposed to put *her* on a boat and keep her contained there for weeks until they landed in Eiad again. Doya was the raging north contained in fur and blood and bone, and he was asking to put her in a cage.

In a way, he was asking the same of Sofya.

He glanced toward her, riding beside him with her hair in a messy braid. Her face was soft, eyes fixed firmly on the horizon, the muscles in her arms flexing as she adjusted her grip on the reins.

Her eyes shifted slightly, catching his gaze, and she tipped her head. "What?"

"Nothing," Asher said, immediately tearing her eyes away. "I feel bad asking you to put Doya on a boat."

"She will be okay," Sofya said. "She has been on boats before—never as long as two weeks, but she will manage. And once we are in Eiad, I will let her roam."

"You can't," Asher said. "People kill wolves as often as they can in Eiad, simply because of our religion. Doya won't be safe running wild in Eiad like she is here."

Sofya made a noise in the back of her throat. "What do you mean, because of your religion?"

"The Wolf is an enemy of the Phoenix," Asher said. "Wolf pelts are sold to the temple for extremely high prices. People can kill wolves for a living and never wish for anything again."

"I will kill *them* and never wish for anything again," Sofya spat. "You must stop the killing of wolves when your rebellion takes over."

"Of course," Asher said. "In our thanks, I'm sure the rebellion will do many things to please Verdeca."

"It is not for Verdeca," Sofya said. "It is for me only."

Doya reappeared, weaving through the trees like a ghost.

"May I ask you a question?" Sofya asked, and Asher turned toward her.

"Of course," he said. "Anything."

She didn't say anything for a long moment, the two of them listening to the wind. "Do you know you talk in your sleep?"

"What?"

"You talk in your sleep," Sofya said. "A lot."

"I'm sorry," Asher said, face burning slightly. "I didn't realize that was something I did. If it's keeping you up, I can sleep a little further away."

"It doesn't bother me," Sofya said. "Do you want to know what you talk about?"

She was being strange, not looking at him. Her tone was off, too.

"If you want to tell me," Asher said.

"You talk about your mother," she said. "All the time. I am sorry she hurt you, Asher. I am sorry I was not there to save you."

Asher stared at the horizon. "I should've saved myself."

"Impossible," Sofya said. "You never talk about your father."

"There's nothing there to talk about," Asher said. "He pulled away from my life, and there was nothing I or anybody else could do about it. So when that happened, my mother took her frustration out on me. I look a lot like him, you know. She saw him in my face every time she looked at me."

"I am going to kill them," Sofya said. "You will not be able to keep me away from them when we land in Eiad."

"It won't stop the pain," Asher said.

"Of course not," Sofya said. "But it could help ease it."

Chapter

THIRTY-FOUR

EMBER MET THE OTHERS where they sat near the Phoenix Flame. They walked to dinner in silence, except for Cerraine's occasional chattering. She led them down a staircase , weaving through hallways and doorways.

Ember was lost within minutes, walking quietly beside Blue.

"The baths are right here, down this hallway," Cerraine said, pointing. "I'll show it to you again after dinner. I know it's pretty confusing to get around here, but you'll get it after a week."

"What is down most of these hallways?" Blue asked, dropping his hand to Hazel's head. The dog leaned into him, and Ember smiled softly. It was good to see both of them bonding. She had been worried, initially, about bringing the dog with them, but it seemed as though it had been good for both Blue and Hazel. Blue had lost a parent, too.

"Libraries, for the most part," Cerraine said. "Some of the rooms are filled with the stone that we use to contain the Phoenix Flame. That's where we pull from when we need to set up a new temple. Oh, and there're always the rooms with food, water, and clothing. A few washrooms, the kitchens. Things like that. But like I said, most of them are libraries. Ancient knowledge, from the time of Saffi herself."

"I don't know that story," Lucasta said, stepping up to walk with Cerraine. "Could you tell it to me?"

"Of course," Cerraine said. "I'd be happy to tell it to you later, or any other story about the temple or Phoenix that you wish to know. For now, though, I will need to step in and help with dinner. Please find a table. I'll find you later and take you to the baths afterwards."

"Thank you," Lucasta said.

They entered the dining hall, which was surprisingly similar to the one at the base of the mountain. Long tables, carved of wood, accompanied by benches. Silver-clad priests and priestesses moved between the tables and sat on the benches. Cerraine made her way to the left side of the room, where an open kitchen was filled with priests and priestesses carrying massive platters of food and pitches. On the right side of the room, a slightly raised dais held a small table and single chair, where the High Priestess was seated, scanning the room.

Ember locked eyes with her, and the slightest smile curved the High Priestess's lips. Her eyes shifted to Lucasta, and Ember slid in front of her, blocking her. The High

Priestess's smile only grew, and Ember forced herself not to squirm under that deep, blue gaze.

"Blue found a seat," Viper said, appearing beside her. "Come on."

Ember didn't break eye contact with the High Priestess as she slowly followed Viper toward one of the tables, where Blue had somehow made room for all four of them. A young priest made his way up the dais, and the High Priestess's gaze mercifully broke.

Hazel, laid out under the table, looked up as they approached, wagging her tail. Ember scratched her between the ears as she slid in between Viper and Lucasta. Blue, on Lucasta's other side, looked around optimistically.

"Who are you looking for?" Lucasta asked, and Ember followed his gaze as it bounced around the room, unable to keep up with him. "Cerraine?"

"No," Blue said, and his tone shut down any further questions. Lucasta turned back to Ember, raising her eyebrows. Ember shrugged.

"No idea," she said, glancing up again at the High Priestess, who was focusing entirely on the left side of the room. Ember found Cerraine amongst the other priests and priestesses, her curly head bobbing around the others. "She was lying about the rooms, wasn't she?"

Lucasta placed a finger against her lips and nodded. "There are ears. We will discuss later."

"Understood," Ember said. She shifted again, her leg brushing against Viper's. She swallowed, turning fully to speak to him as Lucasta again engaged Blue about who he was looking for.

"This place is a maze," Ember said. "Do any of you remember how to get back to the sanctuary?"

"I could find where she said the baths were," Viper said. "But no, I couldn't get back to the sanctuary."

"Beloved of the Phoenix!" Ember jumped as the High Priestess's voice rang out across the room. "Will you please stand with me for the prayer."

Again, it was not a request, and Ember pushed to her feet with the rest of the room. Around her, heads bent, and Ember followed, staring at her shoes.

They had belonged to Verity, she realized. She was wearing her mother's shoes. She hadn't meant to—they must have been living in her closet before Verity had been kidnapped.

It had been so nice to forget. To move on. To try and pretend that she was going to go home and her mother would be waiting for her in the Draco Estate.

But that was another lie.

The High Priestess's voice droned on in the background as Ember's vision began to spot.

Not here, she thought, pushing thoughts of her mother out of her mind.

Or tried to, at least, as it didn't seem as though they wanted to go anywhere this time. They wouldn't budge even as she threw all of her will against them, begging with her mind to get rid of the memories, if only for a little while longer. She couldn't very well leave the room while the High Priestess was praying, but as soon as she was done, she could get out—

Please.

She couldn't afford a distraction now, couldn't afford thoughts of Verity when so much was on the line. The last thing she needed was to have an episode in the middle of the dining room, where everybody would see. Her breathing sped up, coming in short, quick pants. Tears swam in her eyes. Even the gloves weren't enough anymore—her entire body was shaking as her mother's death replayed in her mind again and again.

A pair of arms closed around her waist, accompanied by the faintest smell of paint and oranges.

Despite herself, Ember relaxed into Viper's touch, her body melting into his warmth. His breathing caught as she pressed her back fully against his chest, his heartbeat thundering through her body. His chin rested on her shoulder, his breath tickling her face. His thumb brushed soft circles on her stomach. Comforting her. Easing her breathing.

The prayer continued, but Ember didn't hear a word of it as Viper continued to touch her, to hold her, to keep her safe.

Viper's heart was still pounding.

He'd let go of Ember as soon as the High Priestess had finished her prayer, attempted to collect himself all throughout dinner, didn't speak a single word to her...

And it wasn't enough.

He could smell her, fire and apples, all over him.

She had been a flame in his arms for that brief, stolen moment, and he desperately wanted her back. Every brush of her leg against his was torture. He was going to scream if he had to hear her laugh with Lucasta again.

Existing with Ember Ignis was going to kill him. He was going to go insane if he had to put up with this for the remainder of the month. Not to mention the trip down the mountain and the week at the base of the mountain. And the trip home. And all of the time afterwards. He would never be able to escape her.

And frankly, he didn't want to.

He'd done this to himself, after all. He'd been the idiot who approached the heir of House Draco and inserted himself in her life, and now he couldn't get out of it, no matter which way he turned.

Viper found himself staring at her, and she turned slightly, hair brushing his arm.

She looked up at him, pupils expanding slightly. It took him a second too long to pull away, to drop his gaze to the food in front of him. He hadn't paid any attention to it—he'd simply put it in his mouth. All of it was gray and tasteless.

Everything was gray and tasteless compared to Ember.

So when Cerraine came to collect them, he walked in the back of the group silently, watching Ember walk next to Lucasta. Blue stood with Cerraine, talking to her quietly as they made their way through the halls.

"Again," Cerraine said, raising her voice. "The baths are this way. Don't worry, though, I'm going to walk you to the rooms and come and collect you again later. The baths are *very* busy right after dinner, so we'll wait a little bit and then go down. And don't fear, there are towels and soaps and sleepwear down there. You don't need to bring anything."

"We can't bring anything," Ember said. "Considering our clothes aren't here yet."

There she was. Lady Ignis was back, replacing the anxious mess she'd been less than an hour before. Commanding and entitled again. He knew it was a front, but it was still strange, the shift in her personality.

He hated it, he realized. Hated when she became Lady Ignis.

"I do apologize for that," Cerraine said. "They should be here tomorrow."

Viper didn't miss Cerraine's gaze dropping to Ember's knife, tightly strapped against her arm. The priestess's brow furrowed slightly.

"I'm sorry," Cerraine said. "Is there a reason you carry a knife?"

"Of course there is," Ember said. "I was raised in the houses. My life is at stake, always. All four of us—five, if you want to count the dog—are in danger here."

"I understand," Cerraine said. "But you aren't in danger here, Ember."

"You don't know that," Ember said, and Cerraine smiled softly.

"You're right," she said. "I don't. But our sacerdos are adept at healing and miracles. We'd keep you safe."

"Cerraine," Ember said, her voice surprisingly controlled. "Tell me again about the miracles."

"Unfortunately, I can't. The secrets of the temple and the ancients...you aren't worthy of hearing them. You don't understand how long we've guarded these secrets. If we gave them away to everybody who asked, they would've been stolen long ago. After all, there have been many pilgrims. You aren't the first to ask, Ember, and you won't be the last."

"Oh, I don't doubt it," Ember said. "But I won't steal your secrets, Cerraine. I have no reason for them."

"Wrong," Cerraine said. "You have a war to fight. The secrets of healing…they would be invaluable on a battlefield."

"So you understand, then, how much we'd need you," Ember said. "How many people you could save."

"It's not my place to have this conversation, as much as I wish I could," Cerraine said. "Only the High Priestess can choose whether or not we enter the battlefield. Not me. Not any of the other priests or priestesses. Please, please don't bring this up to any of them. The younger ones…I would hate to see them be punished because of loose lips. It simply wouldn't be fair to them."

Punished.

An interesting choice of words, especially considering the already punishing life the priests and priestesses led. All of them had scarred palms from their sacrifices to the Phoenix Flame—Cerraine's scars were surprisingly neat, but Viper had seen several at dinner where the scars were sporadic, crisscrossing across their hands and arms. Not like Ember's scars—these were shallow, meant to bleed for a short amount of time and then heal once bandaged. None of them were deep enough to require stitches.

But they bled nonetheless.

All of them bled.

"You said some people come here as children," Viper said, attempting to keep up with the hallways. They made their way up a staircase. Hopefully they were nearing the end of their journey—he was sick of the twisting hallways and the endless doors. "Where do they live?"

"Ah," Cerraine said, visibly relaxing. "An easy question. Thank you, Viper. Those under twelve—novices, as we call them—have their own quarters. I'm sure you noticed the little buildings that surround us. There are greenhouses, stables, kennels, heated pens for livestock, and the dormitories for the novices and their guides. Our senior priests and priestess also live in those houses, and we tend to them as well."

"You seem to have an excellent system here," Viper said, and Cerraine nodded, her voice and step noticeably more excited. Her love for the temple, for the people surrounding her, was apparent. This place had raised her better than King Whelyn ever could've, and for that, Viper was glad she didn't know the truth of her heritage.

"Oh, yes," Cerraine said. "The most ancient one in all of Eiad. Older than the houses and the royal family. The temple was the past and will be the future. There will never be an end to the temples of Eiad."

Ember glanced back at him, eyes bright.

There will never be an end to the temples of Eiad.

They'd found their way to force the High Priestess to cooperate.

Chapter

THIRTY-FIVE

THE ROSSOLINKY PALACE WAS a living, breathing creature. It sprawled over acres of land, a monstrosity of glass and gold-veined marble, dome-topped towers shooting in the skies, statues of stone wolves prowling through endless garden mazes, snow lightly dusting the tops of their heads. Figures moved behind massive windows, golden light streaming onto the grounds. Even the *gate* was enough to draw the eye—snowy maidens and bears dancing through ribbons and berries, and it swung open as soon as the two men on either side caught sight of Sofya and Doya, who both shot through the gate without so much as slowing down. Asher was only a moment behind them as they thundered upon the stone path that led to the magnificent front doors, white ringed with gold. The crisp air smelled faintly of flowers.

Sofya dismounted in a single, fluid motion, throwing the doors open and startling the poor servants inside. Asher stumbled after her, legs aching from the ride but unwilling to slow Sofya. Doya was at her side again as she led him into the foyer of the palace, a massive, open room. Walls hung with rich paintings of mousy-haired, stern men, and ringed with guards, small pieces of furniture against the walls in an attempt to make it less cold.

It didn't work. Asher could feel Verdeca's history breathing down his neck, and the feeling didn't go away as she led him down a long hallway, stopping outside of twin doors. She glanced at him for only a moment before flinging the doors open and stepping inside.

Another throne room, this one larger and prettier than the one at the Summer Palace. It was also fuller.

Thousands of soldiers crowded the space, and at the head of the room, on a raised dais, sat the tsar and all of the lords and ladies. Little Siyana Pavlova tipped her head and smiled gently at Asher from where she sat near the end, in between Maximovich and Razin. The lords and ladies of the north had been placed on the tsar's right, in their furs and swords, and the lords and ladies of the south on his left, dripping with silk and jewels. Some, Asher had met at the Summer Palace, but still others he'd never seen before.

He scanned the crowd, searching, searching, searching, his eyes finding Viktoriya and the other seven throughout the crowd, always keeping one eye on the other soldiers and the other on the tsar.

Asher continued looking, continued desperately to find Tyvish within the crowd.

"Sofya Seminoava," the tsar said, and although he did not shout, his voice carried, and all conversation in the room abruptly ceased. "Clear a path for my Fangs."

The soldiers moved without question, creating a walkway directly to the dais.

Sofya began moving, Doya on her left and Asher on her right. When they hit the bottom step of the dais, she knelt, and Asher went down beside her, glancing at her slightly. She blinked slowly at him, and then cast her eyes to the ground, waiting.

"Rise," the tsar said. "It is good to have you home, Sofya."

"Thank you," Sofya said. "It is good to be home."

Asher did not miss the slight hesitation in her voice, the way her eyes darted around the room restlessly.

"And you, Asher of the Bears," the tsar said, turning his attention onto him. "You have done well. This is but a fraction of the soldiers you have rallied, through the lords and ladies that flank me. Good work. They are all yours to take to Eiad, along with the boats that you need to transport them. And do not forget the seven, and the wolves. They will all go with you to aid the cause."

"Thank you," Asher said, inclining his head. "Your country is…incredible."

The tsar smiled. "Isn't it? And excellent work on getting back here on time. Your friend is safe, do not fear. He has simply taken up a friendship with some of the other soldiers and is practicing his archery in the range. He is quite talented with a bow. You are lucky to have him."

Asher was all too familiar with Tyvish's skill with a bow—he'd faced down the end of a burning arrow once before, and he knew that when Tyvish loosed, he didn't miss.

"I'm glad to hear that he's safe," Asher said, shifting uncomfortably. The tsar revealed nothing on Tyvish's success with the southern lords and ladies. "He is a good man. Many would miss him should he lose his head."

"Oh, I agree wholeheartedly," the tsar said. "I've grown quite fond of him. Bring him out, Vika."

With a grin, the Wolf disappeared behind the throne, to where Asher could only assume a secret door lay. After a few moments, she reappeared, Tyvish at her side. He was wearing Verdecan furs, like Asher was, with a new bow strung across his back alongside a quiver of black arrows.

He looked at ease, Asher realized. *Good.*

He thought the room had been silent before Tyvish entered. Now, he could hear the flick of Doya's ears as she looked around the room.

"Asher," Tyvish said, taking a step forward, and Asher didn't realize how much he'd missed the Eiadian accent, the way his people spoke. He took a step forward, and a massive smile split Tyvish's face. Asher didn't know quite how it happened— one moment, he was standing beside Sofya, and the next, he and Tyvish were embracing at the bottom of the dais.

"I'm glad you're still alive," Asher said. Tyvish laughed, brushing dark hair away from his forehead.

"I'm glad *you're* still alive," Tyvish said. The tsar cleared his throat, and the two of them stepped back to where Sofya stood. The tsar had the slightest smile on his face.

"When do you plan to leave?"

"As soon as possible," Asher said, schooling his expression. He and Tyvish would have plenty of time to catch up. "If we can, I'd like to give Sofya and myself the night to recover, but I am willing to begin the march to the coast tomorrow morning."

"I second that," Sofya said. "I can start tomorrow as well. We will have time on the ships to recover."

"Very well," the tsar said, smiling. "You are all dismissed. Except for you, Sofya, and you, Viktoriya. Stay behind—I must speak to you. Somebody give the Eiadians a room and something to eat. I'm sure they have much to discuss."

The next morning, they began the march to the coast, where the tsar's ships waited to carry across the forty thousand men that walked behind Asher and Sofya, who rode at the head of the army alongside Tyvish and Viktoriya. The rest of the seven were spread out amongst the ranks, as were some of the lords.

They rode silently, neither Asher nor Sofya speaking, watching Doya and Vika's wolves as they ran across the tundra, the two nothing but tricks of the eye against the snow and one standing out like a blemish against the earth, their howls filling the air.

He wondered if his parents could feel them coming, feel the army that *he* had raised marching to the Phoenix Palace, marching to destroy what remained of the old Eiad and to raise a new one.

He wanted to see their faces when they heard about Verdeca landing on their shores. He wanted to watch the fear in their eyes when they realized the wolves were here, and they were hungry.

And perhaps he would take Sofya up on that offer to be rid of them—that offer that would guarantee, no matter what happened, no matter who won this war, they would never be able to torment him again.

After a while, Sofya pulled her horse off of the road, motioning the rest of them forward. Asher followed, riding up next to her. She stared back into the heart of Verdeca, eyes scanning it as though she was trying to memorize it—the gray-blue sky, the cold, white ground, the evergreen trees. The small bushes with the red berries, the purple flowers.

"What's wrong?" Asher asked.

"I am trying to remember it," Sofya said. "This will be the last I see of it. This is a broken country, but I have loved it dearly nonetheless."

"I…Sofya."

"I already told you," Sofya said. "Death is waiting patiently in Eiad."

"You're the best soldier alive," Asher said. "Who's to say you'll die in Eiad? You could easily survive the war."

Sofya glanced at him, fingers tightening on the reins.

"It is not the war," she said softly, reaching for the hem of her shirt. She lifted it, fingers white as she gripped it, pulling it up to the base of her sternum.

Asher leaned forward as the lump came into view. It was underneath her ribs, small but not unnoticeable. He couldn't recall seeing it when they spent the night together in Lady Siyana's keep, but he attributed that to the alcohol.

"What is it?"

"A tumor," Sofya said. "It is killing me. I went to the healers last night, again, to see how much longer I had left. It is the second time I have gone since I first saw it. They have given me about five months, and they warned me that the pain will only increase as the months pass. There is nothing they can do. There is nothing I can do. So yes, Asher, I am going to Eiad to die."

Sofya took a long, shuddering breath, and a single tear fell down her face. She brushed it away quickly, and her jaw set. The wind whipped at her braid, pulling small strands out to fly around her face. She didn't look at him.

Asher couldn't speak. He hadn't thought, not even for one moment, that Sofya could die. She was untouchable in his mind, somebody who could dance away from death's grip again and again. Even if he fell in battle, Sofya would survive—she would always survive. But now...it didn't matter. It didn't matter how good of a soldier she was; it didn't matter if she walked off of the battlefield without a single scratch. This would kill her anyway, and nobody could save her from that.

He couldn't save her from that.

It wasn't fair that so much of her life had been spent in a prison. It wasn't fair that he would only get five more months with her.

"Sofya—"

Sofya looked at him, and she gave him a small, sad smile, letting her shirt drop. "I have made my peace with it. I will do my job. I will destroy the royal family of Eiad, as is my duty. I will establish a place for my gods in your country. And then I will be allowed to rest."

She wheeled her horse back to the road, and Asher followed her.

Somewhere, a wolf was howling.

Chapter

THIRTY-SIX

THE TRUNKS HAD ARRIVED at some point during the night, and Ember dressed in her own clothes for the first time in weeks. She made sure to try and dress in a way the High Priestess couldn't find much fault with—soft black pants and a gold sweater. She pulled her hair back into a short plait, tying it off with a ribbon. She wore shoes, too, because the floors of the temple were far too cold for her to move without them.

Ember slipped out of the room, Lucasta still sleeping in her cot. Despite the sky outside just beginning to brighten, plenty of priests and priestesses already moved through the halls, dipping their heads to her. Not out of respect, but out of equality.

The staircase down to the sanctuary was full of people, some wearing regular clothes, like her. Fellow pilgrims, she supposed.

Ember stepped into the sanctuary, staring at the Phoenix Flame in the center. It seemed…subdued right now, compared to yesterday. The voices were quiet this early in the morning, only softly murmuring to her as she slipped by. But it wasn't the main sanctuary she was worried about—it was the small hallway that extended from behind the mosaic of the Dragon, where she noticed a small saying inscribed over the archway that she hadn't seen yesterday.

O flamma et furor, moerores et terror!

Oh, the flame and the fury, the fangs and the terror!

Small, white stone basins of the Phoenix Flame, mounted in the wall, lit the way, burning gently in pools of blood. Flickering flames lit the walls, painting them in shadows.

Nekun wasn't there, yet, and Ember approached the small altar that had been constructed. She knelt, slipping her hand back into her glove. Her eyes fluttered shut, and she focused on her breathing, on the beat of her heart in her chest. Focused on her humanity.

Or what remained of it, at least.

She knew that it was likely that she would have to use violence to convince the High Priestess to side with her. And she didn't mind that. It was necessary. The High Priestess was her greatest chance to slaughter the Order. Juniper Farley would finally answer for her crimes.

And once the High Priestess agreed to provide sacerdos, whether they were fighters or simply healers, she would go home.

And she would prepare.

She would hone her body back into a weapon. She would provide Lucasta the resources to do the same, if she wished to fight. But Ember wouldn't ask her to do so, wouldn't ask her to risk her life for a country she didn't even like. She would pay for Lucasta to go back to Geloj Swesh, or whatever country she chose, if that was what she wanted.

Viper would fight. His siblings would as well—all of the houses would fight, and there was the army as well. That wasn't even considering any allies that Eiad had with other countries. But the temple would be key. Most of the houses' forces were concentrated in central Eiad. If the temple chose the rebellion over the houses, they would be able to sweep in from the north and the south.

That wasn't to say they couldn't fight their way out—they were certainly capable, and they had plenty of allies on their own. But it would be much, much more difficult. The casualties would be immense.

Ember could live with that, though, so long as they were Order and not house.

Footsteps echoed in the hallway, and Ember jumped, reaching for her knife as she twisted to look over her shoulder. The person's shadow preceded them, stretching down the hallway. After another moment, they appeared, and Ember moved to her feet, still keeping her hand near her knife.

Nekun grinned at her as he emerged in the sanctuary.

"Good morning," he said. "Would you like to talk?"

"I would," Ember said. Something twisted in her gut. She knew vaguely what this was going to be about, but she didn't say anything as Nekun gestured toward the hallway, allowing her to leave first. They emerged into the temple proper quietly, with Nekun guiding her outside, away from the rapidly crescendoing voices of the Flame.

The air stung when she first stepped into it, colder than she'd expected, and her eyes watered as her body tried to get used to the chill. The grass was wet with dew, soaking through her shoes.

"How cold!" Nekun said. "It does not get quite this cold in Oscela. We aren't this far north."

"No," Ember said. "I'm not used to it being this cold during the late spring, anyway. I live further south. It's probably closer to what you're used to."

"Oh, yes," Nekun said. "That is good."

They turned silently off the main path onto a side one, toward some of the smaller buildings. The sun was just beginning to come up fully. The iron in her gloves was warming with the heat of her hands.

A small, stone bench appeared beside one of the buildings, and Nekun made his way toward it, Ember following a step behind. It was strange to be in the presence of a foreign noble. It had happened before, of course—they visited other countries, and they'd come to Eiad, too. But something felt different about Nekun being here. They weren't meeting in a throne room or at an official party, and he'd been sent here, by his father, *for her*. Not for Whelyn or Feather or even Asher, if they hadn't heard the news yet.

Nekun sat, and Ember sat beside him. For a long moment, neither of them spoke, Ember waiting for him to say something. He cleared his throat, shifting slightly.

"So," he said. "I did not explain what I meant last night. About my father sending me here for you. We heard the news of your mother's death, and I am sorry, Lady Ignis. I lost my mother, too, at a young age. But I had my father, of course, and my aunts and uncles. But nobody can quite replace a mother, can they?"

"No," Ember said softly. "They cannot."

"Second," Nekun said. "We heard, too, about your prince. Former prince. Asher Cinis is no longer heir to the throne of Eiad, correct?"

"Correct," Ember said.

"Then my father was right," Nekun said. "You are heir, then."

Ember froze.

She hadn't thought about that, not really. It had been one thing to be the Dragon Heir, a role she'd been *born* to fill, following traditions that spanned hundreds of years.

But it was another thing entirely to be the Phoenix Heir.

"I...I'm not entirely sure," Ember said softly. "It hasn't been discussed."

Nekun's expression dropped for a moment—not into unpleasantness, but into confusion—before he smiled again. "There has been much going on. I suppose they will announce it soon."

"I suppose," Ember said. She had the feeling that Feather Cinis would rather shove a hot poker through her eye before giving Ember that kind of position, but Nekun didn't need to know that. "Please, continue."

"Of course," Nekun said. "I told you that my father sent me here for you, and that was the truth. Word spread about your pilgrimage to the temple and the High Priestess. As I told you, my father is the *Pasha* of Oscela, and with the other families within the *Cehan,* they made the decision to send me here to meet you and offer something."

Ember knew, deep in her bones, what the next words out of his mouth were going to be. But she didn't say anything as Nekun continued, watching as he laced his fingers together and twisted his rings.

"There is...talk about Eiadians in Verdeca," Nekun said. Ember lifted her eyes from his hands to his face, and Nekun didn't look away as Ember held his gaze. "Since the royal family is allied with the other countries of the middle continent, it must be the rebellion, no? If they come, can you survive alone, without your allies?"

No. The answer to that question was absolutely not. The houses could stand against the rebellion, and the temple, if need be. But with the might of Verdeca backing the rebellion, they could not.

How dare they.

Nekun didn't wait for her to answer. "My father and the *Cehan* are only willing to offer Oscela's forces if you agree to a marriage."

Royal intermarriage. It was a common enough practice— if Asher Cinis hadn't married within the houses, Ember knew he would've been married off to one of the princesses of the middle and far continents, to either begin or strengthen a relationship with that country.

It hadn't ever occurred to her that Ember would be expected to do the same thing. Dragons didn't get married at all, much less to other rulers. Some of the other houses might offer their children to lower aristocrats or merchants for their own personal gain, but never Dragons.

And then there was Viper.

Ember wasn't entirely sure *what* was between her and Viper, but it was something, and if she were to marry Nekun…

She couldn't think about Viper right now. Ember had to think about what was going to help her people. What was going to save all of them. *She* had the opportunity to save them and crush the Order with one marriage.

Nekun cleared his throat, breaking the silence that stretched between them. "With me, of course. They sent me so we could meet."

"I—yes," Ember said, twisting her gloves. "Of course."

"I'm sorry this came out of nowhere," Nekun said. He patted her hand gently. "You've been through much recently. But there truly is no time to waste if there are Eiadians in Verdeca. I must get word to my father."

"I understand," Ember said. "Could I have a day? I can give you an answer tonight."

They both knew what her answer was going to be. Eiad couldn't afford to lose out on the impressive cavalry of Oscela, or their knowledge in fighting the Verdecans, residing on their northern border.

Nekun simply dipped his head and smiled again. "Of course, Lady Ignis. Enjoy your day."

She watched as he got up and walked away, his shadow dark against the snow. Ember sucked in a breath of freezing air, watching it cloud in front of her as she exhaled. She wanted to scream.

It wasn't that bad. Not really. She was being asked to do so little for so much. It was a marriage. She wasn't being asked to give up her life.

But it felt like that, a little bit.

The bells began to toll, and Ember leapt to her feet, grateful for the distraction. Perhaps Lucasta would be able to give her some advice.

"There she is," Blue said. Viper lifted his head quickly, finding Ember in the doorway, nose and cheeks bright red. Their eyes met, and Viper found the corners of his mouth lifting as Ember made her way toward them. She didn't smile back, necessarily, but her eyes softened slightly.

"Where were you?" Lucasta asked.

Ember, halfway through filling her plate, looked up. "Outside."

"Outside?"

"Yes," Ember said. "I was speaking to somebody."

"The High Priestess, I hope," Lucasta said.

Ember shook her head. "No. I have to wait for her to summon me, anyways. I assume it'll be soon. Somebody else."

Lucasta scowled. "Why are you being so weird about it? Who were you talking to?"

Ember's gaze flicked to Viper, and he could see her calculating as she stared at him.

"I'll tell you later," Ember said. "Let's just eat, okay?"

Chapter

Thirty-Seven

Viper found himself wandering near the Phoenix Flame after breakfast. Blue had gone in search of Kerio, Hazel in tow, and Lucasta and Ember had disappeared immediately after they'd finished eating. It had been so strange, the way Ember had based her answer off of him.

Was there something she didn't want him to know?

He couldn't think of a reason for her to hide speaking to somebody like Cerraine or Kerio, and he knew the High Priestess hadn't called for yet and probably wouldn't meet with her outside, anyways.

No, it wouldn't be anybody like that.

He paced closer to the lip of the Flame, staring down into it. He still didn't know what Ember had heard in it, yesterday, when she'd nearly walked into it. To him, it was only a fire. A bloodthirsty fire, but a fire nonetheless. He couldn't hear anything within the depths.

He really hoped they would go soon. He wanted to be home with plenty of time to prepare for the Solstice.

Solstice was a two-fold holiday, taking place over an entire day. The morning was for worship and prayer, ceremonies rather than celebrations. Noontime was used for small meals and socializing with family and friends—most people took that time to try and get some sleep before the evening, where massive, extravagant feasts would take place. The Solstice—both the temple services and the feasts—were open to all who were willing to attend, the tables open to the masses. Everything was controlled, of course, but even the lowest of the low was welcome to join the tables with the lords and ladies and heirs.

Each part of the celebration demanded different outfits of the houses. In the mornings, they were expected to wear pure white with something distinguishing them from the other houses. Viper's clothing would be stitched in a snake-skin pattern, while other houses would represent their patron animals accordingly. House Vulpus of the Fox, for example, would wear fox-fur around the cuffs of their clothing and their collars. Those would be worn until noon, when preparations for the evening would begin. Then, they would change from those white, divine clothing into masquerade costumes.

Now, *those* were something to behold. These, too, would be based on their houses, each house more extravagant than the last. The avian houses, as well as Ember, would wear wings and each house would wear magnificent, hand-crafted masks, stitched together with fine gold and silver, precious gems, and rare silks. All of it would be imported, and the houses would spare no expense on the masks, nor their gowns or suits.

It was a night that was not easily forgotten by anybody. Viper loved the Solstice, far more than any other holiday. It was one of the few that wasn't based in bloodshed. It was refreshing to simply celebrate after a holiday like the Duels. There would be no cries for blood during the Solstice celebration. It was simply just a ceremony followed by a party that lasted until dawn.

"The High Priestess summoned Arienne last night and she didn't come back." The whisper startled him from his thoughts, and Viper whipped around, finding two young sacerdos walking past him. They couldn't have been older than twelve, a blonde and a redhead, and both of them jumped away from him.

"What?" Viper asked, and the girls exchanged a glance. He swallowed, crouching down to be at their level. "I'm sorry. That was rude. I just heard that your friend is missing? Is she the same age as you two?"

The girls looked at each other, and the redhead cleared her throat. "Arienne. She sleeps in our room, but she left last night because the High Priestess needed her. I—of course she's safe if she's with the High Priestess, though."

"Of course," Viper said.

"She's probably with Marwo and Selene," the blonde said.

"The High Priestess wanted to speak to them, too," the redhead said. "But that was a while ago, and they're older than us. I think they probably got sent down the mountain."

"Maybe," Viper said. He didn't mention the fact that he hadn't seen any girls their age in the village at the base of the mountain. "What are your names?"

"Rore," the redhead said, and tipped her head toward the blonde. "Her name is Celia."

"Thank you," Viper said. "My name is Viper Trunca. I'm a pilgrim here."

"You came with the Dragon, didn't you?" Celia asked, and Viper nodded.

"I did."

"The High Priestess talks about her sometimes," Rore said. "And the Phoenixes. But usually she just talks about *the* Phoenix and *the* Dragon. In the teachings."

"Right, yes," Viper said. "It's important to study the texts. But I must know—what does she say about the Dragon? The woman."

"She doesn't like her very much," Rore said, wrinkling her brow.

"Rore! Celia!" Somebody from across the room called the two girls' names, and Viper smiled at them.

"Thank you for telling me about your friends," he said. "I hope you see them soon."

The girls rushed off without another word, and Viper straightened up, watching the two girls make their way toward another sacerdo, one he hadn't seen before.

And there, in the shadows, Cerraine stood, watching him. Viper didn't shy away from her as she began the walk around the Phoenix Flame, ultimately taking his arm and leading him into the hallway leading toward the Stallion's sanctuary.

"Are you a fool?" she hissed, standing there in the darkness, the anger on her face so like Whelyn Cinis's. He yanked his arm out of her grasp.

"What did I do?" he asked, and he could *feel* the scowl she gave him.

"Don't go poking into things that don't involve you," Cerraine said. "I don't know if you've realized this, but *she hears everything* that happens in this temple."

"Children are going missing in the temple," Viper said. "I need to tell Ember before she speaks to the High Priestess—"

"You're too late," Cerraine said. "She's called Ember to her quarters already. You'll just have to tell her after she's done."

"Do you know something about the children?" Viper asked. "Anything? I can tell you their names if you want."

"I know their names," Cerraine said. "And it's not my place to say, Viper. The High Priestess is allowed to do as she pleases in her own temple. I'm sure the children are perfectly fine."

"I'm sure," Viper said. "But I'm still telling Ember."

"Do as you please," Cerraine said. "But understand the fact that it's your own lives you're risking."

The High Priestess kept her quarters sparse. Rather than the luxury she could've easily had for herself, the woman's room was completely barren, with a thin cot shoved in the corner, a closet,

310

a small desk with two chairs in the middle of the room, and a shelf that contained three books—the volumes of the Book of the Phoenix.

"Dragon," the High Priestess said, looking up at where Ember stood in the doorway. "Please, come in."

"Thank you," Ember said, sliding into the seat across from her. She'd gotten the summons only a few minutes ago and had allowed herself to be led by a remarkably sweaty sacerdo. She'd seen Nekun in the hallway, briefly, and had torn her eyes away from his as she walked by. "Your sacerdos are remarkably efficient."

"Of course they are," the High Priestess said. "I taught them, after all."

They sat in silence for a moment before the High Priestess leaned forward, lacing her fingers together. "Your mother sat in that seat when she was your age. Not asking me for war, but for support. She came without the backing of the royal family."

Ember forced herself not to react. She avoided speaking of her mother. There was too much there to think about, to deal with. But this—this was new information.

"She had just come into power, and she wanted to ensure the temple would be beside her should she need them, for whatever reason. I don't know what she feared would happen. I doubt she thought she would meet the type of end she did. It is interesting, though, that her daughter comes *only* because she has been commanded to do so. Every year, the houses diminish. I met your grandmother as well, although I was only a sacerdo then. I had never seen golden eyes before. I believed them to be a myth until she was staring down at me. She could've eaten you alive, little Dragon. Had you killed with a flick of her hand. I have watched the weakening of House Draco with my own eyes. And now I am going to watch the fall."

Ember clenched her fists at her sides but schooled her expression. The High Priestess was just trying to get a reaction out of her, and she wasn't going to play her hand so easily.

"Why are you telling me this?"

The High Priestess smiled. "Just to give you something to think about. You may plead your case whenever you wish."

Ember swallowed, forcing herself to clear her thoughts before adjusting her posture. "High Priestess. I have come on behalf of King Whelyn Cinis and Queen Feather Cinis and all of those who are loyal to the king and crown of Eiad to ask for your assistance in the war against the Order of the Bear. You and your sacerdos could be essential in ensuring the survival of not only the houses, but the temples of the Phoenix as well. At the very least, High Priestess, I ask that you remain neutral in the war. If you don't send your sacerdos to fight for us, keep them out of the conflict entirely. You cannot win against the houses should you side with the Order, and you certainly cannot win alone. We're not asking for soldiers, High Priestess. But your sacerdos know ancient ways of healing and miracles that are unknown to everybody else in Eiad, and we could use that."

"And my incentive?"

Ember sat back in her seat. "I already told you. The temple will fall if you choose the wrong side. They'll have your head, High Priestess. They'll burn this temple to the ground."

"Of course they will," the older woman said, the hint of a smile on her mouth. "But that is a chance that I am willing to take. And I think that you're forgetting that we have fire too.

You're dismissed."

Ember didn't quite know why the dismissal stung so badly. She knew the High Priestess wouldn't change her mind or her answer, but it was still shocking to hear how flippant she was about taking such a risk. Ember stood and walked toward the door. Hand on the doorknob, she turned, staring back at the High Priestess.

"Your sacerdos will die."

"You would have my sacerdos die for you," the High Priestess said. "But I won't have them die for a cause I cannot support."

"What if it's a cause they support?"

The High Priestess's eyes flashed with fury. "I assure you, Dragon, *my* sacerdos do not support such a foolish venture. Now go. Take your friends and leave. Tell Whelyn that I will not come. Leave tomorrow morning. If you choose not to, my sacerdos will have to step in."

Ember nodded and slipped out of the room. She paused outside of the door, leaning against it. There was something there, something in the way the High Priestess had spoken about the sacerdos.

My *sacerdos do not support such a foolish venture.*

Something wasn't quite right about that. She needed to speak to somebody—Cerraine, perhaps—and find out what the High Priestess had meant by that.

Ember found Viper before she found Cerraine. She'd gone down a few hallways, peering into doorways and hoping to come upon a sacerdo that could point her in the direction of Cerraine, but instead had found Viper sitting in a library by himself, back to a window. She stood there for a moment, watching him. Weak sunlight outlined his figure, casting a long shadow onto the table. He was sketching on a piece of paper, making furious lines with a pencil. A collection of brushes and paints was scattered on the table, in familiar colors—gold and black and red. Dragon colors. A half-eaten orange rested near his hand.

This was the first time she allowed herself to truly think about what had happened between them in the bathhouse. She'd wanted to kiss him that day, and when she thought about it, her fingers tingled in the gloves. She'd let her guard down enough to allow Viper in, to make a place for him in her being. Ember couldn't deny the fact that it scared her. The Order had taken her mother, and it had almost killed her. If they took Viper, too…

No. If they took Viper, she wouldn't allow herself to lie down and die again. She would get him back before they could kill him. Oh, yes. If the Order took him, she would kill every single one of them to get him back.

He lifted his head suddenly, and Ember couldn't move, pinned in place by his eyes, twisting the strings of her gloves. He looked young here, younger than he did at the palace. Perhaps it was something about the air. Perhaps it was only the fact that she was more relaxed here, and she could see him differently—she could see him for who he really was. Viper. Not Lord Trunca, not a Serpent, not even Viper Trunca. Just Viper.

Ember wondered, briefly, if she was just Ember to him, or if she was always Lady Ignis.

She shook off the weight of his eyes.

"Viper," Ember said, swallowing and stepping into the library. It was small, with only two shelves and a handful of tables and chairs scattered around the space. "What are you doing in here?"

"Finding something to do," Viper said, sitting back in his seat. He made no move to cover the paper, but she didn't dare drop her eyes to it. The moment was gone now, and they were back to Lord Trunca and Lady Ignis. Fellow house members. "The rest of you went off after breakfast, so I decided to explore."

"I need to tell you about something," Ember said, sliding into the seat across from him. "Two things, actually."

Viper reached for one of the containers of paint, rolling it between his fingers. "I hope it's about the person you were talking to this morning."

Ember scowled. "If you ask again, I'm not going to tell you."

"Fine, fine," Viper said. "Go ahead."

"First," Ember said. "There's something up with the High Priestess. She was acting weird during our meeting."

"I talked to some sacerdos about that, actually," Viper said. "But continue."

"The second thing," Ember said. "The person I was speaking to. His name is Nekun of Oscela and he is the son of the *Pasha*."

She waited for the realization to settle on Viper's face, their years of schooling coming back to him as he understood how important it was that Nekun was here.

She saw the moment it hit him, a slight widening of his eyes.

"He's here for you, then?" Viper asked. "To ask for your hand in marriage?"

Ember gaped at him for a moment. "How—"

"It's the only thing that makes sense," Viper said. "Why he'd be at the temple, specifically. If he was here for somebody else, he would've been sent to the Phoenix Palace first. Am I right?"

"Yes," Ember said softly. She watched him hesitate, mouth opening and closing a few times. She could see him working toward the inevitable question and answer that were to follow, the necessity of what she'd have to do.

"Are you going to say yes?"

"I have to," Ember said. The answer hung between them as Viper dropped his eyes to the book in front of him. "The High Priestess didn't change her mind. Oscela won't come without the marriage, and since Oscela is allied with the rest of the middle continent, it wouldn't surprise me if they didn't come either."

Please look at me. She knew Viper understood why she had to do it. But Ember also understood what this would mean for her and Viper, for the small spark they were slowly kindling. He stared at the vial of gold paint.

"What do they think they get out of marrying you to him?"

"I'm the Phoenix Heir," Ember said. "I don't know why we didn't realize it before."

"I don't either," Viper said. "We'll have to tell the king and queen about Nekun."

"Of course," Ember said, swallowing. "And, Viper...we'll figure something out."

"I know," Viper said, finally looking back up at her. "I know you will. But you get reckless sometimes. Don't let this be that."

"What do you mean by that?" Ember asked, sitting back.

"You do things without thinking about them first. I understand why you would say yes. But don't do it because you feel obligated."

"Of course I'm obligated," Ember said. "It's part of the role. It's what I'm supposed to do."

"Do you ever think about what you want?"

Silence hung thickly between them.

"This is what I want."

Viper snorted. "Okay. I'll drop it. The High Priestess?"

"The High Priestess," Ember said, relieved. "What did you find out?"

"Sacerdos are going missing," Viper said. "They go to see the High Priestess and then they don't come back. Cerraine knows about it, but she isn't doing anything."

Ember sat for a moment, processing the information. "That...makes sense. She told me that *her* sacerdos don't believe in the court's cause, but I figured that some of the sacerdos had to disagree with her."

"What do you think she's doing with them?" Viper asked, and Ember glanced at the walls, to the small bowls of Phoenix Flame that flickered merrily.

We have fire too.

"The Flame," Ember said. "She's using the Flame."

Viper set the paint down, leaning forward. "No bodies."

"No bodies," Ember agreed. "The Flame is what keeps her safe. It keeps her confident."

"Complacent?"

Ember snorted. "No. She's far from complacent. The High Priestess has an army too, but the Flame is undoubtedly her best weapon. She knows that."

"Of course," Viper said. He picked up the orange, peeling off a slice, his elbow brushing the paper on the table. It turned slightly in her direction, and Ember leaned forward without meaning to, eyes scanning the paper.

Her own face stared back. Even without the coloring, there was nobody else it could've been—high cheekbones, lips pursed in a thin line. Her eyes were sharp, and she could read the disgust within them.

Her annoyance from his earlier words vanished.

"I can't stop painting you," Viper whispered. He traced a knuckle down the paper, and the movement made Ember shiver. She looked up at him, and he stared back. "Has anybody ever told you how unsettling you are? I'm always half-expecting you to grow wings and breathe fire. I can never capture you exactly, no matter how hard I try. That *something* about you. I can't pin it down."

"You've done a pretty good job," Ember said, trying to keep her tone light as she stood to see the paper better.

"You should see my other attempts," Viper said. He stood, coming around to her side of the table to look at the sketch with her. Their arms brushed as he reached for it, drawing the paper closer to them. He looked up from the paper, staring at her face, squinting as though he would be able to find what he was looking for. He snorted. "I don't know what it is. It should be perfect."

"Should be," Ember said. She was watching him, now, and she couldn't quite figure out what it was, but she desperately wanted to reach for him. "Viper."

He looked at her then. "Ember."

The word hung between them for a long moment before Ember took a step forward and lowered her face to his. She could hear him breathing, and she wondered if he could hear the pounding of her own heart, still human despite what she was. There was a streak of charcoal underneath his eye, and as Ember reached up to brush it away, Viper closed the distance. Their lips touched gently at first, Viper's soft underneath her own, the faintest taste of oranges clinging to them. Heat spread through her body, and Ember pulled back for a moment. Even with the gloves, she was trembling.

She had failed to keep him away. Utterly failed, and yet she did not mind at all.

When Viper drew her back in, she went willingly. The sunlight was warm on her face as he kissed her again, his hand reaching around to cup the back of her neck, his fingers achingly gentle as he held her there.

He broke away, resting his forehead against hers, and Ember could feel the blush in her cheeks.

"I—"

Viper shook his head. "Don't. Don't say anything."

So she said nothing. She stood there, forehead resting against his, for a long while, and for a little bit, the world quieted around them.

Chapter

THIRTY-EIGHT

E MBER WENT LOOKING FOR Nekun before dinner. She wanted to give him her answer before they had to leave in the morning, to hopefully get him out of the temple and on the way to either the coast, to send a message to his family, or on the road headed toward the Phoenix Palace.

She found him wandering in one of the greenhouses, occasionally bending down to smell an herb or flower. Nekun looked up as she approached, gesturing to one of the herbs in front of him.

"It's from Oscela," he said. "I recognized it immediately. Here."

He plucked a leaf off the plant, holding it up to her nose. Ember inhaled, her nose instantly flooded with a rich, earthy smell that was *almost* familiar.

"I don't know how to say it in Eiadian," he said. "But in Oscela, we call it *virund*. It's commonly used in our dishes, to help with the flavor. We also use it boiled into tea for medicine, for help with pain."

"Fascinating," Ember said softly, staring at the dirt in front of her.

"It is," Nekun said. "But I know you did not come here to listen to me talk about Oscela's plants."

"No," Ember said. "I did not."

Silence hung between them as Nekun rubbed the leaf between his fingers before allowing the pieces to fall back into the dirt. After a moment, he reached out, taking one of her hands into his. Ember looked up at him, at his gentle brown eyes.

"Your answer, Lady Ignis?"

"I'll enter into the marriage agreement," Ember said softly. "For the sake of Eiad."

Nekun squeezed her hands. "I thought so. I will tell my parents and the *Cehan*. They will be overjoyed to hear the news."

"I'm glad," Ember said softly, pulling her hand away. "Eiad will be overjoyed as well, I'm sure."

"Yes," Nekun said. "And, Ember?"

"Yes?"

"I understand," Nekun said softly. "I can tell there is somebody else. You are only doing this because you must. I, too, am only doing this because I must. We are making sacrifices. Remember, though, Ember—this marriage is but a formality. It is a duty."

"Of course," Ember said.

The bells began to toll, and Nekun gave her another small smile.

"I will see you soon," Nekun said. "Until then, take care."

Ember watched him as he turned and walked out of the greenhouse. There had been something there, in the way he'd spoken about the marriage—*I am only doing this because I must.*

Perhaps there was somebody else for Nekun, too. Perhaps he understood more than Ember had originally thought.

Kerio sat with them at dinner, much to Ember's disappointment. She'd been hoping to speak to Lucasta and Blue about their plan to leave the temple early in the morning, as the High Priestess had been clear on her threats. Getting back to the Phoenix Palace would give them time to inform the royals about Nekun—and to give Nekun time to summon Oscela to Eiad. Time to have a wedding, Ember supposed, before the Order swept in on them.

They ate in awkward silence until Cerraine sat down at Ember's side, and Ember seized her chance.

"The High Priestess is killing sacerdos, isn't she?" Ember hissed, leaning into the other woman. She grabbed her arm, digging her nails in. "Isn't she, Cerraine?"

Cerraine didn't speak for a moment, and Ember ignored the looks she was getting from everybody else at the table.

"I can't tell you that," Cerraine said, her voice equally as soft. "The High Priestess is only doing what she must to keep the temple safe."

"Is she or is she not killing them?"

Kerio, from where he sat across from them, squirmed uncomfortably.

"Ember."

"What?" Ember snapped, turning toward him.

"Cerraine can't tell you. She hasn't seen it," he said. "But I have. If…if you like, I can meet all of you later to talk about it. After the temple has gone to bed."

"Okay," Ember said, releasing Cerraine's arm. "All of us."

Kerio nodded, dropping his eyes back to his plate. Ember's gaze flicked over his shoulder, meeting the eyes of a sacerdo sitting at the other table. The young man looked away quickly, and Ember glanced at Viper. She would have to find Nekun before they left tomorrow morning, to inform him of her decision. If he wanted to ride to the Phoenix Palace with them, she would have to let him, but Ember was desperately hoping he didn't. She wanted that time with her friends, these last stolen moments, before she had to go back to being Lady Ignis. She didn't know when the order to march on the Order would come.

But for now, she simply needed to focus on the High Priestess and what she was doing.

Ember walked to the Dragon's sanctuary after dinner, something pulling her toward the sacred space created for her and her family. She walked through the main sanctuary, sprinkling a few drops of blood into the Phoenix Flame as she passed by and slipped into the Dragon's sanctuary, staring at the mural of the Dragon, at the glowing gold eyes and sharp silver teeth.

It was strange to be back here, where her foremothers had once stood. How many generations of Dragon's blood had been spilled in this space, how many palms split over the Flame? Her grandmother had stood here once. Her mother had as well.

Ember had put her mother aside at the temple. She had something to focus on, something to put all of her energy in. She hadn't had a nightmare last night, for the first time since her mother's death. It was a relief to wake in the morning without the image of her mother's body burned into her mind.

Perhaps, when she got home, she would enter Verity's bedroom.

She gave more blood to the Flame, and then, at the last moment, smeared her bloodied palm across the maw of the grinning Dragon.

Somewhere in the depths of her being, she knew she would be the last true Dragon to stand in this space.

Ember bandaged her hand and slipped her glove back on, making her way out of the room. Maybe Nekun would be outside. She rounded the corner, adjusting her gloves, and froze when somebody stepped out behind her and placed a sickle against her neck.

"Keep walking," the person said. Ember recognized the High Priestess's voice instantly, and a shiver of fear trickled down her spine. "Out into the sanctuary, Dragon."

The curved blade of the sickle could slit her throat if she made even the slightest wrong move, so Ember couldn't reach for the knife strapped to her arm.

Stupid, stupid, stupid.

She'd known better than to let her guard down here.

When they came into the main sanctuary, Ember's heart dropped further. Viper, Lucasta, Blue, Cerraine, and Kerio knelt on the mosaic of the Phoenix, alongside two young priestesses she hadn't seen before. They all looked okay except for Kerio, whose robes were bloodied in several places. A crowd of silver-clad sacerdos surrounded them, each of them holding a sickle. There was nowhere to run—on one side were the sacerdos, on the other side, the Phoenix Flame, which was desperately reaching for Lucasta, who was closest.

Oh, Phoenix. What had gone wrong?

Ember scanned the crowd, searching for a familiar face within those who were standing, and then scowled. The young priest from dinner, who had sat just a table away, was staring at her.

Him.

"Kneel," the High Priestess said, moving Ember into the center of the circle. "Now, Dragon. My patience has its limits."

No. She would not kneel for this woman, not if she could help it. She'd knelt enough.

"*Now,*" the High Priestess said, shoving Ember down beside Viper, pressing the blade of her sickle into her neck. Ember hissed against the sharp pain as the High Priestess pushed too hard. A drop of hot blood rolled down her neck and into the collar of her tunic. Her knees stung with the impact of slamming into the ground.

"I wanted you gone in the morning," the High Priestess said. "I gave you the grace to leave leisurely. But you're incapable of minding your own business, aren't you, Dragon?

And what a shame it was to have Laryn come and tell me about two of my most favorite sacerdos telling secrets to those who are unworthy."

"Laryn, you rat," Cerraine hissed.

The High Priestess snapped at the circle of sacerdos, "Bring her here."

"Don't—"

"*Be quiet,*" the High Priestess said. "Do you know why I've had to do what I've done?"

Cerraine bucked against the two sacerdos that attempted to move her, glancing back at Ember with wide, desperate eyes.

Viper could see Ember's brain working. He watched as her eyes darted from Cerraine, to the High Priestess, to the circle of sacerdos. He watched her as she put the pieces together like a terrible, lethal puzzle.

Somebody was going to die.

And he was going to make sure it wasn't Ember.

Cerraine was forced in front of the High Priestess, still attempting to break away from the other sacerdos.

"Open her mouth," the High Priestess commanded, Laryn. He nodded, kneeling beside Cerraine and digging his fingers into her skin. She thrashed, tears pouring down her face as she whimpered. Her mouth remained shut as Laryn continued to struggle with her.

"Oh, for the Phoenix's sake," the High Priestess said. She brought the sickle down, slashing it across Cerraine's face.

Cerraine opened her mouth to cry out and Laryn moved, striking as fast as a snake. He used his fingers to hold her mouth open. The High Priestess gestured to another of the priestesses, who came forward uncertainly.

"Faster," the High Priestess snapped, and the girl knelt where she gestured, directly in front of the struggling Cerraine.

"Cerraine," the High Priestess said. "stick your tongue out."

Ember lunged.

Viper hadn't even noticed her tensing beside him, but she must've, springing forward as she drew twin knives from her belt. One went flying for the High Priestess's head.

The other lodged directly in Laryn's chest.

The priest gasped as red bloomed from the silver. He collapsed, releasing Cerraine.

Laryn's body slid down, down, down into the Phoenix Flame.

The Flame seemed to *snarl* as it ripped into Laryn's body, devouring flesh and bone and blood.

Nobody had moved as they watched in horror as nothing but robes and a thin throwing knife remained of Laryn.

And then Cerraine began to run. She broke through the circle of shocked sacerdos, rushing for the door. Lucasta and Blue were a step behind her, Ember following with Kerio at her side. Viper followed them, and Cerraine had just slammed into the door when he realized that not a single sacerdo had moved to stop them.

"Oh, Phoenix," Cerraine whispered. "It's locked."

"You stupid girl," the High Priestess said. "You stupid, stupid girl. Did you truly think that would work? Fools. All of you."

"Enough of this," Ember said. "We can talk about this—"

"We *cannot*," the High Priestess said. "I had already given you my answer. You chose to go looking for things that were none of your business."

"Why kill them, High Priestess?"

"Isn't it obvious?" Cerraine said from behind Ember, her words choked with tears. Blood ran down her face from the cut the High Priestess had made in her forehead. "She's preparing for the war."

"The...but you said you wouldn't help us."

"She doesn't support *either* of you," Cerraine said. "The royals or the rebellion. She supports herself. She's cleansing the temple to ensure the sacerdos are completely loyal to the temple before she moves."

"I support this temple," the High Priestess said. "I support the Phoenix and the mission She laid upon my shoulders when I became the High Priestess. I support all of the High Sacerdos that came before. They guarded this temple and the traditions of the sacerdos, and *I will do the same*. Subdue the Dragon and her friends. *I* will deal with Cerraine."

The sacerdos pounced.

Ember didn't know what was real and what wasn't as the sacerdos grabbed her, pinning her to the ground. She screamed then, her entire body crying out.

This was Verity all over again. She tried reaching for her knife, but they had pinned her wrists to the ground, a sacerdo on either side of her.

Not again. Phoenix, not again!

They pulled her to her knees, forcing her to kneel again beside Viper and Blue as the High Priestess again restrained Cerraine and forced her mouth open.

This time, the High Priestess didn't ask Cerraine to stick her tongue out.

She simply reached into Cerraine's mouth, yanked her tongue out, and sliced it off.

The noise that ripped out of Cerraine's mutilated mouth would haunt Ember for the rest of her life. It was not quite a scream, not quite a choke, but something horrifyingly in between, a terrible, wet sound.

The High Priestess tossed the mangled remains of Cerraine's tongue into the Phoenix Flame, staring down at the priestess. Blood poured from her mouth, and she choked, gagging on it as she spat and spat and spat.

"You," she said, gesturing to the frightened priestess from before. "Clean her up. Get her what she needs to heal. Cauterize it." A wicked smile curved across the High Priestess's mouth. "Let's see exactly how many secrets you will tell without your tongue, Cerraine."

Two sacerdos grabbed Cerraine by either arm and hauled her away. Ember tracked her with her eyes until the three of them had disappeared from sight, Cerraine continuing to whimper.

"You *bitch*," Lucasta hissed. She, too, was being held down, but she gazed up at the High Priestess defiantly.

"The Phoenix demands obedience," the High Priestess said. "I do the same. You are hereby banned from entering this holy place again. Get out, Ember Ignis."

The sacerdos did not give them any choice. They unlocked the front door of the sanctuary and threw them all, Kerio included, out into the snow, locking it behind them.

The temple grounds were silent except for the echo of Cerraine's screams.

Part Three

THE SOLSTICE

The Solstice is a two-part holiday: the dawn, which is a ceremony, and the evening, which is a celebration. Both parts are to give thanks to the Phoenix on the day She ascended to her home in the sky. There is no holiday more sacred or more holy, as all are invited to participate in it, even those who are not of the houses. Feasting and dancing will allow the people to bond and feel closer to each other and the Phoenix.

—THE BOOK OF THE PHOENIX, VOLUME THREE

Chapter

Thirty-Nine

As soon as they got to the first house, the five of them moved quickly, immediately searching for warm clothing and bandages and healers. They sat at the table together, eating stew and bread in silence, sipping warmed tea. Lucasta wrapped Kerio's wounds, while the rest of them moved to separate bedrooms in the house.

When Ember was inside hers, the door closed and locked, the tears began.

She stared at herself in the mirror for a moment, at the angry red line around her throat where the High Priestess had come so close to ending her life.

Ember bit her lip to stifle a sob as she shed her clothing and boots, turning the tap on for the bath and standing still beside it as it filled the tub. She added soap, watching as it bubbled up. She slipped inside, blissful warmth enveloping her body as the bubbles covered her. After a moment, the door that connected her room to Lucasta's opened, and the other woman stepped in. She silently joined Ember in the bath, neither of them speaking as Lucasta rested her head on Ember's shoulder.

Neither of them spoke as the water turned warm, and then lukewarm, and then chilly, and then they both got out, drying, and moving away from each other.

No words were necessary.

They understood.

They both understood.

And Ember went to sleep, and felt slightly better, because on the other side of the wall, she was not alone.

She woke crying.

Ember wasn't surprised—it wasn't the first time she'd been jerked from sleep by her tears, and she knew it wouldn't be the last—but it was annoying nonetheless. She rolled onto her back, staring up at the ceiling.

After a moment, she swung out of bed, opening the door to Lucasta's room softly, but she was sound asleep, snoring gently.

Ember wouldn't dare disturb her peace. The fact that Lucasta could even sleep in a bed by herself and stay asleep was...soothing. Comforting. Ember knew that the depths of her trauma, the depths of the nightmares, would never compare to what Lucasta had experienced. It wasn't her place to ask the specifics. She knew enough.

And it was enough for her to know that, as soon as she was done with Juniper Farley and the rest of the rebellion, she was going to burn every brothel from Saffi to the coast.

And she would *slaughter* the owners of those pleasure houses like the animals they were. No—better yet. She would show Lucasta how to kill them, to draw their deaths out in whatever way she saw fit. The prostitutes themselves...Lucasta would know how to help them. Would know where they needed to be and who they needed to be around.

That was exactly what Ember wanted to do.

But for now...

She closed the door gently, stepping away.

Somebody else. She needed somebody else.

And the only other person she trusted enough was across the hall.

Ember stepped into the hallway, knocking softly on Viper's door.

"Viper?"

It opened almost immediately, Viper's face a mask of concern.

"Ember? Are you okay?"

Ember squirmed, suddenly nervous. "I...never mind."

"Ember," Viper said gently, reaching forward and catching her wrist. "Please. Talk to me. Come into the room."

Ember followed him, and Viper gently shut the door behind her. "Should we lock it?"

"Yes," Ember said. "Please."

Viper locked the door and led her to the bed, patting a spot on the edge. "Sit."

She did as he asked, and he sat behind her, just out of her line of sight. "Viper?"

"Just talk," he said. "If you ask me to stop, I will. But just…talk, for now."

"Okay," Ember said softly. "I have nightmares. You know that. But I have them about a lot of things. And I had one about Cerraine, tonight."

The ribbon holding her plait was pulled off, and Viper's fingers began to work through her hair. Ember leaned into his touch slightly as he sectioned off a portion and began to brush it gently with his fingers.

"She was just…another person I couldn't save. And I know. I know that there will be more. You will fight, and so will Blue. And if I can't save you…"

"Shh," Viper said. "Don't talk about that, Ember. I'm going to be okay. Talk about something good that happened today."

"Something good?"

"Yes," Viper said, and his voice was a gentle rumble. Ember's eyes fluttered shut as he continued to brush out her hair. "Something good. Anything. Something small, something big."

"The stew was good," Ember said. "And the bath was hot. And we're all alive. At least…at least we're all alive."

"Yes," Viper said. "At least we're all alive. Cerraine is still alive, at the top of the mountain."

His hands moved to her shoulders, and he began to massage them gently. A moan slipped from her mouth, and her face flushed. She tensed, jerking away from him.

"Ember." His hand gently touched the side of her face. "Look at me."

She forced herself to turn toward him, but she couldn't quite meet his eyes.

He tipped her head up.

And then he was kissing her.

Viper deepened the kiss, pulling Ember into his lap. She shifted her hips, sitting easily on top of him, and he held her there, hands on her hips. Ember gasped softly as he ran his tongue over the seam of her lips, and he did it again, just to draw the sound out of her.

"Viper," she murmured, opening her mouth slightly. Her arms were around his neck, pulling him ever closer. He broke away from her mouth for a moment—that soft, sinful mouth—and buried his face in the place where her shoulder met her neck, where her nightgown had slipped away to reveal soft, pale skin.

He kissed her softly there, her skin warm under his lips, and Ember sighed in contentment.

"This…we…"

"Don't speak," Viper whispered. "Just let me hold you."

Ember did as he asked, and he breathed her in, relishing the feeling of Ember underneath his fingertips. A beautiful, living flame that breathed softly in his arms, her head resting against his.

After a long time, he lay back, taking her with him. He pulled the blankets over the two of them, Ember snuggling up against him. Viper pulled her close, her back against his chest, and whispered softly in her ear.

"Tomorrow," he said. "We'll find another good thing."

"Promise?"

"Promise."

They wasted no time the next morning. All five of them were up before dawn, dressed in warm clothing Blue had found in a chest. They'd re-dressed Kerio's wounds as well and took with them a small pack of bandages and poultice to change his bandages if they needed to before they arrived at the next house.

And then they were off, a ragged group of five—and a dog—who wound their way down the mountain as quickly as possible. They passed the second house after only a few hours—they were much faster going down than they had been going up, and they were pushed, not by the queen's orders, but by the High Priestess's threats. At least to Ember, it felt as though they were being constantly pursued by that horrible woman and her group of ever loyal sacerdos.

Ember wouldn't risk another one of their group being mutilated by the High Priestess. She hoped, selfishly, that Cerraine was okay, if only so that she could speak to her later. To apologize.

To try her best to make it right. She rushed to the front of the group, where Kerio led them, stepping gracefully down the mountain. He had abandoned his silver robes in the house, choosing instead to wear traveler's clothing and a wool cloak, clasped around his neck.

"Kerio," Ember said. "What weapons does the High Priestess possess?"

"Well," he said, glancing over at her, "there are several things. In terms of manpower, she is…unable to compete with either you or the rebellion. But *all* sacerdos are taught to use those sickles from the moment they begin training as a novice. All, including those who are sent to other temples."

"So the sacerdos in the Phoenix Palace…?"

"Yes," Kerio said, nodding. "Them as well. If the High Priestess chooses to call the sacerdos to arms, they will have to fight."

"Has that happened before?"

"Yes," Kerio said. "It's rare, and it hasn't happened in centuries, but yes. High Sacerdos have called the others to arms in times of war. Oftentimes, it was during religious conquests, when the king or queen called upon the High Sacerdo for help in spreading the religion. Your king conquered the north with assistance from the former High Priest, although he didn't provide soldiers, only weapons and supplies. For the most part—in terms of history—the sacerdos attempt to stay out of conflict."

"So lessened soldiers, but all of whom have been training for years. All of them equipped with sickles."

"That's not to mention the healers," Kerio said. "It's not magic, but it's as close as humanity has ever gotten. Mount Saffi houses rare, endangered herbs and other plants, medicines and poultices mixed and created by sacerdos long dead. Some of those vials…I've seen what they can do. People bring their dying to the temple, to give them to the Flame once they've died. But we've been able to save some of them before. Bring people back from the brink of death. It is…incredible. And terrifying."

"What else?" Ember said, storing that information in the back of her mind. Medicines that could revive people from the brink of death…they could potentially avoid *some* casualties.

Kerio's face darkened.

"I…I don't know if it would be possible. I don't know how she would transport it. But…the High Priestess…"

"Spit it out," Ember said. "Now, Kerio."

"I…the Phoenix Flame. If she figures out how to do it, she will undoubtedly unleash the fire upon a battlefield. She'll wait until both you and the rebellion are in the same place, and then she'll set it off."

It would be a massacre.

The Flame would exploit every chink in armor, every weakness. It would slip in through gloves, through pant-legs. And nothing would be able to contain it. It could decimate both armies in minutes.

"She wouldn't be able to get it back, though," Ember said. "Would she?"

"The Flame would burn itself out with no blood to consume. She would walk away unscathed. And if she really did want to re-contain the flame, she would just have to use the tons of white stone she keeps in the temple. She has the materials to make barricades out of it, or even armor, if she could find somebody to craft it for her."

"Wonderful," Ember said, kicking a rock. "How do we prepare for her?"

Kerio glanced at her.

"You can't," he said. "You can prepare for the sacerdos with my help. You can prepare for the rebellion and their allies. But you will *never* be able to prepare yourself for what the Flame will do to your armies. Never."

Chapter

FORTY

T HE CARRIAGES WERE WAITING for them at the bottom of the mountain, and not a single sacerdo asked them questions, simply loading their trunks into the carriages and walking away.

Ember allowed the other three into the carriage before her, the driver stopping her gently.

"Lady Ignis," he said. "Should we send a rider ahead to give warning to the king and queen? Perhaps it would be in our best interest to tell them that you're coming home early?"

"Don't bother," Ember said. "If we move fast enough, the letter won't get there before we do. Better to wait."

He nodded. "Very well. We'll do our best to get you there as quickly as possible, Lady Ignis."

"Thank you," Ember said, boarding the carriage and sliding in beside Viper. "We'll be home soon."

Ember woke with her head in someone's lap. A gentle hand raked through her hair, brushing the knots from it.

Her eyes fluttered opened, and she found Viper looking down at her, smiling softly.

"You're finally awake."

She turned her head slightly, finding Blue sleeping, sitting up, his head resting on Kerio, who was asleep on his shoulder. Lucasta was curled up beside him, his arm slung around her.

Ember allowed herself to smile.

Lucasta was comfortable with him. She felt safe enough with Blue to sleep on his shoulder, with his arm around her. They'd been sleeping in the carriage a lot this week, to cut down on the time needed to get home. There was a pressing need to get back to the palace, to stress to the king and queen that they needed to have a wedding as quickly as possible.

"How long have I been asleep?" she asked.

"Two hours or so. Not long," Viper said.

"Oh, good," Ember said.

"The driver said we'll be home by the morning," Viper said. "You were supposed to sleep through the night, like the three of them."

"Why aren't you asleep?" she asked.

"Because somebody had to stay awake," Viper said. "Just in case something happens."

"Well, I'm awake now," Ember said. "Go to sleep."

"No," Viper said. "I'm not tired, anyways. I'll stay up with you."

"There're only two days until the Solstice," Ember said softly. "We almost missed it."

"I'm glad we didn't," Viper said. "It's my favorite."

"Really?" Ember asked, squinting at him. Oftentimes, the houses favored not the Solstice, which was open to everybody, houses and houseless alike, but their own specific holidays. The Duels were Viper's holiday, just as the Hunt was Ember's.

But she understood where he was coming from—there was a certain *something* about the Solstice, that made the Phoenix Flame burn higher, that made Ember's heart pound faster. Something about their white clothing and glittering masks and gleaming teeth that made the holiday feel much more special than the others. It was almost feral, in a sense, bringing her closer to the Phoenix more than any temple service could.

"Yes," Viper said. "I don't have to try and kill anybody, we aren't hunting or competing in any way. We're just celebrating. And my sisters love it, too, because they get to dress up."

"Ah, the Children's Ball," Ember said. "It's been years since we went to that party."

Viper laughed softly, still trailing his hand through her hair. "Not since we were thirteen."

"No," Ember said. "I was ten. Verity wouldn't allow me to attend the Children's Ball after my tenth birthday. She said I was too old for that."

"You grew up so much faster than I did," Viper said, and Ember shrugged.

"I'm used to it. It was as though turning ten...awoke something in my mother. I wasn't a child after that. I was the heir. And I spent the next years of my life preparing to be the lady. I just never expected it would come so soon."

"How old was Verity when she became the lady?"

"Twenty-four," Ember said. "Her mother was also murdered, possibly by my grandfather, although we've never had any proof."

"Strange," Viper said. "That two Dragon matriarchs would be murdered back-to-back. How long was Verity in power?"

"Let's see…twenty-four…to forty-seven…twenty-three years. My grandmother was sixty-three when she was killed, just as a comparison. I don't remember how long Ferra was in power. My mother had me a few years after she became the lady."

"Have you ever wanted to meet your father?"

"So many questions," Ember said, closing her eyes again. "But the answer is no. I've never felt an absence there. His life, whether he is still alive or already dead, means nothing to me. He means nothing to me. And I have no desire to know if he went on to father other children or have a family. None of that impacts my life. It never has, and it never will."

"Ah," Viper said. "I don't understand you, sometimes, but I suppose that makes some sense."

"No, it doesn't," Ember said. "Normal people would mourn the loss of a father figure. Wouldn't you, if your father was killed? Blue certainly did."

"And Lucasta?"

"Lucasta's family is not my business," Ember said. "If she wishes to tell me, she will. For now, I am content with what I know."

"She's very…private," Viper said.

"Of course she is," Ember said. "What's she's gone through…my trauma can't compare. It is my one wish to gift her whatever revenge, whatever comfort, whatever space she requires. When this war is over, I will do anything for her."

"Why are you two so close? You met not long ago."

"Because she helped save me," Ember said softly. "Now, it's my turn to help save her, if she wants my help. She deserves that freedom. She deserves that love. She is worthy of it."

"So are you," Viper said. "You know that, right?"

Ember laughed, but the sound rang empty in the quiet carriage.

"Oh, Viper," she said, staring at him. "When will you learn that monsters cannot be loved?"

Viper opened his mouth to respond, but at that moment, the carriage slowed, and Ember sat up completely, pulling the curtains aside to look out the window.

"What's wrong?" Viper asked, joining her.

"I don't know," Ember said, jolting forward a little as the carriage came to a full stop. "Stay here. I'll ask the drivers."

She slipped out of the carriage, shutting the door softly behind her. She came around the side of the carriage, up to where the drivers had dismounted and were staring at the road, where a thin log lay, blocking their way forward.

Ember instantly drew a knife.

"Lady Ignis," one of the drivers said, turning to her. "We can't continue until we've moved this. There may be another road, but we'll have to go back, and—"

"I understand. We'll move it," Ember said, listening to the carriage door open and close again. Viper came to stand beside her.

"Why the knife?"

"There've been no storms recently," Ember said. She moved toward the end of the tree, running a hand over it. "And this tree was cut, not broken. Wake up the other three, please. I don't trust this."

Viper nodded, moving back toward the carriage as Ember turned toward the carriage drivers. "Be on your guard."

When the other four came back to her, Hazel trotting at Blue's side, Ember pressed a knife into Lucasta's hand. "I'll help the others move the log. Keep watch."

Lucasta turned to stare into the woods, Hazel winding around her legs.

"The log isn't too big," Kerio said, stepping over it to stand on the other side, squatting to grab it. "We should be able to move it with the six of us."

"Good," Viper said. "I'm ready to get home."

They spread out along the log, and on Kerio's command, they lifted at the same time, the log painstakingly coming off of the ground. As they began to move it off of the road, Hazel let out a sharp, high bark that had Ember turning her head to see what the dog had noticed.

"Ember!" Lucasta screamed.

A knife flew past her head and embedded itself in the tree behind her.

The log fell to the ground with a thump as the six of them scattered, Ember reaching for another knife.

She *knew* it was a trap, but they had no other choice but to walk into it.

"Get down!" Ember yelled, eyes scanning the dark trees.

There—a shadow flashed, and she threw.

Re-training for the Duels had made her accurate again, and the shadow fell to the ground with a grunt.

Ember knew there wouldn't only be one attacker, though. This wasn't just a random person trying to get a hit on the Lady of House Draco.

No, this was the Order of the Bear.

She reached for another knife.

And then they came.

The Order members came rushing out of the trees, brandishing knives and clubs, and from above, Ember could see at least one archer, pointing an arrow directly at her face.

"Scatter!" She threw forward and up this time, toward the archer, and waited for his body to hit the ground before she moved into the trees, pulling her knife from his chest before desperately looking for more attackers.

Ember knew the rebellion was situated in the south of Eiad, but she'd been foolish to believe they wouldn't have pockets across Eiad, even this close to the Phoenix Palace.

Movement on her right side had Ember throwing again. She let out a hiss of annoyance as the attacker dodged the throw, and she moved her hand to her belt, finding only a single knife left. She didn't know where the first person she'd killed was, and although Lucasta still had one of her knives, she couldn't exactly go back now.

She'd have to work with just the one.

Ember drew it, crouching in the underbrush as she waited. *Come on.*

The person moved, and Ember lunged. She didn't dare take the chance with throwing the knife and instead grabbed the person around the waist and dragged them down. They hit the ground with a grunt, and Ember released her right arm, stabbing down with the knife. The woman's blood spurted up, splashing onto Ember's face, and although she gagged, she was already moving, slipping off of the body and staring into the trees.

Nothing moved.

Ember stood, barely out of the crouch, and began to make her way back into the others, who were mercifully untouched.

"Only three of them," Ember said, sheathing her knife and holding her hand out for the one Lucasta held. "It doesn't feel like it was a very organized attack. Might not have been the Order at all."

"It didn't seem like the Order," Viper said. "Like you said, they were…sloppy. Could've just been a random attack—there were plenty of bandits who roam these roads, even before the Order made them bolder."

"Maybe," Ember said. "Let's move the log and get home. I'm sick of being in this carriage."

Chapter

FORTY-ONE

"**W**e're home." **Blue's voice** shook Viper from sleep, and he opened his eyes, turning out the window to find the Phoenix Palace rising above them, glittering in the morning light.

"Finally," Ember said. She'd moved away from him, and her hair was now in a thick plait, her gloves cleanly tied. "We have much to tell the king and queen, but the four of you are welcome to go home. Kerio...you choose which estate you want to stay at."

"I've already offered him a place to stay," Blue said, blushing slightly. "But we should all go in, Ember. We all have things to say. We all saw things differently."

Ember nodded. "Very well. Follow me, then."

They filed out of the carriage silently, guards watching as they made their way into the palace. The halls were eerily still as they stepped through, the hair on Ember's neck on end as she led them toward the conference room. It was likely that somebody who at least knew of the king and queen's location would be there, but as they walked, they encountered nobody but the guards, standing like silent statues along the wall.

But voices flooded out of the conference room.

"Lady Ignis is not fit to assume the dual role of heir and lady," somebody was saying. Ember's hand stilled on the knob, the others falling into place behind her.

Multiple voices rose at once, and Ember couldn't tell if they were in agreement or in protest. Her hands, despite her gloves, began to shake.

"I think she's perfectly capable," a woman's voice this time. It sounded like Nocte Specula, of House Ibis, but Ember couldn't pinpoint it for sure. "She's handled much more than many of us. After all, I don't think many of us believed she'd ever come out of the grief over her mother's passing, nor did we think she'd survive the wound she received from those filthy traitors. She's done remarkably well. She has exceeded my expectations."

"Regardless. She killed my son."

"Your son knew the risks when he walked into that arena. Just because nobody expected Lady Ignis to kill him, does not mean she was in the wrong."

"Enough."

Ember swung the door open, stepping inside. At once, over thirty heads turned to look at her, eyes widening, mouths agape.

"Lady Ignis—" somebody began, but Ember stopped them, raising her hand.

"I need to speak to the king and queen. Without the other houses present."

"You forget yourself," Charles Palin, of House Equo, said, half-rising from his seat.

"No," Ember said softly. "You forget *yourself*, Charles. You forget that I am the lady, the matriarch, of House Draco. Do not forget your place. Do not forget that you are *beneath* me. Leave."

The lesser houses complied immediately, Blue and Viper's respective families casting them worried glances as they shuffled out of the room. Those who remained—Alces and above—continued to stare at their group, their eyes roaming from Ember's bandages, to Kerio, to all of their pale, terrified faces.

"Begone," Ember said. She didn't dare look at the king and queen, who sat silently, observing them all. "Your assistance and presence are *not* required at this meeting. If the king and queen wish to release the information my companions and I are about to share, it will be at their discretion. But I will not tell you."

Alces and Equo stood and left.

"Let them stay." The king's voice was hollow, emotionless. "They are my trusted few, after all. You are the rulers of the three highest houses. Take your seat, Ember Ignis. Allow your companions to take theirs. And then you will begin your story."

Viper sat in his father's seat, Blue a few places down in his mother's. Kerio sat behind Blue; Lucasta sat behind Ember. It felt almost natural, as though they were slipping on a well-loved coat.

He kept his eyes constantly moving, taking in the space. It was familiar to him, but the expressions on those who remained—outright surprise from the queen, resigned emptiness from the king, and confusion on the remaining house members—were not. He couldn't figure out the queen's surprise. Ember hadn't even spoken yet.

Which meant something else was going on.

Was she, possibly, surprised to see them alive?

No, no, that was stupid. She was the queen, after all—what good would it do her to send one of her finest fighters to her death? And besides, she couldn't have known what was going to happen with the High Priestess, anyways.

Ember began their story, the others completely silent. Then, Viper allowed himself to watch her, her hands and her face, the curve of her mouth and the gleam of her eyes. Then, he allowed himself to look at her for a split second, to trace the line of her jaw and the gently slope of her neck.

He met Lucasta's eyes over Ember's shoulder, her face pinched.

Something felt wrong.

But he didn't dare interrupt Ember as she continued to speak, weaving an elaborate picture of what their experience had been like. When she reached her meeting with the High Priestess, the king outright groaned.

"That woman…no amount of money will make her budge. We needed the temple to be on our side."

"Neither will violence," Ember said. "The threats we made never made an impact against her. She seemed completely immune to all of them. Allow me to continue."

As she dove back in, Viper stared at his own hands.

They'd failed, so very miserably. They had been assigned one job, one task, and they had been unable to complete it.

When Ember finished, nobody spoke for a long while, all of them looking at each other.

"This is terrible news," Lord Minus, of House Tigris, finally said. "They have Verdeca."

"Possibly," Ember corrected. "These are only rumors that have been heard by the royalty of Oscela."

"We cannot fight Verdeca, even if the temple had been on our side," Nocte said. "You know that as well as we do, Whelyn."

"I know," the king said. "But we have allies of our own that we can call to our aid. Oscela's offer to wed Prince Nekun to Ember Ignis for their support in the war guarantees their troops. We aren't completely alone in this war, after all."

"But will it even be enough?" Lord Minus asked. "To stand against the might of Verdeca and the rebellion combined?"

"It has to be," the king said. "We simply have no other choice. We either call our allies and fight or lie down and allow the rebellion to run us over."

"And that's still not counting the temple," Nocte said. "They're a small force, true, but if we have to deal with that as well, it's another issue that we have to face. Another battle. We'll have to split our troops in half."

"Not directly in half," Whelyn said. "We don't need half of our army to handle the temple. We don't even need a full quarter to deal with them."

"Regardless," Nocte said. "Splitting up our troops at all is a dangerous game to play."

"And it's one we don't have a choice about," the king said. "We must deal with all of our enemies. We must deal with the temple, with the rebellion, and with Verdeca."

"What if they attack during the Solstice?"

Lucasta's voice was so soft that Viper almost didn't hear her, but the entire room turned to face her.

"I…" The queen didn't finish her statement, exchanging a glance with the king.

"Security will be tight," the king said. "Tighter than the Duels, even. We have hand-selected every soldier who will be there, and access to the public will be restricted unlike years prior."

"She has a good point," Lord Minus said. "It may be wise to close off access to the public entirely."

"No," the king said. "No. Absolutely not."

"Just consider it—"

"The Solstice is a holiday for *all*, and I will not further alienate myself from my people. The Solstice feasts will remain open to the public, is that understood?"

Viper watched Ember as she hummed softly, considering that. He couldn't believe how idiotic the king was being— hadn't he learned his lesson from the first time? Did he not fully comprehend the danger all of them were in?

"I would agree with Lord Minus," she said. "However, I am bound by the king's will. If the gates must stay open, *we* must be on our guard. Every house member should be armed and have guards assigned to them. We should have guards in disguise amongst the feasters as well as those along the walls. If they choose to attack us…it'll be messy. A slaughter."

"I won't allow it to be," the king said, setting his jaw. "Believe me, all of you. I do not wish for a repeat of this spring. I will not see another one of my lords or ladies killed on the palace grounds. And of course, if you are uncomfortable attending, leave your families at home. Lesser children younger than fifteen should be kept at home with personal guards. The lords and ladies *must* attend, especially after the loss of House Pardus, but spouses and all children except heirs are exempt from attending. Besides, the Solstice is in a few weeks. We have time to prepare."

"Very well," Lord Minus said. "I suppose that will be sufficient."

Viper personally felt that it wasn't sufficient in the slightest, but at least his sisters would be home, away from the bonfires and the feasting. He didn't know what he'd do if something happened to them.

"Dignitaries will begin their travels after the Solstice," the king said. "We'll send both lords and ladies and heirs to speak to our allies and have them sign alliances with us. We will need all of them to agree. We may not end up calling all of them to battle, but I'd like to have the option to, if need be."

"Understood," Nocte said. "I would be happy to go, if need be."

"Absolutely not," Whelyn said. "Lesser houses will be fine. I wish to keep the three of you close."

Ember dipped her head, as did the other two. Viper squirmed. It felt strange to hear the king say that, especially after what they'd just experienced.

But that had been the queen's doing, after all. The king hadn't said much when she'd delivered their sentence.

"You are dismissed," Whelyn said. "I will see all of you tomorrow morning in temple."

Chapter

FORTY-TWO

WHEN THE SHORES OF Eiad came into view alongside the delighted shouts of the Verdecan soldiers on board, Asher was the first one to the bow, staring at the port they were approaching, a port that was not in any way ready for what was about to land there. It was the same port Asher and Tyvish had sailed out of two months ago, but back then, it had only been a singular ship, unremarkable, pulling out of port.

But now...now, this ship, with its train of Verdecan ships flying the howling wolf, it could be mistaken for nothing but a declaration of war. Some people on the docks scrambled away, as though Verdeca planned on beginning their conquest right there, while others stood frozen, slack-jawed, watching as the captains guided the few ships they could into port. There were not enough docks for each, not even close, but at this point, it was not Asher's job to get the ships docked. It was to get word to the rebellion as quickly as possible to prepare them for the influx of soldiers that were about to swell their ranks—and their camps.

Asher stepped off the ship, Sofya behind him, and Doya still behind her. For a moment, they stood on the dock in silence, grateful to be back on land, and then Asher was moving, striding toward one of the dock workers, one of those who had frozen instead of fleeing. He couldn't have been older than fourteen, shifting awkwardly as Asher towered over him.

"Get me the dock master," Asher said. "You are loyal to the Bear, correct?"

The boy glanced from Asher, standing with his arms crossed over his chest, to Sofya, with her twin swords, to Doya, and nodded slowly.

"Good answer," Asher said. "Be quick."

The boy didn't hesitate, practically sprinting down the dock as Tyvish and Viktoriya joined them.

"I hate boat," Viktoriya spat, scowling.

"Me too," Asher said.

"I can't say I mind it," Tyvish said, and Asher shot him a look. "The dock master is with us. Hopefully he'll be able to clear out these other ships so we can dock. It's the only port we've got under our control—or at least it was, before we left."

"I'm aware," Asher said. "Hopefully they've been able to take more back since we've been gone."

"Hopefully indeed," Tyvish said. "But with these soldiers, perhaps we can take back more."

"You and I both know that we won't be the ones in charge of them," Asher said. "That's up to Viktoriya, Sofya, and Luria to fight out. I don't want to be in charge of soldiers."

"But they came because of you," Tyvish said. "So in a way, I think you're partially responsible for what happens to them no matter what."

"Perhaps," Asher said softly.

From down the dock, a little, fat man wearing a hideous green hat stumbled toward them, calling Asher's name. The dock master was, quite frankly, an unfortunate type of person that Asher didn't particularly care to work with, but as it so happened, he didn't really have a choice. They needed this dock, and although Asher didn't know the specifics of what the rebellion had promised him, he knew that they couldn't do without him.

"You need to clear this port," Asher said, cutting the man off before he could get a word in. "We need all of your docks for the Verdecan ships."

"I'm afraid I can't do that," the dock master said, snatching his hat off his head and twisting it between his hands. "Those ships are all here in support of the rebellion in some way—most with supplies, but some ships have men."

"Men from where?"

"I don't ask questions, sir, I simply provide them a place to put their ships. You will need to find a new place for the rest of your ships. I will take what I can."

Asher and Tyvish exchanged a glance. "Then you need to point us in the direction of a new port."

"I...I am afraid that most other dock masters are quite loyal to your parents, Prince Asher, sir. They have been providing them troops to keep their ships and products safe. *I* have received no such help from the Order; however, I am willing to stay loyal so long as—"

"I don't care," Tyvish said. "Find us a place to dock these ships. You will get *nothing* if we cannot use these soldiers, is that understood? The Order cannot stand without them."

"Yes, yes, that makes perfect sense, however, as stated, there is little I can do at the moment."

"I'll handle this," Tyvish said softly, placing his hand on the dock master's shoulder and turning him around. "What can I do to make you more receptive."

"You allow such people to speak to you that way?" Sofya asked, mixing Verdecan and Eiadian so smoothly that it took Asher a moment to catch up.

"Unfortunately, yes," Asher said. "I have no power here. My value comes from who I *used* to be, not who I *am*."

"Ah," Sofya said. "I understand."

They did not speak again as they stood on that dock, not even when she slipped her hand into his silently, squeezing once before turning and heading back up onto the ship.

Night was falling when they arrived at the rebellion's main camp, the camp where Luria Van Ela and Juniper Farley awaited their arrival. They'd asked most of the Verdecan soldiers to stay behind, on the ships, and it was only a small group of four that came into the camp—Asher, Tyvish, Sofya, and Viktoriya. And the wolves, of course, ever unwilling to be parted from Sofya and Viktoriya.

"Main tent," Tyvish said. "Luria will be there."

Sofya swung down from her horse, surveying the camp, the endless tents and campfires, all contained within 'reclaimed' farmland, taken by the rebellion for this exact purpose. "You have no room for us."

"You'll have to help us get room," Tyvish said.

"My soldiers cannot fight without first resting from such a journey," Sofya said, scowling.

"Who said anything about soldiers?" Tyvish asked. "I only mentioned you."

Sofya scowled. "Fine."

They moved silently through the camp. Asher could feel the eyes of other rebels following them, watching them, taking in the three massive wolves that followed their group.

There would be no question as to who they were. No question as to what they were there for.

The whispers began slowly, quietly, almost as though the others were scared that even a single word would send the wolves at their throats.

"Verdeca…"

"Prince Asher, right?"

"Phoenix above, look at the sheer *size* of them…"

Viktoriya was practically skipping on Asher's left, grinning wildly at the rebels who openly stared, forcing their eyes away.

"In here," Tyvish said, stopping in front of the massive, main tent, a silver-and-blue Bear flag flying above it. He turned toward them, face suddenly so serious that it almost scared Asher. "Let me go in first and make sure she's awake."

"Make sure who's awake?"

Asher's head shot up, finding Luria Van Ela standing there, massive scar covering half her face, and a small smile curving her lips.

"Well, well, well," Luria said, coming to stand beside Tyvish. "You succeeded."

"He did," Sofya said. "I am Sofya Seminoava, Fangs of Verdeca."

"I Viktoriya Bolshi. Wolf."

"I am Luria Van Ela, leader of the Bears of Eiad," Luria said, in near-perfect Verdecan, inclining her head. "Your coming will turn the tide of this war. We are eternally grateful for your help."

"Tell us where to dock our ships and house our armies," Sofya said. "They need rest, as do we. We can be ready to march in a few weeks."

"There is no rush," Luria said. "There are…other things that must be done before we can even hope to march on the Phoenix Palace."

"Like what?" Asher asked, drawing Luria's attention to him. Her eyes darkened, and she turned back to Tyvish. "Give them Juniper's tent. Let me speak to Asher alone."

"No," Sofya said. "We sleep with our army. Take us back to the ships."

"Of course," Tyvish said. "Whatever you'd like. Just right this way."

Asher watched them go, watched the tip of Doya's tail disappear into the shadows, before turning back to Luria, who gave him a pained, tight-lipped smile. "Come into the tent and sit down. I want to catch you up."

Asher ducked into the tent behind her, finding himself in a massive space, a cot shoved in a corner. Most of the tent was taken up by a table, littered with maps, sheets of paper and bottles of liquor. There was a singular chest underneath the bed, and mismatched chairs surrounded the table. Right now, they were all completely empty.

"Sit," Luria said, pointing at one of the chairs and popping open one of the bottles. "You know the Solstice is in about a week, do you not?"

"I—" No, he hadn't known. Asher had completely forgotten, so deeply entrenched in Verdeca that all of the traditions and holidays of Eiad had completely fled his mind. "I forgot, honestly."

"Understandable," Luria said. "You were in Verdeca for several months. Things have happened here that are deeply important, and I think it's important that you are told. Juniper did a poor job keeping you in the loop when you were here before—I intend to use you to your full potential. First and foremost, we are planning a Solstice strike. We desperately need to break the Dragon, and we know how."

"You're going to kill her?"

"No. Ember Ignis, for some ungodly reason, doesn't seem to be able to die. She's certainly able to kill, though—she killed the Tiger heir."

"Really?"

"She did," Luria said, pausing to take a long swig from the bottle before pushing it toward him. "And then your parents sent her and her little group up to the Mount Saffi Temple."

"I'm not surprised," Asher said. "They'll want to keep the temple away from us."

"We have no interest in the temple," Luria said. "If they choose to side with us, fine. If they choose to play neutral, fine. I know for a fact that they will not choose to side with your parents."

"And you know this how?"

"Gut feeling," Luria said, smiling. "Those are rarely wrong."

Asher bit his tongue—this was the most information the rebellion had ever willingly given him, and he wasn't about to mess it up by opening his big mouth.

"We have brought Verdeca over," Luria said. "Or, rather, you and Tyvish have. But Oscela landed in the north about a month ago. A singular ship. The information is conflicting, but there have been rumors swirling that one of their princes, the *Pasha Daha,* is here in Eiad. He has yet to reach out to us, which means he is there for your parents."

"Oscela," Asher muttered, running through years of geographical and political tutoring, calling to mind everything he knew about that particular country. "Cavalry. Incredible cavalry—probably the best in the world."

"Yes," Luria said. "Luckily for us, you brought us the seven best soldiers in the world, so perhaps that evens the playing field."

"Do you know where in particular he is?"

"The temple," Luria said. "At least, he was."

"He's there for Ember," Asher said. "I'd be willing to bet on that. She's the most eligible lady in Eiad right now, especially if my parents name her heir."

Luria sat up straighter. "Heir?"

"She's the next in line if both of my parents die. They could name somebody else, of course, but if nobody is named, she steps in."

"Good to know," Luria said. "I hadn't even considered that. Phoenix above. Ember Ignis as a queen would be…"

"Terrible," Asher said. "It would be awful."

"That's why we intend to break her," Luria said. "Her Serpent—what is his name?"

"Viper Trunca."

"Him. We're going to take him during the Solstice."

"I…Luria. You got away with killing her mother. Do you really think she's going to let you get away with taking Viper?"

"I don't know," Luria said. "I don't know what she'll do. But we must *try*. We need Ember to break so she's out of the way."

"Then I wish you the best of luck—"

"Oh, good try," Luria said. "You'll be planning the strike, and you're going to get us in."

They'd found a place for the Verdecan soldiers to camp.

Or, rather, Sofya and Viktoriya had. They'd slit the throats of an entire family, living alone on a massive swath of farmland, covered in fruit trees. The Verdecans pitched their tents between those very trees, tied their horses to them, ate from them. It was only a bit further north than the other camp, perfectly situated to march whenever Luria asked.

But that wouldn't be for a little while.

Asher swung down from an apricot tree, one clutched in each hand. He tossed one to Sofya, sitting at the base of the tree with Doya's head in her lap, all three of them taking in the silence and stillness, the warm sun streaming between the trees. They could hear the sounds from the camp about a half mile away, but out here, it was only them and a few songbirds.

Asher sat beside her, closing his eyes and leaning against the trunk of the tree.

He knew, in the depths of his soul, that this type of serenity would not come again until the war was over.

Perhaps this was the last time he would ever experience this peace. He bit into his apricot, sweetness spilling over his tongue, juice running down his arm. Asher could hear Sofya and Doya breathing in time beside him, and although he wondered what she was thinking, he didn't dare ask, unwilling to break the silence, unwilling to interrupt this moment that was so incredibly precious that Asher felt it could shatter in his hands. He wondered if she was thinking about the ever-growing tumor in her body, the little thing that was slowly, quietly, painfully killing her.

Was she afraid to die?

Was he?

Asher didn't know if he was ready to face that question, didn't know if he was even ready to consider the possibility that he might die at all.

They didn't touch, nor speak. They didn't even look at each other.

But they could feel each other there, the weight of their presence enough to keep them both grounded.

Chapter

FORTY-THREE

"**YOUR DRESS IS UGLIER** than mine." Ember looked away from her reflection to find Lucasta standing in the doorway, looking down at the swaths of white fabric that covered her. She'd chosen her own style, with gauzy white fabric stitched with elegant, intricate gold patterns. A scarf covered her head, her dark eyes staring out from underneath it.

"You're right," Ember said. "Lucasta, you look beautiful."

"Thank you," she said. "It's been a long time since I wore the clothing of my homeland. It feels right."

Ember stared down at her own dress. It was still lovely, despite Lucasta's comment, with large, long sleeves and a bell where it fanned out from her hips. She would wear not a scarf, but a small, golden circlet engraved with twinning Dragons.

Beyond that, neither of them were allowed to wear any sort of jewelry or accessories. They would wear the same shoes, too, soft white flats that would make no sound on the floors of the temple for this most holy of days.

"I'm dying to see what animal you picked for your mask," Ember admitted, wincing as a maid yanked a brush through her hair.

"Well, it wasn't as though I already had one built in," Lucasta pointed out. "Hopefully you like it."

"That's true," Ember said. "I suppose that's fair."

"You'll be a Dragon, I assume," Lucasta said, running a finger over Ember's sleeve. "Good choice of material."

"Thank you, and yes," Ember said, relaxing at the maid finally stopped yanking on her hair, instead securing the diadem with small, black pins that blended in perfectly to her hair. "We should be going. The Solstice is the one temple service that you simply do not want to be late for."

Lucasta nodded, stepping back and allowing Ember room to stand up.

"You'll sit with me," Ember said. "But we won't be allowed to sit with the boys. And remember, the sacerdo officiating the service—"

"'Is not to be trusted.' I know, Ember. You can relax."

"I can't really," Ember said. "I still think the king was wrong to keep the Solstice open to the public. The Order can so easily slip inside and we'd never even know until they kidnapped or killed somebody else. I don't understand why they're always so willing to take risks with all of our lives."

"Breathe," Lucasta said. "It won't be you."

"But it could be one of you," Ember pointed out. "And that would be worse."

"I have my own weapons," Lucasta said. "And the guards will be there. Real guards, not like the ones last time."

"Right," Ember said. "I hope you're right. I hope this is just a normal Solstice."

"So do I," Lucasta said, linking her arm through Ember's. "I've heard stories about the food, and I must say I simply cannot wait."

Viper watched Ember and Lucasta arrive from within the sanctuary, watched as they strode through the doors, their expressions almost daring anybody to stop them.

They looked like goddesses.

Beautiful, immaculate goddesses, crafted from glass and steel, adorned with gold. Ember so rarely wore white that Viper couldn't even recall seeing her in it before, but he was so violently aware of her now that his stupid heart tugged him toward her regardless.

"You're staring," Coral spoke softly, and Viper turned his attention toward her, scowling slightly as he gently yanked a lock of her hair.

"Mind your own business."

"She's really pretty," Coral said. "Both of them are. Lady Ignis and her friend, I mean."

"I know who you meant, Coral," Viper said. "I think so too. And her friend's name is Lady Lucasta."

Coral tried the name on her tongue, nodding. "Lucasta. That's not an Eiadian name."

"No, it's not," Viper said. "She's from Geloj Swesh."

Coral, however, was no longer paying attention, now pointing a few rows away. "Lord Blue!"

Viper turned, flashing Blue a smile. Kerio stood beside him, both of them wearing loose, white robes, much like what Viper himself was wearing. Kerio had tied his with his silver sacerdo rope, staring with a hollow expression around the temple.

The temple was almost entirely full by then—only a few, the king and queen most notably—were missing, but despite the crowd, the room was eerily silent. Nothing made a sound, not their shoes, not their clothing, least of all their voices.

"I'm scared," Addie whispered, leaning over the other sisters to get to Viper.

"It's okay, Addie," Viper whispered back, casting a glance over his shoulder at his parents, who were too busy staring at the Phoenix Flame to notice much else. "It'll start soon, and it'll be just like temple is normally, okay?"

"Okay," she whispered, sitting back.

Soft footsteps drew his attention, and then everybody was turning to watch the king and queen come in, both of them wearing their ceremonial crowns. Interesting—Viper couldn't remember them wearing those last year, but perhaps it was simply a show of force, a reminder of the power they still held.

A few moments after the king and queen had taken their seats, two silver-clad sacerdos stepped up and onto the raised platform with the Phoenix Flame and knives.

"Welcome," one of them, a priestess, said, her voice soft but not weak. It carried throughout the temple, and Viper shuddered. The crowd leaned in, entranced by the Flame. "Today is the day of the most high, a day of celebration to the Phoenix Herself. Today is the Solstice."

"There will be no story today." This was now the other sacerdo, a priest. His voice was louder than the woman's but no less evocative. "There will be no group prayers. We invite you to sit in silent prayer until you are called forth to offer your blood to the Flame. Remember, the Phoenix can sense your devoutness, and She is grateful for your offering into the Flame. Remember how you came to be, and how your body will leave this earth. It is all done through the Flame and the fury."

"Whelyn and Feather Cinis are the first invited to the Flame."

The wet, squelching sound of the knives ripping through the king and queen's hands made Viper cringe away from it, flexing his own palm. Addie hadn't given blood before—she'd watched him and the other girls do it, but she'd always been too young, too little, too scared.

But she would have no choice today, just as he didn't.

He was glad they would all be going home with him after this, and there they would stay when he, his parents, and his older siblings left for the palace in the evening.

Row by row the sacerdos went.

The next was Ember and Lucasta, although only Ember stood, making her way slowly toward the Flame. She extended her hand, allowing the sacerdo to slice through the flesh there. The blood began to pour silently, dripping into the Phoenix Flame. It leapt, devouring her offering.

On and on it went.

Row by row, palms were split, cleaned, bandaged. Row by row, the Phoenix Flame grew as it gorged itself on their sacrifice.

Until it was finally their turn. Viper's parents stood, his older siblings close behind, and then they were stepping out of the pew, into the main aisle of the temple. He could feel everybody's eyes on his back as he made his way up to the front.

Behind him, Coral began to cry softly, but nobody stopped, nobody moved to comfort her.

There would be time for comfort later, Viper had learned when he was young. There would be time for their mother to kiss their wounds and tell them sweet, placating words to make them feel safe.

But right now, they all had to give a sacrifice.

So he would give.

And when the knife cut through his skin, his blood a crimson stream that poured into that greedy Flame, Viper didn't shy away from it.

"It's finally over," Ember muttered to Lucasta, watching as the last maid slit her palm to feed the Flame. "Phoenix above. That was excruciating."

Lucasta nodded in agreement, sitting back as the sacerdos again stepped up to the Flame, which was roaring in its stone prison. It burned higher than Ember had ever seen it before, and even the two sacerdos took a step back from it, casting terrible shadows on the wall behind them.

"Go forth, and be blessed," the priestess said. "Remember the Flame. Remember the fury."

Ember couldn't move faster—she and Lucasta fell into step behind the king and queen, House Tigris and House Nocte coming after them. They filed out of the temple silently, the king and queen turning down a hallway, and the houses moving toward the main doors. There would be no socializing after this temple service. That would happen later, starting in the afternoon.

"You're welcome to eat or nap when we get back to the estate," Ember said. "We don't need to be back until late afternoon, so you have at least two hours before you have to start getting ready. Unless you need more time than that."

"I don't know how much time I'll need," Lucasta said. "I'll speak to the maids about what I want to do. Hopefully they'll be able to give me an estimate on how much time I'll need."

"Very well," Ember said. "It still feels…wrong. For us to keep this celebration open. For us to even *have* this celebration. I understand keeping the feasts for the houses and perhaps even the elite, but the rebellion can slip in with the poor. Not to mention that everybody will be wearing *masks*. It feels so stupid. So…reckless. I'm almost tempted to not show up, but I would never get away with it."

"I understand," Lucasta said. "Never fear, friend. We'll be okay."

"I hope you're right," Ember said softly.

Chapter

FORTY-FOUR

"VIPER. IT'S TIME."

Coral's hands, which had been tying his mask on, stilled on the back of Viper's head. "Are you nervous?"

Viper paused for a moment as her small, deft hands tied a knot in the back, keeping the mask tight to his head.

"In a way, yes," Viper said softly. "But that's how the Solstice is. When you go, you'll understand."

"I don't want to go," Coral said, and Viper turned toward her, taking her hands into his.

"Then you don't have to," Viper said. "Nobody will make you go to the Solstice celebration. You can stay home."

"Good," Coral said, resting her forehead against his. "I hope you have fun, Viper."

"I hope so too," Viper said. He kissed her forehead. "Have fun with the younger girls tonight."

She held his hand as they descended down the stairs, to where his parents waited at the bottom of the stairs. "Very nice, Viper."

Viper dipped his head toward his father. His entire family—his little sisters excluded—wore Serpent masks, although he'd kept his outfit simple, nothing more than a pair of pants and body paint in the pattern of scales. Most of the men would be bare chested, painted with the pattern of their patron animals, and the women would be in gowns.

"The celebration starts in about thirty minutes. Your siblings are already there," his father said. "Let's go."

Viper followed his parents outside, to the carriage. His sister, Boa, smiled at him from inside. "You look nice, Viper. I'm sure Lady Ignis will have a hard time keeping her eyes off of you."

Viper whacked her arm, his mother glancing at them disapprovingly.

"Oh, calm down, Viper," Boa said. "It's so obvious you have a thing for her. No reason to try and hide it."

"Enough," their mother said. "We're going to the Solstice. You two need to act like adults, not children."

"Oh, mother," Boa chided. "Let us breathe. It's a celebration, after all."

"It's the Solstice, not a birthday party. Behave."

Boa grinned, leaning back in her seat. "Very well."

Viper exchanged a glance with her, holding back a smile, and Boa grinned back.

Ember stared at herself in her mirror, gently reaching up to adjust her mask.

This outfit was beautiful.

It had been commissioned shortly after last year's Solstice, with Verity's help, and Ember felt as though she was wearing a piece of her mother with her. Where most women would wear a gown, Ember was wearing a pantsuit. The suit, stitched from black silk, had long, light sleeves, and the bottoms of the pants were wide, allowing her to wear boots.

But it wasn't the suit that drew the eye—it was the wings. Golden, heavy wings, strapped around her shoulders, underneath her sleeves, brushed the ground as she walked. The frames of the wings were made of bone, delicately placed together. Golden fabric had been placed on top of it, and that had been stitched with details.

The mask, like her suit, was black, sweeping away from her face like a second set of wings. Her hair had been braided into a large bun on the back of her head, keeping it out of the way of the black ribbons that held her mask in place. She wore short golden boots, and her lips had been painted a deep shade of crimson.

She wore her gloves, as well. Several small, hidden slits in the sides of her suit would allow her access to her knives, although her Dragon-head's knife was sheathed on her arm, in plain view.

There was no point in hiding that, at least.

"Lady Ignis," somebody said softly from the doorway. Ember turned, finding a young maid standing in the doorway. "Lady Tersus has requested your presence in her bedroom."

"Very well," Ember said, following the young woman out and toward Lucasta's room, near the other end of the hallway. The door was thrown open, and when Ember entered, she couldn't help but gasp.

Lucasta had themed her outfit around the scorpion.

Her dress was a soft orange color, with a high, elegant collar and long, tight sleeves. Her dress, unlike Ember's, was straight all the way down, ending just above her ankles, where delicate bangles jangled. They encircled her wrists as well, and large hoops hung from her ears. The top of her dress was stitched with a delicate lace pattern. She turned slightly, showing her the back, where gold metal was used to create the ribbed pattern of a scorpion's back.

Ember reached up to help adjust Lucasta's mask, small bells jingling on the sides as she did. The mask was crafted from an orange-brown metal, intricate metal work in the shape of scorpions, framing her dark eyes. The ribbons holding it in place were orange as well, all of it elegant and lovely and perfect for the dark-haired beauty wearing it all.

"Your craftsmen are incredible," Lucasta said, looking down at her dress. "This dress…"

"It's beautiful," Ember said softly. "You look amazing, Lucasta. You're going to be the prettiest one there."

Lucasta laughed, batting Ember's hand away. "You're ridiculous. Let's go."

"Oh, gladly," Ember said, linking her arm through Lucasta's. "I'm so excited to show up with you."

Lucasta leaned into her, grinning. "Ah, Ember. Only you would be so lucky as to show up with me."

The bonfires were roaring, the tables were laden with food, and a line of horses and carriages extended from the back entrance of the palace. The Solstice celebration would take place in the gardens—there was no room inside for the massive group that was about to congregate. Across from Ember, Lucasta shifted excitedly.

"This is fun," she said. "I'm actually…excited about this."

"Good," Ember said, giving her a small smile. She felt nervous more than excited—already, there were so many people here, and despite the guards forcing people to lift their masks, Ember knew it wouldn't matter. They didn't know what the rebellion members looked like.

Ahead of them, two horses arrived at the gates, the riders dismounting and lifting their masks. Their own carriage was waved on without question, trundling toward where several servants stood, waiting for them. The carriage came to a stop, the door opening. A servant extended his hand toward Ember, and she slipped her hand into his, stepping out of the carriage.

Lucasta followed close behind, and the carriage was waved on, to wait somewhere else. Ember exhaled as she looked around the gardens, taking it in. Lucasta slipped her hand through Ember's, tugging her toward one of the tables. "I'm hungry."

Ember followed her easily, allow Lucasta to move from table to table, quickly noticing the theme. Each table was themed around a certain patron animal—the first one, as expected, was for the Dragon. Large slabs of charred meat, seasoned carefully, were accompanied by a variety of charred sides; potatoes, carrots, fruits, and cheeses. Lucasta made herself a small plate, a black-clad servant placing a small sample of meat on the plate. Ember made her own plate, the two of them standing slightly off to the side as they ate, watching people flood the garden. The two of them, however, were given a wide berth.

"It's your wings," Lucasta said, stabbing another piece of meat. "They know who you are, and they're afraid."

"Good," Ember said. "I don't want them anywhere near me."

"Let's go to the next table," Lucasta said, giving her plate to a nearby servant and plucking a flute of champagne from his tray. As they walked, more house members arrived, each in intricate, beautiful outfits. All of the avian houses wore wings as well, but they were stitched from feathers rather than leather. House Olor arrived only a few moments after Ember and Lucasta, the carriage doors opening and allowing Blue, Kerio, and Blue's mother and brother, out. Even Kerio wore the white-feather wings of the Swan, which was impressive, the boys shirtless and painted white. Blue noticed them immediately, making his way to them with Kerio close behind.

"This is better than last year," Blue said, snatching a potato off of Ember's plate. "More food."

"Don't you feel off, Blue?" Ember asked softly, leaning into him as Lucasta dragged Kerio to get food. "Doesn't this feel weird?"

"Yes," Blue admitted. "It does. But there's nothing we can do now. I'm sure you're armed. I am too."

"I'm nervous," Ember said. "Something is going to go wrong."

"I don't doubt it," Blue said. "I'm just hoping our group makes it out okay. I don't think we can take another hit like last year."

"No," Ember said. "We can't."

Neither of them could afford to lose anybody else.

Blue glanced over his shoulder at where his brother and mother were speaking to House Vulpus, his face softening slightly. Other than Ember, he was part of the only family in the court that had lost somebody to the Order

"I don't think my family is worth their attention anymore," he said. "Unless they target them because of my association with you. But I doubt it, honestly. I don't provide anything other than my commentary. It's Lucasta and Viper that we need to keep an eye on. Especially Viper. Even with your engagement to Nekun…anybody with half a brain knows that's nothing except a political alliance."

Both of them turned toward where Lucasta and Kerio were eating, the two of them almost moving on to the next station as Blue and Ember watched. "Viper isn't here yet. We'll keep him close when he arrives."

"Very well," Blue said. They made their way toward Lucasta and Kerio, who were on House Tigris's table.

"Ember," Lucasta said, handing her a bowl. "Eat."

Ember lifted it to her nose, inhaling deeply. "What is it?"

"I don't know," Lucasta said. "But it tastes like Kiellian food. I believe it's curry. It's like…a stew?"

Ember dipped her spoon into the bowl, lifting it to her lips.

"Mmm," Ember said, having another spoonful. "It's spicy, but…it's really good."

Lucasta grinned. "I know. I told you so."

"Give me a bowl," Blue said.

"Absolutely not," Lucasta said. "Not until you have food from the first table."

"Fine," Blue said, stomping back to House Draco's table, making a small plate before rejoining them. He ate quickly, depositing his plate and holding his hands out for a bowl of the curry. Lucasta obliged with a smile, watching the two of them eat.

"Viper's here," Kerio said, nodding toward the newest carriage. "All of the people from that carriage have been wearing snake scales and masks."

"Good," Blue said softly. "Keep him near us."

Ember nodded, stepping away from the group and toward Viper's family. He was the last to exit the carriage, behind his sister and her wife.

Viper stopped short when he caught sight of her, his hand on the carriage door.

"Ember," he whispered, taking a step forward. She extended her hand, relieved when he took it.

"Dance with me," Ember whispered back, leading him toward the center of the garden. "Please."

"Anything," Viper said. "I'll do anything you want."

She was breathless as he followed her, other partygoers turning to stare at the two of them.

The Dragon and the Snake.

Lady and lesser son.

Fools, both of them.

They watched as Viper gently placed a hand on her waist, the other lacing with her fingers. Ember placed her other hand on his bare shoulder.

The band began to play, a waltz Ember knew instantly, but she allowed Viper to lead the two of them, his eyes glimmering underneath his mask.

Nobody else danced. They only watched as the two of them spun across the garden.

She felt as though she were floating.

The song was a blur, a brief moment in time that Ember grasped it, held it close to her heart.

And when it finished, Viper brought his hands up to her face and drew her in, brushing his lips over hers in a tantalizing movement that left her reaching for him. She smiled.

"Viper—" Ember said, taking a step forward, reaching out for him. A half-smile graced his mouth as he took a step forward, and then collapsed in front of her with a grunt of pain.

Ember screamed, unable to help herself, as she collapsed to her knees beside him. An arrow protruded from the back of his knee, and Viper groaned as he pushed himself up, his eyes going wide as he noticed something over Ember's shoulder.

She could barely move fast enough to draw her knife, bringing it up to meet a sword. The tip of the sword, held by a large woman, dragged across Ember's forehead as the other woman drew back, baring her teeth like a wild animal. Ember bit her lip to keep from crying out in pain. Underneath the woman's mask, violet eyes glittered with excitement and bloodlust. Short, white-blonde hair shone under firelight. The sword was the final thing Ember needed to know for sure—the intricate designs cut in the steel of wolves and snowflakes.

The Wolf of Verdeca was here.

Stupid, stupid, stupid.

She *knew* that they were going to attack, she *knew* that they were all in danger, and she'd allowed the king to talk her into this anyways. She shouldn't have allowed Viper and the others to come. The risk was too great, and she'd gambled with their lives.

"Guards!" Ember didn't know who shouted, but it didn't matter—all that mattered was protecting Viper.

The Wolf roared, rearing back for a split second.

A split second too long.

Ember leapt to her feet, pulling another knife from her boot and bracing her feet.

It was a repeat of the spring.

It was all the same as the spring.

No.

Ember set her jaw.

They would *not* kill Viper. She would not allow it.

She would kill every one of them before she allowed them to kill Viper.

With the masks, Ember couldn't recognize friend from foe, house from houseless, rebellion members from guards.

Chaos. It was chaos again.

The screaming had begun, accompanied by the sound of steel on steel. People rushed around them, running to or from the violence within the garden. Out of the corner of her eye,

Ember watched a woman trip and fall over the hem of her gown, sprawling on the ground.

Ember pressed her attack on the Wolf. How in the name of the Phoenix had they allowed her to bring a *sword* in?

Ember was at a clear disadvantage. Two knives—one of which was designed not for combat but throwing—couldn't hold against the Wolf's steel. Not for long.

But hopefully it would be long enough for Viper to get away. Long enough for somebody to drag him away, to get him to safety.

Through the fire and the blood dripping into her eyes, Ember caught sight of a woman's arm rising and falling, a knife glinting in her hand. Was she house? Order? It was hard to tell in the darkness, but when she whipped around, Ember's heart stopped.

She knew that face. It haunted her. It mocked her in dreams, staring at her with a sneer.

The queen.

And the man she crouched over had lost his crown, and Ember watched as the king took his last, shuddering breath before lying still.

The queen threw the knife, picked up her skirts, and ran for the palace walls.

The Wolf rounded on Ember again, but a high, long whistle from the other side of the garden had the Wolf ripping her mask off her face and hurtling across the nearest bush, pushing a torch over on her way. The bush nearest to Ember caught fire, and she stumbled away.

She looked down, panting, and panic flooded her body again.

He was gone. Viper was gone.

She pulled her own mask off, scanning the garden with a type of desperation she'd never felt before. There was Lucasta, with Blue and Kerio, holding their own against a couple of Order members as they defended Blue's brother, Norvin.

There—a flash of gold hair and scales in her peripheral. Ember started moving, desperate to reach him. She jumped over somebody, cowering on the ground by a table. Two Order members had him by the arms, and his head slumped. She couldn't see any wounds other than the arrow sticking out from his knee, but he seemed to be unconscious, and that alone was enough to make bile rise in her throat as she ran at them.

Somebody stepped into her path and Ember didn't stop, drawing a knife as she hurtled into the woman with all of the force she could muster. They went down together, toppling into the dirt. She jerked her head up, but Viper, and the rest of the Order members, including the Wolf, were already gone.

Ember covered the woman's body with her own, her knife pressed against her throat. She blinked back tears, blood dripping from her forehead as she stared down at the woman.

At the scar marring her face.

This was the woman who had killed her mother.

The woman who had kidnapped Viper.

Well, wasn't this nice.

Ember leaned in, smiling against the shell of the woman's ear.

"Ah," Ember whispered, the woman shuddering as she pressed the knife deeper into her skin, as if she knew. As if she knew taking Viper had been the most foolish thing the rebellion could've done. As if she knew that Ember was going to take her payment in blood and fire. "I'm so glad you're here."

EPILOGUE

THE LAST THING SHE remembered the taste of was blood. Sometimes, even days later, she still imagined that she could taste it. The way it coated the back of her throat. The inside of her cheeks. Gagging her, drowning her in salt and thick clots. That taste drove her from nightmares, haunted her waking hours. She could taste, too, the metal they'd heated to cauterize the wound, to keep her from choking to death on the blood.

It was strange, to be without a tongue. Strange to not be able to speak beyond a few terrible, gargled noises, dredged up from the back of her throat.

Oh, this was a cursed existence.

Sometimes she almost wished the High Priestess had slit her throat instead of her tongue.

The priestess laid in the darkness, staring up at the sky above. Beside her, the Flame raged, still craving more blood, more salt, more bone.

She could hear it whispering now, in that strange ancient language that was nearly familiar but always out of reach. Words that were almost recognizable but just *barely* too foreign to understand. Cerraine could hear the hatred within, the rage rumbling just beneath the surface. The ancient fury of a god long caged.

The priestess's hands curled into fists.

She did not deserve this.

Kerio did not deserve to be banished.

And it was not the Dragon's fault that it had happened. Not entirely, at least. She had been too curious for her own good, too willing to poke and prod at the High Priestess until she bit.

It was the High Priestess who had done this, despite the Dragon's provoking. It had been the High Priestess who had reached into her mouth and cut out her tongue.

No more.

No more could Cerraine allow this to continue.

She stood slowly, shakily, lips sealed. Always sealed. She no longer tried to speak. The results were too embarrassing.

There were things that lurked in the temple. Shadows and secrets hovering just beyond the reach of the Flame, skirting around the tunnels below. Things that were not meant to be seen.

And that was where Cerraine needed to go. Outside forces would do nothing against the High Priestess. She was too set in her ways, too secure in the loyalty of the sacerdos, to even consider that there may be another way. The war would destroy her eventually, yes, but at what cost?

How many would die by the flame and the fury before she was struck down? How many would die screaming as the original fire, borne of nothing but hatred and terrible magic devoured their flesh and blood?

Cerraine cast a quick glance over her shoulder, watching the Flame.

That was what she needed to temper. That was what she needed to *kill* if there was any chance of slowing the High Priestess. Without the Flame, she was only a woman with her human army. And women could be killed.

Nobody moved in the halls as Cerraine slipped through the shadows, her lips pressed so tightly together it almost hurt.

Through an archway, underneath a door frame.

She gently lifted one of the stone bowls from the wall, the tiniest bit of Flame nestled inside. It clearly hadn't been fed recently—it would've been leaping toward the sky if it had been.

Down down down down.

Into the depths of the temple.

The air was stale here, her feet making soft indents in the mounds of dirt and dust that covered the stairs.

The door at the bottom of the stairs was unlocked.

Cerraine pushed inside, gently placing the Flame on the floor as she gazed around the massive stone blocks that filled the space, glittering with different colors. Many of them were the white that already ringed the Flame, sacred stone that could contain—but not kill—the Phoenix Flame.

But there were others.

Stone of deep red, veined with gold. Small shards of silver stone glittered on the floor. Black stone occasionally broke up the white.

Something in here could be enough.

Something in this room could kill the Flame before it could be unleashed.

And Cerraine was going to find it.

Acknowledgments

For you, reader.

Thank you Mom and Dad, for always being my first beta readers and supporting my passion for writing. I couldn't do it without you.

To Aliza and Lucia, my buddies. You two are getting so big! It makes me feel crazy. You impress me every day.

To Grammy and Grandpa, Abu and Aba. I love you guys more than I could ever express in writing. Your continuous encouragement keeps me going on some of my hardest days.

To Tita and Uncle Johnny, and all of your fur babies. I hope we can see manatees again sometime!

To Uncle Ed, Aunt Katia, Lexi, Eddie Tyler, Hanna, Sophia, and Olivia.

To Bryce. Let's get fried rice sometime soon.

To Ava, Jordan, Jo, Maddie, Amanda, Mia, and Kaitlyn. Thank you for all of your support and for coming out to my first author event. I cannot put into words how much it meant to me. (Horse.)

To Hailey. I miss you, and I wish you lived closer to me.

To Judi Wess, my incredible editor. I will never stop appreciating the work you've done for these novels.

To Thea Magerand, for another incredible cover.

To Sarah Lahay, for your amazing formatting work.

To Hazel, the best dog a girl could ask for.

For everybody who has asked me when this book was coming—this one's for you.

Love always,
Amelia Wood

www.ingramcontent.com/pod-product-compliance
Lightning Source LLC
Chambersburg PA
CBHW051134300726
48978CB00011B/268